# DESIGN OF DECEPTION

## J E FRIEND

ISBN 978-1-9991192-0-1

Publisher: Dark Cellar Publications, darkcellarpublications@yahoo.com

Author: J. E. Friend

www.jefriend.com

Cover Designer: A. E. Hellstorm at Flying Elk Photography

http://www.flying-elk-photography.com/about-book-covers

Editing: J. Gray

Book Designer: A. F. Stewart

*For my husband Steve, whose love, faith and encouragement kept me at the keyboard.*

# CHAPTER 1

Abby exited the elevator onto the darkened hallway of the 15th floor. With each step, the click of her heels echoed on the well-polished marble tiles. She held her head high and her shoulders back, keeping herself erect, ignoring the exhaustion that racked her body. Knots formed along the base of her neck. She rubbed them absently, hoping to ease the tension, as she made her way past the vacant reception desk in the dimly lit suite towards her personal office. Her footsteps softened to dull thuds as she stepped off the tiles onto the carpeted corridor that led past the cubicles of the junior partners and associates.

She continued making her way in the dark, not bothering with the lights. She'd wait until she was in her windowless office, then flick the switch. There were still a few things to take care of before she left for the weekend, things that put the last pieces of her plan into place. But she had to be quick. She needed to get in and out without being detected, which was the reason she was here after hours. The deserted office would buy her the privacy she desired.

The events of the day made it seem endless, but she felt satisfied with what she'd accomplished and was confident no one suspected what she'd set in place. With the office empty, she'd grab some files and head home before anyone was the wiser. She also needed to delete some emails and documents from her computer to be safe.

It was long after the business day ended when she unlocked her office door and switched on the light. The room flooded with the bright glare from the overhead fluorescence fixtures. As the room filled with light, a cold sensation of dread trickled down her spine when she saw the figure in the room. Chuck sat behind her desk, with his hands folded in front of him, a cold, knowing look in his eyes. He turned to glare at her as she entered.

*'What was he doing here? He didn't have a key, which meant he either broke in or secretly made a copy. He was sneaky enough to take her key and copy it, but she didn't know what he hoped to gain by doing so. She could ask him, but thought better of it. It would only start a fight, and after the day she had, that was the last thing she wanted. It was becoming blatantly obvious that she'd have to end things with him soon. The relationship had run its course, and she was preparing to make some big changes in her life. Changes that didn't include him.'* She smiled at him to break the tension, but his face remained stony. Abby pulled back her shoulders to brace herself for whatever lay ahead, then spoke.

"Chuck, you surprised me. What are you doing in my office?"

"I think a better question is, what have you been up to? I know something's going on. You've been out of the office all day. No one could reach you. That's out of character for you."

Abby considered what he said. Sure, she'd missed a few of his calls today, but there were none from anyone else in the office. She wondered to herself if he was grabbing at straws, or did he know where she was and what she was doing? She thought, *'There was no way he knew. It was too soon. No one would know before Monday. Then I'll be long gone.'* She took a slow, deep breath before responding, deciding it was better to feign ignorance.

"I don't know what you're talking about. My phone wasn't off. I had it set to vibrate. I've been in meetings all day. I couldn't respond to you. By the time I finished; it was after hours. I figured I'd message you on my train ride home." She replied calmly as she made her way further into the room.

"You know exactly what I'm talking about. It's this case. It's turning bad. I think you're the one behind it. If I can't get Miguel off, they're going to kill me. Is that what you want?"

"Calm down Chuck. You're being melodramatic," she said. "It's a vehicular manslaughter case. As long as you do your job, you'll be fine."

Chuck jumped abruptly up from the chair, kicking it back with a violent force as he did, forcing it into the wall behind him with a loud crash. A deep gouge scarred the wall where it connected. With a few steps, he breached the distance between them and grabbed her shoulders. His fingers dug into her tender flesh, with his face only inches from hers. He continued.

"You stupid bitch! What the hell did you do with my file? You're the only one other than me who knew its existence, and now it's gone. If that gets into the wrong hands, I'm screwed!"

"Take your hands off me, Chuck." Abby's tone was icy. Startled, Chuck's grip loosened. "If you lost a file, you'd better find it. I'm not responsible for your misplaced work documents. There's no way you're blaming me for your incompetence. I think you'd better leave my office. We can talk about this again next week when you've calmed down."

"Calm down? Miguel's in jail. Do you have any idea what that means? I promised his father he'd be free by now, and I've just heard from the Crown Attorney's office. They claim to have evidence that will put him away, possibly for life. The same evidence that until yesterday I'd hidden away. I know it was you. Trust me, you'll pay for this."

He shoved her roughly. She stumbled to regain her poise as he turned to leave. Then he paused and continued.

"When I tell the partners what you did, you won't have a job next week. Mark my words! I'm not going down for this. You are!"

He shot her a look of disdain. The depth of his hatred was clear on his face. Then he stormed out of the office, slamming the door. The pictures on the wall rattled from the force. Abby felt her knees go weak. She stretched out her arm and grabbed the filing cabinet, steadying herself before continuing. It was time to put everything in motion. She no longer had a choice. The small window of opportunity she'd left herself just slammed shut.

Determination set in. She walked over to her desk, pushed the chair back in place, and collapsed into it. She looked back at the door before leaning forward to turn on the computer. It chugged and sputtered before the monitor flicked on, filling the screen with her documents and icons. She scanned it until she found the file she was looking for and sent it to the printer. With deliberate precision, she began the meticulous task of deleting the files that could tie her to this mess, being extra careful to empty the trash bin. She had a small virus she planned to upload and infect her computer when she finished. One that would take care of anything she may have missed and make it impossible for the tech guys to retrieve her deleted files. There were still a few documents and personal items she needed to grab from her desk and stuff into her briefcase.

Finally, she opened the centre drawer and felt around at the back. Her heart raced when she couldn't locate what she was looking for. Then she felt the smooth plastic tube with her fingertips. She curled her fingers around it, pulled it into her grasp, and dropped the lipstick into her briefcase before locking it. Satisfied that she had everything, she paused, took a deep calming breath, and sauntered to the printer to pick up the now ready document.

Her heart raced. No matter how calm she appeared, she knew she needed to pull off the biggest lie of her life as she headed away with her best friend, Madison, for the weekend. Madison would know something was up if she wasn't careful. The only reason she agreed to go to the chalet was that it afforded her the distance she needed when everything came to light. If Madison became suspicious and found out what was going on and how dangerous it was, she'd want to help and end up caught in the middle of it all.

When this was all over, she'd fill her in. Madison would be angry, but she'd be safe. Until she was sure everything was under control, it was important to keep Madison in the dark, which would be difficult, as she had an uncanny way of discovering things. Abby would have to be careful.

Returning to the task at hand, she scanned the pages in front of her to verify that everything was in order and added her signature to the bottom. Then she placed her signed resignation letter and her office keys neatly on the centre of her desk, inserted the USB with the virus into her computer, grabbed her briefcase, and left her office for the last time.

# CHAPTER 2

The heavy metal door leading to the alley was all that stood in her way. Madison pushed on the release bar and heaved it open. A smothering, thick blanket of humidity assaulted her as she stepped out. Her breath caught as she adjusted to the change from her air-conditioned studio to the stifling air of the city. Moisture clung to surfaces like tiny drops of dew, unusual for this late in September. In her left hand, she held her suitcase, which she rolled along on the ground behind her. She made her way to her SUV and hoisted it up onto the back. Then she slipped behind the wheel, turned on the ignition, and cranked up the air. She brushed humidity dampened curls out of her eyes, slid her sunglasses into place, and put the SUV into gear. She checked her rearview mirror before backing out of her parking spot and easing into the flow of traffic in the city's core. A wave of relief overcame her as the cool air blasted from the dash and brought her body temperature back down.

Madison worked her way through the snarl of the downtown traffic before merging onto the Expressway. It wasn't much of an expressway during rush hour, but it was still the quickest route. She looked at the clock on the dash and realized that she'd be later than she expected.

She continued on her route to the suburbs to pick up her best friend, Abby, so they could enjoy a relaxing weekend at her chalet in Ellicottville, New York. These getaways allowed them both to temper their pace and rejuvenate from the hectic day-to-day pressures of city life.

The last few days she'd been stuck in the city, forced to endure the current heatwave. The thought of embracing the cool, fresh mountain air exhilarated her. She could only manage a few long weekends a year because of her work schedule. But she was grateful that somehow Abby always coordinated to go away with her.

These escapes enabled them to each put aside the pressures of work, even though their careers couldn't be more dissimilar. Abby spent her days as a criminal lawyer. With her hard work and determination, she landed a position with a prestigious law firm, and she was well underway to becoming a junior partner. It was only recently that she'd rethought criminal law. A tidbit that had just came to light.

Madison was a fashion designer. After she gained experience with some local designers, she started her own company. With the money she inherited from her parents, she bought a building in the downtown garment district, turning the lower level into her studio and the upstairs loft into her living quarters.

Madison pulled off the highway towards the small suburban bungalow Abby owned. Madison turned into the driveway of the well cared for home with its well manicured yard, and she chuckled to herself. They were best friends, but so different. She preferred the mixed diversity of living downtown with all it offered. Abby worked in the city, but was a suburban girl at heart.

Hearing the car pull up, Abby was on the porch with her overnight bag. She locked the front door, waved her hand in greeting, and sprinted down the steps towards the waiting SUV. The tailgate lifted so that she could toss her bag in the back. She climbed in the front, gave Madison a brief hug before buckling her seatbelt and settling back to enjoy the ride.

They'd grown up next door to each other and had been friends for as long as they could remember. The girls enjoyed play dates, holidays, and sleepovers as the two families grew closer. Their friendship survived high school crushes, losses, and university. Over the years, they became more than just friends; they were each other's family. When Madison's parents died in a car accident, the summer after she graduated high school, it was Abby's parents who took her in, helped her settle her affairs, and filled in the void. They were closer than most sisters.

As they made their way to the USA border, they chatted, expecting to be delayed by the heavy weekend traffic. Instead, they were pleased that the border crossing wasn't as bogged down as they expected. Soon they were on the I90, headed towards Ellicottville, New York. After the stifling city smog, they were eager to get out of the SUV and breathe in the fresh mountain air.

They made good time, and before they knew it, they were approaching the town, as the now darkened sky burst with beautiful spatters of white, green, red, and blue. A fireworks display erupted, lighting their way. The town had strung banners throughout the downtown core, welcoming visitors to a 50s and 60s tribute. Madison grinned as soon as she saw it.

"Oh, this is going to be fun." Madison laughed. "If I'd known, I could have whipped us up a couple of poodle skirts, so we'd fit right in."

Abby groaned.

"I'm glad you didn't know! I don't think I couldn't dress the part, as well as having to put up with the music for an entire weekend! Don't get me wrong! Some of it's great, but there is a lot of hokey music from that era too." Abby chuckled as they continued driving to the chalet.

Madison turned the SUV into the driveway, gravel crunching under the tires as they made their way. The chalet on Hencoop Lane was just a short distance from the Holiday Valley Ski Resort. Sensor lights illuminated the area as she parked the vehicle, flooding the surrounding grounds with a soft glow.

Madison loved her chalet. It brought back the sense of home and family. Her parents often brought her here for family vacations, and they always rented this chalet. It was here where she learned to ski. When it went on the market, she bought it because of how much her parents loved this place and her fond memories here. The chalet helped her feel close to her parents. Here she set up all her family mementos after she rescued them from storage. She would always feel their loss, but in this place, she still felt close to them. Her parents would have been happy.

The interior décor was a far cry from the stark minimalism of her loft. In the chalet, she used comfortable overstuffed furniture in rich earth tones, choosing to soften the masculine look with cream carpeting and light oak tables. She had small treasures from her childhood scattered around the room. A piece of needlework her mother made, her father's collection of antique pipes, and framed family photographs graced tabletops. The effect was both homey and inviting.

The chalet had four bedrooms, two with an ensuite. One bedroom was for Abby. The other was Madison's. Madison let Abby decorate her room to suit her own personal taste and style so that she'd always feel at home. When they entered the chalet, they deposited the food they bought in the kitchen. Then they headed upstairs to unpack and change into PJs. They always stayed in on the first night.

The city heat was long forgotten, as nightfall brought in crisp cool air, leaving the interior of the chalet feeling cool. Madison knew she would have to hurry downstairs to start a fire and warm things up. After unpacking and changing, Madison made it downstairs first, so she built a fire. A few minutes later, Abby came down dressed in yoga pants and an oversized sweater. She paused in the kitchen and poured them each a glass of wine before joining Madison, who was stoking the now roaring fire. Madison had prepared some snacks. She'd covered the coffee table with an assortment of cheese and crackers, along with a variety of junk food for them to enjoy.

"So tell me, how is everything with Chucky? You haven't mentioned him lately." Madison asked, as she nibbled on a piece of licorice.

"You're awful!" Abby exclaimed as she threw a pillow at Madison. "You know he hates being called that. But I have to admit it is funny watching how it gets his back up." Abby wanted to keep the conversation about Chuck light. The memory of his rage still weighed upon her.

"It's hard not to tease him. He's always so puffed up and full of himself. He thinks he's the best thing to happen to you."

"Well, it helps that we're in the same field and attend the same functions. Usually, he's fun to be with and makes me laugh. We have a lot in common, but there's no sizzle. I think he's more serious than I am. He started talking about us living together, but I keep putting him off. I may have to end things because we're not heading in the same direction anymore."

"Then just tell him! It's obvious the two of you don't have a future, but if you want to have the whole suburbia thing, husband, kids, and a dog, you know you need to move on. How will you ever find what you want if you're unavailable? Don't close yourself off from other possibilities."

"You're one to talk," Abby laughed. "When was the last time you had a boyfriend? I can't remember the last time you went on an actual date."

"Ha, ha, ha, I date. It's just in my line of work most of the men I meet are gay. Call it an occupational hazard. I keep busy with work and I like the way my life is uncomplicated. What more do I want? Some guy who's going to tell me what to do, and when to do it? No, thank you."

Abby stared at Madison and asked what had been weighing on her.

"You don't like Chuck, do you?"

"No, I don't. I'm sorry. I've tried, but there's something off about him. I can't put my finger on it, but there's something that's not quite right. I promise as long as you're dating him, I'll be nice."

"Thank you, that's all I can ask."

The spreading warmth of the fire replaced the slight chill that emanated from the chalet when they first arrived. The smoky scent of burning wood added to the ambiance of the natural setting. Warmed and relaxed, the two women chatted until the wee hours of the morning before exhaustion set in and they headed up to bed.

MORNING ARRIVED and with it a ray of glorious sunshine that brightened the sky. The humidity from the previous day was gone. Abby was the first one up and donned a pair of running shorts and a t-shirt before she slipped into Madison's room and tossed a pillow at her sleeping form to awaken her.

"Get up sleepy head. It's time for a run. You need to work off all that wine and junk food you ate last night."

"Ugh. Give me five minutes. I need to splash some water on my face, brush my teeth, and tame my hair first."

"O.K. I'll go down and set up the coffeemaker so it'll be ready when we get back."

Madison threw back the covers and hopped out of bed. Once ready, she joined Abby downstairs and who handed her a water bottle as they slipped out into the sunlight. They headed to town to check out the activities scheduled for the day. Allowing them to see if there was anything in particular that interested them. Both were avid runners and found the exercise motivating, enabling them to clear their minds and focus on whatever lay ahead as well to keep fit and healthy.

Instead of their usual pace, they settled on a light jog, keeping to the soft shoulder away from the flow of traffic. The gravel offered a gentler surface on which to run, knowing they'd be doing a lot of walking on hard pavement later. As they approached the town, they noticed activities already crowded the streets, even at this early hour.

Music vibrated through speakers throughout the downtown core. They heard Elvis' sultry voice fill the air with 'I'm All Shook Up'. The streets were brimming with people of all ages, from babes in buggies to seniors on scooters and everything else in between.

Their run continued looping up and down the side streets, allowing them to note programs they could check out later. Sweat drenched their clothing as they ran back up Hencoop Lane. It was then that Madison noticed someone was occupying the chalet next to hers. Not that they would bother them. The neighbouring chalet wasn't that close, and the trees between the properties provided enough privacy. The large numbers of cars parked in the laneway suggested it was a party weekend, although there was no one in sight.

# CHAPTER 3

Dean laid down his binoculars on the sideboard and crossed the room towards Don Fernando, adjusting his holstered revolver as he went. The Don sat in the middle of one of the chocolate brown sofas, his immense frame dwarfing it. His first name was Don, but everyone referred to him as 'The Don' as he demanded unconditional respect and obedience from the people he surrounded himself with. He was a hard, vengeful man. One who always got what he wanted, no matter the cost.

"They're coming in now," Dean stated, drawing deeply on his cigar.

"They aren't suspicious?" questioned Don Fernando.

"No. They aren't aware of anything."

"You're sure it's her?"

"Yes, I'm positive. I compared her face with the picture you gave me."

"O.K., let's make sure we set everything in place. Tonight has to go according to plan. When everything falls into place, that will solve our problem. But timing is everything. You need to check with Tony and see if he's completed his task. He had little time. I don't want any screw-ups."

Dean glanced out the window one more time before leaving in search of Tony. Tony was unpredictable but loyal to The Don. Dean felt Tony was a loose cannon with a quick temper. Tony was The Don's first choice for solving unwanted problems that required a violent end.

Dean found Tony standing in the hall, leaning against the wall, cleaning his nails with the tip of the large knife he always carried. Dean signalled for him to join them. Tony slipped his knife into its sheath and followed Dean back into the living room.

WHILE WAITING FOR TONY, Don Fernando sat and stewed over all the trouble the woman had caused him over the past several months. It was time to settle the score. No, it was long past the time. After tonight, she wouldn't interfere in his business ever again. From his vantage point, he could sit back and watch it all play out. But if he did, how would she know who was responsible? She wouldn't know for sure he was the reason she was going to die. That was unacceptable. He wanted her to know. The DON needed her to know. He had to be there to see her reaction. See the fear and dread in her eyes, as she realized how helpless she was. A slow smile spread across his lips, almost reaching his cold, black eyes, as Dean and Tony entered the room.

"Sumpin' making you happy, boss?" Tony asked as he crossed over to unroll the blueprints out on the table. Not waiting for a response, he continued. "Here, I'll show you where the device is located. We could set it off remotely, and no one would be the wiser. I can also enter without being detected, wait for her, and knock her out. That way, she can't leave before the explosion. I would enjoy the second choice."

Don Fernando heaved himself to a standing position with great effort. Waddled over to the table to look at the plans, nodding his approval as Tony explained everything. Tony was excellent at explosives. That, his willingness to get his hands dirty and his dedication were a few of the reasons The Don had him in his organization. Plus, he never asked too many questions, just followed orders.

"Ëes, perfection, no?" asked Tony.

"It'd better be. I don't want any screw-ups. That bitch has pushed me too far. I want her to know it was me who brought her down. I want to see her face when it happens." Don Fernando looked out the window towards the location in question, his hatred clear from the glare in his eyes.

"It'll be difficult, boss, but not impossible. You could watch from here with binoculars. You'd..."

"That's not good enough," He cut in. "I plan to be there! I want to see her reaction when she realizes her fate. She needs to know it was me! She needs to know why! Nobody crosses Don Fernando!"

Dean and Tony exchanged looks. It didn't surprise them that The Don wanted to be there. It would just be more problematic than they thought. The Don's lack of mobility meant more security and a longer delay on the detonator. But neither would try to dissuade him. His voice had the air of authority and finality to it. There was no question they would have to ensure the proper outcome.

"I'll arrange it for you, Sí." Tony rolled up the blueprints and left the room to work out how he could make The Don's demands happen. Being able to get him out safely would take time. He'd have to change the setting on the detonator to delay it from going off too soon or make use of the remote instead. There was no use arguing with The Don when he set his mind. He was the boss. He got what he wanted, no questions asked. Tony knew all too well that anyone who crossed The Don didn't live long enough to make a second mistake, and Tony wouldn't put himself in that position. He valued the family and where he stood within the organization too much.

Tony went to the kitchen, where he spread the blueprints out on the table, checked the exit locations and where the device was. It would be difficult, but not impossible. He could arrange for the boss to be sitting on the sofa in the primary room when she returned. This would allow Don Fernando to see her face-to-face, speak his peace, and leave before the explosion. It would mean that either he or Dean would have to be present to make sure that they left the bitch unconscious, and hold her in place to prevent her from escaping while The Don spoke to her. Not as simple as just using the remote, but it would give The Don the satisfaction he wanted. Keeping him happy was part of Tony's job. Being in the room with The Don was definitely a job for him. He'd enjoy knocking her out. Yes, he'd go in with the boss. Once he'd incapacitated her, he could get The Don to safety before using the detonator. Dean could be the lookout.

He mapped it out, calculating how long it would take to get Don Fernando out, once he'd rendered the target unconscious. The Don's sheer size meant evacuating him would take a considerable amount of time. But if he tied her up or killed her before the explosion, they might discover it during an investigation. Knocking her out was the only choice. It ensured it would look like an accident. The coroner would attribute a head wound to the explosion if there was anything left for the medical examiner. He'd already loosened the fittings on the gas. The explosion would destroy the detonator. The bumbling locals would think it was a gas leak set off when they lit the fire. Tony took his time to determine the safest distance from the building in which to detonate the device. Once he checked and rechecked all of his figures and calculations, he rolled up the blueprints and went back to show the boss.

"Everything's in place," Tony smirked. "It won't be too difficult. You can sit and watch, say what you want, and look her in the eyes. Then I'll knock her out. I could use chloroform, but a good blow to the back of her head would work, too. I don't expect there will be much left to identify her with, let alone any unusual trauma. Once she's unconscious, we'll leave and use the detonator at a safe distance."

"She's not alone," The Don commiserated. "There are two of them. We have to be sure to take care of them both. I'll need you both on hand. Tony, I want you inside with me. The pleasure you get from inflicting pain will be invaluable. Dean, you stay outside and make sure nothing goes wrong. It's your job to see that things go as planned. I don't want any surprises. If they don't come inside together, dispose of the friend however you want, but it must look like an accident. I would prefer if they died together in the explosion." Don Fernando gulped down the last of his drink, dismissing them. As Dean and Tony left the room, he leaned back onto the sofa, his mind envisioning what lay ahead.

"WELL, the rest's up to us, Dean. It looks like we'll both need to be there. The Boss wants this done and over with. His daughter's wedding's comin' up and he wants Miguel back before then. He has to be back well before the wedding, without this hangin' over his head. So much trouble caused by one connivin' little bitch."

Dean watched Tony out of the corner of his eye. Tony was nervous. He always resorted to poor grammar when he was, but Dean knew it wasn't the job that was causing this. It was the fear of disappointing The Don. The only time they could detect his poor roots was when he was nervous. As smart as he was, it was amazing to watch him slide down the chain of command. It was for this reason Dean knew Tony would never move up within the organization. Dean was always calm. This little scenario would play out, and he could gain control of the situation. He was always in control. Unlike Tony, very little fazed him. Dean stood, observing Tony's behaviour as he dragged deeply on his cigar.

"Tony, calm down. The boss is in the other room, everything's in order. You have nothing to worry about. Have a cigar. That will relax you. It's a Cuban."

"You won't catch me with one of those things. They stink." Tony glared as he moved further away from Dean and the smell of his cigar.

"There's not much left to do now, but wait. They have to leave and go into town so that you can finish setting up. When they leave, I'll follow them. We don't want to take any chances that they'll bring someone back with them. That could get very messy." Cigar clenched between his lips. He turned and looked out the nearest window.

"I'll tell the boss and go with you. We can duck out before they head back, and be waiting for them."

"No. You need to set everything up and help The Don get there. He needs to be in position before they return. I'll follow and monitor them. When I see that, they're heading back. I'll text you. That will give you plenty of time to check the device, which is your specialty. I'll blend in and ensure everything goes according to plan."

Tony glared at Dean. He hated when Dean took control, but knew he was right. Dean had a knack for blending in with the locals. Tony's look was harder, more criminal. He couldn't just blend in, and he knew it. He took a deep calming breath before setting off to make some adjustments to the second device he planned to plant, and left Dean staring out the window through his binoculars.

# CHAPTER 4

The aroma of brewed coffee permeated the air as they entered the chalet. The run to town was exhilarating, and their bodies still glistened with sweat. As tempting as the rich scent of coffee was, Abby decided she wanted a shower first. She needed to peel the damp running gear from her body and feel the refreshing warm water wash away the sweat. Madison's stomach growled as the rich bouquet filled her nostrils. They didn't eat supper last night, and she was hungry. As appealing as the coffee was, getting out of her soiled clothing also came first.

"The coffee smells amazing, Abby! I'm starving. This morning, we need a substantial breakfast. A long run always helps me work up an appetite."

"I agree, but you're cooking. I made the coffee, got you up, and dragged you out for a run. I think I deserve a little TLC. I'm heading up for a shower. I need to wash so that I can enjoy my coffee."

"I'll grab a quick shower, too. Then I'll come back down and get breakfast started. You can take your time, Princess."

Abby shot Madison a look before laughing at her remark. Madison smiled back and gave her a quick wink as they both headed upstairs. Abby would take her time in the shower. That would ensure that Madison had plenty of time to prepare breakfast, not that Abby doubted she would. Madison was the better cook. Abby enjoyed how creative she could be, even with eggs. If she came down too early, she might have to help, and that could be disastrous.

Once upstairs, Madison slipped out of her running clothes and turned on the shower. She waited for it to come to temperature before she stepped in and allowed the invigorating massage from her shower jets to ease her sore muscles. The hot, steamy water ran down her body, rinsing away the sweat and dirt that clung to her. The jets soothed out her tired muscles and refreshed her skin. A brisk rub with her towel to dry herself, followed by moisturizer, and she was ready to cook. She went to her closet and picked one piece from her lingerie line, a copper silk-lined, silk velvet robe. Slipping into it, she tied it around her waist and headed to the kitchen.

Madison derived great pleasure from cooking. It was also something she excelled at. She learned at her mother's side and found the process was a back to basic, comfortable feeling from her childhood. When she was growing up, her mother spent hours in the kitchen with Madison at her side, and she always seemed to know just the right spices to bring out the flavour of whatever dish she was making. Madison learned this art and had created many unique dishes herself over the years. Abby never mastered cooking, something Madison found funny, considering Abby was Ms. Suburbia, the one you'd expect to be at home in the kitchen. In the city, whereas Madison had a cornucopia of restaurants to choose from but still preferred to cook for herself. She prided herself on her gourmet abilities and felt much of what she prepared was better than what she could find at most restaurants. At least she knew the ingredients were always fresh.

This morning's breakfast would be simple, comprising lightly scrambled eggs with a dash of oregano, Roma tomato slices with fresh feta, slices of avocado, juice, and coffee. Abby had already made the coffee, so the rest was up to her. She selected a classical piece to play on her music streamer. Rich musical tones filled the air. Madison loved classical music and found it relaxing and enhanced her creative inspiration, whether she was designing or cooking.

"Oh god, Madison, you and your ridiculous taste in music. Can't you play something more modern?" Abby groaned as she came down the stairs in an oversized t-shirt, her short dark hair still damp from her shower.

"Well, you wanted me to cook, but then again, I didn't want you to cook. We want to be well enough to go out later."

Abby whacked her playfully on the shoulder and observed Madison's beautiful new robe. She stroked the material, noticing the delicate softness of the velvet.

"This is exquisite. I know it must be one of yours, but I don't remember it. Was it on the runway? Or is it from your private collection?"

"It's from my private collection. I only made a limited number and only one of each colour. If you'd looked in your closet, you'd have noticed the one I made for you in emerald green. You didn't think I'd forget you, did you?"

Abby squealed in delight and ran back up the stairs to her room. Her work as a criminal lawyer required her to be demure and serious. But when she received a gift, she still displayed a childlike enthusiasm. Abby loved clothes and looked forward to anything Madison designed, knowing she always had something made that was only for her. Her parents brought Abby up with the belief that the clothes made the person, and so far in her career, she had found this to be true. Clients took her more seriously when she dressed in quality, well-made suits than at any other time. It was a blessing that Madison had become a designer. Madison's sense of style made all the difference in her career. But her position had also helped Madison. Reporters often interviewed Abby while wearing one of Madison's unique and distinctive designs. This created more business for them both.

Abby slipped out of her t-shirt and donned the robe, then rushed downstairs and embraced Madison before twirling around for inspection, flashing her well-muscled legs. Her excitement at receiving a beautiful gift shone through. The luxurious silk lining skimmed her skin like a tender kiss. The silk velvet was rich and soft. She beamed at Madison.

"Oh Madison, I love it. Thank you for having this made for me. I love this fabric. It's so rich and opulent. You may take chances on the runway, but anything you make for me is classic."

"Breakfast is getting cold, so let's eat while the eggs are still hot. There's a lot I want to do and see in town today." Madison replied, brushing off Abby's compliments.

They sat on the high stools at the breakfast bar, enjoying their meal while discussing what they planned to do in town. When full, they leaned back, taking the time to sip their coffee and enjoy the warm rush of caffeine. When she finished her coffee, Abby got up and put the dishes in the dishwasher before heading upstairs to dress. Madison continued sipping her coffee and walked to the large picture window in the living room. While enjoying the beautiful view of the countryside, she finished her coffee.

# CHAPTER 5

By the time Madison and Abby arrived back in town, they found the crowds heavier than they were during their run. Large groups of people were already forming around the various activities set up throughout the principal streets. The thought and creativity required to organize the number of events relating to the fifties and sixties overwhelmed them. As they walked along the busy streets, they joined in on a variety of activities, even taking part in a quick game of hop-scotch. While they played, a small cluster of individuals stopped to watch. They laughed and took turns tossing a small rock to the next square, before hopping on one foot or two as the grid required, before carrying on, engaging with some bystanders.

When they finished their game, they continued down the main street, stopping to take in the various displays in shop windows. Abby stopped in front of one of the smaller boutiques in town. It carried unusual books and handcrafted items. This store was her favourite, and she never failed to go in and have a look around. It was a treasure trove of undiscovered wonders. There were items from local artisans, antique books, and even some first editions. Together they explored the well cared for displays, hoping to find something new, a hidden gem to take back home. Madison often found unusual items here to decorate her loft or chalet, adding to the eclectic feel.

While examining an interesting piece of pewter, Madison noticed through the mirrored reflection of the display case a tall man standing not far behind her. He was well over six feet; his dark hair was close-cropped and streaked with silver. Although he was slim, his t-shirt clung to his chest, outlining well-developed muscles. There was something familiar about him, something she couldn't quite put her finger on, but she knew she saw him somewhere before. Out of the corner of her eye, she watched him turn and move to the front of the store. She liked the way his faded jeans fit and how he swaggered as he went. He was confident, exuding sexuality, but there was also a hint of danger. She turned to Abby.

"Abby, do you see that tall man on the other side of the store?" Madison whispered, motioning to the front door.

"No, not really. All I can see is the top of his head. Why is he cute?" Abby stretched on tiptoes to get a better look.

"Yes, but, um, well, that's not what I meant. He seems very familiar to me. It's as if I've seen him somewhere before. I just wondered if you'd seen him, too. Oh well, never mind. It's not important. I probably saw him when we were goofing around outside. Let's go check out the bandstand. I understand the mayor is joining a 50s and 60s group that only plays a few times a year. I bet it'll be fun."

"Lead the way. This is your thing."

They strolled down the main street to an empty parking lot with a large tent set up to provide shelter from the sun. There was a platform erected at one end to serve as the bandstand. On the stage, the musicians had already set up to perform a soundcheck. They left most of the tented area open, and people were positioning themselves to watch the show and maybe enjoy a little dancing. Madison and Abby stood to one side and waited for the band to finish and begin the show.

The band comprised a mismatched group of characters. The lead singer was an attractive, tall, slim man dressed in a black suit with a bright purple shirt. One of the guitar players was more flamboyant and wore a black and white zebra suit with a red shirt. The drummer wore a ratty old t-shirt and jeans with a head of curly hair minus the halo in the back where he was thinning. The mayor was on bass and made an interesting figure with his long hair pulled back into a ponytail, displaying his extroverted, flashy personality. Although the band rarely performed together, they were fantastic. The feel of the 50s and 60s was so strong that the still gathering crowd danced to the varying beats. Many of the young girls, and even some of the more mature women, were vying for eye contact with members of the band. It was enjoyable to watch, and the girls were having fun.

Madison enjoyed herself as she observed the crowd. Watching people was a hobby of hers, and there was an array of characters here. She kept her eye on the various people, noting their different characteristic quirks and irregular style choices. This gave her some great design ideas. She rummaged through her bag, brought out her paper and pencil, and sketched.

Abby turned and saw what Madison was doing and rolled her eyes. This was supposed to be a get-a-way from work, but Madison never seemed able to let go. She worked everywhere and anywhere. At least with her own work. As long as she didn't have a file under her arm or a brief to prepare, she could separate herself from work more easily. But that didn't stop the thoughts from creeping in if she was working on a more disturbing case. She turned to Madison.

"It's no wonder you're not able to commit yourself to a relationship. Every time a guy gets romantic, you probably get inspired and go off on a drawing tangent." Abby laughed.

Startled, Madison looked up at Abby and back to her sketch pad.

"O.K. I get the hint. I'll put away the sketchbook. I don't have men on the brain, I never have. I have no interest in complicating my life like that right now. Besides, men our age are married, divorced with kids, or confirmed bachelors."

"If not now? When? There are still plenty of men who are

career-minded and have advanced themselves in business first. I think it's about time you started living again, and I don't mean work. You need to feel passion that you can only get from a relationship. That would certainly add new flavour to your designs. You should allow yourself to be loved Madison. You won't regret it."

"Well, I'll take it under advisement. Who knows! Maybe someone here will stir me in a way no one else has been able to for a long time."

"I'm taking that as a challenge. From this point on, my eyes are wide open in search of someone to get your juices flowing. Beware, I may find him."

"Sure you will. We'll see. Just keep in mind we don't live in the States."

As the band finished the last song, the sun had set. The milling people left to find food or head home. Madison and Abby stayed to watch the band members take down their equipment and stow away their instruments.

"What about the lead singer? He's your type."

Madison laughed, "Yes, he is, but if you noticed, he's also wearing a wedding ring."

At that moment, an attractive woman with a small baby girl in a stroller approached the stage. The lead singer was all smiles as he gazed down at them.

"Daddy's little sweetheart." He sang out to his infant daughter.

"See? What did I tell you, Abby? That pretty blonde with the stroller is his wife. I knew he was married. Most men my age are married with families. I want children someday, and I know one day I'll have to do something about it. Maybe I'll have one on my own. I don't need a husband to have a family, and the man I planned to have a family with is gone."

"That was a long time ago. Cory wouldn't want this for you. He would want you to be happy and move on. Remember, you can't live in the past."

"Maybe what you should look for is your own Prince Charming.

We both know Chucky isn't it. Then maybe you'll lay off me while you do your own search."

"All right, I won't say another word. And stop calling him 'Chucky'. I don't think I like it either. It makes him sound like the creepy doll from that horror movie."

# CHAPTER 6

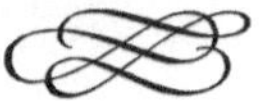

The sun set on the town's activities. The residents drifted home for supper and the visitors headed off. Madison and Abby went to a local restaurant for supper to enjoy the Cajun grilled chicken and a glass of wine.

"I'm glad I went with comfortable instead of glamorous," Madison stated while rubbing her none existent stomach. "I always feel stuffed when we eat here. It's got to be the great food and wonderful service. Sometimes it is nice to have someone else prepare the meal."

"Stop acting like you have a stomach. You spend too much time running to get fat. I am built closer to the ground, so my stomach is showing."

Abby laid down her fork and leaned back. With supper finished, they lingered over a half litre of wine. The server approached and cleared away their dishes. After checking if they wanted anything else, he returned with the bill, which Abby grabbed, beating Madison to it.

"This one is on me," Abby stated as she pulled out her wallet and signalled to the server for the debit machine so she could pay.

When they finished their wine, they went outside, surprised to find that the evening air was still warm, although it had cooled off, now that the sun had set. Madison draped her jacket over her arm. Together, she and Abby strolled along the busy street. Plenty of people were still milling around, looking in shop windows and enjoying the various activities along the sidewalks. After checking the time, they decided it was too early for the popular bars to be in full swing, so they opted to try a little obscure out of the way one, where the Mayor's regular band was playing. They found the bar easily enough, even though the entrance was up a stairwell over one shop, almost hidden. They paid their admission and headed up the narrow stairway to the second floor, which served as a nightspot. It was already busy, because the space was small and could only accommodate a few patrons. They set the band up near the entrance and were part way through their first set. The crowded dance floor made it difficult to move across to the bar, which was at the back of the room.

After a quick discussion, Madison decided she would stay near the band and grab a small, round table. Meanwhile, Abby ventured to the back to get some drinks. The band continued the 50s theme but added some more contemporary songs to the mix. Madison swayed to the music while she waited for Abby. The mayor saw her, caught her eye, and smiled. She smiled back. She'd never met him, but had attended several functions where he was present. 'He's unusual-looking,' she thought, 'but there was something about him that was also welcoming. Only in small-town America could such a man get away with not conforming to the political norm.' Madison chuckled to herself. When she looked up, she saw Abby was returning with two glasses of wine. Abby placed the glasses on the table and explained to Madison that she ran into a group of guys on a bachelor weekend. They asked the girls to join them for a drink. It was an impromptu bachelor party for one of them. They were all down from Toronto, to hang out and have fun. Madison rolled her eyes at Abby.

"Come on, Abby." Madison groaned. "Do you want to get involved with that? I thought bachelor parties involved strippers and gambling. They're probably all drunk and horny, looking for a couple of party girls to help them out."

"I don't think so, Maddie. There are about twenty of them, and they all seem nice. They bought us these drinks, even though I didn't say we were coming back. I think they're just bored with all the guy talk and are looking for some stimulating and attractive women's company."

Madison sighed.

"O.K., if that's what you want. I'll go make nice with a bunch of drunken men. It will just confirm why I don't want one. But the minute my warning bell goes off, we're out of here."

"Deal! But when you see them, I think you'll agree."

Hesitantly, Madison picked up her glass and followed Abby to the back of the room, where the men had huddled around the horseshoe bar, drinking. Each of the men smiled and greeted the girls as they approached, moving to give them space at the bar so they could set their drinks down. They even relinquished their chairs. After a quick round of introductions, they all fell into simple conversation.

*'It's amazing,'* Madison thought as she stood talking to one man in the group, *'Abby's right! Twenty attractive, clean-cut guys out celebrating the fact that one of them was getting married. They weren't hitting on them; they were just looking for some female company. This was exactly what Abby said. It must be the lawyer in her that helps her spot both honesty and insincerity in people, after having to deal with so much dishonesty in her line of work.'*

Madison noticed several were wearing wedding rings and not trying to hide the fact that they were married. They talked about their wives and families. This impressed her. In her experience, guys went away, pretended that they weren't married, always on the lookout for a little fun on the side. The groom, Glenn, was the only one who seemed to be excessively drunk. He singled Madison out and talked non-stop about his fiancé and how much in love they were. He told her that the wedding was going to be at the end of

October and that they were heading to the Dominican for their honeymoon following the reception.

Madison made her way through the group, talking to each of them one by one, enjoying the diversity of their lives and backgrounds. One fellow, Jamie, a mechanic, reminded her of her dentist. When she told him this, he leaned in and asked to taste her toothpaste. She chuckled and shook her head as she moved on. Soon she realized she had long since lost sight of Abby. She tried to find her in the sea of people but wasn't successful. She figured if Abby didn't show up, she'd go in search of her.

The diversity of the men was why she enjoyed herself so much. Some were very articulate, others more boisterous. But they all seemed very nice. She even enjoyed the harmless casual flirting from the single ones. It was fun to have so many men pay attention to her with no expectations. They just seemed to enjoy talking to her. As a joke, a married man put his arm around her shoulders and asked her to marry him. She laughed, slipped out from under his arm, and questioned in mock shock what his wife would say. She had long since turned from wine to water, as the bar was hot, and she preferred to keep her wits about her when she was out in public. It was part of the cautious city girl in her coming out.

She spotted Abby out of the corner of her eye, near the front of the bar. She noticed Abby was in a deep conversation with a man she didn't recognize from the group. From Abby's expression, she could tell she wasn't happy with the conversation, or maybe it was just the man himself, but she wasn't attempting to break away, either. Madison noticed that there was something familiar about the man. At first she couldn't quite place him, and then it hit her.

*'That's it! He's the guy from the store. Everywhere we went today! It seemed he was there, just off to the side, just far enough away not to be creepy, but close enough to be nearby. It was as if he'd been following us all day. I'd better go see what's going on and put a stop to this. He's ruining Abby's mood.'*

As she headed over to where Abby and the man were talking, he looked up, saw her approach, then he turned and walked away, exiting the bar. As he left, Abby turned, noticed Madison coming towards her, and she met her halfway.

"Who was that?" Madison asked.

"Who?"

"The guy you were talking to. He upset you. What did he say?" Madison questioned.

"Oh, him. He, uh, he just made a bad pass, that's all."

"Are you sure? It seemed like more than that to me. He was the guy I mentioned to you earlier. Has he been following us?" Insisted Madison.

"It's just a coincidence. Stop being a mother hen Madison. You know I can take care of myself just fine. It's you I'm worried about. I've left you alone with all those men for far too long." Abby replied.

"Yeah, alone, in a bar full of people." Madison chuckled.

"Forget about it. We're here to have fun."

"O.K., if you're sure."

Still concerned, Madison kept a close eye on Abby. It didn't feel like a coincidence for her. It wasn't the only bar in town, and if he wasn't following them, it's just as likely he'd have ended up some-where else. Madison continued watching Abby, noticing that her mood had changed. She seemed out of sorts. It was obvious her mind was elsewhere. That guy said more to Abby than she was letting on. Madison was sure of it. At least he'd left. So he wouldn't be bothering her again. But something happened between them.

There was nothing she could do if Abby wasn't honest with her, so the best thing was to enjoy the rest of the night. If anything was bothering Abby, they could talk about it later. It was hard not to enjoy the evening. The men were a lot of fun. They bought drinks and danced with the girls all night long. As the evening progressed, Madison learned they had rented the chalet next to hers, which explained all the cars she noticed parked there. When they discovered this, the best man suggested that they all share cabs back and invited the girls over for a late-night BBQ. Madison and Abby hesitated, considering that if they felt uncomfortable, they could walk back to their chalet whenever they chose. In the end, they agreed on the condition that they could contribute something.

The bartender was kind enough to call a local cab company and arranged for several cabs to pick them up. Soon, they were all crammed together into cars and minivans on their way back to the chalets. Abby and Madison shared the backseat of a cab with Glenn. He pulled out his phone and began showing Madison pictures of his fiancé. While Madison was distracted, Abby pulled a tube of lipstick out of her pocket. Put it in the little cosmetic bag Madison always carried in her purse before settling back, deep in thought, as they returned to the chalet.

WHEN THEY ARRIVED, they spilled out of the cabs and onto the dewy grass. Some men headed back to their chalet to get the BBQ started, and a handful waited outside for the girls to get what they needed and return. As they started back to Madison's chalet, Abby paused, placed a hand on Madison's arm, and turned to her.

"Madison, I'll get something out of the freezer and grab that salad you made earlier. You go ahead, I'll only be a minute, and I have to pee. I promise I won't be long and they're waiting. If we both go home, one or more may follow us, and that could prove awkward. I'll be quick, not even long enough for you to get into trouble."

"Fine, but don't leave me alone too long. I know they seem nice and respectable, but it is a bachelor's weekend. They might have other things on their minds, especially if they keep drinking. I'd feel safer with you there. Maybe I should wait out here?"

"Sure, wait here. I'll be right back."

Madison watched Abby make her way up to the chalet. There was something very odd in her manner, but Madison still couldn't put her finger on it. Abby wasn't acting like herself. Something happened this evening to change her mood. The more Madison thought about it, the more convinced she was that the man in the bar had something to do with how upset Abby was. Although, when he left, she seemed to enjoy herself again. But something was different.

'I'll talk to her about it later. If anything's really bothering her, she'll let me know when the evening is over and we're alone.'

# CHAPTER 7

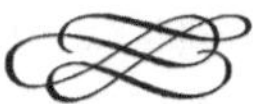



"**S**he's coming now." Tony declared from across the darkened room, letting the curtain fall back into place. "She's alone though. The other one isn't with her."

"Don't worry. The other one won't be far," The Don growled. "This is her house. I'm sure she'll be along shortly. There's nothing to be concerned about Tony Dean's outside. He'll keep an eye out for her. As soon as she shows, he'll take care of her, even if he has to knock her out and leave her outside the door. The explosion will still finish the job. Now shut up! I don't want her to hear us."

WITH HER HAND on the doorknob, the hairs on the back of Abby's neck prickled with moisture from the beads of sweat that formed. She hesitated before opening the door and turning on the living room lights. Someone was in the chalet. She could feel it. Maybe she should trust her instinct and turn around and leave. There were so many people next door, one of them would come to check the place out for her. As she switched on the light, a lump formed in her throat, and her heart sank.

"Hello bitch." Don Fernando rasped, "How's it feel to know you're going to die, and I'm the one responsible?"

Abby felt her knees buckle. She reached for the wall to support herself. There, in the middle of Madison's couch, sat Don Fernando. His enormous frame diminished the size of the overstuffed sofa. He'd slicked his black hair back, which added to his evil, sinister appearance. He was a vile man. Even by looking at him, there was no mistaking the criminal intent behind his eyes. To her right, she could see another man. He had a gun aimed level at her chest. This one was a broad, muscle-bound Neanderthal of a man. Tattoos snaked across his forearms. He hid his eyes behind dark glasses, even though it was night, and a thin moustache skimmed his upper lip. Abby shivered.

Her mouth went dry as she tried to swallow. Fear inspired perspiration beaded her upper lip, which she licked to moisten her tongue. She couldn't run. Although Don Fernando might not stop her, but the man with the gun could. She had limited options. Thank god Madison wasn't with her. She knew this was her mess, and hers alone to deal with.

"What do you want?" She croaked. "I did nothing."

"Maybe not intentionally, but you knew what you were doing was wrong. You went against the wishes of your firm."

"I was following protocol. The law required full disclosure. The truth would have come out, anyway! Please tell me what you really want?"

"I already told you. I want you dead. But first, I wanted to see your face when you realized what was going to happen. I wanted to smell your fear. Did you think you could cross me? That I wouldn't seek my revenge? You're a stupid woman. Nobody double-crosses me. You know too much, so now, bitch, it's time to die."

There was a quick movement beside her and then a flash of pain, searing, burning pain. Her legs buckled out from beneath her as she crumpled to the floor. Waves of darkness threatened to overcome her as she watched Don Fernando struggle to stand. His henchman rushed to his side to grab his arm, aiding him to his feet before they both left. Nausea overcame her, and she vomited as she tried to push herself up, succumbing to the weakness. As darkness overtook her, her last thought was, *'You lost, I'm not dead.'*

~

*'ABBY'S TAKING TOO LONG,'* Madison thought. *'Something's wrong. Did she imagine it, or was there someone else in the chalet? She thought she saw a shadow move behind the closed curtains before the lights went on.'*

She excused herself for a moment, leaving the conversation she was having with several of the men to head towards the chalet. Staring at the living room window as she went while she tried to make sense of what she saw. In her peripheral vision, she glimpsed movement in the bushes next to her. An arm darted out, grabbed, and dragged her back. A hand clamped over her mouth, preventing her from moving. Suddenly the ground shook, forcing her and whoever grabbed her backward. As the sky erupted with a blast of flames, her body freed from the person who'd seized her as she slammed onto the ground. The air from her lungs expelled from the impact. Pain seared through her as bits of burning rubble landed on her exposed flesh. The smell of smoke and fire filled her lungs; she gasped and coughed trying, to clear the suffocating odour. Shock and pain filtered through her muddled mind as it tried to disconnect from what she saw. Overcome with shock, she lay helpless and watched as her chalet became engulfed in flames. She heard people screaming around her. She struggled to stand, but found herself pinned back to the ground. Her mind cleared as the hand reached out and tried to cover her mouth again. She bit down hard. A curse sounded behind her, and she screamed! "ABBY!"

# CHAPTER 8

bby! Madison heard the name screamed into the air. It wasn't until she felt the ache in her throat that she realized she was the one screaming. She struggled to get up. The heat from the flames kept her back. A heavy cloud of smoke and the choking stench of burning wood filled her nostrils. Falling embers landed on her, searing into her tender flesh until she flicked them away. She could hear someone from the neighbouring chalet shouting to call 911. She stared in horror as her mind tried to register the sight before her. From the ball of flames that licked at the bare husk of burnt timbers, the gaping hole where her living room once stood, and the complete pandemonium of people running around the area without purpose or focus. She leaned forward, trying to get her feet beneath her to stand. When she found her footing, she stumbled towards the burning rubble, still screaming Abby's name.

She felt intense pain from the loss which tore through her. Her heart ached as the reality of the scene in front of her sank in. All around her was chaos. Pieces of debris littered the ground. Flames shot upwards, brightening the night sky. The explosion reduced the chalet to burning rubble. The severe emotional loss overwhelmed her. A loss she hadn't felt since that summer fifteen years ago. That was the summer when she lost her boyfriend Cory, and then her parents.

Cory's death was because of drunken recklessness. That year, her graduating class went to the river to continue celebrating following the ceremony. Everyone was already drunk when a group of boys crossed the trestle bridge over the river. No one heard the train approaching, and in the dark, the engineer couldn't see them in time to stop. By the time the horn blared, it was too late. Cory was the last in line, lumbering along in his drunken stupor, oblivious that most of his group had already reached the safety of the other side. When he heard the train, he ran but with too much to drink; he stumbled and fell. By the time he got to his feet, it was too late. She would never forget the sound of the train wheels screeching as the conductor applied the brakes before it slammed into his body, dragging him underneath. Horrified screams filled the air as teenagers ran in all directions. Her own scream caught in her throat as she fainted in horror.

While she was still reeling from Cory's death, she sank into a depression, refusing to leave the house until her parents forced her back into counselling. Through every step, Abby was there, offering whatever support she could. For the rest of the summer, Madison walked around like a shadow of who she once was. As she climbed out of her depression, tragedy struck again. On their way home from the movies on a cool, wet night, a drunk driver killed her parents, forcing Madison so deep into despair that Abby doubted she'd ever recover.

In the weeks following the accident, Madison lived dangerously. She took chances with her life, not caring whether she lived or died. The tremendous loss overwhelmed her, and she felt she had nothing left to live for. Her rationale dangled by a thread, which Abby pulled tight to keep from breaking. Abby wouldn't let Madison self-destruct. She pushed Madison back into counselling, pulled her from the edge, and kicked her hard enough to get her to fight back.

It was Abby and her family who helped Madison climb out of her depression. She got the counselling she needed and rebuilt her life. She went back to school and was finally happy. Everything she had, and everything she was, she owed to Abby, and now Abby was gone, too.

# CHAPTER 9

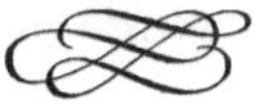

Once she was back on her feet, Madison started towards the burning chalet, screaming Abby's name. But someone thwarted her efforts and grabbed her from behind and restrained her. A hand clamped back over her mouth, once again silencing her. She struggled against whoever prevented her from moving. Madison was being pulled backward as another arm wrapped around her waist, restricting her movements. She could feel the firmness of his body as she thrashed, trying in vain to get free.

"Be quiet." A voice hissed into her ear. "It's too late for your friend. If you go inside, you'll die too. I'm only trying to help you. I think the explosion was deliberate, and whoever did it could still be around. Be silent!" The hand slipped from her mouth as she nodded.

"Let go of me. She's still in there. Oh, my god! Abby's inside!" Madison sobbed. Tears rolled down her cheeks, mingling with the soot and ash as she tried to jerk from his grasp.

"I said to be quiet. Do you want anyone to hear us? You can't help her now. She's already gone. Between the explosion and the fire, she didn't stand a chance." The voice behind her reasoned while keeping a firm grip on her arm.

The aching, hollow sensation of grief overcame her. She turned to him, pressed her face into the soft material of his t-shirt, and let the tears flow, seeking the comfort of human touch, allowing him to hold her long after she stopped struggling. She sagged against him as his arms loosened around her. For a moment, she felt comforted, but the horror of what she'd witnessed cracked through her consciousness as fear slipped back in. This was a stranger. He wasn't from the group were with all evening. There was a faint trace of a cigar clinging to his clothing. None of them smoked. With his grip loosened, she twisted and broke free. She ran towards the woods behind the chalet, trying to put distance between herself and the mystery man. Her instincts kicked in as her mind raced. He stopped her from going into the chalet, told her to be quiet. He knew Abby was inside, but he did nothing to help her. The man prevented her from going inside and saving Abby! He might be the reason she's dead. Why was he right outside her chalet, just before it exploded? Tears of sorrow and frustration blurred her vision while she tried to find answers. There was something familiar about his voice. Something that made her feel uneasy. The deep huskiness of it echoed in her ears.

'*Oh God!*' She thought, '*It's the man from the bar.*' She remembered the husky sound of his voice when he and Abby were talking. She remembered how upset Abby was and how she'd brushed it off. Was he responsible for this? Madison pushed herself harder, trying to put as much distance as she could between herself and the man who followed. Wishing she'd worn different shoes and drank a little less wine, she begged her legs not to give out. There was no telling what he would do with her when he caught her, especially if he caused the explosion. She needed to get away, to find a safe place to hide until she could figure everything out.

She could hear his footsteps pounding on the firm earth. He was right behind her, calling to her in a hoarse whisper. '*Abby wouldn't have told him her name. She was too careful when they went out, never wanting to attract unwanted attention. The only way he could know my name would be if he'd been spying on us. He was everywhere they went today. That guy was at every turn, every stop and event. He must have followed them all day, but why? What did he want?'*

Her breath escaped with short, raspy spurts. Sweat ran down her face, mingling with the tear-stained soot dripping in her eyes, burning them. She wiped her face with her sleeve as she ran, smearing her mascara as it mingled with her sweat, blinding her. Her foot slid on a damp patch of fallen leaves before she tripped over a protruding root. Madison's hands splayed in front as she went down, preventing her face from connecting with a jutting tree stump. Her right knee slammed into a jagged rock, pain jolted, vibrating up her leg.

Desperately, she tried to scramble up, but her feet slipped out beneath her on the damp forest floor, making her attempts futile. Just as her footing became more secure, his hand grabbed her by the shoulder. Roughly, he lifted her and twisted her around to face him, his other hand clamping onto her arm.

"Stop running. I'm here to help you. If you want to live, you'll come with me." He hissed.

"Stay away from me, or I'll scream."

"Go for it." He sneered. "You'll just let the men who killed your friend find us. They're not the kind to leave loose ends. If you would just shut up and listen, you'd hear them in the woods. I can tell you, whoever else is up here, it isn't the police. If the police were looking for you, they'd be calling out to you, identifying who they are, and let you know they were trying to help. I wasn't the only one who saw you run up here."

Madison listened, heard twigs snapping, and the soft pounding of running feet on the damp ground. It wasn't a search party out looking for her. It was the sound made by a lone person. She looked up at him. As she stared into his pale eyes, she knew she had no other choice but to trust him. He had saved her life, and she couldn't outrun him. Her knee throbbed, and she was exhausted, both emotionally and physically. In her heart, she knew he was right. If he didn't cause the explosion, then whoever it was wouldn't be pleased, knowing she escaped. This man stopped her from harming herself by entering the burning building. If he wanted her dead, he could have just let her go. She'd have died if she made it inside. Even if the flames weren't too intense for her to enter, the fire had gained momentum, and she would never have made it out. What remained of the chalet after the explosion became engulfed with flames by the time she ran.

She turned and looked back, just making out the glow of the smouldering remains of her chalet in the distance. She could hear the faint sound of sirens as the fire department approached. They would be there soon, but not soon enough. There wasn't anything left for them to salvage. All they could do now was to stop the fire from spreading to other chalets and the surrounding forest.

Tears burned in her eyes as she watched the charred timbers fall, flames still licking at the hollowed shell, knowing her best friend was gone and with her a lifetime of memories. Abby wouldn't be there tomorrow. She'd never hear her voice again. Abby was gone. The sorrow tore at her heart. Tears pooled in her eyes before they spilled out and rolled off her cheeks in a steady stream. She'd already suffered so much loss in her life. This time, she wasn't sure she'd recover.

HE STOOD WATCHING her in silence, mindful of the footsteps as they headed off in another direction. The man wasn't sure whether he should comfort her. He sensed how great her loss was and how much it affected her. It took all of his restraint not to wrap his arms around her and pull her close. She looked so vulnerable. He reached out to touch her shoulder, and before he knew it, he pulled her into his embrace, offering her the comfort she needed. He held her and soothed away her sorrow. Madison buried her face in his chest, again smelling the faint aroma of a cigar. But this time, she also picked up the hint of his musky cologne. At five foot eight, she wasn't short, but he had to be well over six feet for him to make her feel so small and helpless.

Abruptly, he pushed her away. He had to keep this professional. He saw the startled look in her eyes as she searched his face to understand. His jaw clenched as he looked over her head into the forest behind and led her further up the mountain.

"Quickly, they're looking for you. We have to get out of here."

Madison resisted before she gave in. Over her shoulder, she just made out the glow from her chalet. But she heard creaks and groans as the final timbers fell. Voices rose from the woods behind her. Although muffled and unable to see anyone, she knew he was right. They heard someone shout orders for the forest to be searched, and she was sure it wasn't the local fire and rescue. Somehow, whoever did this knew Madison wasn't inside when the explosion went off, and now they were looking for her. He kept a firm hold on her arm. His grip tightened as he led her away, deeper into the forest, up into the foothills of the Allegany Mountains and beyond.

# CHAPTER 10

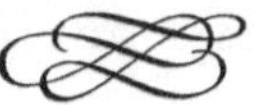

"Come on! You've got to move faster. I can hear them just behind us, and if we don't keep going, it won't take them long to catch up. If they do, it'll be all over." His hand was still around her wrist as he pulled her along deeper into the forest. "I'm pretty sure they don't know you have help, but they must know you weren't inside when the bomb went off. We'll have to find somewhere to hide until they give up for the night. In the morning, they'll send dogs out to pick up your scent if they don't find you before then. It'll take a while to organize a dog search, and they won't risk that while the police and fire services are still hanging around, so we have some time." He hissed.

Madison wanted to yank her arm free of his grasp, but she heard whoever was in the woods with them and thought better of it. She knew she was taking a chance by following him, but she didn't have a choice.

"I know a place," she gasped. "There's a small cave just over the crest of the mountain. We could hide in there for a while. It's not big, but it's well hidden. I used to play there when I was a child." Madison's mind jolted *'Why am I trusting him?'*

"O.K., you lead the way, but keep up the pace. We can't allow them to catch up."

Madison shook his hand from her arm as she pushed forward, keeping to a light jog. Her face stung from the branches that lashed her as they sprinted through the woods, ever mindful of the voices behind them. The soft wet ground caused their feet to slip out to the side as they ran, slowing their progress. The voices grew further away. They'd either turned in a different direction or fell behind. Madison wasn't sure how much longer she could go on. Sweat beaded her face as she exerted herself up the steep incline. Tears continued to brim her eyes. She felt his other hand reach out and tighten on her arm as she slipped on the damp leaves beneath her feet.

"It's just a little further. Up behind those bushes. Few people know it's here. It's so well hidden. I only found it by accident." She panted.

"That's good. We need whatever coverage we can get before we go any further. We need the chance to make a plan and figure out our next move."

Madison stopped in front of a group of bushes and pulled them back to reveal a small, dark opening in the rocks just over the ridge.

"This is it? We'll never fit in there." He groaned.

"The entrance is small. That's why few people know about it. Even the locals don't bother coming here. But inside is much larger, almost like a room. Although I haven't been here for many years, I'm sure there'll be enough room for both of us."

Madison got down on her hands and knees and crawled into the opening. It was smaller than she remembered, and she hoped he'd squeeze through. Although the entrance was narrow, he wiggled through with some difficulty. The cave itself was also not as large as she recalled. But her memory was through the eyes of a child when everything seemed larger by comparison. When he stood to his full height, his head skimmed the roof of the cave. The floor had a limited area. It would just accommodate them both if they had to sleep here, and there was no way he'd be able to stretch out.

"You're right! It's small!" He said. "At least we'll be dry if it rains. But the rocks will be cold and damp. I pulled the bushes back over the opening so that it's hidden again. In the dark, if you didn't know where it was, it would be impossible to find."

Madison turned to face him, just able to make out his features, as only a slim glimmer of moonlight allowed her to see where he was. Until now, she'd followed him with blind faith, believing him when he told her she was in danger. Now, with the running behind them, at least temporarily, she had questions. She was alone with this stranger in a cave. No one knew where she was. If he intended to harm her, she'd just made it easier for him. He could kill her here, and they'd never find her body. If he was trying to help her, then what she needed most from him were answers.

"Who are you?" She shot out.

"I'm Carl." He stated, as if his name explained everything.

"Carl? Carl who? How do you know what's going on? Why were you there? Who killed Abby?" Madison fired questions at him. Even though she felt devastated and confused, she took control.

"It doesn't matter. I knew what was going to happen. I couldn't get there in time to stop it. But I saved your life. Now I have to figure out a way of keeping you alive."

CRACK! The sound of Madison's hand as it connected with his cheek echoed through the tiny cave. In the dim light, the outline of a red handprint was visible. His eyes narrowed as he looked down at her, struggling to control his temper.

"How dare you!" She spat. "You knew we were in danger, but you didn't warn us? Why didn't you call the police? You bastard! It's your fault Abby's dead."

Carl grabbed the wrist of her still raised hand, locking it in his steely grasp. He yanked her closer and lowered his face until he looked into her eyes.

"Don't try that again." He hissed, "If I called the police, they'd have aborted the plan, for the time being. But understand this, they would have made a second attempt. I might not have been there to save you. Then you'd both be dead."

Madison glared at him. He still wasn't answering her questions. Her best friend was dead, and he had the knowledge to prevent it. She wanted to kill him. Her sorrow turned to rage as her mind whirled with possibilities. She needed more information. Madison didn't understand why he wasn't telling her what she wanted to know. She had to have something to tell Abby's parents, something that would help them make sense of this tragic loss.

Madison took a slow, deep breath, calming her fury. She knew she needed to reel it in, take control and bottle it up to for later. It wouldn't help for him see her anger. She still wasn't sure whether he was working with them, whoever 'they' were. She didn't know him, but she was sure he'd just saved her life. What she didn't know was why. Maybe this was a ploy to get her away from the police so that he could lead her back to the murderers. No matter what happened, she would not be a victim. She was a different person now than she was the last time she dealt with tragedy. Then she'd been a victim.

She couldn't change what happened to Abby, but she'd be in control and aware. She would find out who did this and make sure she brought them to justice. Once she gained control of her emotions, she started questioning him again.

"Who killed her?"

"It was a mob hit. It's that simple," he admitted.

"What's so simple about a mob hit?" She urged. "Who was the target?"

"Your friend Abby. She was a lawyer, right?"

"Yes," Madison replied, biting down on her lower lip.

"Well, she stepped on some big toes. The information I have was that she was supposed to get a mob boss's son off on a murder rap, but she changed her mind. She let prime evidence fall into the Crown Attorney's hands. The boy went to jail, and his father wanted his revenge. She had client/lawyer privilege information. It was information that could bring down his entire organization and family. He wouldn't let that happen."

"And me? It was my chalet. I'd have been killed too."

"To them, you were just an inconvenience, collateral damage, so to speak. They had to make it look like an accident, and it had to be in the States. The family didn't want to take a chance of getting caught crossing the border. Somehow they found out you were coming here, and they made use of the opportunity."

"Then it's my fault. If I hadn't planned this trip, Abby would still be alive." Madison, weakened with exhaustion, sank to the ground.

"She may be alive today, but not for long. There was already a price on her head. They would have gotten to her somehow. It may have taken a little longer, but they still would've stopped her. If need be, an accident in Canada, a car crash, fake suicide, anything. They have someone on their bankroll that worked in proximity with her and was feeding them information. Somehow, in the next few weeks, she would've ended up in the States and they'd get to her then. She was an obstacle in their way and a danger to the organization. They needed her gone."

"They killed her for doing her job?" Madison cried. "She was honest. She didn't work like that. Abby would never have deliberately put a man behind bars. And she would never make a deal with the mob. She is, or she was, a criminal lawyer. Abby defended criminals. She didn't put them away. She believed in innocent until proven guilty. They only went away if she lost a case, and the last case she was working on, she won."

"That may be, but this time, her winning meant the son of the mob boss went to jail. I think it was a sting operation." He tried to explain.

"Oh my god, what was she into?"

"Try to rest Madison. We'll give it a few hours and then head out."

"How do you know my name?" She regarded him with fear because she never told him her name.

"As I've told you. I was trying to stop this from happening. To help, I needed to learn as much as I could about both of you. I knew who Abigail Monroe was because of the hit the mob put out on her. But I had to learn who Madison Kerr was, too. I knew you'd be here.

I wished I could have saved you both." Carl finished with an air of finality.

Madison watched him as he sat down, attempting to get comfortable on the cold stone floor. She was sure he wasn't telling her everything. She needed to find out what he was keeping back. It was difficult to see him in the dark, dank cave. She could just make out his features. She remembered what he looked like when she saw him in town. He was handsome, but not in the GQ Magazine way. His face held more character. His eyes were a pale turquoise, which she'd noticed when he was comforting her. Carl's close-cropped dark hair that was streaked with silver showed he could be close to forty. He leaned back against the wall of the cave with his eyes half-closed, his long legs stretched out. She continued to look at him, trying to get a sense of who he was, as she tried to prepare to get some rest.

He was at home in his faded jeans and jacket. Blue jeans and t-shirt type of guy, she thought. What was he doing mixed up in a world of power suits and the mob? What was his connection to all of this? His eyes opened as he returned her stare.

"Are you finished?" He asked.

"What?" she replied, startled, unsure what his question meant.

"Are you finished assessing me?" He ventured. "I assure you, I won't kill you while you sleep."

Madison put her purse under her head as a pillow and rolled over so that her back was towards him. What in the hell did he mean by that? Assessing him indeed! But wasn't that just what she'd been doing? She only wanted to be sure he wouldn't harm her. Madison remembered the steely glare he gave her when she slapped him. She was embarrassed that he caught her looking at him, but these were very unusual circumstances. He was too full of himself for her to worry about now. She shivered as her body relaxed from the adrenaline that had pumped through it. Quietly, she let tears of sorrow run down her face and drip onto the dirty cave floor as she cried for Abby.

# CHAPTER 11

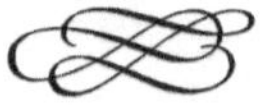

"Have you found her?" Don Fernando demanded as Tony entered the cabin.

"No boss, there's no sign of her."

"Well, then keep looking. She can't be far. And where's Dean? He hasn't checked in yet."

"There's no sign of Dean either. He disappeared right after the explosion. Or he may have followed her, or he might lie low. He should have been outside the chalet, keeping a lookout before the bitches came home. So I'm sure he took off when the cops showed up. He knows how to make himself scarce and getaway. I don't know where he is, but I'm sure he'll show up soon."

"He'd better turn up soon, or else. I don't like screw-ups, and the other one getting away is a screw-up. Take care of any loose ends! I have to get back to the compound. I've arranged for a car to come for me, and it should be here shortly. I need you to stay here and keep looking for her. As far as anyone knows, I wasn't here. No one saw me, and they can't trace you to me. So if anyone sees you, there's no problem. I rented the cottage under an alias, but in case the cops come around asking questions, cover your arms. Your tattoos are very distinctive. I know you know how to handle the cops. I'm sure you can come up with a suitable cover story about why you're here."

"Si, I know nothin'. I was out in the town, and when I came back, the chalet was on fire. I never saw who was staying there and I don't know who rented it or who it belonged to. The cops may sniff around for a bit, but they'll leave me alone. I'll let them know I'm here to check out vacation spots for my girl. She wanted to go on a skiing trip and heard Ellicottville was a nice place."

"Fine. Just be careful what you say. Don't give them too much and watch the Spanish! I want you to do a sweep of the chalet. Clean and wipe down every surface. Make sure there's nothing to link us to this and then search again. Keep me posted. I'll see you when you get back to the compound."

With that, Don Fernando heaved his massive frame up from the sofa to leave. Tony grabbed The Don's overnight bag and took it out to the waiting car. The Don knew when to leave. It was well before dawn, and the police hadn't started going door to door to ask questions. There was enough to be done to keep Tony busy for a few days, and to ensure that there wasn't any evidence left behind. At least Tony was thorough. The Don wasn't getting his hands any dirtier than they already were with this mess. He shouldn't have risked going to the chalet, but the temptation had been too great. It was a close call getting out on time. Now he needed to leave and find peace in his own environment. He would go to the compound where he would find serenity, and he could forget this unfortunate situation. He needed to recharge and get back to the business at hand. They'd taken care of the problem. With the lawyer out of the way, there was nothing more to worry about. Even if they didn't find the other girl, there was no way anyone could link them to this. It might be a good idea to consider having it appear that the other one was behind the explosion. That way, if they didn't find her, it wouldn't matter, and then finding her would be up to the cops.

*'Where the hell is Dean?'* Don Fernando thought. *'It wasn't like him not to check-in. He'd better show up soon, or else he's a dead man. I'd hate to lose a good man, but no one crosses me!'*

~

TONY STOOD at the front door and watched as the car that carried Don Fernando drove out of sight.

*'Christ, heads were gonna roll. The Don didn't look happy. Could Dean have betrayed them? I saw that bitch running away up the mountain, and I'm sure I saw someone else following her. If it wasn't Dean, then there's someone else to take care of when I clean this mess up. I want to be the one to catch her. I'll enjoy making her suffer for all the trouble she'd caused. But if Dean double-crossed The Don, I'll make him pay. The Don will want his revenge taken out slowly and painfully. Inflicting pain is my specialty. If Dean switched sides, his treachery would put the boss over the edge, and who knew how far things would go? The Don has a soft spot for Dean, but I also have ambitions within the organization, and The Don's affection for Dean is in my way. For now, I'll give Dean the benefit of the doubt, but if I find out he's crossed the line, I'll take care of him myself. A slow and painful death.'* Tony stepped back from the door once The Don was out of sight, closed it, turned the lock, and closed the blinds.

*'The Don wants me to hunt the bitch down and take care of her. I can't let her get away, or he won't be happy. Is it possible she knows something? I wonder if the lawyer told her about the evidence? If she knows anything and can get to the cops before we find her, there'll be hell to pay. I can't let that happen. I'll make sure I find her, and when I do, I'll enjoy wrapping my hands around her neck and squeezing the life out of her. She's a looker, so maybe I'll fuck her first and then kill her. There's no reason I can't enjoy my work. Hell, when I'm done with her, I'll split her in two!'*

Tony chuckled to himself as he began the tedious process of going room to room to do a sweep. Slowly and carefully, he began tossing evidence into the fire and any of their belongings into bags to take back to the compound. With expert precision, he removed all signs that could tie any of them to this place. He dusted, polished, and scrubbed every surface, wearing gloves so that he wouldn't leave prints behind as he went. He packed his own belongings, leaving enough out for the next couple of days. When he finished, he sat down with the pile of Dean's things and went through them. Other than basic, almost generic clothing, and some expensive cigars, there was nothing that gave him a clue where Dean was. There was also nothing there that could identify Dean as an infiltrator or as a member of the family. His entire ID was missing. That alone wasn't suspicious. Dean was very skilled at what he did, but something wasn't right. Tony felt he needed to understand it. Dean wasn't coming back to the chalet, so he packed up Dean's possessions and added them to his pile to take back to the compound.

After a final survey of the chalet, he took everything out to the garage and locked all of their personal items in the trunk of his rental. From now on, he'd be careful to wear gloves when he was inside to avoid leaving prints behind while he waited to see the outcome of the investigation into the explosion. In the meantime, he'd continue searching the woods for the bitch.

# CHAPTER 12

$\mathcal{M}$adison awoke, restless, after a few hours of disturbed sleep. Even though she was exhausted, she'd spent much of the night crying over Abby's death. She turned gingerly on the cold, damp, rock floor of the cave, noticing how stiff she was. She shifted her body onto her back before opening her tear-swollen eyes. When she did, it startled her to look up into Carl's clear aqua ones, as he leaned over her in the dim, still moonlit cave.

"What the hell!" she exclaimed, as she tried to push herself further away from him, only to hit the back of her head on the rock wall. Her hand shot up to rub the now tender spot.

"It's O.K., you're safe. I wouldn't attack you. I was just about to wake you. We need to get going while it's still dark. They won't expect us to make a move until morning, and the darkness will be the perfect cover. By now, they'll have figured out we've found somewhere to hole up for the night."

"I wouldn't expect you to try anything. I've already hit you once, and I'd hate to hit you again," Madison replied indignantly, trying to sound braver than she felt.

"I told you that wouldn't happen again. Do you keep anything useful in that purse of yours?" He asked, motioning to the handbag that she'd slung across her body before the explosion.

She looked down at her purse. Even though she used it as a pillow, she'd almost forgotten that she had it.

"Sure I do. Let me see." Madison said as she began rummaging through her bag. "My wallet, a couple of protein bars, a bottle of water, cell phone, keys, some cosmetics, brush, sketch pad, pens, and a pocket knife." She finished rhyming off most of the items she found.

"A pocket knife?" He asked, as his eyebrow rose quizzically.

"It's one of those army jobs, you know, scissors, screwdriver, corkscrew, utensils, etc. I find it comes in handy now and then."

"I guess I'm lucky you didn't decide to use it on me last night," He teased. "We should get something in us before we move on. I hope you don't mind if we share the protein bars and water. It may be a while before we have time to eat again. I think we should only split one bar and part of the water. That way, we can make it last. There's a clearing not far over the ridge. From there, we'll try to get a signal with your cell phone. I'll call someone I know to help us."

"Are we going to call the police?"

"No, I've already told you. The police can't help you. I have a friend I'll call. He'll track us down and get us out of here safely and undetected."

Madison broke one of the protein bars in two and handed half to him. They each took small sips of her water to conserve it. Madison was thankful that she had put them in her bag before leaving the chalet yesterday. She wasn't sure why she did. Maybe it was a premonition.

Carl ate most of the protein bar, swallowing a big mouthful of water to wash down its chalky texture. He wanted to get moving as quickly as possible, but he didn't want her to see how anxious he was to do so. There was no need to fuel her fear or uncertainty. He needed to make that call so they could put distance between them-selves and the explosion site.

Madison watched him as he ate, taking small bites of her protein bar while she did. He appeared relaxed and unhurried. It was almost as if he was at home, being on the run. She could tell from his demeanour that he wasn't a stranger to dangerous situations. The longer she was with him, the more curious she became about who he was, and whether she could or should trust him. She needed to know more.

"Who are you planning on calling? How could he be better at sorting this out than the police? You know we need to report this. I'm sure they're looking for me. It was my chalet, and so many people knew I was there. Oh, God, I have to talk to Abby's parents. They can't hear this from a stranger. Her parents need to hear it from someone who loves them and Abby. They also need to know I had nothing to do with this." She knew she was rambling, but couldn't stop herself. She exhaled. Tears brimmed her eyes, threatening to spill over. She brushed them away with the back of her hand.

"It won't matter. The police will have already notified her next of kin. An explosion like that will be big news. Didn't you see the people from the chalet next to you? They had their phones out, taking videos and pictures. By now, it will already be all over social media. Those responsible will try to pin this on you, especially since you escaped. I'm certain they've made sure they can trace the explosives back to you. These people are experts at covering their tracks."

"No one who knows me would believe I'd kill Abby. I loved her. She was like a sister to me. If you knew so much about 'them,' why didn't you stop them?" Anger flashed in her eyes, replacing the tears.

"I couldn't stop them," he replied. "Once the wheels were in motion, there was no stopping them. They would have aborted one plan for another until they got the job done. I'm sure they've made it look like you're responsible. They'll find an angle, possibly jealousy, or something she had that you wanted, boyfriend, career, lifestyle, something like that. The public will buy it. They always do."

"No," she whispered, "there's nothing." Her voice caught in her throat as her eyes welled once again. Abby's dying was unbearable. But to think that her parents would be told she killed Abby that was unthinkable. They were her substitute family. They would never believe it.

Carl could sense the pain she was in, but knew there was nothing he could do. He wasn't a stranger to pain, but dealing with fresh loss was always the most difficult. He popped the last piece of the protein bar she'd offered him into his mouth, allowing her time to pull herself together before he forced them to move on. When she wiped away her tears, she abruptly stood, grabbed her bag, brushed the dirt from her pants, and jutted out her chin in determination.

"Let's go. You're the one who said we had to get out of here while it was still dark. If we're going to make it before 'they' start looking again, then we'd better get a move on."

Carl stood up, shaking his head. *I'll give her credit. She's got guts. Thank God. Otherwise, she'd never survive what's ahead of her, and we'd never get out of this. I think she's done all the crying she's going to do for now, and that's a good thing. I need her strong if my plan is going to work.'*

Carl led the way, squeezing out of the cave opening and holding back the bushes so that Madison could get out with ease. It was close to dawn, but the sky was still a deep blue. Bright glittering stars filled the sky, and the faint filtered glow of the moon was visible, casting a dim light on the forest floor. Carl hesitated as he looked around to get his bearings before he chose which direction to take. He paused and looked down the mountain to where the chalet once stood. No matter how brief his glance was, she caught his look and followed his gaze. There was nothing left. The fire was out, and she could no longer see her chalet. From this distance, all she could make out were the fire trucks and flashing lights from police cars. Along with Abby, she'd also lost all of her precious keepsakes from her childhood. The mementos of her parents, even the small pearl ring Cory gave her. Everything was gone. She vowed to herself that she would get whoever did this. If it was the last thing she did, she would see that justice was done, justice for Abby. There would be no more tears until she avenged Abby's death. Madison took a deep, calming breath. She'd faced too much death in her life already. She squared her shoulders and lifted her head high before marching past Carl in the direction he'd shown her.

～

CARL NOTICED an immediate the change in her, the determination and self-assured pose of her posture. Something happened. He wasn't sure what, but something somewhere deep inside had changed. She seemed resolved. It wasn't an acceptance, but an understanding. There was a lot she would face in the weeks to come, but her still blissful ignorance was important. What he didn't tell her was that she was useful to him. The minute he saved her life, she'd become part of his plan. He needed her, needed the information she had, whether she knew it or not. She had access to information that would make all the difference. But first, he had to earn her trust. It was the only way his plan would work. It wouldn't be easy. She didn't trust him, but another obstacle was that she didn't seem to like him either. Not that it mattered what she thought. She was stuck with him for the time being, and a bit of trust would go a long way. As things moved forward, he'd do his best to protect her.

She was fiery with a strong will; that much was obvious. When she learned she was stuck with him, it wouldn't sit well with her. Not that she had a choice, but he would do his best to keep her safe. He almost found her attitude amusing. In fact, under other circumstances, seeing her indignant and fuming would please him. It was her suffering he couldn't handle. There was more going on here than the loss of her friend. He could tell old wounds had opened up, ones that had never healed. When he got back, he'd have her file sent over to see what it said. He'd been more interested in Abigail Monroe than Madison Kerr when preparing for this.

"Let's get moving." She said with determination. "You said it was dangerous to stay here. The faster we get going, the faster we can get out of here. Then I can find those responsible and make them pay. Abby didn't deserve to die, no matter what she did or didn't do. I want to help catch who did this to her, and for her parents to know what really happened." Madison slung her bag over her shoulder as she tore her eyes away from the scene below and continued forward.

Carl followed her lead. His eyes darted from side to side as he watched their surroundings. They'd only traveled a short distance when he grabbed her from behind. He clamped his hand over her mouth and held her still. This time she didn't struggle, knowing he had a reason, but that didn't stop her from feeling outraged. With his hand pressed against her mouth, he turned her to face him. Anger flashed in her eyes until she noticed his free hand was at his own mouth, signalling her to be quiet.

They held this position in the darkness, listening to the surrounding sounds. Something unexpectedly broke the silence with a movement to the left, then followed by the sound of a snapping twig. Her expression changed from anger to alarm as she searched his eyes for a sign. They stood together, careful not to move, and listened to the surrounding forest. They held their breath until they were certain whoever or whatever they heard had drifted back down the mountain.

"O.K., I think we're safe. It may have only been an animal, but I'm not sure." Carl whispered. "The faster we get away from here, the better. Let's keep moving."

Under the cover of darkness, they continued to move forward. They took their time as they made their way through the forest until vibrant streaks of orange and pink crested the mountain with the first signs of daylight. As the clearing appeared ahead of them, they could see the break in the forest. Carl moved into the clearing after motioning Madison to stay behind, where she would still hide in the safety of the trees. There, he used her cell phone to contact help. His call was brief, and in less than two minutes, he turned back towards her.

"We'll have to make our way towards the other side of the McCarty Hill State Forest. There's a small back road there. My friend picked it as the perfect meeting place. It's in an area off the major roads and will be difficult to find. I know the spot, but this territory is more familiar to you. I'll let you lead the way through the forest. When we're close to the meeting place, I'll take over. We should get there sometime later this afternoon. Then we'll have to stay hidden until nightfall. When it's dark, my friend will arrive, and signal to us."

"Fine. I know my way, and I think I know the road you're talking about. Can I assume we're to stay away from roads and paths on our way?" Madison questioned sarcastically.

"I think you already know the answer to that," he affirmed.

Madison inspected her surroundings so she could get her bearings. She regretted not adding a navigation app to her cell phone. But she was certain they'd have traced its signal. They'd already traveled a respectful distance in the dark, but now that they were at a high point of land, it wouldn't be hard to find the right path and head in that direction. The first rays of sunshine streaked the sky to her left. Therefore, she was facing south, and she knew the shortest route out of the forest. She pointed in the direction they needed to take.

They were careful to keep to the thick wooded areas and well away from the roads, pathways, and areas that naturally attracted hikers and adventurers. Before dusk, they reached the meeting spot. A thin, rarely used dirt road that was overgrown with weeds, long grass, and brush tangled along the edge. They settled back in the woods to wait and watch. The road, covered in a mixture of dirt and gravel, was old and not well maintained. From their vantage point, they couldn't see a single light, showing that there weren't any cabins nearby. The remoteness of this location made the spot perfect. Not a single car passed them as they waited, just out of sight.

Madison had dozed off when she heard the muffled sound of gravel crunching under tires, signalling an approaching vehicle. She snapped awake and listened. It pulled up the road and parked along the side, lights off, close to their hiding spot. She squinted at what appeared to be a beat-up pickup, rust showing through the cream and burgundy paint. The short box on the back had a Tonneau cover that was custom made. She realized it was patina, and it was designed to look old and beat up. The driver turned off the engine before slipping out of the cab. He wore a cowboy hat, boots, and blue jeans with his quilted jacket. She couldn't make out his face under the shadow of the hat. He walked around to the wooded side of his truck, glanced around, and then appeared as if he was going to relieve himself.

"That's the signal," Carl said as he rose to a half hunched over position. "Quickly! We have to get in the truck before we're seen."

Madison followed him with the same hunched over posture, running to keep up with his long strides. As they exited the woods and onto the tangled brush at the road's edge, the cowboy reached over and opened the passenger door, flipped the front seat back, revealing a panel that slid to one side, granting access to the covered back. The cowboy tipped his hat. 'Howdy'. His eyebrows raised when he saw Madison up close. He nodded towards Carl, who nodded back.

"Climb in," he said. Madison hesitated, so Carl pushed past her, and squeezed into the opening, and stretched out along one side of the padded compartment in the back of the truck. She looked at the cowboy again, and he smiled at her. This reassured her, so she followed Carl and squeezed in beside him. The cowboy slipped the panel back into place, and she could feel the truck shift as he climbed back in and started the engine.

Madison lay in the back and bumped with the movements as the truck drove along the dirt road. The padding did nothing to prevent her from feeling every pothole and groove on the surface. She couldn't stop herself from rolling and banging up against Carl. But each time she did, she squirmed back to her own side. She held her tongue. Not asking any more questions, hoping he would fill her in when he saw fit. This proximity to him made her feel ill at ease, and she didn't trust herself not to say anything scathing. It seemed like an eternity before he spoke to her through the darkness.

"I'm sorry. It's necessary to keep hidden. I designed the truck for this purpose. You never know when it will be necessary to move someone from one place to another undetected. They'll be looking for two people, not a single man driving alone. When we get to a safe place, I'll explain as much as I can to you. The cowboy is Hank. He works for me. He's been waiting close by in case I needed him. We go back a long way, and I trust him with my life. He's resourceful and knows how to get things done. He'll take care of everything and get us to safety. Don't worry! You're not in danger. Now that Hank's seen you, he'll make sure of it. He's always been a sucker for a damsel in distress."

She wasn't sure of anything Carl said, but one thing she knew was she liked Hank on sight. He had a straightforward way about him, and his smile was bright and true. She doubted he was behind what was happening to her, and judging by how surprised he was to see her, Carl hadn't filled him in. If Carl wouldn't level with her, maybe Hank would.

As she struggled to lie still in the back of the truck, she thought of Abby. Trying to figure out what Abby did for someone to want her dead. If Abby knew how dangerous it was and that it would get her killed, would she had done things differently? If she'd gone to the chalet instead of Abby, would that have changed anything? Then Madison remembered how determined Abby was to go in alone. She insisted Madison stayed behind to wait, which was unusual. It was as if she knew something wasn't right. Her mind flashed to the scene where Abby and Carl were talking in the bar. Did he warn her? Did Abby know she was going to die? If Madison had died, would that have made things easier for the killer? Now it made sense why they were after her. She was at a loose end. Her stomach clenched at the reality that to these people, she was expendable.

Until this was over, and as much as she wanted to grieve for Abby's death, it would have to wait. When she saw those responsible paid, then she would grieve, not before. She had to stay focused and try to get as much information out of Carl as she could. Only then could she go to the police. She needed proof that Abby was murdered and that the explosion wasn't just an accident.

# CHAPTER 13

hey'd roped the area around the chalet off while the police and fire department sifted through the ashes, searching for clues. They discovered evidence of a bomb and detonator, and now classified it as a crime scene. Several officers strung up yellow caution tape to cordon off a larger area, so they could continue with the investigation. Tony tried to get close enough to find out what they knew, but an officer guarding the perimeter cut him off. He considered disguising himself as a cop and joining their efforts, but he knew he couldn't pull it off. Dean would have blended in. Damn him for disappearing. A smile spread across Tony's lips while he surveyed the large number of the people still milling around. He could still dress up as a cop and get information from the witnesses. They wouldn't know the difference.

He left and pulled out a generic uniform from his trunk. He always was prepared for anything. A few minutes later, dressed in uniform, he wandered through the crowd. He wanted to know what people saw, and he knew there was always someone willing to answer a few questions after such an event. He noticed a group of men from the neighbouring chalet who were still standing around, stunned by the devastation. His mood brightened as he made his way towards them.

*'These must be who the bitches were with last night.'* He thought, *'Well, let's see if they can tell me anything. One of them might have seen which way the girl went. Maybe even give me a clue as to Dean's whereabouts.'*

Tony pulled out a notebook, took purposeful strides as he headed towards the small group of men.

"Hello, do you mind answering a few questions?" He continued before they could respond. "Can any of you tell me what you saw here last night?"

"We already talked to the cops." One retorted.

"Well, that was the night shift. You know how it is. Sometimes they forget to fill the day guys in. Do you mind telling me what you saw?" Tony questioned, using his most polite voice.

"O.K. sure. We met these two girls last night."

"Abby and Madison." Another interjected.

"Yeah, that's right. Abby and Madison. They were nice and fun to be around. We invited them to come back to our chalet for a BBQ. They headed to their chalet to get something to contribute and join us."

"Was it just a barbecue, or did you have something else in mind? I understand they were both attractive young ladies." Tony hinted.

"No, it was nothing like that. Our best friend is getting married, and we came down here to celebrate with a bachelor weekend. I'm sure some of the single guys may have hoped, but no one expected anything. They were just fun to be around. Anyway, Abby went to the chalet, and Madison waited outside and talked with a few of the guys. She thought Abby was taking too long, so she went to get her. Just after she left, we heard the explosion."

"Do you think this Madison set the explosion?" Tony asked to get them more comfortable talking to him.

"No. It was Madison's chalet. There's no way she would have done this. Something or someone else caused the explosion."

"Did you notice anything after the explosion? Someone you

didn't know hanging around, or someone running away, or anything else like that?"

"Yeah, Stu mentioned seeing someone running up the mountain."

"Which one's Stu?" Tony hissed.

"Ah, um, he's gone already. But he told the other cops he saw two people running up the mountain after the explosion. One was following the other. He couldn't tell if it was a man or a woman. Whoever it was, was too far away. The cops said they'd look into it, so I'm sure they made a report. If that's all, we have to get going. We all have to be back at work tomorrow."

"That's O.K. you can go."  Tony's eyes drifted in the direction where 'Stu' saw people running away. 'It must have been her, and it had to be Dean following her. No one else would have been nearby. This is a good thing. That meant Dean will take care of her.' A smile crept to Tony's face as he considered this, failing to notice the confused looks he was getting from the men he'd just spoken with, having already dismissed them from his mind. They didn't matter to him now. He got all he needed from them.

"The hunt is on bitch." He hissed aloud as he made his way back to the cabin to avoid the 'real' police.

Tony resolved that Dean's sudden disappearance had something to do with the missing girl. He just didn't know how or why. Dean must have gone to look for her. She was of no importance, but they couldn't be sure, so now he would make her pay. Dean may have chased her up the mountain and into the forest, but if it was Tony, he'd kill her there. They may never find her body. But that wasn't Dean's style. He wouldn't kill her. He'd capture her and bring her back to the boss unless he'd deceived them all and was helping her. If it was the latter, Tony would bring Dean down too. If Dean went against The Family, it would be his chance to move up, maybe even be The Don's right-hand man. Secretly, Tony hoped Dean had turned on the family. Then finding her would be up to him, and he'd be able to take care of her in his own way, something he'd enjoy.

# CHAPTER 14

Madison bumped along in silence in the truck's bed. She found herself lost in thought as she tried to understand how she'd ended up in this situation. Until now, they'd only stopped once at a rundown, out-of-the-way motor inn. Hank requested the room furthest from the motel office so that he could slip Carl and Madison in unobserved. Instead of supper, they ate potato chips and drank stale coffee before heading off to bed. Carl and Hank shared one, leaving Madison in a bed to herself. At night, she tossed and turned in a fitful sleep, and often woke from the nightmares of the explosion that plagued her.

It wasn't until the second day that Hank felt they'd put enough distance between themselves and Ellicottville and looked for a place to eat. Hank found a roadside diner with a convenience store attached and pulled over. He parked at the rear of the building so no one would notice when Carl and Madison climbed out from their hiding spot. The three of them headed inside to eat their first proper meal since going on the run. Hank handed Madison a ball cap as they made their way inside so that she could tuck her hair up into a ponytail and shield her face. Once inside, Carl led them to the back of the diner and positioned himself so he could watch the door. Hank and Madison sat across from him.

"The hat was quick thinking, Hank. It helps to disguise Madison." Carl took a swig of his coffee the server had just served them. "At least the coffee's good. I hope the food will be too. I'm starving."

Hank cast a sideways glance at Madison.

"I think it would take more than the hat to hide her, but it helps. You look good in a ball cap, Madison."

Madison hesitated. She wasn't comfortable with either of them and hated the situation she was in. She was biding her time. All she wanted was to ask where they were going and how they were going to find who killed Abby. But she held her tongue and smiled at Hank instead. She shifted further into the corner of the booth, took in the chipped Formica tabletop and the torn red vinyl upholstery. The paint on the walls bubbled and peeled, faded posters tried to cover the dismal repair of the diner.

Madison peeked out from under her cap at the only other patron. His t-shirt was dirty and riddled with holes, his stomach protruded where it didn't quite meet his pants, as he sat hunched over his plate, shovelling in his meal. Sensing he was being watched, he turned towards her. Gravy clung to his grizzled beard as he smiled at her. A large gaping hole where only a few posts of teeth remained. His partially chewed mouthful clung to the posts and his tongue. Madison shivered in revulsion and turned back to her companions.

Soon the server approached with their food. Carl chose a hot beef sandwich, Hank a burger, and fries. Madison wanted a salad but doubted the freshness of it and went with chicken strips and fries instead, assuming they'd come from the freezer and would be safe. After depositing the plates of food, the server returned with the coffee pot to top them up.

Both men ate with a ravenous appetite while chatting about nothing in particular. Madison just picked at her food. Although she was hungry, the puddle of grease congealing underneath it turned her off. She ate half of a chicken strip and some fries before pushing her plate away.

"I'm going to go next door and get some snacks for the ride."

Carl looked up at her, his eyes searching hers before he responded.

"Fine. I'll wait for you out front. Hank and I are almost finished. Do you need cash?"

"No, I have some."

"Just make sure you only use cash. If you use your debit or credit card, they can trace the transaction."

"I'm not an idiot! I know that!" Madison snapped as she stood, waiting for Hank to let her pass.

Hank stood up so she could get by and watched her go as she left the restaurant before turning back to Carl.

"You'll have to tell her something. She's emotional, reeling from shock and getting pissed off. The combination is dangerous. I don't understand why you just don't level with her."

"It's not for you to understand. I know we go back a long way, but you work for me. I'll tell her what she needs to know when I feel she's ready." Carl leaned back in his seat. "She won't do anything stupid. Madison doesn't have a passport with her, so she can't cross the border back into Canada, and where else can she go? She has no one else."

"You're underestimating her. I think there's a fiery temper to match the hair under her cool demeanour."

MADISON DIDN'T LOOK BACK as she left the restaurant. What she needed was a plan. Being left in the dark didn't sit well, and neither man was giving her anything to go on. The little overhead bell tinkled as she entered the convenience store. She glanced around and it surprised her at how well-stocked it was. Noting the very thin woman who sat behind the counter, she nodded at her in greeting.

Madison made her way along the snack aisle, chose some items, but not until she checked the stale date: you can never be too careful. Satisfied that she had enough for a little while at least, she made her way up to the cash to pay. She could see Carl through the dirty window waiting out front, and it angered her. She wasn't a prisoner, although he was treating her like one.

After placing her choices on the counter, she rummaged through her bag, looking for her wallet. With her cash in hand, she looked up and noticed a stack of newspapers on the rack by the cash. On the front page was an aerial view of what remained of her chalet, with both hers and Abby's pictures. The caption read *"Designer Kills Lawyer"* as Madison's gut rolled as she read the headline. She looked up at the cashier and handed her the money. Her mind raced. She had to get away and talk to the police. If she didn't, she'd always be a wanted woman. There was no way she was going to rot in a US prison. Now she knew her next move.

"Do you see that man outside?" Madison asked the clerk, motioning to Carl.

The woman only nodded.

"That's my ex. He's been following me. He's got a nasty temper. I have to get out of here before he finds me. Do you have a backdoor I can use?"

The woman hesitated, looked towards Carl, and then nodded.

"Go through the staff door," she replied. "At the end of the hall is the door to the back lot. But you'd better be quick. The owner doesn't want people using it."

"Thank you."

Madison grabbed her purchases and sprinted to the door. She needed to put some distance between herself and Carl and find a place to hide while she figured things out. She prayed the cashier didn't recognize her from the newspaper and alert the police. At the end of the hall, she saw the exit door and pushed forward. When her hand wrapped around the doorknob, she risked a glance over her shoulder and relief flooded over her when she found she was still alone. She turned the knob, stepped out into the bright sunshine, and right into Hank. Her heart sank. Hank grabbed her arm, and in her struggle, she dropped the bag of snacks.

"Let me go!"

"I'm sorry, Madison. I can't."

She lifted her leg to kick him as Carl turned the corner towards them. Madison knew it was over and put her foot back on the ground. She couldn't fight them both.

"Good job Hank. You were right."

Defeated, Madison looked between the two of them, Hank's hand still wrapped around her arm as Carl bent down to pick up the dropped bag.

"You're not safe here. I thought I made myself clear."

"Nothing's clear. You still haven't told me where we're going or why."

"Fair enough. I'm taking you to my ranch. You'll be safe there. Then we can figure out a way to get you out of this mess. In the meantime, I swear on my life you won't come to any harm if you stick with us."

Hank let go of her arm and mumbled an apology. She looked at each of them, resigned herself to her fate, and climbed back into the truck.

# CHAPTER 15

Madison shifted in the back of the truck, stretching out the stiffness she felt after the long ride in cramped quarters. They'd stopped several more times at back road motels, enabling them to take turns showering and resting, but she still didn't have any answers. Hank prepared for the trip. He'd mapped out a route, so they rarely needed to travel the major highways. He even supplied some generic, although too large, clothing for Madison to change into. Neither Carl nor Hank spoke much about where the ranch was located, and Madison stopped asking, especially after Hank showed her another headline from a local newspaper. *'Canadian Designer Wanted for Killing Lawyer.'* It was then she realized she wasn't only being hunted by the people responsible, but now the police were looking for her as well. Carl was right. She became quiet and withdrawn as she tried to sort things out. The hardest thing for her to rationalize was the knowledge that Abby's parents would believe she did this. That she'd killed Abby, their daughter, and her best friend. Now the most important thing for her was to clear her name.

SHE STRETCHED and slid back the panel to look out at the warm Arizona sky. Carl was sitting up front with Hank, allowing her to sleep in the back. He'd finally told her that his ranch was in Arizona. Noticing that she was awake, Hank pulled over so she could get out and join them in the cab. Now that they were far away from Ellicottville, they no longer had to hide.

When she climbed out and into the front of the truck, she took in the vast fields that stretched out in all directions. They were in the middle of nowhere, but both Carl and Hank assured her they were on Carl's ranch. The sheer vastness of it overwhelmed her. Other than a small group of buildings in the distance, there wasn't evidence of anyone else for miles. Ahead, she could see the large ranch house Carl told her was his home. Nothing could prepare her for how big the house was that stretched out before her. There was more to him than she knew.

The house was a sprawling single-story building, built with raw timber. Large windows graced the front, which was surrounded by a porch that seemed to wrap around as it disappeared along both sides. She turned to take in the smaller houses set off behind the barn, forming a little community all on its own, and wondered who lived there. They pulled up in front of the house just in time to see the front door swing open.

"Well! It's about time!" exclaimed the portly woman who emerged from inside. "There's work to be done, and supper's ready. Come on now."

She motioned for them to come in with the large wooden spoon she had clutched in her right hand. As they got out of the truck, Madison watched the woman. The woman seemed stern but with a friendly air, and there was something about her that made Madison want to get to know her better. She wondered if it was Carl's mother. Her steel-grey hair was close-cropped, and she wore faded overalls with a plaid flannel work shirt. She had a simple food-stained apron tied around her waist. She stood on the porch with her legs apart and her one hand on her hip as she shook her head at them. Something was commanding about her that even Carl seemed intimidated by, which pleased Madison.

"It's good to see you too, Rose." Carl snorted as he went inside, dropping a kiss on the top of her head as he passed, leaving Madison standing in the dirt driveway. Rose turned and followed him in.

Hank walked around the truck and placed his hand on Madison's elbow as he led her to the house.

"Don't worry about Rose. Her bark is worse than her bite. You should see her when Carl's away for a longer period, then the warmth of his return is almost comical." He whispered as he led her to the house.

"He goes away a lot?"

"Well, that depends on many things. The ranch is his haven. He uses it to get away from the 'real' world. This is where he lives when he's not on a job. He never brings a stranger here, which is why I'm surprised he brought you. Rose will have a lot of questions. This is the first time he's brought his work home."

"Tsk, I'm not his work!" She retorted. "As of a few days ago, I didn't even know he existed. If things were different, I wouldn't know him now. All I want is to be back in Toronto with Abby before any of this happened."

Carl growled as he stepped back outside to see what was keeping them. "Get Madison inside before Rose comes back out after us. We don't want to keep dinner waiting."

He stood scowling as he held the door open with his foot, allowing Hank and Madison to squeeze past. The aroma of cooked food filled her nostrils. Madison took a deep breath and realized she smelled freshly baked biscuits. She could see that Rose had already set the dining room table for four, so it was obvious she expected them.

"Rose, this is Madison. She'll be our guest for a while. I know Hank told you she was coming. Is the guest room ready?" Carl asked before plunking himself down at the table. Rose nodded to Madison in greeting.

"Sure, I got everything ready," Rose responded. "I just don't know what kept ya from making the call yourself. All I ask is that you keep her outta my kitchen. I don't like strangers messing with my kitchen." Rose smiled as she said this and extended her hand to accept the one Madison held out to her. "I'm Rose. I take care of things around here. I was just kidding about the kitchen. I do all the cooking, but come in and join me for a chat any time. You'd never know I almost raised Carl, the way he behaves." She finished with a wink.

Madison giggled. "Pleased to meet you! I promise to stay out of your kitchen except for chats, but I don't plan to be here that long, anyway." She warmed to Rose. There was something about the way Rose didn't cow to Carl that she found inspiring. Rose may be gruff on the outside, but there was a lot of compassion behind those knowing eyes.

"We'll see," Rose said as she served up a large bowl of stew and dumplings, glancing up and down Madison's thin frame. "Here, you need some meat on your bones, missy. Eat up."

They ate in silence, enjoying the delicious, thick, hearty stew and fluffy biscuits. It had been days since she'd eaten a proper meal. After supper, Madison offered to help clean up, but Rose wouldn't hear of it. With her stomach full and nothing else left to do, she leaned back in her chair and looked around at the inside of the ranch, trying to get a feel for the man who had either rescued her or kidnapped her. She still wasn't sure which.

She loved the open concept of the interior. The kitchen seemed to be the heart of the house, with its central location. This appealed to Madison. Kitchens should be the heart of the home, the area where families gathered. The living and dining combination stretched across the front on one side. Large windows flanked the porch, creating what must be well-lit rooms when the sun was shining. She didn't know where the bedrooms were and what was on the other side of the ranch house, but if the rest was anything like this, it must be impressive. She liked the comfortable way he'd decorated the room. The simple furniture had a country feel. It felt warm and inviting, not at all what she expected. A part of her thought she'd find hard, uncomfortable, and unyielding chairs, much like Carl.

After excusing herself from the table, she made her way to the living room and sat down in a comfortable armchair before she picked up one of the day's papers she found piled on the coffee table. It shocked her to see pictures of Abby and herself on the front page of the first paper. The headline read 'Designer Blows up Lawyer in Jealous Rage!' She read the article in which 'Chucky' claimed Madison was interested in him. When he turned her down, Madison went off into the deep end, killing Abby. They even quoted him saying that he planned to go with them. But under the circumstances, he felt it would have been uncomfortable, as Abby didn't know Madison had hit on him. He had stressed how sorry he was that he didn't go and that maybe if he had, things would have turned out differently.

"That bastard!" Madison exclaimed as she slammed the newspaper back on the coffee table in a rage, just as Carl strolled into the room.

"Which bastard?" He asked, "Me?"

"Don't be ridiculous. I haven't had time to decide if you're a bastard or not. Have you read this paper? Do you know what they're saying about me? I don't even like Chucky. There was something about him that always felt slimy to me. I didn't think he was good enough for Abby. I urged her to break up with him and find someone better. Why would he say that I was interested in him? He knew I despised him. It makes little sense. None of this does. I have to talk to the police and let them know what happened. At the very least, I have to call Abby's parents and tell them I wasn't involved!"

"It's too late for that now. This 'Chucky' character could be involved in what happened to your friend. Talking to the police won't help. The articles say that they want you for questioning. They'd arrest you. And then what? Until we can clear your name, you need to trust me. I'm sure that by now, they have planted enough evidence to convince even the biggest skeptic of your guilt. What this boyfriend of Abby's hoped to gain by saying those things, I don't know. Maybe he's trying for his five minutes of fame, but my gut says he's involved."

"Five minutes of fame, all right! He wouldn't have any fame if this hadn't happened. He was just your typical sleazy lawyer. Most of his clients were 'low life' the rest of the firm wouldn't bother with. He is a bottom feeder. He hitched a ride on Abby's star, and he was hanging on for dear life." Madison retorted, swiping the paper off the table with her hand.

"Easy now! There's not much you can do. I'll check with some of my people to see how I can help you. This is a lot bigger than you realize."

"Then why don't you tell me what's really going on here? I'm caught here in the middle of whatever this is, and I think I deserve to know what I'm up against!"

"I agree, but I can't tell you everything just yet. You're too head-strong for your own good. I'm not sure I would tell you even if I could." Carl finished, turning and leaving Madison to fume.

"Don't worry about Carl," Hank assured, as he entered the room. "He hates it when he's not in control. When he's had some space and information, I'm sure he'll share what he can with you."

Madison looked up into Hank's boyish face. His smile made his brown eyes sparkle. With all the running over, she noticed him for the first time. He was handsome, with sandy-brown hair that curled around his ears. He sported a Vandyke, and when he smiled, his teeth were even and white against his sun-tanned face.

"Here, let me show you around. Maybe getting your bearings will help you feel more at ease." Hank said, offering an extended hand. Madison looked him in the eyes and took his hand as he helped her stand, thankful for the distraction. She was also curious to see the rest of the ranch, hoping it would unlock some of Carl's secrets.

Hank began with a tour of the inside of the ranch house. As they went, Hank described how Carl designed and built the place, choosing the kitchen to be in the centre because it was where the family gathered. A room to the right of the living room was Carl's 'office'. He kept it locked, so she wasn't able to see it. The next room was the TV or screening room. At one end, there was a large 110-inch movie screen, flanked by two bookcases filled with DVDs and CDs. Overhead was a projector that allowed the movies to be viewed on the big screen. The furniture consisting of overstuffed tan leather chairs and sofas set up so that they could see the screen from any seat.

"Isn't it great?" Hank asked.

"Well, yes, but he must spend a lot of time in here for him to have set up a room like this. Does he watch a lot of movies?"

"No, Carl doesn't use this room. He set it up for the families of his ranch hands. I'm sure you noticed the small houses located out in the back. They belong to the ranch hands. Each one has a house for his family. It's a long way into town to see a movie or rent one. So he buys all the latest movies and stocks them here. They have the choice of taking them back to their homes, which I'll show you later, or come up to the main house and watching in here. It's almost like going to the movies. Look, you'll notice a door to the outside on the far wall, which allows them to come and go whenever they want. The room is soundproof, so it doesn't disturb the rest of the house. Now, here's what makes this room special. This panel in the wall opens up to a concession stand." Hank pushed a button, and the panel opened to reveal the full concession stand, with candy, chips, chocolate, pop, and a real movie theatre style popcorn maker. Madison couldn't help it. The room impressed her.

"Wow, this is something. I'm surprised though. He doesn't seem the type to care so much about other people."

"There's a lot about Carl that you don't know."

"Let's keep it that way," Carl growled at them from behind. "Your room's ready for you, Madison. Hank, I'd appreciate it if you'd check with the foreperson to see what's happened in your absence. She can see the rest tomorrow."

"Sure." Hank chuckled as he left.

"That was rude!" Madison snapped.

"Not any ruder than talking about me behind my back. Your tour is officially over. I'll be your guide for any future tours of my ranch. Now follow me. I'll take you to your room." His tone told her not to argue. She let him lead her down the hall towards the bedrooms in silence.

Carl stopped in front of a door at the end of the hall on the left and opened it, revealing a room so well decorated that it seemed at odds in this rural setting. Someone decorated the room in varying shades of cream and in a variety of textures and patterns. The dark mahogany antique furniture contrasted with the fabrics. A large four-poster bed was in the centre of the back wall. Cascades of cream chiffon ran down the posts and puddled on the floor. A small sitting area with two armchairs on either side of a drum table sat underneath a large picture window. He opened the doors to the armoire to reveal an impressive entertainment centre. Madison was in awe. She couldn't fathom this being his choice of décor, and wondered to herself who decorated it.

"You'll find what you need in the cupboard and dresser drawers. I had Rose pick up some clothes and toiletries for you. I guessed a size small, so I hope that's right. This room has its own ensuite, so you can have some privacy. If you need anything, I'm right across the hall. Rose has a private suite off the kitchen, and Hank has his own house out in the back. You should know that Rose operates her kitchen like a clock. Breakfast is at 7:30 a.m. sharp, so you can either set the alarm, or I can knock at your door when I head in to eat. The TV works, and there are some movies in the cabinet. You'll also find some books on the shelves on a wide range of topics if you'd prefer to read. In the desk drawer, you'll see that I supplied an art pad and some pencils. I want you to be comfortable while you're here. Take some time tonight to relax and unwind. Tomorrow, I'll show you around, and maybe I'll have some news for you." Carl explained, while motioning around the room. The first sign of a smile played at his lips as he observed her expression.

"Thank you." Was all that Madison could mumble before he let himself out.

*'A bath would be nice.'* Madison thought while walking across the room, feeling the lush carpet beneath her feet. The clean style carried into the ensuite, which boasted a deep soaker tub and separate shower stall. The vanity had a small array of toiletries that she assumed Rose had set out for her use. She ran the bathwater before checking the cosmetics bag on the counter. In it, she found some basic cosmetics. They were all new in neutral shades, a toothbrush, toothpaste, brush, shampoo and conditioner, even a hair clip. He'd supplied everything she needed. On further inspection, she found a hairdryer and straightener under the sink, along with some feminine hygiene products. There was even a plush cream robe hanging on the back of the bathroom door. Madison slipped out of her clothes and settled into the soothing bathwater, laying her head back as the tension left her body.

Feeling relaxed for the first time in days, she stepped out of the tub and dried off before donning the soft robe. She combed through her hair and partially dried it, allowing the natural curls to take hold before leaving the bathroom. When she went back into the bedroom, she noticed someone turned the bed down and draped a simple white cotton nightgown across it. She realized it must have been Rose. Madison felt gratitude. After changing into the nightgown, Madison realized how physically exhausted she was, and turned in for the night. She could work things out tomorrow. She'd read all the articles on the explosion first thing in the morning. The coffee table was full of them. Then she could evaluate where things stood.

WHEN CARL SAW Madison settled for the night, he headed back to his office, unlocked the door, sat down at his desk, and stared at the thick file that had arrived with information on Madison. He flipped it open and stared down at the 8 by 10 glossy of her, which was included in the package. It was a promo picture. He'd read the file, having decided it was time he learned more about Miss Kerr. He pored over the pages, digesting the details. When he finished, he closed the file and leaned back in his chair. *'That explains so much,'* he thought. Now he understood her tenacity and vulnerability.

# CHAPTER 16

Tony's frustration choked him, knotting in his bowels. He couldn't believe that it had been over a week since they'd taken care of the lawyer, and yet they were no closer to finding her friend. She vanished. He slammed his fist into the wall, caving in the drywall and bloodying his knuckles. Dean had contacted The Don and informed him he was following a lead as to her whereabouts, but Tony didn't trust him. He believed Dean was the one that chased her up the mountain. If it was, he should have captured her and brought her in by now. During all this, The Don discovered the lawyer might have made a copy of the file and thought Madison may have it. If she had the file, he needed to get it from her, which was why they were still searching for her. It didn't sit well with him that Dean wouldn't divulge any information about where he was or where he thought she went. It just seemed all too convenient.

Tony felt that Dean's disappearance was too timely for it to have been anything but a setup. The Don disagreed. He bought Dean's story about seeing her slip off with someone that night, saying that he had followed them. But if that was true, why hadn't he made a move yet? Claiming he didn't want to call attention to himself and that he was waiting for her to be alone before grabbing her didn't bode well. The Don wasn't gullible under normal circumstances, but with Dean, all bets were off. Tony knew The Don was grooming Dean for greater things, and it enraged him. He should be the one The Don groomed! He'd shown his loyalty time and time again.

*'It should be me!'* he fumed to himself. *'I have been a loyal part of the organization for years. Bringing her in would have cemented things, guaranteeing my role in the family business. The Don seems to think her getting away was my fault. He forgets I was inside the chalet with him and the lawyer. That it was me who knocked her out and got him to safety before the explosion. Dean should have been able to take care of the other one. If he was outside watching like he should have been, he'd have her. He just continues to get in my way.'* Tony thought, *'There's no way in hell I'm letting that bastard get the best of me. I'll prove his responsibility in the bitch's escape. Then, The Don will know which of us he can trust.'*

Tony pulled up the search bar on his computer, determined to learn everything he could about Dean and the designer. He may have poor roots without a formal education, but he was resourceful. He might find a connection, linking them together. At the very least, he might find a hole in Dean's background, something that would help him and help to get rid of Dean. Even if there wasn't anything, maybe it was time to make it look like there was.

MADISON TRIED to break through the door. This time she could stop it! All she had to do was get in. She kicked at the door, screaming for Abby to hear her. Stop! Why wouldn't she listen? The door melted away, and she could see Abby. Abby turned towards Madison. Their eyes locked before she mouthed 'I'm sorry', as the scene played out. She watched as Abby flew into the air, her body catching fire as the explosion hit. First, her skin melted away, then muscle; all that remained was her skeleton. The skeleton's jaw slipped from the skull and crumbled to ash. Somewhere in the distance, she could hear screaming. She realized she was the one screaming, and someone was shaking her, holding onto both shoulders in a firm, insistent grip. She was dreaming.

"Madison, wake up."

As the voice broke through the fog of her dream, she could feel hands on her shoulders, holding firm but shaking her. She sensed the dampness on her cheeks that were wet with her own tears. Her throat ached, and her tongue stuck to the roof of her mouth, she realized from screaming. The screams she heard through the fog of her nightmare were her own. Slowly, she opened her eyes, noticing for the first time that it was Carl who sat on the edge of her bed, trying to awaken her. Bewildered, she looked into his eyes.

"You were screaming. I thought someone was in your room." He looked down at her tear-stained face and water-filled eyes, sensing a deep sadness made him feel protective of her. He pulled her to him to offer her comfort.

Without thinking, Madison slipped into his embrace and allowed him to hold her. It felt good to lean on someone, to feel the comfort of another human being, to have someone hold the bad dreams at bay and make her feel safe. She slipped her arms around him, seeking the warmth and strength offered within his embrace. Her hands felt the strong bare muscles of his back, while her cheek rested against the soft curls of the hair on his chest. There was something about the way he held her that made her feel safe. Her mind didn't register who was holding her, although deep down, she knew. She felt his hand as it stroked her back, soothing away her fears.

'No! This can't happen,' she thought, 'I don't know him, and I certainly don't trust him.' Now fully awake, she realized the situation she was in. This needed to stop. She pulled back from Carl and wiped the tears from her face with the back of her hand.

Startled at the sudden change in her demeanour, he paused, looked into her eyes, and asked, "What's wrong?"

"Nothing's wrong. I just had a bad dream. I'm fine now. You should go back to your own room. I'm sure you need some sleep." She muttered as she settled back down on the bed, pulling the covers up to her chin, dismissing him. Carl's face showed his confusion, but he shrugged his shoulders as he stood up and turned to leave.

Madison couldn't help but notice as he left the room that he was wearing long pyjama pants or that his shoulders were so broad that his back tapered into a 'V' as it reached his waistband above his slim hips. He was tall and lean, with muscles that roped his shoulders and arms, no doubt from the physical demands of ranch work.

*'He really is attractive. It's too bad he was such a miserable jerk most of the time. If not, and under different circumstances, it might draw me to him. That wouldn't happen, not here, not now, and not with such a pig-headed mule!'*

She felt determined to keep as much distance as possible between them. She needed to concentrate on getting back to her own life and finding out who killed Abby. Any distractions would just get in her way. With a newfound resolve, she settled back in bed and tried going back to sleep.

AS CARL MADE his way back to his room, he puzzled over her nightmares. She was strong, but whether she was strong enough was yet to be seen. In the days to come, he knew her strength was going to be tested, and things would get worse before they got better. Now wasn't the time to tell her everything, but he needed to tell her something.

His chest was still damp from her tears. He paused, allowing himself to relive the sensation he felt from holding her. When she was vulnerable, she was gentle and all woman. He could still smell the soft scent of the herbal shampoo that clung to her lush auburn curls, filling his nostrils. Her large emerald eyes, pooled with tears, had for a moment looked into his with complete trust. It wasn't long before that look had clouded over to stubbornness.

*'Damn her! This was going to be harder than I thought. I knew she was stubborn and strong-willed, but the innocence and trust are unexpected*

*and have thrown me off guard. I will have to get tough and not let her softer side get to me. It could ruin everything. Too much work has gone into this already. I can't let anything distract me from my end goal. Helping her will help me reach it, but it will come at a cost.'*

Carl punched an indentation into his pillow before laying his head into the hollow. He stretched his arms up under his head, linking his hands together as he planned his next move. The running was over. Now it was time for action. He continued to lie there as he roughed out a plan, thoughts rolling in his head until daylight crept into the room. By the time he got up to shower, he'd laid out his next move in his mind. It was time to set the stage for the next act.

# CHAPTER 17

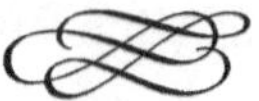

The Don sat behind his enormous mahogany desk and trimmed the end of a Cuban cigar with neat precision, using an ornate gold cigar cutter. His chocolate brown leather swivel chair was custom made to accommodate his vast size. He turned in the chair and looked out of his window to the compound below while drawing deeply as he lit the end of the cigar, inhaling its rich flavour and aroma. His private line rang. Knowing it would be important, he reached over to answer the call himself.

"Hello, Don." A deep rich voice cut through the line before he could speak.

"Ah, Dean, so you've finally checked in again. When are you bringing in the merchandise? I'm running out of patience."

"I'll have her soon, but…"

"But what? I don't like loose ends, and you know I like ultimatums even less."

"It's not an ultimatum. It's a request, or maybe a reward, for a job well done. I know you're going to question her and see if she knows where the lawyer kept her confidential files, but she has to be kept somewhere while you do this. We may get better results if we treat her like a 'guest' at first. So, while you're questioning her, and before we dispose of her, I'd like to keep her in my room. I'd like some time with her before we take action."

Soft laughter drifted across the line. "So you want a little piece of her? I can't blame you. She's quite beautiful. I'm surprised though. I thought you liked them more complacent. I doubt you'll get that from her. Everything I have on her suggests a fiery temper. No matter, if that's what you want, it's done. You can have her in your room for up to a week if it takes that long. But after that, we take care of business. I'll expect you here before the end of next week. No excuses." The line went dead as The Don disconnected the call. Dean cursed. He didn't get to finish, not that it mattered. He knew The Don would grant him what he wanted as long as he kept in his good graces. For now, all he could do was bide his time. Getting her to the compound would be difficult, especially with the shorter timeline than he wanted.

MADISON LAY on her back in the middle of the big, soft bed, blinking as the gentle glimmer of sunlight filtered through the curtains. She stretched out and, for the first time in days, allowed herself the luxury of an unhurried morning. The bad dreams ended when Carl left her room last night. It embarrassed her she'd allowed him to comfort her and how reassured she felt to be in his arms. But that was last night. This was a whole new day. A gentle rap at the door broke the serenity.

"Come in."

The door opened, and there he stood. The sheer height of him filled the opening. His head was just below the top of the frame. His broad shoulders blocked her view of the hall. Madison blushed, remembering the warmth of his embrace and how gentle he had been last night. She glanced up at his face, searching his eyes, hoping to see a hint of concern. But the look had hardened. Gone was the compassionate man who held her only a few hours ago.

"You want revenge? It's time to move. Rose has breakfast waiting. You'd better get going. We have a lot of work to do." With that, Carl turned and left her doorway, closing it and calling out, "Oh, and dress in comfortable clothes!"

Madison stared after him, shocked by his behaviour. With him, there was no consistency. He was an enigma. She was more confused by Carl than ever before and didn't know what to make of him as she threw the covers back and slid out of bed. The dresser revealed yoga pants and t-shirts. She grabbed a set and dressed before brushing her teeth, running a brush through her hair, pulling it back into a neat ponytail. Not wanting to feel rushed, she made her bed and surveyed the room. Satisfied, she felt she was ready for whatever the day had in store. She had a surprise for him. She had done some thinking overnight and had a plan of her own.

Carl was a puzzle she didn't have time to solve. So she steeled herself against his attitude, knowing he was just a means to an end. If he could get tough, so could she. She wanted to get back to her own life, and it seemed he was the only one in a position to help her. Pulling her shoulders back with a newfound determination, she left the bedroom, noticing the enticing smell of breakfast wafting down the hall. The wonderful aroma filled her nostrils, causing her stomach to growl in hunger. Other than last night's dinner, she hadn't eaten a proper meal in days, and she was starving.

She strode with confidence into the dining room, her back erect and her head held high. Her resolve and strength were clear. Hank and Carl already sat at the table, which was laden with food. Hank greeted her with a warm smile. Ignoring her, Carl's head hung over his breakfast of eggs, hash browns, biscuits, and sausage as he shovelled in his food. Rose walked in and eyed the setting, from Hank's smile to Madison's upright posture to Carl's hunched over figure. She marched up to Carl and cuffed him on the back of his head. Startled, he turned and gaped at her.

"Where's ya manners? You weren't raised in a barn. And with company here too!" She barked in disgust.

Carl's head rose sheepishly. Hank slapped the table and burst out laughing. *'Only Rose could get away with that.'* He thought as Carl shot him a warning look. Hank disregarded Carl's glare and continued to laugh. Rose stormed back into the kitchen to get Madison a plate.

"You know, Rose is a stickler for manners in front of a lady, Carl. She won't put up with you being rude to Madison. Nothing gets by her." Hank chuckled. "I guess Rose doesn't like the way you're behaving, with your head bent over your food like that. It seems a waste not to enjoy the company of a beautiful woman."

Madison blushed at Hank's compliment, watching as he stood, sauntered over to where she was still standing, and pulled the chair out for her. She smiled at him as she sat down, allowing him to push her chair in. Carl turned his head and glared at her. His eyes never left hers as she squirmed in her seat. Satisfied at her reaction, he sat back and smiled as Rose entered with a warm plate and placed it down in front of Madison. Her hand rested on Madison's shoulder as she spoke.

"Take no mind of him. He's prickly like a thistle on the outside and solid granite on the inside." She chuckled. "Actually, he's someone you can depend on when things are tough. Your being here tells me things are tough for you right now. You needn't worry. Carl will help you out. Now eat up. There's plenty more where that came from."

"Thank you for your kindness, Rose. I don't know how dependable Carl is because I don't know him. But I don't have a choice, so I'll have to take your word for it. Right now, everything's beyond my control. I hate being left in the dark. Things seem pretty bleak. I'm thankful for the help. I don't understand why any of this happened. But thank you for your hospitality. Breakfast looks amazing."

"If you're all finished having fun at my expense, Miss Kerr and I still have work to do. Hank, is the room ready?" Carl cut in.

Hank nodded and looked at Madison, watching as Carl stood and motioned for her to follow.

"Miss Kerr." Carl held his hand outstretched, showing she should join him. Madison just glared at him. She'd just sat down and hadn't even started her breakfast. She wasn't going anywhere until she ate. The tone he used made it seem as if she had repulsed him. She didn't care. He was a means to an end. And she felt deep in her gut she was going to need the energy this breakfast provided. He scowled at her while he waited. She sensed Rose would be all over him if he didn't let her eat.

"I don't know what you have in mind, but it's time to tell me what your plan is, and how I can get back to my own life."

"Don't worry. I have a plan."

"You can't expect me to continue taking your word in blind faith. I need to do something so that I can get back to Abby's family, and we can grieve. If you really have a plan, I expect you to fill me in. You said it was a mob hit, so then prepare me for what lies ahead. I can't do this without knowing what I'm up against."

"I agree. Finish your breakfast, and you'll find out what I have in mind."

Madison struggled to control her anger and took her time eating. Her mind mulled over the possibilities of what Carl's plan was. As she chewed on her last mouthful, she slid out of her chair and nodded to Carl to lead the way. Hank jumped up and joined the procession to the back of the ranch house.

Madison looked at Hank. Her eyes pleaded with him for information. His smile was sympathetic, but only shrugged his shoulders. It didn't take long for her to realize that Hank wouldn't go against Carl, but it still didn't hurt to have an ally. Someone who might be in her corner and go to bat for her if need be. At least he was friendlier and more approachable. Maybe she could rely on him to be a buffer between herself and Carl. He didn't seem to have a problem letting Carl know when he wasn't happy. She needed to develop a friendship with Hank. It may make all the difference.

AT WHAT SEEMED the furthest point in the house, they stopped in front of a locked metal door. Carl keyed in the password, and the lock clicked open, granting them access to the room beyond. Upon entering, Madison's step faltered. Apprehension gave way to shock. The room held an arsenal of weapons, an indoor shooting range, and a fully equipped gym. In anger, she spun around and glared at both of them.

"What do you expect me to do? I thought you were going to tell me what's going on, and how we can change it. I don't understand what all this has to do with helping me?" She exclaimed, as she motioned with her arm at the surrounding room.

"It's nothing as dramatic as you think. I'm going to train you. You said you wanted to be prepared. I'm going to get you physically ready for what's ahead. I'm assuming you've never shot a gun before, right?"

"No, I haven't." She snapped. Ignoring her tone, he continued.

"Well, we have only a few days to test your strength and for you to develop an eye for shooting. There's a lot at stake here, and we can't take any chances. You wanted to help, and you wouldn't let me take care of this for you, so the only choice I have is to prepare you."

"I'm sure if you're my target, I'll get it right the first time!" Madison retorted.

Carl shot her a warning look. She nibbled on her bottom lip, regretting her outspokenness. If she didn't control her temper, she would get herself into more trouble than she wanted.

"Before we start, you'll need these." He tossed protective eye and ear wear at her, which she caught with ease.

"You're going to work harder and longer than you ever have before. There isn't much time to get you prepared. And for both of our sake and safety, you need to be as ready as possible. You're going to learn how to operate a small, light-weight handgun. I've checked my stock, and I've already picked one out for you. Once I give it to you, it will be yours. I expect you to always keep it with you. No exceptions. It will be in your holster at the table when you walk around the ranch, and on your bedside table at night, or under your pillow, if you prefer. You need to feel so comfortable with it you can't imagine it not being a part of yourself."

Carl strode over to a wall that housed a variety of various sized handguns, reached out, and picked up one of the smaller guns. He examined the sights and weight and checked the chamber before he turned the handle of the gun towards her for her to take.

"This is a Taurus PT145. It's your new best friend. You'll find it's small, easy to handle and conceal. The total weight is 23 ounces with a 3 ¼ inch barrel. It's a semi-automatic, double-action with night sights. The magazine holds 10, plus 1 shot in the chamber. Never point it at someone unless you intend to use it. It's loaded and ready to go. The safety is on. Once we go through the safety basics, I'll show you how to load and unload it. Only then will you practice on the target. When we're done, and you are comfortable with it, I'll show you how to disassemble and clean it."

Madison took the gun in her hands. The cold blue metal felt foreign to her touch. She listened to Carl's safety instructions as she moved the gun more firmly in her grasp. Although she had never held a gun before, she felt a strange reassurance with it now, tight in her grip. She adjusted her goggles and ear protection before she turned her attention to the target when Carl told her to. In her mind, she reviewed Carl's instructions on how to fire the weapon. With careful precision, she raised the gun, disengaged the safety, and aimed at the centre of the target. She squeezed the trigger, felt the recoil as the first shot left the chamber. She continued firing off all the rounds in rapid succession. When she finished, Carl brought the target in to examine it. All shots were dead on.

"Oh my God, you're a natural!" Hank expressed with excitement. "Carl, did you ever..." He cut himself off when he saw the icy glare in Carl's eyes.

"Do you think this is a game? If you already knew how to shoot, why'd you lie?" Carl growled at her.

"You're an idiot. If I knew how to shoot, I'd have saved us both the time. Did it ever occur to you that in my profession, a steady hand and a trained eye are essential?" Madison turned the gun so that the handle was facing Carl as she handed it back to him. "Let's get on with the next lesson. The less time we're forced to be together. The happier we'll both be."

"That's fine by me. The next lesson is how to disassemble and clean your weapon. When you're proficient at that, we'll find out what physical shape you're in."

# CHAPTER 18

Madison followed the care instructions of her *'new best friend'*. She took it apart for the first time, checked to see if the gun was loaded, before she disassembled it under Carl's guidance, putting the pieces in order on the table. She soaked the bore with a cleaning solvent, then wrapped it around the cleaning rod and inserted it into the muzzle. Then followed with a bore brush and a dry patch, which she repeated until the patch came out clean. Then she took a cotton mop attached to a cleaning rod, added a few drops of lubricating oil, and lubricated the bore and all moving parts before wiping the gun down. Carl made her repeat the steps until she could almost do it blindfolded.

Once confident with her performance and ability, he turned her lessons to the physical side of training. Here, he pushed her hard. He started her off running on a treadmill, escalating the speed and incline, waiting for her to say she had enough. She was just as stubborn as he was and refused to give in. He wanted her to run as fast and as long as she could, to see how long she could keep up the pace. By the time she finished, sweat ran down her face in rivulets, beads dripped from the end of her nose, and sweat soaked her clothing. When she got off the treadmill, he handed her a towel and a bottle of water. He allowed her a short recovery time before he tested her physical strength and agility.

Carl found he admired her ability to endure the torture he put her through. She was in good shape and could tolerate what lay ahead. He continued to push her throughout the day, only stopping for lunch when Rose entered with a tray of food. When she saw the exhausted condition Madison was in, she raised her eyebrow and shot Carl a searing look. In here, she wouldn't interfere, but that wouldn't stop her from giving him a piece of her mind later, and he knew it.

MADISON SURVIVED Carl's demands and vigorous training, she never complained, or let him see how close she was to collapsing. He assumed she was tougher than she appeared, or more stubborn than he thought. He thought it was more than likely the latter. Carl didn't think he'd met anyone who was as determined, or as infuriating, as she was. These qualities he admired in her.

Hank had long since left the training area. He found he couldn't watch the physical demands Carl had placed on Madison. He had to leave, or he and Carl would have had words. That didn't prevent him from waiting nearby for what he knew would be hours of intense training. He only left to tend to matters concerning the ranch. He knew he'd have to put an end to the training and lead Madison out before she collapsed in exhaustion.

After the day she had, she would need a long hot bath and a hearty meal. The meal he'd already arranged. He spoke with Rose when he left the training area and explained part of Carl's training program to her. Rose agreed, as she'd seen for herself how tough it was when she delivered lunch. Rose said she would make a meal of steak, potatoes, and vegetables with some fresh biscuits. She'd even make a hot apple pie for dessert. As the day crept into the late afternoon, Hank couldn't take it anymore. He prepared to storm in and end the session when the door opened.

Madison came out first, wiping her face with a well-used towel, her head held high. The evidence of her exhaustion was obvious. Her hair, damp with sweat, clung to her head. Madison's face was flushed and continued to glisten even after wiping it with the towel. Her drenched clothing clung to her, but she was determined not to show Carl how worn out she was. It took almost everything she had to walk out of the training room. There was no way Carl was going to beat her down. She rotated her head to loosen the muscles in her neck as she passed Hank and smiled at him. Hank fell in step beside her and handed her a fresh towel. She mumbled a thank you before wiping away the sweat that still oozed from her pores.

Hank looked over his shoulder and gave Carl a look of disdain. With that single glance, he let Carl know he felt Carl had gone too far. Carl ignored Hank. He knew he'd pushed her too hard. But they were both stubborn, and neither one would give in. He wanted her to say she had enough, but she didn't. He respected her for it but knew she would hurt tomorrow, and tomorrow she'd have to be back at it. They still had a lot of ground to cover before they'd be ready to move.

"You have enough time to get cleaned up before supper, Madison. I know Rose is making something delicious. When you're done, she'll throw the steaks on. Do you need anything?"

"No, but thanks anyway, Hank. A hot bath and a change of clothing are all I'll need before we eat. I'm starving, so I won't waste time." With that, Madison headed off to her room to get cleaned up.

BACK IN HER ROOM, she closed the door behind her, leaned against it, and took a deep breath. She pushed herself away from the door and padded to the bathroom. Sweat soaked her pants through which clung to her as she peeled them down past her hips and dropped them in a sodden pile on the floor. She finished stripping out of her wet clothing before running the water, debating whether a shower would be better, but opted for the relaxing effect of a soak in a hot tub. She threw in a handful of Epsom salts, climbed in, and laid back, feeling the tension ease out of her exhausted muscles as the steaming water enveloped her. Without realizing how tired she was, she drifted off to sleep.

# CHAPTER 19

Over an hour passed after they left the training room, and Madison still hadn't shown up for dinner, so Hank went to find her. He knocked at her door. When he didn't get a reply, he tried the handle. Finding it unlocked, he pushed it open and called out to her. When she still didn't respond, he pushed the door open wide and looked in. She wasn't there. He was about to leave when he noticed a light coming through the open door of the washroom, which was ajar. *'She must still be in the bathroom.'* He thought as he walked over and rapped on the door. As he did, the door swung open. She was still in the tub with one of her slender, long legs draped over the edge, while the other was bent at the knee and angled against the tiled wall. Her head rested on a bath pillow, with her curls floating in the water. She didn't see or hear him in her deep slumber. He felt embarrassed that he walked in on her while she was still in the tub, but sleeping in the tub was dangerous. Hank glanced down, averting his eyes as he backed out of the washroom. He closed the door before knocking on it and calling out in a loud voice that supper was ready.

Madison awoke with a start and realized she was still in the now cool bathwater.

"Hello?" she questioned.

"I'm sorry about coming into your room, Madison. I knocked at your door first, but you didn't hear me. So I got worried and came in. I realized you were still in the bathroom, so I knocked to let you know supper was almost ready. Rose is just waiting for you to put the steaks on the barbecue."

"That's O.K. Hank. I must have dozed off. I'm sorry about that. Just give me a minute, and I'll be right out. I'm starving. I don't want to ruin Rose's supper."

Madison grabbed a towel and dried off, and pulled the plug from her bath. As the water drained out, she towel-dried her hair and ran a comb through her thick curls. She then applied some moisturizer to her face. Madison debated using some cosmetics that were supplied for her, but thought better of it. She wasn't here to impress anyone. After wrapping herself in a towel, she opened the door and peered out to see Hank still stood in her room. She was thankful she took the time to wrap herself in a towel. In the future, she should lock the door. Not that Hank was inappropriate, but it was better to be careful.

"Hank, could you please hand me my clothes off the bed? The faster I get dressed, the sooner we can eat. Just give me a minute, and I'll be ready."

Hank scooped up her clothing and handed it to her. He admired how beautiful she was. She didn't need make-up. Her skin was flawless, only marred by the few freckles that graced her shoulders and sprinkled across the bridge of her nose. She was a natural, wholesome beauty. Although he was sure she could look glamorous if she wanted. He hoped she'd feel up to riding with him after supper. There was still so much for her to see on the ranch. She deserved some playtime mixed in with the back-breaking training schedule Carl had set for her.

True to her word, it only took her a minute to throw on a pair of jeans and a sweater. As they were about to leave her room, Madison turned to Hank.

"Would you mind not saying anything about my dozing off? I don't want Carl to think he got the better of me today."

"Don't worry, I won't say a word, but I think he's working you too hard. I understand the urgency, but it seems a little excessive to me. Carl told me what happened in Ellicottville. I wanted to tell you how sorry I am about your friend and everything."

"Thanks. You're the only person who seems to be."

"Aw, if you mean Carl, he never wastes time being sorry. He's more action than emotion. But you don't have to worry. If anyone can help you clear your name, it's him." He finished with a grin as he pulled open the door to find Carl standing there with his arm raised in the air to knock. He took in the sight of the two of them as they left her room. Her hair was still damp from her bath. He turned and scowled at Hank.

"I thought you were going to get her and bring her right back?"

"He did, but I was still enjoying my bath. So I invited him in while I got ready." Madison snapped as she turned and marched towards the dining room.

Carl grabbed Hank's arm and held him back so that Madison couldn't hear his angry words.

"She's been through a lot. I don't think now is the time to add another notch to your bedpost, Hank. Leave her alone. I don't want her distracted during our training."

"It's my understanding that her training's done for the day. I don't recall you saying that she couldn't socialize with anyone but you. Who said I was looking for another notch? Maybe it's time to find someone permanent. She has all the qualifications of someone worth spending the rest of my life with. And if things didn't work out, at least we'd have some fun. Something she deserves, I think." Hank retorted, before chuckling to himself. Carl was acting a little jealous of someone he claimed to have no interest in. Even Carl wasn't immune to Madison's charms. Being such a thick-headed mule, he wouldn't figure it out for himself, anyway. He wasn't standing in Carl's way, but he wasn't backing down either. If

Madison wanted to spend time with him, then that was her choice. Why shouldn't he enjoy her company, no matter what Carl said?

"Well, I'm starving. Let's not keep Rose waiting any longer. You don't want her blowing a gasket if her meal's ruined." Hank stated, leading the way back to the dining room.

~

TENSION FILLED the air at the table. Carl continued to scowl as he watched Hank flirt with Madison. His playfulness made her relax. She flirted back, seeming to enjoy the attention and light-heartedness. Carl wasn't sure why, but he found this even more irritating.

Madison enjoyed the easy banter she'd established with Hank. It felt good to relax and unwind after the gruelling day she had. Every muscle in her body ached, and all she wanted to do was head straight to bed when supper was over. She just had to keep up appearances for a little while longer. When they finished eating, she could excuse herself and go to bed.

By the time Rose set the food out on the table, it amazed Madison to discover how hungry she was. She attacked her meal with a ravenous appetite, almost not tasting the tender steak or the butter-laden baked potato. It wasn't until she helped herself to seconds that she slowed down and tasted how delicious everything was. As she took her last bite of the still-warm apple pie, she leaned back to observe her dinner companions. It was then that she noticed the tension that developed between Carl and Hank. Hank continued to ignore the angry looks Carl shot at him when he spoke to her.

"Madison, do you know how to ride a horse?" After she nodded yes, her mouth still full of pie, Hank continued, "Well, Carl's got some beaut's here on the ranch. Maybe after you're finished, we could go for a ride. We could travel more distance. It would give you a chance to look around the ranch and get some fresh air after being cooped up in the training room all day."

Madison felt exhausted and was on the verge of declining when Carl cut in.

"I think she'd better just go to bed after the day she's had."

Madison glared, stood up, and threw her shoulders back. He wasn't getting the best of her.

"I can answer for myself," she snapped. "I'm fine. A ride would be nice. Thanks, Hank." She replied.

"That's fine with me. Then I guess we'll all go. Hank, why don't you get the horses saddled? I'll walk Madison down to the barn in a few minutes. I have a few things to discuss with her first."

Hank shrugged his shoulders, left the room after flashing Madison a wide grin and a quick wink.

"If you have so much energy left, I mustn't have worked you hard enough. I guess a nice long ride will tire you out." Carl retorted.

"I don't think you're used to strong women. Otherwise, your futile attempts to tire me wouldn't be so amusing." Madison returned.

"Not used to strong-willed women? Ha! You obviously don't know Rose very well!"

"And you don't listen very well! I said, strong women, not strong-willed women."

Carl shot back with anger. "With you, there doesn't seem to be a defining line."

With an icy chill, Madison replied, "If I'm so hard to get along with, then why are you insisting on coming along for the ride with Hank and me? I'm sure you'd have a much better time by yourself, and I know I'd have a better time without you scowling around."

"As appealing as that sounds," Carl snapped. "I think I'll stick to the plans. You'll have to put up with my 'scowling' for now. You'd better grab a jacket. It'll be cooler when the sun goes down."

Madison went back to her room and grabbed a jacket before following Carl down to the barn. He was the most infuriating man she'd ever met. He pushed her buttons. Well, she'd show him. She could take anything he could dish out. Deep down, she knew he was only coming along to push her into complete exhaustion. At least she'd be on horseback and not walking around the ranch. He wanted her to admit how tired she was, but she could take it. She was glad she'd been working out since college. Otherwise, it would have been impossible to survive Carl's excessive pace. She knew she was in good physical shape, but she had to admit this was tougher than anything she'd experienced before.

When she entered the barn, the sweet smell of hay mixed with the sharp pungent odour of horse manure assaulted her nostrils. Hank stood in the centre, holding three fine horses by the reins. He had them all saddled and ready to go. For her, Hank had chosen a gentle mare, a rich chestnut with a white star on her nose. He introduced her to the mare, named Star. Madison stroked the mare's nose and talked to her in a soothing voice before putting her left foot into the stirrup and swinging herself up into the saddle. The muscles in her legs screamed in protest as she did. Tomorrow she'd feel worse, but it was a small price to pay to keep her pride. Carl and Hank each settled themselves into the saddles of their respective horses before Carl took the lead. They began their ride in silence. It wasn't long before the tension between Carl and Hank slipped away as they both pointed out the unique sights on the ranch. They passed by the dozens of small bungalows belonging to the ranch hands. Hank pointed out his to her as well, thinking if she needed an escape, she could come there and find him, if need be. It wasn't long before they were all chatting like old friends. They forgot the harsh words while they continued around the ranch as the sun set before calling it a night.

# CHAPTER 20

When Madison awoke, her body groaned in protest with each movement. Every muscle ached. She'd thought she was fit until she experienced the regime Carl put her through yesterday. She was fit, but not fit for war. Carl designed his program to train soldiers, not civilians. Her own stubbornness was the reason she was in so much pain. She wouldn't give him the satisfaction by saying she had enough, so he kept pushing her. To top it off, she shouldn't have gone riding last night. Instead, she should have gone straight back to her room, soaked again in a hot tub, and stretched out her muscles.

Now she was paying the price for her impetuous behaviour. She rolled over in bed, hoping to find a more comfortable position. It was no use. The only thing left to do was to get up, stretch, and dig out some Advil. Carl would make her pay for her hasty decision, so she'd have to keep the Advil to herself. If she didn't, he'd ridicule her for it and be quick to point out that part of her discomfort was from the ride. Then they'd both dig in their heels as he put her through today's training, and by the end of the day, she'd feel much worse.

As she flexed and stretched her muscles, feeling the burn as they moved under protest, she wondered how her life had taken such a drastic turn in such a short time. Less than a week ago, she was packing for a weekend away with her best friend, and now she was training for the fight of her life. If only she could turn back the clock. If she could, she'd convince Abby, even at the last minute, to spend the weekend with her in the city. Then maybe everything would be different. They'd both be alive and at home. Maybe.

# CHAPTER 21

Over the next several days, Madison trained hard. Every muscle in her body screamed in objection as she continued the demanding pace Carl put her through. Her body ached each night as she climbed into bed, sometimes even too tired to eat the meal Rose prepared. Rose gave her some more Epsom salts for her bath to help her ease her sore, tired muscles. It annoyed her that Carl still hadn't explained what she was training for, but it felt like a marathon.

The little Taurus had proven to be very accurate. She had become so accustomed to it; she kept it in the drawer beside her bed. She holstered it to her hip every morning before she left her room and could assemble and disassemble it blindfolded, as she'd proven this afternoon when Carl gave her the last test. After that, he broke off their sessions, even though it was only mid-afternoon. Now, for the first time since Abby's death, she found herself with a little time on her hands. Time she could use to read over the growing pile of newspapers and articles about the explosion.

She picked up the Taurus and fastened it in the holster, and slipped it into the bedside table before heading to the kitchen. Rose wasn't there, so she made herself a light snack and grabbed a bottle of water before she headed to the living room. She scooped up all the newspaper articles she could find about the bombing. Madison stepped outside onto the porch to enjoy the warmth of the afternoon sun as she prepared to arm herself with as much information as she could before going off with Carl to where ever he was taking her.

Settled on the well-padded porch swing which faced the road, she opened the water and basked in the warm sunshine. She compiled all the articles in chronological order to enable her to read the news in order; she read through each article, not stopping until she'd finished every one.

The consensus, she discovered, was that she murdered Abby in cold blood over Abby's boyfriend. Of course, that was because Chuck had leaked that scenario. There was no sign that Abby's parents had spoken with reporters because of their grief. One article had a picture of Abby's parents going through the motions of burying their daughter when Madison knew the coffin would be empty. There wouldn't be anything to bury after such an explosion and the intense fire. The thought that they may believe her guilty tore Madison apart. No matter how well Abby's parents knew her, these headlines were sure to leave some doubt. The realization about this hurt almost as much as losing her best friend.

She stacked the newspapers back in order and stared out at the paddock where Hank and some of the other ranch hands were working with a spirited young horse. She wondered how a rancher became mixed up in a mess like this, but she knew from the training room that Carl wasn't your typical rancher. There was more to his story. She may never know everything, but it was time to find out how the training was going to help her clear her name and get back to her own life. She had a business to run. With everything that had happened, she hadn't even picked up a sketch pad. There was something about having your whole life thrown upside down that curbed the creative process.

She hoped Carl would bring some answers to her questions and concerns. Until now, he'd been closed-mouthed about his plans. She knew he would have to tell her something, and soon. She could tell by how anxious he seemed; it was almost time to get moving. There was no way Carl would end the sessions if he didn't think she was ready. That much, she figured out. The one bright thing through all of this was that Hank's playful charm had made the last few days bearable. But even he wouldn't tell her what the training was for. He wouldn't divulge anything, no matter how hard she tried, although she suspected he knew.

Getting her life back was imperative, and that could only happen once she cleared her name. Without Carl's help, she doubted she'd be able to. She didn't have enough information and didn't know where to start. She hoped his plan was as well thought out as his training program. Then she could get back to her own life and put all this behind her. Madison wanted to place flowers on Abby's grave, say goodbye, and grieve with her parents. Something she couldn't do as long as the police suspected her.

If it took much longer, all the hard work she put into building her design label would be for nothing. She knew her business would suffer from adverse publicity. Madison felt helpless at not being able to check-in and see how things were going. She knew her design team could handle the most recent orders, and she trusted them to continue, but something like this could ruin her.

She knew she had to contact her production manager, George. Let him know that he'd have to continue running things without her until further notice and that it was business as usual. It was important for her to give him the go-ahead and full authority to run things in her absence. She wanted him to know that the news reports were false. She'd advise him to hire a PR person to put a spin on things if the company was going to survive. The only problem was that Carl took her cell phone, and she had no way to contact the office.

She piled the newspapers on the end table on the porch, placed a rock on top to prevent them from blowing away in the breeze before she slipped back into the house. She saw no one, which meant she went unnoticed. Madison crept down the hall towards

Carl's study, knowing it was the only place she'd find a phone line. She paused at the door and listened to hear if anyone was inside. It was quiet. So she tried the door, and to her relief, found it unlocked. She pushed the door open and peered inside. The room was empty. Carl's phone sat on his desk. He'd disconnected all the other extensions, making sure she didn't have access to one. Madison looked back over her shoulder and closed the door behind her, strode over to the desk, and picked up the receiver. She listened to determine that there was a dial tone before she dialled the number and waited for someone to pick up.

"Good afternoon, Madison Kerr Designs. How may I help you?"

"George?"

"Madison?"

"Yes, it's me. Listen, George. I only have a little time."

"Where are you? This place is crawling with reporters and cops! The things they're saying about you in the news are awful. We've been sick with worry."

"I'm sorry, George. I can't tell you where I am, but I need you to know I didn't do this."

"Save it Madison, we all know you wouldn't hurt Abby. Everyone here knows how close the two of you were, no matter what the papers say. How can I help?"

"George, what I need from you right now is your strength and the reassurance that you can handle things. You'll have to continue to run everything for me while I work this out. I don't know when I'll be able to call next, but I will try to contact you again soon."

"Everything is being handled. You don't have to worry about a thing. Just get yourself out of this mess. So far, no one has cancelled their orders, so things are still looking good. Sometimes in our line of work, a scandal has its advantages."

"O.K., yes, that makes sense. Get the PR guys to spin this out. Depending on how long I'm away, you'll find preliminary drawings for next season in my office. You know what we discussed for the next line? Order the fabrics. I trust you to polish the sketches and have the samples mocked up so that we can be ready when I return. Take care, George. I'm putting my faith in you."

"Be careful, Madison. I don't know what you're mixed up in, but please be careful."

"I'll do my best, ciao George." Madison sighed as she disconnected the call.

"What the hell do you think you're doing?"

Startled, Madison jumped, placed the phone back in its cradle, took a deep breath before she turned to face Carl. He stood blocking the doorway, his arms crossed in front of him. His eyes glazed with anger. She didn't hear the door open or him come in.

"I had to call my production manager." She stated.

"How stupid can you be?" He challenged her.

"What the hell are you talking about? I've lost my best friend. Her parents, whom I love as my own, think that I killed her. Some mob boss wants me dead. I'm wanted by the police. Do you think I'm going to lose my business as well? What else do I have left?"

Madison's chest heaved in anger as she returned Carl's steely scowl. Tears threatening to fill her eyes, but she refused to allow them. He marched further into the room, closing the distance between them in quick, easy strides. His hands clamped onto her shoulders as his eyes bore into hers. His expression changed as she returned his glare. Madison forced herself to look into his eyes, expecting to see pure anger. She sensed how mad he was. But when she looked up to return his stare, she saw something else, something other than anger. Something she was sure she couldn't have read right. Just behind the anger, she saw compassion and a hunger that she couldn't quite explain.

CARL WATCHED as confusion replaced the look of anger. He continued to look into Madison's deep green eyes. His hands still held her shoulders in his grasp. His eyes shifted from hers to her soft, full mouth. Her tongue darted out to moisten her lips as she spoke. Carl lowered his head and captured her lips with his own, cutting off her words. At first, his lips were soft against hers. Then their lips parted as their mutual need and intensity increased. A fever created out of the mixture of the anger and frustration between two people who should never have met ignited as the kiss deepened. Without thinking, Madison slipped her arms around his shoulders and allowed her fingers to nestle in the hair at the nape of his neck. Carl wrapped his arms around her as he pulled her tight against his body. Their tongues explored the depths of each other's mouths as passion flared, blurring the lines of common sense, allowing them to forget everything but the need growing between them. Carl walked her backward until she felt the wall pressed against her back, trapping her body against his. He pressed against her as his desire deepened.

Madison could feel his arousal as it pressed hard against her abdomen. She realized what was happening as her thoughts waded forward in her mind as if through a heavy fog. Something inside her snapped. What was she doing? Kissing this man who enraged her! This man, who all but held her captive, worked her to the bone and made no qualms about what he thought of her. She had to stop this. She pushed him back and pulled away from him, turning her head, breaking the kiss.

"Stop!" she hissed, angrier at herself than at him.

CARL STEPPED BACK and looked at her. He'd scared her. He hadn't meant to, but then he hadn't planned on kissing her, either. Her response had been real. He was sure of that. But now she'd put an invisible wall up between them. Carl felt her response. He wanted her. His need ebbed away. But she had stirred him, and he knew she wanted him too. He wasn't surprised that she pulled away. If he'd learned anything about her, it was that she was stubborn and liked to be in charge. Here, everything had been out of her power, and this was something she could control.

"Whatever you want Madison. I know you wanted me too, but it doesn't matter to me. Just stay off the phone. Phone calls put everyone at risk. You don't know if your office line was bugged or if someone traced the call. You'll be happy to know we'll be leaving in the morning, just before dawn, so pack a bag and be ready for my word," he replied, motioning for her to leave. "I'll make sure I lock the door this time."

MADISON THOUGHT of a retort as she stepped out into the hall, but decided against it as she made her way back to the living room. There was no reason to start an argument. They still had to get through supper tonight, and she needed more information before they headed out in the morning. The kiss meant nothing. It was just their reaction to the anger and how close they'd been working. She wasn't foolish enough to think there was anything more to it. It was nice to know she wasn't the only one affected by it. A smile played on her lips as she thought about how uncomfortable he'd be for a little while yet.

"What are you smiling about?" Hank asked as he walked down the hall towards her.

"Oh, nothing much. Did you hear? Carl's ready to go. Too bad I still don't know what I've been training for or where he's taking me. Do you think he'll tell me before we leave?"

"Yep. I knew you were ready. I think he's going to give you the breakdown tonight after supper. How about a walk before we eat? Rose said supper would be ready in about 45 minutes, so we have time."

"That's a good idea. I've spent too much time locked indoors with Carl. I would enjoy some fresh air while the sun's still shining."

Hank offered her his arm, led her through the front door and out into the warm Arizona sunshine. She slipped on a pair of sunglasses before leaving the porch. Being with Hank was so easy. He wasn't pretentious and could make even the worst situation seem better. Madison found him playful. Their conversations were easy and lively as they headed towards the barn. It was refreshing, after all the days locked up with Carl's dark moods, to have someone to talk to. Madison asked Hank if they could visit the barn. If she was leaving tomorrow, it would allow her to say goodbye to Star. Together, she and Hank walked up to the stall. Star stuck her head out as she heard Madison dig into the oat bin. Star lowered her head for her nose to be stroked as she ate oats out of Madison's hand.

When Madison finished feeding and saying goodbye to Star, they realized it was time to head back to the house for supper. They dawdled as they walked, enjoying their time together, as the sun cast a pink glow along the western horizon. When they approached the house, they noticed Rose standing on the porch, her legs spread and her hands on her hips.

"Well, it's about time." She snorted.

"What?" Hank asked, feigning innocence.

"I said 45 minutes to supper, not an hour!"

"Oops, we're sorry about that, Rose. It's my fault. We walked down to the barn so that I could say goodbye to Star. According to Carl, we're leaving tomorrow."

"What do you mean, you're leaving tomorrow? Carl?" Rose turned to Carl as he stepped out onto the porch.

"We're both heading out tomorrow." Carl cut in. "We have some business to take care of. You know we've been preparing to leave Rose. That's what all the training has been for."

"Well, I wish someone would fill me in on the comings and goings around here." Rose huffed as she went off to get supper on the table.

# CHAPTER 22

The normal banter during supper was absent. Carl's sudden announcement dampened the mood around the room. Rose frowned at Carl from across the table, almost daring him to say something to her so that she could speak her mind. She knew that when they left, both Carl and Madison's lives would be in danger. She had become close to Madison over the past week. Rose found Madison to be a genuine and determined young woman who had suffered her fair share of hurt.

Rose had filled in some of the missing pieces for Madison, explaining that she'd been working for Carl's family since he was a little boy and that she had become a substitute mother to him. She knew Carl was helping Madison out of a difficult situation and that they'd have to leave to take care of it. But it didn't prepare her for the suddenness of the departure. Rose's cautious revelations of Carl and tidbits of his past; helped Madison feel more at ease with him.

Rose observed Hank as he held his playfulness in check. He was avoiding the angry glares Carl shot from across the table. Rose felt Madison was ready from the discussions she'd overheard, but she would miss her and be worried about her safety. She knew Carl would do his best to protect her. There were always unforeseen variables, and Carl couldn't control the outcome. Rose suspected that both men had developed feelings for Madison. It explained the tension in the room.

MADISON HAD JUST FINISHED EATING when Carl announced it was time to head to his office to discuss their plan of action. Madison was glad to get up and distance herself from the hostility of the dining room. She wanted to say goodbye, but thought she'd have a chance before they left in the morning. Instead, she excused herself and thanked Rose once again for a lovely dinner.

*'Finally,'* she thought, *'Carl is going to fill me in on what to expect. There is no way he'll want me to face what's ahead unprepared.'*

Madison followed Carl out of the dining room and down the hall to his office in silence. She didn't trust herself not to speak her mind or say something that would set him off. Once they were both inside the office, Carl locked the door, motioning for her to have a seat.

"Do you think locking the door was necessary? I doubt either Rose or Hank would follow us here, after how uncomfortable everyone was at dinner."

"Who said I was locking anyone out?" Carl challenged.

Madison bit at her bottom lip. Her mind flashed back to the kiss that took place in this very room only a short time ago. Was he planning to continue where they left off, or was he just trying to unnerve her? Her emotions were raw. She needed him, to be honest with her, not to seduce her. He smiled at her, as if he could read her thoughts.

"Don't worry, I'm not planning to kiss you again. As pleasant as it was, we have more important things to discuss."

"I'm not worried. I wouldn't have let you, anyway." She retorted, just a little too fast.

With that, Carl closed the distance between them in two quick strides. His hands grasped her shoulders as he stared down, looking deep into her eyes. Madison lifted her face to his, jutting out her chin in defiance. Carl dropped his gaze from her eyes to her lips, noticing that they had parted. They tempted him to capture them in his, but he released her.

"You are the most infuriating woman I've ever met. You had better learn to keep your tongue in check. Where we're going, a smart mouth will get you killed."

"Killed? Isn't that why I've been training so hard? So that I won't get killed? I know how to keep quiet, but it's about time you told me where we're going. I need to understand what I'm up against. I have worked hard for you and met all your requirements, but I don't have the foggiest idea of what's coming or where we're headed."

"Ah, and here's the catch. I can't tell you where we're going. I can only tell you that in the next couple of days, you will come face to face with the man responsible for your friend's death. His name is Don Fernando. His 'family' calls him The Don. He is a powerful and dangerous man. As the head of one of the largest crime families in the northern states, he's someone to be feared. He killed your friend because she was part of a ploy that sent his son to jail, instead of getting him off on a murder charge. The police charged their son, Miguel, with killing a Senator's daughter. From what I know, he was traveling with her up in the Georgian Bay area when she died, which is why his trial was in Canada. I don't know the circumstances of her death, but I know Don Fernando arranged with someone from your friend's firm so that Miguel to go free. Your friend found out the truth, and somehow a file that incriminated Miguel landed in the Crown Attorney's hands. That file has gone missing from the evidence locker, and that changes Miguel's case. They thought Abby might have made a copy of the information that they'd use against Miguel in the trial. That's why there was a hit put out on her. I believe someone from her firm set her up to take the fall if what you've told me about her integrity is true."

Madison stood gaping at Carl. Her jaw dropped in shock. This was more information than she expected, but also less. How could he not tell her where they were going? Did she hear him correctly? He expected her to go off with him in blind faith to face a mob boss, but he wouldn't give her any more information than that. Her mind raced. She had already put so much trust into this man by coming here. Could she trust him to finish the job and catch Abby's murderer? It didn't seem like she had a choice. She would follow him and continue trusting him until she could find justice for Abby. Madison considered various scenarios, trying to get a sense of what lay ahead. Her mind drifted away from what Carl had told her. She refocused so that she could pay attention.

"You need to pack light. Only dark, comfortable clothing, and don't forget your gun. It will fit down the boots I got you if you use the ankle holster. That way, you can conceal it better. There's a small backpack in your room for your use. Bring nothing unnecessary or that could identify you. That means leave your wallet here. Madison? Are you listening to me?"

"Um, sorry, yes, I'm listening."

"You heard what I said, didn't you?"

"Of course I did. I'm not deaf."

"But you didn't react." He challenged. "Where's the fire I expect in your eyes? I thought you'd explode and demand that I tell you everything. I know I gave you a lot to digest, and it's hard to grasp everything, but this isn't the reaction I was expecting. Instead, you're just standing there, not saying anything. Are you sure you're OK?"

"I'm fine. There's just so much to sort out. I never realized that Abby got mixed up in that. I remember reading about it in the papers. Abby never discussed the details of a case, even with me. I also realize that pushing you won't make you give me more information, so I'm just listening to what you have to say."

"Well! Well! Well! This is a side of you I didn't know existed. I'm not complaining, mind you, just surprised. OK! You'd better get a good night's sleep. We'll be leaving before dawn. I'll come to wake you in the morning and arrange for Rose to pack us some food for the road. We won't have time for breakfast before we leave, but I'll grab us some coffee and muffins. Do you have questions other than where we're going?"

"Just one. Why are you involved?"

THE FRANKNESS of her question startled him. He wasn't sure how much more he should divulge. But realized if she knew some of his background, maybe she'd have more confidence in his ability to keep her safe and to see this through. He turned to his desk, pulled out a file, and handed it to her.

"That file will give you some information about me. You can look it over, but I'll give you the breakdown. I'm a retired military, ex-Green Beret. I've continued to use my special skill set to help those in need on a contract basis. Here it was the Senator. He first contacted me because he wanted me to help bring down that branch of the mob. The Senator discovered his daughter's involvement with Miguel Fernando. He worried about her safety, and for good reason. Now he's worried that a trial without the incriminating evidence will allow Miguel to go free. I'm not a humanitarian. I get paid for what I do, and I get paid well. I am also a rancher. This is my haven from the violence I see on a day-to-day basis."

Madison stared at him. Whatever she had imagined, this was not it. He was a professional. Did this for a living. And yet he was taking her into the middle of it. She picked up the file and flipped through it under Carl's watchful eye. When she finished, she placed it back on the desk and looked at him, waiting for whatever came next.

"Are you satisfied?"

She nodded.

"Good! Now, show me your Taurus."

"My what?" Madison turned, startled.

"Your gun. Show it to me."

"I don't have it with me."

"Of all the… I told you to carry it with you everywhere. You never know when you'll need it."

"But..."

"No buts! When I said to carry it everywhere, I meant everywhere. Even if you think you're safe, you may not be. That's what I've been drilling into you for days. I can't believe you don't have it with you. Maybe you're not ready."

"Don't worry. I won't make that mistake again. I'll take it everywhere. I'll even carry it to the bathroom when I shower. I don't want to disappoint you. You know how hard I worked for you. I just thought with training over, I could take a break. But you're right. I'll never know when I'll be in danger, and when I'll need it. Who knows! Maybe it's you I need protection from."

With that, Madison turned to leave. Her body vibrated with anger. But when she reached the door, she hesitated, recalling that Carl had locked it from the inside with a key. Her dramatic exit ruined. She couldn't wait to get back to her room and enjoy what little peace she had left before being trapped with him any further. Her only choice now was to wait for him to unlock it. It was that or to ask him to do so. She waited.

Carl took his time getting to the door, enjoying how uncomfortable she was. He reached over her shoulder and unlocked the door, now regretting that he'd locked it. He needed her to trust him and be well-rested before they set out in the morning. The anger that raged within her would take hours to subside. He also needed a good night's sleep, but he still had a few things to take care of. He watched her make her way down the hall to her room. Before he reached up to close the door, Hank's hand shot out to stop him.

"Carl, we need to talk."

"I was wondering how long it would take for you to come here." Carl walked toward his desk and sat down, waiting for Hank to close the door and join him.

"You can't still be thinking about going through with this plan. Anything could happen. You can't control the risks. It isn't fair to put her in this situation, and you know it. She doesn't know what she's getting into." Hank uttered as he locked the door before he sat on the chair across from Carl.

"There's no other choice. She's so bull-headed and stubborn. Do you think she'd sit meekly by waiting for me to take care of things? Can you imagine telling her she'd only get in the way? The minx would probably follow me, anyway. At least this way I can monitor her. You don't have to worry. I've set everything up to protect her and allow her to make peace. At least her being there will help me put an end to all this. I want this contract finished."

"She's a powerful woman, Carl. I think if you gave her the benefit of the doubt, she might surprise you. Let her know the real danger, so she can make an informed decision. Leaving her in the dark is taking her life into your hands. Do you want to be responsible for her death?" Hank placed his hands on the edge of the desk and leaned forward.

Carl ran his hand through his hair. Hank had some good points, but he had no choice. If she didn't come with him now, who knows what would happen? Her going was essential. The plan wouldn't work without her help. She didn't know it yet, but she was going with him into the bowels of hell. God help her if she didn't follow orders.

"You know I didn't have a choice, Hank. The way things went down; this was the only alternative. I wish things were different, but they're not. Just back me up, and we'll all get through this in one piece. You'll need to be ready for my signal to get us both out of there."

"I've always stood by you. That won't change. She was in the wrong place at the wrong time. But keep in mind, she's innocent in all this, and I don't want to see anything happen to her."

"Neither do I." Carl finished.

# CHAPTER 23

Tony looked around the dingy motel room. He was certain that he'd left nothing behind. They trained him to clean up and not leave a trace. Tony wiped everything clean. This was something he excelled at, cleaning and leaving a scene so spotless that there was no way to link it back to him. Even though The Don hadn't contacted him, he knew it was time to head back to the compound and wait for Dean. The Don was positive that Dean would bring the package back with him. Tony wished he'd found her first. He wanted the opportunity to set the puta straight. He looked forward to watching the terror in her eyes, knowing that she was at his mercy. Tony wanted her death to be slow and painful for all the trouble she'd caused. He desired to have complete control over her before she died. He wanted to be the one to kill her.

There was something about killing that turned him on. Just thinking about his hands around her neck and all the ways he'd make her suffer gave him an erection. He loved the fear in their eyes when reality set in. For him, it was the best type of aphrodisiac. If Dean showed up, then the girl would be with him. Then he'd get to enjoy ending her life. The Don promised him the pleasure of taking care of her. Dean didn't handle those jobs. They left them to Tony.

He took great pride in ridding The Don of these inconveniences, especially when he could take his time. The girl being brought to the compound meant he could. When he finished, he'd arrange for her dismembered body to be dropped into the Everglades, removing all traces of her existence.

The Don thought Dean wanted to fuck her before they got rid of her, and that's why he requested that she be in his room, but that wasn't Tony's concern. If Dean brought her in, he could have her. When Dean finished, and the Don turned her over to him, then it would be his turn. The Don always trusted him when it was time to get rid of a problem, and this girl had turned into a big problem.

Both women should have died in the explosion. But she got away and then Dean disappeared. It was all just a little too convenient. Dean's explanation that he followed her and waited for the opportunity to grab her and bring her in didn't sit well with Tony. From what he knew of Dean, something else was going on. Or at least what he thought he knew about Dean. Now he wasn't so sure if he knew him at all. As far as he could tell, Dean didn't exist before he came to work for The Don. There was no paper trail, and over the last couple of weeks, Tony had exhausted every avenue trying to find something, anything. It was as if Dean had just materialized. How had he become an integral part of the organization? There were too many unanswered questions. Soon he'd have his answers. It was time to plant the seeds of doubt with The Don. Then maybe he could get rid of Dean as well.

Just before dawn, Carl made his way to Madison's room to awaken her. The room was still dark. Only a small glimmer of light filtered through the half-opened door from the hall. He shook her awake.

Startled from her deep sleep, Madison reached under her pillow and whipped out her gun. Without waiting to see who was in her room, she aimed it. With the swiftness of her actions, Carl's eyes widened in shock as he heard the soft click of the safety being disengaged.

"Madison, it's me." He whispered, his voice hoarse, his heart pounded in his chest.

Even in the dark, he could see that her eyes never left his as she lowered her weapon, switching the safety back on.

"I guess I trained you well. Is your bag ready?"

Madison nodded and gestured towards the small backpack on the chair, her gun still in her grasp but now resting at her side.

"Good. I'll give you a few minutes to get ready. Nothing fancy, just plain black clothing, and pull your hair back into a ponytail to keep it out of your eyes. I see you've become comfortable with your gun. Don't forget to strap it to your leg. I put the ankle holster on your bedside table. You'll have to adjust it until it fits tight around your ankle. Then, when you're ready, meet me in the kitchen."

Carl slipped out as quietly as he came in. Madison shook her head in disbelief. Last night, after their disagreement, she put the gun under her pillow instead of the bedside table. She'd been close to firing without knowing who it was. This realization unsettled her, but she wondered how many times he'd been in her room without her knowledge. She wasn't sure why she put the gun under her pillow last night, but now she felt confident she was ready. She slid out of bed and padded to the bathroom, where she splashed some water on her face. This wasn't the time for makeup. She planned to head out bare-faced. After slipping into a black turtleneck and slacks, she tamed her thick curls into a ponytail and brushed her teeth. She picked up the Taurus from the bed and transferred it to the ankle holster before she strapped it around her ankle. She slipped her wallet with her ID into the bedside drawer, knowing it would remain there until her return, if she returned. On a whim, she opened her purse and pulled out her Kobo and makeup bag, and slipped them in the backpack. With the bed made, she picked up the backpack and threw it over her shoulder before heading down the hall to the kitchen.

A small light illuminated the room from over the stove. Darkness blanketed the rest of the house. She found Carl leaning against the counter, waiting for her, also dressed all in black. He handed her a travel mug of coffee and a muffin before stuffing a small bag of food into his pack.

"We're eating on the run. I want to get out of here before Rose or Hank wakes up. They will only delay us, so let's get a move on."

"You're still not going to tell me where we're going? No details about what to expect when we get there? Do you expect me to trust you?"

"You don't have a choice. It's you, trust me, or you don't. But if you're coming, I'm leaving now. I thought you wanted to see this through? That you wanted to face the people responsible for your friend's death and to help me put an end to all of this?"

"Abby. Her name was Abby! Of course I do," Madison spit between clenched teeth. "Let's just go. The sooner we get this over with, the sooner I'll be free of you."

Carl led the way out of the ranch house with long, quick strides. The still dark sky made it difficult for Madison to see where he was taking her as they continued on foot away from the house. At the rate he was moving, she needed to jog to keep up with him as he moved at a swift pace crossed the yard. He seemed oblivious to the fact that she could fall behind, and it infuriated her. She expected nothing less from him. He'd trained her hard, like a well-tuned soldier. The thought that she was going to war jolted her and sank in with the reality of what her life had become.

The shadows and the soft nickering of the horses indicated when they passed by the barn. They continued past the group of houses where the ranch hands lived. Madison paused at the faint flicker of light coming from Hank's house and had to sprint to catch up with Carl before she became disoriented in the dark. Just ahead, she could make out what appeared to be a dense area of brush. It was there that Carl stopped. She knew they were still on his ranch, but she didn't recognize this area and wasn't sure where they were. Carl pulled away some of the loose branches, revealing a jeep painted a flat black covered in a camouflage mesh. He reached across the vehicle, removed the mesh, and rolled it up before storing it in the back.

"This is our ride. The plates are untraceable, and the registration is phony. No matter what happens from here on in, we don't exist. If you have any papers or identifying items with you, now's the time to ditch them. The mesh will help us hide the vehicle when we get to our destination. That way, it will still be there for our escape."

"That's not a problem. My wallet and ID are back at the house. I only brought what you told me to. I'm a good little soldier." With that, Madison clicked her heels and saluted him.

His eyes narrowed.

"Hilarious." He snarled. "It's that attitude that will get us both killed. Help me finish clearing away the brush, and we can get going. I didn't tell anyone we were leaving so early, and if we're any longer, Hank will find us."

"He already has."

Both Madison and Carl whirled around to see Hank standing behind them. In the shadowy light, Madison could just make out his figure. His arms hung by his side, but she could see that his hands tightened into fists. Madison smiled when she saw him. No matter how angry he was, she knew it wasn't her he was mad at. Hank didn't smile back, but continued to stare at Carl.

"Sneaking off wasn't part of the plan."

"It was necessary."

"Bullshit! You wanted to be in control. You always need to be in control. This whole situation is a mess. It's dangerous! No matter how careful you are, you can't control the outcome. Madison is putting her life on the line with you. Yes, I know it's also about her friend. But Rose and I care for her, and you have her up to her ass in this shit, and now you've tried to deny us the chance to say goodbye. It would be better if I went with you instead of Madison. I'm already trained."

"Hank, you know I won't let anything happen to her. You also know that I can't take you with me. It would ruin everything. The plan has to stay as it is if it's going to work. Otherwise, we're all as good as dead. If you go off half-cocked, how will I cover it up? I'm good, but not that good. I need you here in case of trouble, and when the time comes, to get us out."

"If you two macho jerks have finished, maybe you'll both listen to me." Madison glared at them.

"Ouch, Madison. You could kill a guy with a look like that." Replied Hank.

"I may just do that Hank if we don't get this over with. I have been training hard for this mysterious 'plan' that I still know nothing about. Now I'm following Carl with blind, unfounded faith here. It doesn't instil confidence, having the two of you at each other's throats. I'm leaving with Carl, just like we planned, and I'd like to get going before daybreak." She leaned over and picked up her backpack. "Are you ready, Carl?"

"Wait for a second Madison. I didn't mean to offend you. I just had to be sure everything was O.K. I know how hard you've trained, but this situation is dangerous. I want you to know I am only a phone call away. If you need anything, anytime, day or night, call, and I'll be there."

"I appreciate that Hank. I'm sure I'll be fine. If I need you, I'll call." She leaned over to brush a light kiss on his cheek. Instead, he turned his head and kissed her full on the mouth. The brief kiss ended almost as soon as it started. Then he turned to Carl.

"I know you'll be fine, Madison." He said as he shot a warning look at Carl and headed off back to the ranch house.

"Oh, now I get it. There's a little something going on between the two of you. That explains why Hank's behaving like a mother hen." Carl snapped.

"If there is, then it's none of your concern."

"I think it is after the kiss you gave me yesterday." His eyes bore into hers.

"I gave you!" she sputtered.

"Yes, a very memorable kiss. I know it would have led to somewhere, such as my bed, if I pursued it. I know you wanted me."

"Humph, if you'll remember, I broke away from your kiss. And me in your bed, only in your dreams." She challenged.

"Yes, and often," he whispered.

Madison swallowed against the lump that grew in her throat. He was letting her know his attraction to her. How was she supposed to handle that information? She'd felt it too, the sexual tension that charged between them. Under the circumstances, it was normal. They'd worked so hard and close together. He'd become her protector. He saved her from dying with Abby in the explosion, gave her a place to feel safe, and he was attractive. No, this development did not surprise her. Well, it didn't matter, anyway. Nothing was going to happen. She was sure of that. They were on a mission to clear her name and get the proof of who killed Abby.

Carl stowed both of their backpacks in the jeep's rear with the camouflage mesh before sliding in behind the steering wheel of the driver's seat. He waited for her to climb in beside him before he started the engine. The headlights flashed against the well-packed earth.

"We're off. There are only a couple of things I want you to remember. First, trust me, no matter what happens or what you hear. I promise I will always look out for you and protect you. Also, after today never use my name. You need to pretend you don't know who I am, and you need to treat me as if I'm your captor."

"What?"

"You heard me."

"You tell me not to use your name. That you want me to trust you? I think under the circumstances, that's a little difficult."

"I don't care how difficult it is, it's necessary. Follow my instructions if you're going to get out of this alive. Where we're going, I don't want them to know who I am. Anonymity is imperative in my line of work. So just do as I say. We'll be driving for a couple of long days before we have to ditch the jeep. From there, we'll be on foot.

We will use daylight to drive, but when we park and continue on foot, it needs to be dark."

Madison fell silent as she pondered what the hidden meaning was behind what Carl had said. It would be difficult, but she would try. She was comprehending how dangerous the situation was, and didn't want to jeopardize their safety. She would refer to him as 'hey you'. He'd love that. She smiled to herself, taking pleasure in knowing that anything she could do to annoy him worked for her.

According to Carl, it was going to be a long drive, so she settled back in her seat and made herself more comfortable. Carl didn't allude to what lay ahead, making it difficult to guess their destination. He wasn't one for idle chatter. So the ride would be long and quiet. Madison shifted in her seat and closed her eyes to rest, unsure of how much rest she would need for what lay ahead. After the restless night she had, she knew sleep was important.

CARL GLANCED OVER AT HER, noting that she had relaxed and was dozing off. She looked so peaceful sitting there with her eyes closed. A wave of doubt went through him. Was he doing the right thing? Could there have been another way? No, not really. But she didn't know the full extent of the danger that waited for them. If he gave her all the answers she wanted, maybe she wouldn't have been so determined to come along. But he couldn't take a chance. If she knew everything, she'd want to go to the authorities. That would ruin all the work he'd done. She became an intricate part of the plan the moment he stopped her from entering the chalet. Madison was now a means to an end. She was his key to completing the job he began so many months before.

# CHAPTER 24

Tony cursed again as he checked his watch. The Don was being taken for a fool. Of course, he wouldn't admit it. He trusted Dean, but Tony didn't. Tony didn't understand why The Don placed so much faith in what Dean had to say, but Tony's warning bells were going off. Whatever was going on, they'd know soon. Tony almost salivated at the thought of being able to expose Dean. But first things first, the girl. He wanted to feel his hands around her neck, feel the life drain out of her as he squeezed her throat, feeling the crunch as he crushed her windpipe. Soon! It would happen soon. Whatever game Dean was playing, The Don wouldn't let it last. Then he'd get permission to dispose of her. But first, he planned to toy with her, make precise cuts into her flesh. Not too deep at first. No. It wouldn't do for her to die too fast. The cuts had to be just deep enough for her to suffer. When she lay there bleeding, her body writhing in pain, he'd fuck her, and hard. That's what she deserved, and all she was good for. That's all any woman was good for. She survived the explosion, which made him look like an incompetent fool. He was nobody's fool. He paced the room in anticipation.

"Ah, Tony, relax." The Don drawled as he hobbled into the room.

Each step was a painful effort under his massive girth as he noticed how agitated Tony was.

"I can't. Dean's up to something. I can feel it."

"You may think you feel it, but that's just your jealousy of him getting in the way. He wouldn't go against the family. Only people I can trust belong in the inner circle, and I trust Dean."

"I hope you're right, boss. I don't understand what kind of game he's playing, but I'm sure he's playing one. He should be here by now. He shouldn't have taken off like that in the first place, without first checking with you. It makes him look suspicious. How long could it take to hunt her down and bring her back?"

The Don chuckled.

"You're always suspicious, Tony. That's why I have you so close. I trust your judgement with taking care of a problem. But in this case, you're wrong. I know Dean. He wouldn't double-cross me. Dean wants what's best for the organization. He has a different way of achieving it than you." The Don plopped down on the large leather sofa and prepared one of his Cuban cigars with meticulous care. He snipped the end to perfection before lighting it and taking a deep inward draw of smoke.

Tony walked to the window and looked out at the surrounding forest. There was only one road that led to the compound, which was blocked by a large, guarded gate, and an eight-foot electrical fence protected the surrounding area. Through his binoculars, he looked up the road, watching for an approaching car. No one was coming, although he expected Dean to use a different route. He wasn't the type to march up to the main gate. That would be too obvious, and Dean was never obvious. He'd sneak in, slipping in the back, right through security. For him, it would be a piece of cake. He designed the latest system, and if there was a way to breach it, he could. It was another reason Tony didn't like him. He knew too much and kept his knowledge to himself.

The Don had misplaced his trust in Dean, of that Tony was sure. He wished The Don would listen to him and have faith in his gut instinct. Tony's gut never let them down. The problem was The

Don thought Tony felt jealous of Dean, and that was what sparked Tony's mistrust. That may be true. But if he knew where she was, she'd already been here.

"Shit!" Tony cursed.

"Relax, Tony. Dean will be here soon. He'll have the girl. When the time is right, I'll let you have the honour of disposing of her." The Don grinned, the curl of his smile didn't quite reach his black eyes.

Tony smiled to himself. He liked the thought of that. He'd already worked out how he would torture her before he killed her. There was more than enough time to envision it over the last few days. He could see every detail in his mind, the nuances of pain inflicted to draw out the most pleasure for himself to enjoy. Once she was inside the compound, he could take his time. There was a bare cell downstairs, ready for her. He had shackles fastened at different spots on the wall, with his tools out of reach. No one would know she was there. He enjoyed watching how people reacted while being tortured. Yes! He would have to wait a little longer. If Dean didn't show up by dusk the next day, The Don would let him hunt both of them down like the dogs they were. No matter what, things would work out for him. It was a win/win situation. He would have the girl at his disposal, and if Dean messed up, he'd be able to take care of him, too. He just needed patience.

WHEN NIGHT FELL on the second day of travel, Carl pulled the jeep off the main road. Madison glanced around and saw nothing for miles but trees and the deserted back road they'd driven up on. There were no houses or buildings in sight, no sign of lights in the darkened forest, nor a glimmer of human life. Carl turned the jeep into a small grove of trees and parked. When the jeep lights went out, it plunged them into almost complete darkness. The foliage of the forest was so thick overhead that it was difficult to detect the glow from the moon and stars. Under different circumstances, Madison would have loved the setting.

She enjoyed looking up at the stars while surrounded by nature, but they were in the middle of a war, one she wasn't sure she could win. Madison knew they must be near their destination because they were leaving the jeep behind. She felt a tightening in the pit of her stomach.

"From here, we're on foot," Carl whispered. "Give me a hand to cover the jeep with the camouflage mesh. It will help keep it hidden from sight. Then we'll grab our backpacks and get moving while it's still dark. We'll use the cover of darkness to help with the element of surprise."

"On foot to where? I saw nothing around for miles. There are no buildings or houses. Nothing. Just how far will we be walking?"

Madison threw her backpack on the ground and grabbed one end of the mesh and helped Carl cover the jeep. He then took branches and smoothed out the tire tracks, erasing them from sight.

"Where we're going is less than a mile away. It's hard to see from this road, but they designed it that way. The people we're after like their privacy, so from now on, we'll have to be careful. There are security cameras set up along the main road and at random locations in the trees. I know where they are and how to avoid being seen, so stay close behind me. From here on in, you'll have to trust me. No matter what happens, follow my lead. We both have a part to play in all this, and I'll need you to believe that I won't let anything happen to you. O.K.?"

"That doesn't sound promising. I almost feel like a lamb being led to the slaughter," Madison replied weakly to add humour to their volatile situation. "But I've come this far, and I've already put my faith in you. I'll do what you ask."

Carl was stunned. She didn't realize how close to the truth she was. If anything went wrong with his plan, they'd both end up dead. Physically, she was ready, but he wasn't sure about her emotional state. He hoped for her sake she'd follow his lead and that her training had prepared her well enough for what lay ahead. If not, it wouldn't matter if she trusted him.

"One more thing Madison," he turned to look at her, his hand outstretched, "The gun. You need to give it to me. When I can, I'll give it back to you."

She stopped dead in her tracks and stared at him. She couldn't believe what he'd said. Did he just ask for her gun? Now? When they were heading off to confront the man responsible for Abby's death? She must not have heard him correctly.

"My gun? You want my gun! Are you crazy? We've just spent weeks preparing for this. You told me to make the gun a part of me, and now you expect me to give it up? Only a couple of days ago, you freaked out on me for leaving it in my room!" Madison spun away from him.

Carl grabbed her arm, stopping her. She wouldn't turn to face him. She didn't want him to see the tears of frustration that filled her eyes. The gun may have been small, but it gave her a sense of security.

"I'm sorry. I know this makes little sense, and I don't have the right to ask you this. But you have to trust me. You'll understand everything soon."

"Soon! So you keep telling me." She fretted. "'Trust me,' you said! Now you want to take the gun away from me? The one you told me to always carry with me. Why not tell me now? Why don't you bloody well tell me what's going on here? You've had me follow you with blind faith. I barely know you, and even Hank seemed to think you were up to something. If he was concerned, why shouldn't I be? He's known you for years. I'm an idiot for believing in you." Madison jerked her arm out of his grasp. She lifted her pant leg and pulled the gun and its holster from around her ankle and slapped it into his open hand. "Here, I'm done. You deal with this your way. I'll go to the police and take my chances." She turned her back on him to leave.

A metallic click stopped her in her tracks.

"I'm afraid you can't do that."

She turned to face him. He had her gun pointed at her. Carl gripped the gun in his hand. His eyes were cold and emotionless.

She'd never seen that look from him before, and it sent a shiver down her spine.

"I need you to come with me. You no longer have a choice here, Madison. The time to back out is long past. You wanted to be a part of this, and now I can't let you leave. But I won't let anything happen to you, either. I promise you that."

"You stand there with a gun pointed at me and expect me to believe you? I was a fool to have ever trusted you. If you're going to kill me, get it over with!" Tears spilled out and ran down her cheeks, glistening in the moonlight.

"Madison, if I wanted to kill you, you'd already be dead. I've had plenty of opportunities. It would have been easy. I could have killed you on the mountain when I first found you, or in the forest before Hank picked us up. You don't know what's going on and I want to help you. Going to the police would be a mistake. They'd arrest you for Abby's murder, and there'd be nothing I could do. The people responsible would get away with it. Is that what you want?" Carl asked, lowering the weapon.

"No," she replied. Tears of frustration still blurred her eyes as she brushed them away. "I'll go with you for now. I'll follow your lead, but if you don't start being honest with me, I'll stop at nothing to see that you're brought down, too."

"Don't worry, I understand."

Carl holstered the Taurus and strapped it to his ankle. He slipped his arms through his backpack and fastened the strap to his waist before handing her pack to her. He waited while she secured it. Madison followed Carl. Her heart ached from the sorrow that filled it. Less than a month ago, her life was perfect. Then, in the blink of an eye, everything changed. She could no longer call Abby and hear her voice. If she didn't clear her name, she'd never be able to face Abby's parents or feel the warmth of their love. They'd always believe in her guilt. She'd spend her life either on the run or in jail. It was too much to bear. So far, she'd been able to hold on, but for how much longer? That stupid gun made her feel invincible. Now it too was gone. She was at the mercy of a man she didn't know. All the time they'd spent together training had been for this. Now, he took away the one thing that made her feel safe. She knew Hank better than Carl, even though she'd spent hours alone in the training room with him. It was Hank who she'd spent her free time with. It was because Hank trusted Carl that she had. Now she wondered if it was a mistake.

The uncertainty of her thoughts and questions weighed on her mind as they continued to walk. She realized that Carl's route seemed to be random. They weren't following a clear path, but he still seemed to know where he was going, almost as if he'd been there before. Whatever her reservations were, she'd have to let go of them for now. It didn't matter anymore. She'd chosen her path, and the outcome unclear. Her future lay in his hands.

# CHAPTER 25

Carl had been honest about at least one thing. Wherever they were going, it wasn't far. The moon was still high in the sky when, after a short, emotional walk, they reached a dense hedge that formed a barrier, blocking their way. Carl ran his hand along the hedge to check the height, and every so often, he stuck his arm into the thickness of the branches. To Madison, it appeared to be a living wall. It was too high and thick to get around or to climb over. Even though she wondered what he was doing, she didn't ask. She didn't trust herself to speak to him without emotion. Their last conversation had drained her and left her raw. To ask him now what he was doing and to have him tell her he 'couldn't explain' would be more than she could handle. So instead, she stood there, watching him as he checked the hedge. She couldn't see where it started or stopped in the darkness, but she knew it was immense. It was so high she couldn't see over it. She looked both left and right, trying to see where it ended, but it seemed endless.

"Got it."

Carl turned and smiled at her, his hand still buried in the twisted leaves and branches. As he pulled his arm out, Madison heard a dull snap. At first, she thought he broke off a piece of the hedge, but to her surprise, part of the hedge shifted. She then realized that he'd hit a trigger that allowed the hedge to open like a gate, granting them access to the other side. Carl pushed it, creating a small opening in the hedge. Through it, Madison could see that the hedge was at least three feet deep. The space wasn't large, but it would allow them to pass through without too much difficulty.

"How did you know that was there?" Madison gasped.

"I do my homework. I knew where we were going. It's my job to find the best way to get in undetected. We still have some more obstacles to get through, but we're almost there."

Carl pushed against the gate of the live hedge until it opened. He motioned to Madison, who stepped through, feeling the hedge as she went, surprised to find that it was real. She ran her fingers across the leaves, feeling the waxiness of them. The foliage was dense with thorns, scratching her hands and snagging her clothing. The sharp thorns tore across her flesh, leaving behind thin lines of beaded blood. She couldn't believe that Carl had thrust his hands through the hedge like that. They'd be scratched and bleeding. After everything he'd put her through, she revelled in the thought that he must have felt pain when he searched for the trigger.

Once they were through, Carl pulled the gate closed, and Madison realized just how right he was about the obstacles ahead of them. The next hurdle stood just a few feet away, a large chain-link fence topped with multiple spirals of barbed wire. As she reached out to touch it, Carl slapped her hand down.

"It's an electric fence. Touch that, and you'll get thrown back into the hedge. It might not kill you, but you'd get a jolt, and it would alert those on the other side that someone is trying to get in."

"So how are we supposed to get around it, then?" Madison asked, shaken, realizing how close she came to touching it.

"You don't have to worry. I have another trick up my sleeve. Follow me, but be careful not to touch the fence. Move along closer to the hedge. It's thorny, and you may end up with scratches, but it's far safer."

Madison looked back at the now solid hedge and realized she'd never find the opening on her own if she had the chance to escape without him. They inched along, keeping close to the hedge, moving only a few feet at a time. Carl brushed his foot over the ground, tapping it as he went, feeling for something either on the surface or just below. They traveled a couple of yards from the gate when Carl stopped. With a satisfied smile on his face, he bent over and ran his fingers through the grass before finding what he was looking for. He cleared away the earth and grass to reveal a large metal ring. Carl gave it a few quick tugs before realizing he needed more leverage. He shifted his position, and after a good hard pull, a large section of the earth in front of him lifted. Madison watched in awe. She knew now more than ever that there was more to him than she knew. She watched as he struggled under the weight of the lifting earth before pulling it open, revealing a trapdoor hidden in the ground.

"O.K. Madison. You go first, but you need to be careful. You'll have to turn around and climb down the ladder. I'll be right behind you. The hatch door is heavy, and I need to close it. Let's hope no one notices we disturbed the earth. When it closes, there won't be any light, so you'll have to use whatever you can from the moonlight to get down. Before I come down and close the hatch, I'll need you to get out of the way while you can still see where you're going. Get to one side and stay against the wall. Make sure you're far enough away from the ladder so that I don't hurt you, but don't go too far. You need to wait for me."

"What's down there?"

"It's a passageway. They designed it for quick secret escapes, but we're going to use it as a secret entry."

Madison peered into the dark hole. She couldn't see the bottom and didn't know how deep it was. Madison slipped past Carl, mindful of how close the fence was. She got down on her hands and knees and lowered her right foot into the opening, feeling for the first rung of the ladder. As she descended, she kept looking down, hoping to see the bottom, but the moon just cast enough light, and she could see only the first few feet of the ladder. She looked up at

Carl's silhouette in the dim moonlight. Her heart raced as panic set in, and her mind filled with doubt. What if it was a trap? What if he was going to lock her in this dark, damp pit? She swallowed and continued her descent down the ladder. Her hands clutched on the rungs as she went.

The pit wasn't as deep as she first feared. She realized as her foot first found solid ground. It was only a little over twelve feet deep. She felt relief as she placed both feet on the ground and moved to one side, feeling the cold, damp concrete wall as she pressed against it and moved out of the way.

Madison looked up, expecting to see Carl in the opening, ready to follow her down. Instead, she saw the faint glimmer of night light fade as the hatch shut. She broke out in a sweat. Her first thought was that he'd locked her in the tunnel. In a panic, she felt around the wall, searching for a direction to take. A scream caught in her throat when she heard Carl's voice break the silence. "It's safe to use a flashlight now." He brushed against her when he stepped off the ladder.

Carl pulled a flashlight out of his bag and switched it on, revealing a long, narrow tunnel. Madison looked around, trying to take in her surroundings and get her bearings in the underground. She noticed the walls were rough, unfinished concrete, and were cold and damp to the touch. That explained the dank, musty smell of mildew that filled the air. The flickering light filled the narrow passageway with shadows. It was impossible to know how far it went, as the tunnel curved out of sight about twenty feet ahead.

"We're almost there. After we get out of here, everything will change. I wish I could tell you that this is your last chance to change your mind, but we both know it's too late for that. You can't wait here. And you can't go to the police. Your only choice is to follow me. But you have to listen to me and stay close."

"If I could change anything right now, it would be to have never left home. You pulled a gun on me today and then told me once again that I don't have a choice. How very noble of you. I think the only way I will get my name cleared and for this to end is to go along with you. You're stuck with me now. Keeping my eye on you is the only way I'll be sure you don't double-cross me. But yes, I will listen to you and stay close."

Carl chuckled.

"No matter what you believe, I'm not the one you have to worry about. From here on in, don't use my name. It would ruin everything."

Madison nodded, resigning herself to the situation for the last time. She felt the anxiety of the unknown fill her, along with the curdling sense of dread in the pit of her stomach. With all the security and walls to pass through, she now understood the gravity of the situation. Underground tunnels, hidden passageways. Deep down, she felt like she was entering another world. But in this world, she was going to meet The Don and his 'family,' and everything was uncertain. Even if she could clear her name, she doubted she'd live through this, no matter what Carl promised.

Carl continued, leading them through the passageway. There were a few slight turns as the tunnel twisted through the underground, but no doorways or other tunnels veered off from this main one. This was the only way in. They walked almost as far underground as they had through the forest, their footfalls making soft thuds on the dirty concrete floor. Ahead was the end of the tunnel, their exit blocked by a massive metal door, studded with rivets that signalled the end of their journey.

Carl turned to Madison and placed his hands on her shoulders. He looked into her eyes. She returned his gaze, noticing for the first time in the dim light of the flashlight the pale gold flecks that were mixed in with the turquoise. Those eyes were honest. Something she hadn't noticed before. When he spoke, she heard the sincerity in his voice.

"Well, Madison, from here on in, everything changes. You're strong, and you're going to need your strength. Please have faith that I'm on your side, no matter how things appear." With that, he released her and reached out to pull open the door.

# CHAPTER 26

The door swung open, revealing a well lit passageway beyond the tunnel. In the hallway ahead stood a dozen armed men, weapons raised. Carl grabbed Madison's arm as her mouth dropped open, but not a sound passed between her lips. A lump formed in the pit of her stomach as the cold sensation of dread spread through to the very marrow of her core. Her mind couldn't connect to the scene in front of her. The sight of men with guns aimed at her shifted into her consciousness, and the reality that she was going to die dawned on her.

She was sure they had been quiet, but somehow these men knew they were coming. The men kept their aim and stepped aside as a large man hobbled out from behind them. He wore his dark hair slicked back. His face was red from the exertion he needed to move his enormous mass. A thin moustache dusted across his upper lip. He grinned at her, and her flesh crawled beneath his gaze. His voice was deep, and there was a faint trace of a Spanish accent as he first spoke.

"Ah, Dean! I knew you'd come through for me. You're a man of your word. Tony doubted it, but I never did."

Madison shot Carl a look of shock mixed with hatred. Her mind raced. Why the hell did this man call Carl Dean? She shivered as she understood how precarious the situation was. These men knew they were coming, and they'd prepared themselves. That could only mean Carl had warned them. Was he working for them? Had he set her up? She remembered his words about having faith, no matter what. His expression was blank as she searched his face for a sign. He didn't even look at her. She realized she had no choice but to follow his lead. She had to be careful. One mistake could be deadly. Then she remembered him telling her not to use his actual name. She still felt confused, even though she resolved herself to play naïve. If she died, no one would know, and everyone would still believe she'd killed Abby. There had to be a reason for the weeks of training, but now she wasn't sure what good it was. Her head swung back up to look at the large man as he spoke again.

"Frisk her for weapons, Tony. Not that I don't trust you, Dean, but I have to be careful. You never know where a woman will hide a weapon."

Before she could react, one man grabbed her and slammed against the wall as he forced her feet apart. He ran his hands up her legs and along her body. She grimaced as he squeezed her breast. With one hand, he pushed her head to the wall as he slid the other down the front of her pants.

"That's enough, Tony. I don't think she has a weapon hidden there." The Don interrupted.

"Don't worry, Don. She's not armed. Do you think I'd bring her here armed?" Carl/Dean replied. "I've checked her for weapons."

"Oh, my god." Madison gasped when the man released her.

The Don chuckled.

"I see you still have a way with the ladies, Dean. She didn't know what you were up to. Very well. Everything is ready. I'll let you have her for a while, but I think you'll find her more trouble than she's worth."

"What the hell is he talking about?" Madison questioned, her eyes pleading with Carl.

"You've been had puta. By the time we are both done with you, you'll be begging for me to kill you." The man named Tony shot in.

"That's enough Tony."

Tony turned around and glared at Dean, his hatred clear. Dean was acting as if he was in charge. Tony still didn't trust him, even if he brought the girl in like he said he would. There was something off. He couldn't put his finger on it, but he knew it in his gut. She wasn't afraid until the guns were on her. That meant somehow she thought she wasn't in danger. He pondered how Dean managed that.

"Tell her Dean. Tell little miss nosy just what's going on here. Or maybe you'd like me to do it. I'd get a lot of pleasure outta knocking you down. She seems to think you're some kind of hero. Misplaced, but you can still see it. I'd love to describe to her just what I'm going to do once you're finished with her."

Madison felt her stomach roll. A knot formed deep inside. She swallowed down the bile that threatened to spill out. Madison didn't know what this tattooed creep was talking about. She knew he was referring to Carl as Dean, but why? Was this part of his cover to expose the 'family', as he called it? Or was it something else? Something darker? Could he have been lying to her the entire time? One thing was for sure: she needed to be wary of Tony. Still pressed against the wall, she stared at him, taking in his dark hair and the vicious scar running down his left cheek. This was one man who wouldn't think twice about taking a life. She realized his involvement in Abby's murder. Maybe he was the one who killed her. From what she'd witnessed so far, he seemed to get great pleasure from inflicting pain. Her breast still ached from him squeezing it, and her skin crawled where his hands touched her body.

She knew she was here to help Carl bring down the mob and get justice for Abby. But to come face to face with those responsible wasn't something she'd prepared for. An involuntary shiver crept up her spine. Whatever happened, everything from here on in was out of her control. Carl trained her to fight, but not against so many armed men. He took her gun, her only way of protecting herself. Something inside her snapped. She whirled around to Carl.

"You bastard!" she spat. "What the hell kind of game are you playing? I trusted you, I belie…" Pain split through Madison's skull as she slumped to the floor in silence.

"What the fuck Tony? Why the hell did you hit her?"

"She was annoying me. When you made your arrangement with The Don, you never said she had to be treated any differently than we would a regular prisoner. You got a soft spot for her, Dean? Why? Does she give good head?"

"Fuck off Tony."

Carl leaned over Madison and picked her up in his arms, noticing a trickle of blood in her hairline where the butt of Tony's gun connected when he silenced her.

"Not so fast Dean."

Carl/Dean stopped.

"What is going on here? Do you have feelings for her?" The Don sneered. "Is that what this is all about?"

"No Don. I didn't want her to be fighting a headache when I fuck her later. It takes the pleasure out of the act. I'd much prefer her to be feisty, and if not feisty, at least wanting it. Rape isn't my thing."

The Don chuckled. "Still the same old Dean. O.K. You have some fun with her, but when I say so, you'll give her to Tony. Of course, only once I've questioned her. I don't care how much the two of you hate each other. He's the one who will finish the job. Take her to your quarters, and later I want you to bring her to me. Oh! And make sure she washes first. She stinks of fear."

The Don left, turning in the narrow passageway, shifting his substantial girth with difficulty. The dozen armed men stepped back to allow him to pass before surrounding him as he headed back out of the underground and into the compound. Only Tony and Carl remained, staring at each other in contempt. Madison lay limp in Carl's arms. Tony looked at Carl before he leaned over and spat in her face.

"She's going to have a headache, no matter what. Take the little puta now. But know this, before I kill her, she'll have a real man between her legs."

"In your dreams, Tony. When you get ahold of her, I'm sure she'll be happy to die, if not beg for you to end her misery." With that, Carl pushed past Tony, holding on tight to Madison.

# CHAPTER 27

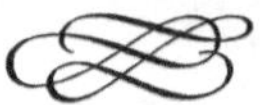

Madison remained unconscious as Carl made his way through the compound to his quarters. He was worried. She was out for too long. Damn Tony. There was no reason for him to hit her. He was showing what a Neanderthal he was. Carl entered his room and kicked the door closed before he laid Madison down on his bed. His quarters at The Don's were ornate, not at all to his taste, but everything The Don owned was that way. Heavy ornate furniture, gilt mirrors, dark red upholstery, and bedding. It looked more like an old brothel than the home of one of the most powerful Dons in the States. But his room was large. It had its own private washroom, seating area, and bar. It suited his needs.

He took a deep breath and considered what had just happened. Things were moving faster than he thought. He had to figure out a way to get the evidence and get them both to safety. Tony was eager to get his hands on Madison, and if they weren't careful, she'd be at his mercy. He'd seen that look in Tony's eyes before. God help him if he touched her again. He promised to protect her. It was going to be more challenging than he thought. Tony held a grudge against Madison for surviving his 'explosion'.

He looked down at Madison and swept a lock of hair from her brow. She'd have a nasty bump when she woke up, but it was better than the alternative. Tony could have just killed her. Sure, it would piss The Don off, Tony breaking the deal they made, but not for long, because it would please him that Tony dealt with her. Tony would be punished because The Don needed to find out what she knew, and if there was a duplicate file hidden, but Carl doubted Tony cared.

He heard Madison murmur as she stirred on the bed. He'd have to tell her the truth, at least part of it. There was no way he could avoid it now. The only way to persuade her to continue going along with him was to fill her in. It was a long shot after what had just happened, but it was all he had. He heard her moan and saw her eyelids flutter. Carl had to take care of her. He went to the washroom, grabbed a glass of water, two Advil and a face cloth dampened with cool water, and placed it on her brow. Caring for her wasn't what he expected, but it happened. He found her strength and tenacity admirable. It was because of this he was determined not to let anything happen to her.

Together, they had a part to play in an unpredictable game. But he vowed to take care of her. He just had to get her to trust him again, if it was possible. He picked up his remote and turned on the stereo, allowing the soft sound of classical music to fill the air. The music would muffle their voices and render it impossible for them to be heard if someone was listening in. It was a practice he had begun long ago, just to be prepared in case he needed to mask a conversation. Like all areas of the compound, he knew they bugged his room.

"Ugh, what happened? It feels like I split my head in two." Madison whispered as she brought her hand to her forehead, her eyes still closed.

"You'll have a headache and a painful bump for a few days, but it could have been worse."

Madison's eyes flew open. She tried to sit up too quick, but the throbbing in her head forced her back. Carl put his hand on her shoulder to steady her.

"Take it easy Madison."

"Oh my god, who are you? First, you tell me you're Carl, and then I find out your Dean. You're some sort of soldier of fortune, then a mob associate, which is it? Did you enjoy playing me for a fool, you bastard?" she hissed between clenched teeth.

"My actual name is Carl, you know that. Dean is a cover, which is why I told you not to use my real name. If I told you what was going on, it would have ruined the look of surprise and shock I needed you to show back there. It had to be real. If you knew what to expect, I doubted you'd be able to fake it. I told you the Senator hired me to ensure Miguel stayed in jail for his responsibility in his daughter's death. That part is true. I had to develop a cover to infiltrate the family. I've been undercover here for a long time. Do you think I would train you just to hand you over?"

"I, I, I'm not sure." Madison laid back, her pallor pale. "My head hurts so bad I can't think straight."

"Don't worry. Tony will pay for that. It was a test to see if you meant anything to me. I passed." Carl declared.

"I could have told him that, and then he wouldn't have had to hit me. What did he use, a sledgehammer?" She moaned.

"I'm glad to see you still have that wonderful sarcasm. Here, swallow these Advil. They will help. Now lay back, and I'll explain everything to you."

"Finally, and all it took was getting conked on the head."

Carl gave her a warning look before he continued.

"The first thing you need to remember is that we can only talk candidly when the music is playing. I'm certain they bugged my room, as is the whole compound. The large man you met is Don Fernando. I told you about him back at the ranch, but you may have already heard of him or at least read about him in the papers. He's a powerful mob boss, always working at the edge of the law. Until now, there hasn't been enough evidence to bring him in."

Madison nodded.

"He ordered the hit on your friend. She made a deal with him, or someone in her firm did. Whoever it was backed out. It seems her boyfriend got her involved in throwing a case."

"No way! Not Abby! She dedicated herself to the law." Madison cut in. "She wouldn't have been involved."

"But, according to her boyfriend, she was. He was the one The Don contacted. There was something in his background, something illegal that made him agree to it. From there, he found a way. Unfortunately for Abby, he put her in the middle of it. He needed her pull and position within the firm. Somewhere along the line, her conscience got the better of her, and in the end, she couldn't go through with it. When she backed out, The Don's son went to prison. In The Don's eyes, that was unforgivable, so he demanded retribution. Her boyfriend Charles gave her up. He even led them to where you both would be that weekend. He gave The Don the address and directions. Although, if what you say about Abby is true, it might be possible that Charles set her up to take the fall for his own mistakes. Maybe he couldn't accomplish what he set out to do, and Miguel went to jail, anyway. He knew The Don would want justice, so he gave him Abby. You were a thorn in Charles's side, so he asked The Don to take care of you, too. It seems he didn't like you very much. The Don didn't care. He thought it would appear more like an accident if you were both killed."

"That asshole! There was something about him I knew was smarmy. I tried to warn Abby that he was a lowlife, but she wouldn't listen. The feeling was mutual. I hated him. I thought he was going to be detrimental to her career, but I never thought he wanted her dead. In the end I was right about his character if what you're saying is true. So when he got into trouble, he arranged for Abby to die, and I could have died too, all to save his own sorry ass. I could still die, and he would still be responsible for my death. I don't think these people plan for me to live, especially now that I've seen their faces."

"No, they don't. They think I want to use you for sex. I'm afraid I let them think that. It was the only way I could get permission to have you in my room and keep you safe. The Don has allowed me to 'keep' you for a short time. I'm hoping that will give me enough time to get the proof I need."

"What if it isn't?"

"Then Madison," he declared. "I'll have to figure a way to get you out of here, and fast. Otherwise, Tony will make his move. He will use you and then torture you to death. Here in the compound, he will have all the time he needs. He's a sick, twisted bastard. Before the explosion, he asked The Don to let him cut away at your friend, piece by piece, so that he could enjoy listening to her scream in pain. The Don refused his request, as he wanted it to look like an accidental explosion, from a faulty gas line."

"Oh, my god. He's a monster!" She cried. "Why would he want to drag it out like that? You'd think he'd be happy to get it over with. Not that I want to die, but if I have to, I'd want it done quick."

"He gets pleasure out of hurting people. That's why Tony would make you suffer. He's sadistic. You're his failure because you lived. He wasn't able to complete his mission. So now, to ease his self-imposed guilt, he will make you pay in a slow and painful way. I believe he also plans to rape you. It would be his ultimate way of degrading you. Not that I'm going to give him a chance. I promise you, Madison, if you listen to me and follow my lead, I'll get you out of here."

"So, what do we do now?"

"First things first. Here's your gun back. You can't keep it on you right now, but I'll find somewhere to hide it in the room and let you know where." Carl said, handing the still holstered gun to her across the bed.

Madison felt speechless. The last thing she expected was to get her gun back. She reached out for it, finding comfort in the leather and cold steel. She rested it on the bed, her hand wrapped around it.

"They won't find out?"

"No. They've already checked you for weapons. They won't expect me to hand you one. Why arm my prisoner? It would allow you to kill me, and who would be stupid enough to do that?" he said with a wink. "I want you to keep it in your ankle holster. The Don expects women to wear dresses. I'm sure he'll arrange for you to have some while you're my 'guest,' so there won't be a way to hide it. I have a wall safe. We can lock it up, if need be, or find somewhere that you can access it in an emergency. I'm expected and allowed to wear a weapon at all times, only so I can protect The Don, of course. I'm sorry, but we will have to share the bed. The only other option is a love seat, and I'm not sleeping there. We can't be too careful. Anyone from the family can barge in, and they can't find the gun. You can't wander around the compound, which means you'll spend most of your time in this room. You'll only leave with me or an armed guard, but if possible, I don't want you leaving with anyone but me. If anyone else comes for you, it may be a trick and, for God's sake, never leave with Tony. Scream blue murder if he ever comes into the room, and you're alone. I'll speak with The Don about allowing me some extra time with you for my pleasure, without Tony's interference, my reward for bringing you in. For the time being, you're going to pretend to be falling under my undeniable charm." He chuckled. "Remember, I am supposed to be enjoying all your carnal pleasures."

Madison smiled at him, relaxing at the playfulness of his words.

"Oh yes! I've seen such a beautiful display of your charms until now. You're a slave driver who wants his own way. You're deceitful, and I'm not sure how to trust you. Now you want me to pretend to sleep with you and like it? If I can pull all of this off, I'll deserve an academy award."

"If you pull this off, I'll have one made for you."

CARL RELAXED, sensing that Madison had accepted everything he'd told her. He'd been honest, but only to a point. He'd laid almost everything out and was once again surprised at how well she was adjusting to her current situation. The road ahead was dangerous, and he needed her on board. Hank tried to persuade him to let her in on it before, but the element of surprise was the best attack. She couldn't fake the look of hurt and confusion on her face when The Don found them. The Don believed and trusted him. That's what he needed right now.

Tony was another matter. His suspicions were going to cause trouble, but Carl was certain he could handle Tony. They hired him as muscle and nothing more. That's why Tony had such a chip on his shoulder. He couldn't move up in the organization, because The Don had already set his limits, which was why he was so driven to be the best at what he did. Plus, he enjoyed the violence.

Carl had been working to infiltrate The Dons 'family' for over two years. During that time, he'd moved up the ranks. Now he was The Don's most trusted right-hand man. He had the right connections to set up the perfect background cover, and no one was the wiser. The Don investigated him before he had access to the organization. He'd passed all the tests, and now he would bring them down. To Carl, it was personal. It had to do with more than Abby's death. He didn't even know her, and it was more than the commitment to the senator regarding his daughter. Those were just convenient pieces of the puzzle that gave him the connections he needed to gain entry. His grudge went back further than that to when The Don was young, and The Don's father was running the organization. Not that he'd tell Madison about it, not yet.

The previous Don had killed Carl's parents to take over their company. His parents were important corporate leaders, but what the old Don didn't realize in his greed was that his parents wouldn't allow their corporation to be publicly traded. When they realized that there was an attempt at a hostile takeover, they worked out a deal with the board of directors. Then they sent Carl off to live with his grandmother and Rose at the ranch before traveling abroad. They assumed they'd be ok, but they assumed wrong. The previous Don caught up with them and arranged for the 'accident' which took their lives.

Carl grew up living with his grandmother until she died when he was twenty-one. Then he inherited the ranch and Rose, all under a new name, thanks to his parents. Their company continued under the board of directors, and they sent dividends to his account. He never wanted for anything.

He rebelled at the whole corporate world that was thrust upon him, choosing to leave the day to day running of the now multi-million dollar company to the board of directors. Instead, he went off to pursue his own interests and ended up training with the Green Berets. When he was ready to settle down and learn the running of the company, he discovered that Don Fernando's father had tried to take over the company years before. The more he investigated, the more obvious it was that the previous Don caused his parent's death. It was then he formed his plan and put it into action.

He had the proof of The Don's involvement, but not enough to have him arrested. Then that Don died, and his son took over. Now, he also had to make The Don's only son suffer. Life in jail would ensure that. There were just a few more things he had to do. Things that would prove The Fernando's involvement. He wanted The Don and his whole 'family' to fall. He wouldn't let Madison know the full truth, not his personal truth. The less she knew, the better. He had to keep an emotional distance from her. Carl didn't want her too close because if it came down to it, and he had to make a choice, he'd take down The Don over saving her life. He hoped it wouldn't come to that. But one life was a small price compared to all the lives at stake in the future if he didn't bring The Don and his family to justice.

# CHAPTER 28

Madison sat in silence, considering Carl's revelation. *'No. Here he was, Dean. She needed to think of him as that. So much hinged on how she behaved and how she responded to The Don's questions. Would he ask her outright about what she knew? Or would he allow Tony to torture the answers out of her? How would she know what the right answers were? Abby divulged nothing about a case to her. She believed in following the letter of the law and would never jeopardize client/attorney confidentiality.'* It broke her concentration when she heard Dean's phone ring. He answered it right away and listened to whoever was on the other end. When the call ended, he turned to her and spoke for the first time since his admission.

"That was The Don. I don't know what he's up to, but he wants us to join him for dinner. He told me tonight you will be his guest. He said he'd send something down he wants you to wear. You'll have to wear it. No matter what it is. I expect it will be some sort of dress. He'll want you to look feminine. Put in the effort to please him. That's the only way you're going to get through this. You can't take your gun, so we might as well put it away now. Go grab a shower. When you're done, I'll have one too."

Madison went to the washroom, closed, and locked the door

behind her before she undressed. She released her hair from the ponytail and ran her fingers through it, working out the knots. Madison felt surprised when she grabbed a towel off the shelf, at how soft and plush it was. She did not lose the paradox of how luxurious her imprisoned surroundings were.

She showered, washing away the grime from the tunnel and the offending smell of 'fear' as The Don called it. Being careful as she shampooed her hair, her fingers gently probed the tender spot where Tony hit her. She wouldn't be able to wear the gun, once again stripped of the security it gave her. Carl was careful to explain how insistent The Don was that women wear dresses, and wearing one wouldn't enable her to hide the gun. He believed women should look like women, which she found odd in this world of crime and violence. When she finished showering, she would find out what that meant. Her first thought was that of a ghastly floral chiffon creation with ruffles.

Clean, she stepped out of the bathroom, wrapped in her towel to see what she was supposed to wear tonight. Hanging on the door to the wardrobe was a long, silk, red sheath dress with thin spaghetti straps. The irony was, he'd sent one of her own designs for her to wear. Everything was red, right down to the underwear and matching shoes. She picked up the gown and noticed it was the correct size. She spun around to face Carl.

"It's my size! How did he know?"

"I'm sure he knows a lot more about you than either of us realized. I'll shower while you dress, then you can have the bathroom to finish getting ready."

When Carl finished, he came out of the bathroom, clean and shaven, with a towel wrapped around his hips. He noticed she was already wearing the gown. It skimmed her fine figure; the front draped low between her breasts. Her hair was still damp, but she hurried past him, back into the bathroom to take care of that. The door closed behind her, and he heard the hair blower start as he dressed in a suit and tie, finishing with a splash of Armani Diamonds. When the hair blower stopped, the door opened, and there she stood teetering on the high heels, her curls tamed to elegant waves. She appeared to be a guest at a fine hotel rather than the prisoner she was.

"You look beautiful Madison."

"Thank you, Dean." She replied, trying to get used to the name he went by here. "How shall I act towards you? Shall I pretend to be enamoured by you or should I show you fear or hatred? Maybe a little mixture of both. I'm sure it will be the most believable."

He chuckled. "Enamoured might be best. First, it will piss off Tony. Second, it may be more believable. You could throw in some fear, at least when you are near Tony. That would be believable after he assaulted you earlier. I think you should show fear and humility towards The Don as well, but not to me. It will honour him to know you fear him. As for hatred, well, The Don may think you're too big of a risk if you're fighting me tooth and nail. I'm hoping to extend your 'stay' for as long as possible to get the evidence we need. We'll have to be careful. I've already searched the room for a hidden camera. So far, The Don hasn't had one installed, but he may. He may use the cameras to watch as I dominate you in bed, to verify that's what I wanted you for."

"What? But that's supposed to be an act. We aren't going to actually..." She took a step back as she realized she might have to do more than just sleep beside him.

"Don't worry! If we have to, we will get under the covers and pretend to perform. Your virtue is safe with me unless you don't want it to be." Carl finished with a smile that looked deep into Madison's soul.

"Anyway, you don't need to worry about that now. It's showtime. You are a beautiful woman who is so infatuated with me you're having a hard time keeping your hands to yourself. But you're a lady, so you're composed and doting." He offered his arm to her as he led her to the door.

"Doting?" Madison repeated, as she raised her eyebrow at him.

"Well," Carl laughed, "You know what I mean. I realize doting doesn't describe you at all. How about hot-tempered or a spitfire?" he asked, trying to appear serious.

Madison punched him in the arm with a playfulness. "Watch it, buster, or you'll regret those words."

"See Madison. You've got this. You're already acting like a lover." He smirked before she took his offered arm and headed to the lounge to meet with The Don for cocktails.

# CHAPTER 29

The Don was already sitting in an oversized chair when they entered the lounge. Two armed guards flanked him. He had a whisky in one hand and a cigar smouldering in the other. Tony sat scowling at the end of one sofa, nursing a beer. He looked uncomfortable in the tight-fitting suit, with the unmistakable bulge of a gun underneath his jacket.

"Ah, Miss Kerr! Welcome! Forgive me if I don't stand and greet you. Right now, you are my guest, but I want you to understand the rules here. While you're my 'guest,' you're expected to dress as a lady when you're out of Dean's room. I have supplied a few choices for you. There are expectations of femininity as far as women are concerned. I expect you to remain in Dean's room at all times unless I've asked to see you. If you escape the room and choose to wander around without a guard, I can't ensure your safety. You're Dean's responsibility while you're here. Anything you do wrong will be a mark against him. So keep in mind, if you don't follow these simple rules, I will turn you over to Tony. He will take care of you. But I would like the chance for us to have a chat first."

She shivered at the thought of what Tony would do in order to 'take care' of her as she turned her head and glanced his way. He rose and walked over so that he could position himself at The Don's left, staring at her with contempt. His dark eyes, liquid pools of hatred, glared across at her.

"Do you understand what The Don said?" Tony barked.

"Yes."

"Yes, what?" Tony snapped.

"Yes, Sir?"

"No, you stupid bitch. Yes, Don. You're addressing The Don, not me."

"Now Tony, let's not be too hasty." The Don drawled. "I like the way it sounds when she calls me, sir. The little snit doesn't understand what the term, The Don, means, but she knows what sir means." The Don leered up at Madison, his thin moustache curling up in one corner with his upper lip.

"Now that we understand each other. I have a very nice bottle of Gaja for you to try. I know you prefer reds, and before you decline, remember you don't have a choice. While you are here, I expect you to do everything I say, without question."

The Don signalled to one server at the far end of the room, who filled a glass with the offered wine. He placed it on a tray and delivered it to her, along with a whisky on ice for Carl. Madison took a tentative sip, wondering if he poisoned it. The smooth, rich flavour filled her mouth before she swallowed it. Smiling, she nodded a thank you to The Don, as she knew he'd expect. It was a fine wine. She made a mental note to get a bottle when this was all over, if she survived.

After they served the drinks, an awkward silence filled the room. No one spoke. All eyes on Madison. She glanced out of the corner of her eye at Tony and The Don, being careful to keep her eyes averted. Madison couldn't remember a time where she'd felt more uncomfortable. She shifted in her seat and wondered if at some point The Don was going to question her, or if they didn't talk business at these 'social' events. Madison looked at Dean, hoping for a sign, but he avoided making eye contact with her. She refused to look at The Don or Tony, but she could feel Tony's eyes on her. His undisguised hatred made her feel like an animal trapped in a cage.

As she glanced around the room, she tried to get a sense of the man who lived here. She took in the heavy mahogany paneling and ornate trim carved into it. There was no evidence of a female's touch. It was all masculine. This didn't surprise her. She was the only woman present, and she hadn't seen another woman since she arrived. Although she'd barely touched her wine, she noticed that everyone else had finished their drinks.

"Not to your liking, Miss Kerr?"

"No, it's very good. I was just savouring it."

"Leave your glass here. You'll get a fresh one with dinner. Dean, escort Miss Kerr to the dining room. I look forward to having her beauty grace us at our table. Please sit her to my left. I think she and I have some things to say to one another."

"As you wish."

Tony scowled, not happy about giving up what she assumed to be his regular seat at the table. She placed her wineglass on the coffee table and rose from the chair, smoothing down the front of her gown as she stood. Carl walked over to her and bowed before he took her by the arm and led her to the dining room.

As they walked, he leaned close to her ear and whispered for her to keep the conversation light and to let The Don take the lead on what they talked about. She just nodded.

The dining room was just down the hall. Under different circumstances, the elegance of the room would have impressed Madison. The oversized table could sit more than a dozen people, but only four places were set. A place setting was at each end, one in the middle, and one on the left side very close to the one end. They did not set it for comfort or mutual conversation, but so that the only actual conversation would be between herself and The Don. As they reached her seat, Carl pulled out her chair. When she moved to sit, he put out his hand to stop her. She then understood they expected her to wait until The Don made it to the seat next to hers. One of the staff pulled out his chair. He plopped down, then turned and nodded at her, showing that she could now sit. The Don motioned for Tony to sit in the middle, whereas Carl was to take the place at the far end of the table. It was a place of honour, but it also created the most physical distance from where she sat, meaning he couldn't hear their conversation if The Don whispered. Madison bit her lower lip. A nasty habit, but one she couldn't seem to stop. She worried about the expectations The Don had concerning their 'conversation'.

Expecting the worse, it surprised Madison when The Don started talking. He engaged in typical dinner party pleasantries. Not what she'd expected, but it relieved her. Throughout the meal, she was on the edge of her seat, ever cautious that she would say the wrong thing or that the conversation would turn and become an interrogation. The food, which she was sure was delicious, tasted like sawdust in her mouth. She took a small bite, chewing thoroughly before swallowing, using it to delay her responses to find the right words. She needed to appear to be eating and enjoying her meal so that she didn't offend The Don, who already showed his displeasure with her unfinished glass of wine.

The masquerade and false pleasantries at dinner took its toll on her. She had a hard time reining in her temper, aware that anything she said could be taken out of context. When all she wanted to do was spit in their faces, accuse them of Abby's murder, and bring the police down on them, but she couldn't. She'd never in her life met such dangerous people. Her fear didn't matter. This was an act, and she had a part to play. What she found most surprising was that Carl seemed unaware of how angry she was with him. He'd learned nothing about her while they trained together. If he did, he'd know that she wouldn't take his deception well. That was his mistake. She would work out her own plan to get out of here before the Don decided to 'give' her to Tony. She thought she couldn't trust Carl, and it was time she started taking care of herself.

Tony's proximity left Madison feeling exposed and nervous. She could tell he was waiting for her to say or do something wrong, hoping for the chance to intervene. Madison hadn't counted on him sitting so close. She'd wrongly assumed Carl would sit next to her. At least he pretended to want her safe. Tony had something else in mind. She squirmed under his direct gaze. She sensed he was trying to read her and discover her hidden secrets. He would get the best act she could muster now, and any time, she had to be near him.

By the time the meal ended, she felt her nerves strained to the breaking point. She'd barely tasted anything, eating only to nourish herself and maintain her strength. She may as well have eaten cardboard for all she cared. Tony's presence threw her off. Somewhere deep down, she knew he would be the greatest obstacle in her quest for justice. But for now, she was thankful to be under Carl's protection. She wasn't sure how safe that was, but it was better than what Tony had in store for her.

The meal finished when they served coffee and dessert. The Don motioned for Carl and Tony to move closer to his end of the table so they could all talk. Carl got up and moved to position himself next to Madison so that Tony couldn't sit there. Instead, Tony chose the seat opposite her. His eyes bore into hers until she forced herself to look away.

"What a lovely guest you are, Miss Kerr, although not much of an appetite, I see. Was it not to your liking?"

"Everything was delicious. I just wasn't hungry, I'm afraid."

The Don chuckled. "I'm sure that has something to do with the position you've found yourself in. Never mind, we don't talk business at the table. Tomorrow will be soon enough. Dean will bring you to my study right after breakfast. We have much to discuss."

Madison swallowed hard, uncomfortable with the way The Don was leering at her. Tomorrow was an ordeal she wished she could forego. She wondered if Carl would be with her when she went for her 'talk'. At least she'd find his presence reassuring. What she hoped more than anything was that Tony wouldn't be. He made her nervous. If he was there, it might mean it was to intimidate her or to use physical means to get her to talk.

"Well, Miss Kerr, if you'll excuse me. I'm going to retire for the night. Dean, you may take her back to your quarters. Now you can have Miss Kerr all to yourself. How you've kept your hands off her so far, I'll never know. I'll bid you adios." The Don said as he lifted his substantial girth from his chair, using Tony's offered arm to assist him. "When you tire of her, let me know. Tony is champing at the bit to get his hands on her. Mind you, don't take too long, or I'll have to call an end to your little tryst myself."

Madison stared at The Don and Tony as they left the room, her mouth slack-jawed. Tony cast a snide grin at her over his shoulder as he left, sending a shudder down her spine.

"He spoke as if I wasn't even in the room!"

"Remember Madison, even though he treated you as a guest tonight, you are his prisoner. As far as he's concerned, he's being more than fair to you. He would have killed you already, but he is allowing me to find 'pleasure' with you before you have to die."

"But..."

"Not that I intend for you to die, but we must carry on this charade until I get the information I need."

"Yes, I realize that. I'm sorry I doubted you. But so much has happened. I'm finding it difficult to trust anything or anyone. Tony gives me the creeps."

"As well, he should. If he gets his hands on you, you won't just die. He will humiliate and degrade you first. By the time he's done, you'll wish you died in the explosion."

"In that case, if you have no choice in the end but to hand me over to him, please kill me first. I think it would be kinder and gentler."

"If it comes to that, you have my word."

Carl draped his arm across her shoulder and pulled her close.

"Now," Carl continued, "I think you should prepare yourself to act out a night of passion."

"What!"

"By now, The Don will have a camera set up in my room. I'm sure that was part of the reason he invited you to dinner. He'll want to be sure that I'm enjoying you to the fullest. I hope you can handle that. We will have to get naked and go through the motions of making love. It's the only way to convince him."

"But…"

"I know you haven't been with anyone for a long time. So I hope being naked won't make you uncomfortable."

"How the hell do you know that?" She snapped.

"Believe it or not, it's in your dossier. I'm not saying that we are going to make love. Just pretend that we are and that we're enjoying it. You remember how to, don't you?"

"You're a bastard, you know." Madison sneered.

"Yes, I'm sure I am. People have called me worse. Do you think you can pull this off?"

"Oh, you don't need to worry about me. When we get in front of the camera, even you won't know if I'm acting or into you. Just you remember, it's for the camera."

"Don't worry, spitfire," Carl responded. "I'm no more interested in you than you are in me. I like my women willing and gentle." He snickered.

Carl kept his arm around her shoulder as they headed back to the bedroom, careful to maintain the pretence in case they were being watched. For all intents and purposes, they looked like a couple heading for a blissful night of passion.

"I'll scan the room to find the camera, and then we'll know what angle will give us the most privacy. It will be more believable if you resist me. I'll signal you to get undressed. That way, you'll know that we're being watched, and then we can begin the show. You should resist and refuse. I may get a little rough. Before throwing you on the bed, I will remove your dress. Are you O.K. with that?"

"Don't worry. I'll try to give you a performance worthy of an Oscar. I'm not surprised you like it rough that's the only way you'd get a woman into your bed! Just don't enjoy the show too much. Remember, I'm only acting."

"Don't worry Madison. I think I can control myself. As I told you before, I like women who want me. And I don't use force. The rough part is for the camera. The Don won't expect you to be willing."

With that, he swung open the door to his suite and motioned for her to enter. The first thing she noticed when she stepped inside was that someone had brought in a bottle of wine and two glasses and placed them on the table in the sitting area. That proved that someone was there while they were at dinner. At least she knew it wasn't Tony. The thought of him in here made her flesh crawl.

# CHAPTER 30

As they entered his room, Carl's eyes darted around, searching to see whether they'd set a camera up. Then he saw it. A small red light flickered, almost hidden amongst the books on his bookshelf. He wished it wasn't there, but there was nothing he could do. The show they now needed to put on would make them both uncomfortable, but it was necessary.

"Enough of this Madison. I want you naked." Carl winked at her with his back to the camera before sitting on the end of the bed. His eyes glanced at the bookshelf. Madison followed his eyes and took a brief look in the same direction, also noticing the small red camera light just visible on the shelf. She smiled and tousled her hair before replying.

"Do you think I'm going to just get naked for you?"

"You don't have a choice in the matter. Remember, you're my prisoner."

Madison scowled at him. What he said hit a nerve. She was his prisoner. But she couldn't think about that now. She had to allow this little scenario to play out. If she didn't make it believable, who knows what The Don would expect them to do? He may want a live performance. She shuddered. If anyone thought it was an act, The

Don would find somewhere else for her to stay. She'd be in real danger if she ended up in Tony's hands. Then she had a thought. Something that would make her nakedness feel less intimidating. Something she hoped would make him feel uncomfortable. The act of being naked didn't bother her. She worked in the fashion industry and had modelled a few times, and nakedness wasn't the issue. The issue was the possibility of intimacy and the fact that they'd both end up naked on the bed.

"Well, I have an idea. What if you got naked for me first? That way, I can see how much my body pleases you." Madison smiled at him through half-closed eyes.

Carl shot her a quick look. She was trying to embarrass him, but it wouldn't work. Her request may benefit them both. If they were going to pull this off, they needed to undress. He wasn't shy, and if he got an erection, it would prove to whoever watched that it was real. He'd also enjoy knowing any evidence of his arousal would embarrass her. She wouldn't know where to look. He smiled at the thought.

"Anything to make you happy." He replied as he rose and began removing his clothing, drawing it out as he folded each item and placed it on the chair. First, the tie, and then his jacket. Each item came off in slow progression until he was down to his boxer briefs and socks. The combination was almost comical, but he soon discarded them in quick order.

She squirmed as she watched him. This wasn't what she had in mind. She wanted him to feel embarrassed, not displaying this confidence. He turned towards her, unabashed. It didn't embarrass him at all. He was very proud of his well-toned body. Madison was the one who was uncomfortable with him standing before her, naked, as he exuded raw sexuality. She tried not to look further down his body, past his eyes, afraid that she might see his arousal, or worse, to find that he wasn't. That would mean she wasn't having the same effect on him as he had on her.

He walked up to her and caressed her right cheek as he continued past to dim the lights. He went to the stereo where he chose appropriate mood music, setting the volume just high enough to drown out whispered conversations. Madison stood rooted to her spot, afraid to move or look at him as he set the stage for their 'performance.' This was far from what she expected. She felt something stir deep inside, the awakening of her long asleep sexuality. It shocked her to realize her attraction to him and that she wanted him. The thought appalled her. It couldn't be. Not this man, and not in this place. She wrapped her arms around her body, trying to shake the feeling.

In his nakedness, Carl continued over, opened the wine, and poured them each a glass before handing one to her. He raised his glass in a mock salute and drained the contents. Madison took a tentative sip and then followed suit, allowing the richness of the red to warm her insides. Carl then poured a second glass and walked to the bed. Placing his wine on the bedside table, before he slid onto the bed, laying on his right side, his head propped up on his arm, his gaze focused on her. Madison couldn't help but look at him, taking in his every male aspect, from his broad shoulders that tapered into narrow hips, his well-toned muscles to his obvious arousal. She missed none of it. Her eyes traveled back up to his face, where his eyes sparkled as a slow smile played on his lips.

"Now it's your turn."

Madison nibbled her lower lip, trying to decide her next move, before remembering she had a part to play. This was all an act. Her eyes locked onto his, observing his expression as she let her hips sway to the music. She danced for him, allowing her body to tease him with its rhythmic movements. Madison lifted one of her legs to the edge of the bed and lifted her gown to reveal a silky, shapely calf as she slid her hands down to remove her shoe. She followed with the second leg, in the same manner, dropping both shoes to the floor. Then she turned to walk away, looking over her shoulder as she went.

She wanted to tease him, touch him ever so slightly, so he'd know what he'd be missing in this game of make-believe. Madison paused and whirled around, allowing the fabric of her dress to cling to her body and emphasize her curves. She approached the bed. Her eyes locked on his. She ran her hands up his legs, teasing him. Her face leaned close to the area that made him male. Madison then stopped and sashayed away. She turned back, dropped one shoulder strap, then the other, letting the whole dress slither to the floor in a puddle of silk. She turned and stood before him in a matched set of delicate red lace panties and bra.

CARL'S MOUTH DROPPED OPEN. God, she was beautiful. He watched as she danced towards him, undoing her bra from behind as she got closer. She clasped her bra to her body, shimmied her shoulders, leaning forward to give him a glimpse at the rise of her breasts, teasing him. She turned and tossed her bra back at him over her shoulder, careful to have her body angled away from the camera. With her back still to him, she slipped her fingers into the top of her panties and lowered them with slow, deliberate movements. Once they passed her well shaped bottom, she let them fall to the floor, stepped out of them, and left them there. She tossed him a look over her shoulder, her glorious auburn curls falling around her face. Naked, she turned around to meet his stare. Their mutual state of undress wouldn't intimidate her. At least as a woman, her arousal didn't show.

Carl leaped from the bed and threw back the covers. In two quick strides, he stood a few mere inches in front of her. His eyes never left hers. Without hesitating, he scooped her up in his arms and carried her to the bed, where he lay her down and slipped in beside her, covering them both, hiding their bodies from the camera's lens. Heat rose from their naked flesh at each point where their bodies met. Madison inched away and tried to prevent them from touching.

Carl shifted his body so that he looked down at her and leaned in as if to kiss her ear. Breaking the spell, he whispered. "You realize I am going to touch you for this to be believable. I hope you're O.K.

with that. I know that this is an uncomfortable situation. If things were different, this wouldn't be necessary."

Madison choked back a tear. For a second, she'd forgotten where she was. She found herself caught up in the moment with a man her body wanted, even if her heart didn't. She turned to face him and whispered 'yes' as she kissed him with a deep passion on the lips. Her fingers tangled in his hair as she held him close. His need and arousal pressed into her thigh as he returned her kiss.

Carl let his hand slide down the side of her body, following every dip and curve. His lips left hers as he began a trail of small soft kisses from her neck down to her breast, where his mouth captured her aroused pink nipple, teasing it between his teeth. A gasp escaped her lips as a deep need raced from her breast to the depths of her groin. She was aching with a long-forgotten sense of arousal and the sexual hunger she now felt. His every touch was like a fire of warmth and need, burning her deep to her core.

Carl grasped her other breast in his hand, feeling the firm, soft roundness as he kneaded it. His hand never left her breast as he licked and kissed Madison down to her navel. His tongue flicked in her navel, sending shivers of pleasure through her. He continued lower until he was kissing her just before her mons. Carl paused and looked up at her, and noticed her expression of bliss, her eyes half-closed. He knew he should stop here, but he couldn't. Carl waited to see if she stopped him as he went further, but she didn't. He continued kissing her, his own need blurring the realm of appropriateness as he heard her groan.

Madison gasped in pleasure as she felt Carl's warm breath against her. She should stop him. Deep down, she knew this was wrong. They didn't need to be this intimate, to be believable. But her common sense hovered away from her body, which was lost in the delicious sensations he was creating. She didn't want it to stop, she realized, as waves of passion rose through her. She'd never felt such desire, and she knew she wouldn't stop him, no matter how far he took it.

Carl began trailing his kisses back up the tenderness of her belly, once again capturing the opposite nipple. He'd tasted her arousal. He needed to feel himself deep inside her. Carl needed to hear her say 'yes.' As he worked his way up her body, tasting her sweet flesh, he moved his hips between her parted thighs. He kissed her chin and looked down into her half-open eyes. She shifted, opening herself to him.

"I need you," Carl whispered to her, his eyes locking on hers. "Say yes."

Passion clouded her eyes as she sighed. "Yes."

Carl didn't hesitate. He looked into her eyes, trapping them with his gaze. He lowered himself until his lips brushed hers before deepening the kiss. Her eyes widened as he entered her.

He pulled back. His eyes continued to stare into hers as he moved within her, her hips lifting to meet his. She wrapped her legs and her arms around him, pulling him to her. Her lips parted to receive his kiss again. Locked together, the pace of their pulsing movements increased as they reached the height of their desire until they both lay sated in satisfaction, their bodies still tangled together.

Carl kissed her once more before lifting his body from hers, shifting so that he lay beside her. Once on his side, facing her, he pulled her deep into his embrace. She curled into him. Her body still tingled with passion.

"I didn't intend for that to happen." He whispered, pressing his lips to her forehead.

"I know."

"No regrets?"

"None."

Carl reached over to pull up the sheet that slipped down during their lovemaking to cover them. He picked up the remote and turned off the music. Then, wrapping his arms around her again, he drew her close so that every inch of their bodies touched. Madison pulled her tumbled curls from her eyes and kissed him goodnight before settling into the crook of his arm. They remained wrapped in each other's embrace as they drifted off to sleep.

~

IN THE CONTROL ROOM, Tony fumed as he watched what had transpired in Dean's room. 'She enjoyed it too much.' This wasn't what he expected. 'Where was the fight? Dean should have forced her to comply, not seduce her. The sex should have been about Dean's pleasure. She should have been terrified, not an active participant.' Tony became enraged and slammed his fist on the desk, sending the computer mouse bouncing to the floor.

"I'll show her how a man treats a puta. When The Don tires of Dean's delays, then she'll be at my mercy. I think I'll tape what I do to her and force Dean to watch. I'm going to enjoy having him watch her squirm beneath me, tied to my bed, knowing she doesn't have a choice. When I have had enough of her, that's when I'll cut her, one cut for each day since that lawyer died, making her death slow and painful. Yes, that's the perfect way to make her suffer."

Tony's agitated state calmed, as he planned how he would take his time while he tortured Madison. Deriving pleasure as he pictured her screams each time his knife cut into her flesh. He was very skilled with his knife. He knew where to cut to cause immense pain but minor damage. That way, he could draw out her suffering. Tony leaned back with his eyes closed and masturbated while his visions of torture played out in his mind.

# CHAPTER 31

$\mathcal{M}$adison rolled over onto her back, her body still warm with sleep. A smile played on her lips as she recalled the vivid dream she had of lovemaking. She felt the bed move and turned to look deep into Carl's cool turquoise eyes as he rolled over to face her. Her face flushed with embarrassment as she realized it wasn't a dream. The ache and tenderness she felt were from the passion they shared last night. It was supposed to have only been for show, but they both got caught up in the moment. She'd let things go too far, and they'd succumbed to the passion. His arms reached out to pull her close, kissing her.

"How d'ya sleep?" Carl asked, feeling Madison tense up.

"Fine," she responded, averting her eyes.

"Look at me!" he commanded.

Madison couldn't help but obey. She looked up as his eyes locked onto hers. Carl's filled with kindness and compassion as he smiled at her. She couldn't help but smile back.

"Don't regret what we did. I won't let you tense up and pull away from me. We both deserve this. You only live once, Madison. When you find happiness in whatever form, you grab onto it with both hands. We both know how unpredictable life is. I know how your body responded to me. You wanted me as much as I wanted you. There's no use in denying it, and there's nothing to be ashamed of."

She smiled, her face lighting up as she hugged him close. She wouldn't admit it to him, but she feared she was only a vessel for his desire, that he'd used her to show his control to The Don. His words forced the doubts from her mind, realizing that what happened between them was mutual. He hadn't used her. He'd wanted it as much as she had. Now she could relax and enjoy the feelings that he'd awakened, maybe even explore them again. She wasn't a fool. It wasn't love, but it was possible she was going to die, and the sex made her feel alive.

Wrapped in his arms, she could feel him grow in response to her warm body. She languished, knowing that she could get such a rapid reaction without even trying. He leaned over her and brushed his lips to hers before intensifying his kiss, which she accepted.

THE DON ENTERED the surveillance room where Tony was still watching Dean and Madison on one of the many monitors. He noted the disgusted look on Tony's face before checking the status of Dean and his prisoner. It pleased him to see how upset Tony was by the whole thing. This would work to his advantage. When angered, Tony made outstanding work of his punishments. There would be no mercy for the girl.

"So Tony! Tell me, how are things going in there? Did Dean have to fight her and force himself on her, or was she willing?"

"They're going at it like fucking rabbits. The little puta can't seem to get enough of him." Tony replied, jerking his thumb towards the monitor.

"Ah, Tony. You sound jealous. Don't worry. You'll get your turn. Dean just wanted her for a little while, as his reward for finding her. When he's done, I'll give her to you to dispose of. Then you can do with her what you will. I don't care, as long as the end result is the same. The woman dead with no connection of it to me."

"You can be sure of that, boss. I'll take great pleasure in seeing the end of her."

⁓

"IT's time to get up and showered sleepyhead," Carl announced as he gave a playful slap to Madison's bottom.

"Just five more minutes," Madison mumbled into her pillow as she swatted the air where he'd been standing only a short time before.

"No, now." He growled.

With that, Carl yanked off the covers, scooped her up in his arms, and carried her to the washroom, where she could hear the water was already running hot and steamy. Madison squirmed, pretending to fight him off. With his mouth near her ear, he whispered. "In the shower, we can talk without being heard. They'll get suspicious if we're always playing music." Madison relaxed. Carl was being careful, and she should start trusting him. She wanted to know what their next move was, and he couldn't tell her if anyone could hear them. In her mind, the plan had changed. Making love to him wasn't supposed to be part of it. It made her feel connected to him. She found a softer, gentler side that she didn't expect, and it blurred the lines, making it difficult to separate the man she'd slept with from the man who trained her. Now, she realized, he was her only hope of salvation. As they entered the washroom, Carl held her, allowing her body to slip through his arms until her feet were on the floor before he pulled her close and nuzzled her neck.

"Now that behaviour won't get us clean." She laughed.

"Who said we can't play while getting clean?" He chuckled.

Together, they stepped into the shower. It was large enough to accommodate them both. The hot water ran down their bodies while they lathered and washed clean. Under the cover of the running water, Carl explained what the next steps were.

He told Madison about the vault he assumed housed the evidence The Don kept from every crime that he'd been involved in.

He kept those records against the advice of others because he felt if he needed something taken care of, he'd find the right person to do it somewhere in those files. In them, he'd find someone whom he could blackmail or manipulate to get the job done, which would remove the immediate connection to the family.

"If you know the vault exists, can't you just get the police to come in with a search warrant?"

"Unfortunately, it doesn't work that way. The police have to have probable cause. As it stands, there is nothing to tie The Don to any crime. The cops have their hands tied in the matter. I need to find it and gain access. I only found out about its existence just before The Don had Abby killed, or I would have worked on getting what I needed long ago. Do as I say, without question from here on in. I'll be looking for the vault. Once I find it, I'll have to get past security and remove the file about Abby and anything to do with Miguel and the Senator's daughter. Then we'll have to get out of here. We can only go to the police once we have the evidence we need."

"I understand what you need to do, but what I don't understand is why I am here? I'm a designer, not a spy. Without your training, I wouldn't even have the rudimentary knowledge of a handgun."

"I am sorry that you had to be involved. When you didn't enter the chalet and took off up the mountain, I had to come up with something. We both know how that would have ended if The Don had sent Tony after you. I couldn't let that happen. I was in a position where I could step in and help you. The biggest problem was that I couldn't come back to the compound without you. The Don expected me to bring you in. So I did. I needed to maintain my cover and your safety, so I arranged for you to be here with me."

Madison's hand flew to her mouth, and she took a step back. He hadn't planned on saving her from the explosion. It was a fluke that she survived. Tears welled in her eyes as she turned away from him, opening the shower doors. Carl grabbed her arm and pulled her back.

"What's different?"

"Everything! You were going to let me die. I'm just a pawn in your game. What we did in the other room… Oh my god. I trusted you. You used me."

"Look at me!"

She lifted her chin and looked him in the eyes. Anger and indignation boiled within.

"I didn't use you. What we did was mutual. You took part and enjoyed it. There are still things I can't tell you, but you have to trust me. I'm your only hope for getting out of here alive."

"You're right! There is no choice for me. I will work with you to get what you need and see this through, but when this is over, I want you to tell me everything."

"I promise." He urged. "Now get dressed. We have to head to the dining room for breakfast. The Don sent word he will expect us, and then he'll want to talk with you. Just answer his question as best as you can. You can't tell him we were at the ranch or anything about your time there. You'll need to say that you broke into a cabin in the Allegany Mountains and hid there until I caught up with you. I made you believe I was going to help you, and I brought you here. I only just found you, and we've only been together for the last three days. Use the anger that you're feeling to your advantage, and make him believe you didn't know where you were going. If he asks about last night, tell him sex is sex. Sometimes you need a release. He'll buy that. Be stubborn about answering his questions, or he'll be suspicious. But answer him before he allows Tony to intervene. Do you understand?"

"Yes, I do. I can remember all that, but what if he asks me about Abby and the trial? How am I supposed to answer those questions?"

"If what you've told me is true, that's the simple part. You know nothing about Abby's trial cases. She was a professional and never discussed the details. Anything you know came from the media. Just tell him he'll keep pushing until he's sure. Hold out as long as you can. Don't give him too much right away, but for God's sake, talk before Tony steps in!"

"O.K. I'll answer as honestly as I can, except for how we met and where I was before I ended up here. What if he has Tony involved right away and I can't stop him? My head still hurts from where he hit me yesterday. I'm not sure how much I could take before I tell him things I shouldn't."

"You don't have to worry. The Don only uses violence on a woman as the last resort. He never watches. As long as he's getting something, he won't let Tony near you. I plan to have access to what I need long before the deadline to turn you over arrives. Now, we have to get up to the breakfast room before he sends for us."

At that, the inter-compound phone rang, signalling to them it was time to head up. Madison slipped into another dress she found hanging in the closet. This time, it was a simple wrap. She ran her fingers through her damp curls so that they would settle on their own and brushed some mascara on her lashes before brushing her teeth. Dean finished dressing while she was getting ready, and together they headed up for breakfast.

# CHAPTER 32

Madison found they hadn't set the main table in the dining room for breakfast; instead, they'd set out a buffet. There were dozens of dishes laid out, enough to feed a small army. A butler was building a plate of food for The Don, who sat off to the side at a smaller table that would only accommodate four. She looked from the table back to Carl, and then she noticed that a large group of armed men entered the dining area and were loading their plates. Carl handed her a plate and motioned for her to help herself. She chose some fresh fruit and scrambled eggs with hash browns and looked around to see where she could sit. The men were taking their plates out of the dining area to eat elsewhere, and Carl was still getting his breakfast when The Don called her over.

"Miss Kerr. Please join me."

Madison hesitated and looked over her shoulder at Carl. He nodded to her, so she made her way to The Don. She put her plate down at the space across from him. Before she could sit, a butler appeared at her side to hold out her chair.

"Please sit, Miss Kerr. I would stand, but it has become more and more difficult for me to do."

She sat in the seat and allowed the butler to push her in closer to the table. Soon, Carl and Tony were occupying the other two seats. This was more intimate than last night's dinner. They were all so close that her knees kept touching Carl and Tony's. She shifted her body so that she could avoid further contact with Tony. He couldn't keep his dislike for her from registering on his face. He scowled before he shovelled in his food.

Carl risked a sideways glance at Madison, observing her obvious discomfort before digging into his own meal. Madison took a bite of her eggs, feeling very uncomfortable and dreading the possibility of having to make polite conversation.

The Don was enjoying his heaping plate of food. He enjoyed too much food and not enough exercise, but that didn't prevent him from being a formidable figure. The Don didn't need speed and agility to accomplish the sense of fear he'd already inspired in Madison. He had others to inflict pain, but the respect and loyalty he commanded from his men showed how truly terrifying he could be.

The meal was delicious. For the first time since leaving the ranch, it surprised Madison to find that she had an appetite. She was sure it had something to do with last night's activities. Madison blushed as she thought about it. She lowered her head, hoping that no one had noticed her blush. The last thing she wanted was for Tony to notice. He'd already been looking at her with pure hatred. She wasn't sure what would set him off and how far he would go before anyone could stop him.

The conversation was general, with no reference to the interrogation that was yet to come or to the viewed events from last night. The Don was a gracious host, even to his prisoners. It was only a matter of time before the tone of their discussions would change, and she'd have to answer questions. She went over the 'correct' answers in her mind and found herself distracted and unaware of the sudden lull in the conversation. Madison only noticed when she felt all three pairs of eyes staring at her. She'd missed something The Don had directed at her. She looked up and met their stare.

"Madison, The Don asked you if you had everything you needed and if there was anything he could get you to make the rest of your stay more comfortable." Carl repeated for her.

"I'm sorry. Please forgive me," she answered. "I was lost in thought. These are unusual circumstances. I believe I have everything I need. Thank you for your attention to detail. I suppose the length of my stay will determine if I need anything else."

The Don chuckled. "Yes, the circumstances are unusual. I guess it's normal for your mind to wander with uncertainty. It's clear that we need to start our brief discussion sooner rather than later. Dean can bring you to my office in an hour so that we can chat. I have many questions."

The Don motioned for them to leave. When everyone left the room, his butlers assisted him to his feet. With the aid of two men, he stood, catching his breath under the strain of lifting his body, and began the trek to his office. Each step took great exertion as he made his way down the hall. He was thankful that his office was on the same level and not too far from the dining room. The Don paused and mopped his brow with a hanky, drying the beads of perspiration that formed there from the tremendous effort required to move from one room to another. He knew it was only a matter of time before his weight bound him to a wheelchair. That was why it was so important for his son to be free. He needed him here so that he could start grooming him to take over. His mind worked, but having a wheelchair would lessen the impact his presence made at any of the family meetings. He needed his son to be the face of the family. He'd still run things but from the sidelines. His wayward, bullheaded son needed to come back and learn so that he could command the same respect from the family. This stint in jail will have humbled him, but he can't rot in a Canadian prison. At least, they didn't have the death penalty, but now was the time for action.

As corrupt as Charles Mitchell was, he hadn't fulfilled his part of the bargain. The jury should have found Miguel innocent. Mitchell promised that getting him off was just a formality, that he could control Abby Monroe and manipulate the evidence. Mitchell had been wrong on both counts, and somehow the evidence ended up in the hands of the Crown Attorney's office.

When The Don found out, he had someone break into the Crown Attorney's office and steal the file, but it was too late. All he could hope for now was that the missing evidence would cause a mistrial. Without it, they'd have nothing with which to hold Miguel. What he wasn't sure of was if the Monroe bitch had hidden copies of the file somewhere else. He knew there was nothing in her office or on her computer. Her home was clear as well. He needed to question the Kerr woman to see if she knew anything or anywhere Abby would have hidden a copy.

Without that file, it would look, as it should have, like an accident. He would deal with Mitchell next. For now, he had to focus on Miss Kerr and what she could tell him. If she knew nothing, it would be time to turn her over to Tony. Her death would be a waste, but he didn't like loose ends.

He settled himself in his chair and contemplated if he should allow Dean to stay for the interrogation. Tony needed to be there to intimidate the girl, but Dean's presence could give her a false sense of security, causing her to let her guard down. This may work to his advantage. He didn't enjoy watching Tony at work. His methods were cruel, and women shouldn't suffer. Tony enjoyed inflicting pain on them too much. Yes, he would have Dean remain in the room. Dean may manipulate her into giving him everything he wanted to know.

There was a soft knock at the door, and Tony entered. He made his way forward, nodding his greeting to The Don, who motioned him to have a seat on the far side of the room, where he would be in the position to look straight at Madison while The Don questioned her.

Tony knew this was the best position for him to be. He could use the strength of his glare to intimidate her into talking, knowing full well The Don would prefer that they didn't use violence in his office or in front of him. Tony hoped it would be necessary. He wanted to see her pretty face marred with bruises and to watch Dean's reaction as he left the marks. Something was off with Dean since he returned with the girl. A little violence towards her may force his hand. He slid on fingerless gloves in preparation.

The Don noticed Tony's gloves and sighed. Tony was becoming a liability. As an enforcer, he was invaluable, but sometimes certain situations needed a more subtle approach, something Tony was incapable of. When this was over, he would have to find a unique position for Tony, something further from the immediate fold of the compound.

"Tony, I want you to restrain yourself when Dean brings the girl in. Allow me to question her without comment or reaction from you. If I need you to step in, I'll let you know. Your presence here will be intimidation enough, I think."

Tony swallowed hard, not wanting to say the first thing that came to his mind.

"Whatever you say, Boss."

CARL WALKED Madison back to his room after breakfast. He wanted her to gather her thoughts and to calm herself before meeting with The Don. Not wanting to give away the thoughts that muddled through his brain, they walked in silence. Madison was so lost in thought, trying to remember all they'd discussed, that it surprised her to discover they were at the door to the suite.

The music they had left on when they left was still playing, and Madison went into the washroom to splash cold water on her face. She went to the closet and pulled out a sweater as the bitter sense of dread overcame her. Her body trembled.

"What are you doing?"

"You told me The Don prefers women to be feminine. I'm cold, and I figured it would be better if I wore a sweater with the dress and refresh myself, so it appeared I tried."

"Good thinking. I can't believe how calm you are. Do you have any more questions before I take you to his office?"

"I'm not calm, but I'm glad looks that way. The situation is out of my control, and there is nothing I can do about it. Freaking out won't change anything, and I need my wits about me. One mistake, and we both know what happens. Now, where should I be looking for the evidence you want?"

"I said I'd be looking for it, not you. Today, neither of us will be. This will be the first of several 'interviews' with The Don. If you answer as I've instructed, he will get enough to be satisfied until he can check out your story. When he discovers that there is more, he will call you back in. At some point, he will pull out his file on your friend and his son. I want you to watch where he stores it and tell me. That's where I'll find my file. Once I have what we need, I'll get us both out of here."

"Your file?"

"Yes. There is something I also want from his files."

"Are you going to tell me what that is?"

"Eventually. Right now, it's not important."

Madison watched him. He still had so many secrets. Every time she trusted him, she learned something new to show why she shouldn't. There were so many variables that could put them both in danger. She wished he trusted her as much as he expected her to trust him.

"What if I have the opportunity to look for it? Do you want me to?"

"NO! It's too risky. If you get caught, I can't guarantee your safety."

"If you get caught, you still can't guarantee my safety. Don't you think the primary aim outweighs the risks? I can't leave my life and safety completely up to you. I won't promise not to look if given the opportunity."

Madison turned from Carl and slid her feet into a pair of heels. She walked back to the washroom and checked her hair and makeup. Madison looked fresh and feminine, just the way The Don liked. She returned to the room and avoided looking at Carl. She could see from the corner of her eye he was struggling to control himself, which meant he realized the truth behind her words. With both of them looking for the file, they may get out of here in one piece.

# CHAPTER 33

It was time to head out for the meeting. Madison was nervous, but tried not to show it. Her stomach rolled and clenched. What lay ahead was a matter of life and death. Hers! She took one last look in the mirror, having pinned her hair up, leaving a few soft curls down to frame her face. She kept her makeup simple and understated, along with her dress. Carl - no, here he was, Dean waited for her.

Carl placed his hand on her elbow as he guided her out of the room and down the hall to The Don's office. He hoped to remain for the interview, but he wasn't sure. It wouldn't do to allow her to fall prey to Tony's cruelty, but what happens in the office was beyond his control. The Don made all the decisions in the compound. Although, that didn't mean Carl wasn't able to manipulate situations to meet his needs.

The procession down the hall to the office took longer than she expected. She knew they passed the dining room and assumed the office was behind the door, out front of which were stationed two armed guards. There were many guards posted at different points along the route, some setback, but others, like the two in front of the office doors, stood with weapons in hand, making their presence known. Automatic weapons slung over their shoulders. Sidearms clipped to their belts. Madison swallowed and smiled her biggest smile as she faced the guards in front of the office before speaking.

"Hi, how are you today?" They didn't respond or acknowledge her. Carl cut in.

"We're here to see The Don. He's expecting us."

With that, one man turned and knocked at the door, which Tony answered. He eyed Madison with a look of lust mingled with disgust. He stood back to allow her to enter, but not far enough that she wouldn't have to brush past him. The guards moved to opposite sides of the doorway, allowing her room. Carl fell in behind her.

Tony stepped in front of Carl and put his hand on Carl's chest to stop him.

"Not you."

"Now, Tony, let's not be too hasty. I think Dean can join us today." The Don called out from behind his desk.

Madison had stepped into the room. She turned back to face Carl and hesitated as Tony held him up. She watched the exchange of looks between the two men and realized they hated each other. This would be a problem if they kept having pissing matches. The Don relished in the display, knowing he could control the outcome of any sparing between the two with a single command. Tony stepped aside and allowed Carl to enter.

"Welcome, Miss Kerr. Please come in and have a seat." He said, motioning to the single chair positioned in front of his desk. "You'll have to excuse my rudeness for not rising to greet you, but my knees are troubling me."

Madison made her way to the chair. She found The Don perplexing. She knew she was a prisoner, but his manners and decorum made her feel like a valued guest. Madison thought it was a ploy to unnerve her and catch her off guard. She couldn't allow that to happen. Madison would be gracious, but also prepared for him to turn.

She was here to be questioned, and if she didn't have the right answers or refused to answer, she knew the tables would turn. Madison tilted her body to settle herself onto the proffered seat, crossing her legs at her ankles, knees to the right, her hands folded on her lap. She smiled at The Don before greeting him.

"Hello, sir. I hope I can answer whatever questions you may have."

Carl rolled his eyes. If he'd learned anything about her over the last few weeks, he'd learned to tell when she was being sarcastic. She spoke her mind, sometimes a little too much for her own good. He prayed she'd get control of herself and follow the story they'd made up together. The Don wouldn't be looking for the lawyer's files today. Today would be about verifying where Madison had disappeared, too. Who helped her, and where Carl found her? He hoped she was as good an actress as she was with a gun.

Carl felt Tony's eyes on him, knowing he was growing suspicious. He was also becoming a problem. Carl would have to do whatever he could to ensure Madison never found herself alone with him. He hoped that whatever transpired it wouldn't end up with her getting killed. He cursed to himself for his rash decision to follow her that night, but if he didn't, Tony would have already killed Madison.

"I hope you have found everything to your satisfaction, Miss Kerr."

"Yes. You have been most gracious." She replied.

"Although you are currently my guest, we have a few things to discuss." The Don replied.

Madison shuddered, knowing what would happen when she stopped being his guest if Carl couldn't get her out of the compound. The words to ask him were on the tip of her tongue, but she got control of herself. She just nodded in response.

"First off! Let me tell you how sorry I was to hear about your friend's untimely death."

Madison's eye snapped up to look at him. Her rage registered.

*'Ahh there's the spitfire my reports told me about,'* The Don thought, leaning back in his chair, observing her. The anger only flickered,

but it was there. He enjoyed she showed so much restraint. When the time came, he'd like seeing her break. Maybe a little of Tony's methods would be a good thing. She needed to learn that they killed her friend on his orders, but not yet. First, he wanted to gain her trust and try to find out what she knew. He wanted to know why she wasn't in the chalet when it blew up, and where she went after that. He needed to know if someone had helped her. And if so, who?

"So, Madison. You don't mind me calling you Madison, do you?" he paused, looking at her. She shook her head. "I understand you were with Abigail Monroe before the chalet exploded. It was your chalet, wasn't it?"

"Yes, to both." She willed herself not to volunteer information or to take his bait.

"So why weren't you with her inside the chalet? Not that I'd want to see you dead, but I'm surprised she went in alone. I also heard on the news that you arranged the explosion out of jealousy. Is this true?" He baited her.

Madison felt like someone had slapped her in the face. He was taunting her, using his own cover story to get a reaction out of her. She could feel the heat of her anger creeping up, her face flushed with it. She opened her mouth to speak but was quick to close it, swallowing and take a breath before answering.

"I wish I had been with her. Maybe then she'd be alive."

"Or you'd both be dead."

"I didn't go in because she asked me to wait while she got something. We were joining some friends at another chalet. She said she'd be back soon to join us. When the chalet exploded, I tried running back in, but one man from the next chalet stopped me by holding on to me."

"If you didn't do this, why did you run?"

"When I broke free, I ran towards the chalet, hoping that Abby wasn't inside when it went up. That's when I heard the two men."

"Two men?"

"Yes. One said, 'Only one bitch was inside. We have to find the other one, or the boss will be pissed.' That told me it wasn't an accident, and that I was in danger."

"You said, two men. What did the other one say?"

"I never heard him speak."

"So, how did you know there were two men?"

"I assumed there were two men. The first one had to be talking to someone. I guess the other person could have been a woman."

The Don chuckled.

"What's so funny?" Madison quipped.

"I'm sorry. You're right, this isn't a funny situation, but under the circumstance that you are describing, I find it hard to believe that a woman was involved. So yes, I can guess you were right in assuming it was a second man. So after you heard the two men and ran, where did you go? Did you have help?"

Madison took a slow, calming breath, reviewing the story she and Carl concocted to cover his involvement.

"I ran up the mountain, staying clear of the ski runs and sticking to the wooded area. My family rented that chalet for years, and I went there every weekend as a child, so I know the area very well. There's a cave halfway up the mountain. If you didn't know it was there, you wouldn't find it. At one time, the entrance was easy to see, but the forest has since grown up around it. Now the entrance is hard to find. I heard the men in the forest looking for me, but I felt safe where I was. I spent most of the night in the cave, and slipped out before dawn, figuring the men had long since given up."

"And where did you go from there?"

"I went to the other side of the mountain and followed one of the back roads. I figured I could hitch a ride to safety. When I found the first gas station, the headlines in the newspaper made me give up on that idea. So I took a scarf out of my bag to wrap around my hair, threw a pair of sunglasses on, and went into the store. I bought some basic supplies with some of the cash I had and headed back to an abandoned cabin I passed in the woods. I stayed there, hoping to figure a way out of this mess. Then Dean found me. He can tell you I put up quite the fight, too."

The Don chuckled again. Yes, he could very well imagine this hellcat putting up a fight. It looked like he needed to have another chat with Dean.

The Don continued firing questions at Madison, one after the other, attempting to catch her off guard and find a hole in her story. What had started as a friendly question-and-answer conversation between the two of them soon turned into a gruelling game. It was a game in which he was the master. He continued questioning his 'guest' in an unrelenting manner, never wavering from his goal. Madison held up under the strain. Pausing as often as she could to avoid being caught in a lie. He felt pleased with the outcome of the interrogation, and The Don called it to an end. With his next words, Madison's vision blurred with tears as relief overcame her.

"Well, you seem to be a very resourceful young woman. I'm sure you gave Dean quite the run for his money. I think that's enough for today. We can continue this tomorrow. You can go. I have other business to attend to."

"But Boss..."

"That's enough, Tony. When I want your opinion, I'll ask for it. Dean, escort Miss Kerr back to your room. After lunch, I'd like to have a word with you. Miss Kerr can eat in your room today. No need for her to come out until supper. Miss Kerr! Supper will be formal, so wear something appropriate."

Just like that, he dismissed them. Madison looked back at Carl, hoping for a reassuring look, but his face was stony. She stood and thanked The Don before turning to leave. Tony's eyes never left her as he watched her get up to leave. Carl was by her side, ensuring he was between her and Tony as they made their way out of the office and back to his room.

# CHAPTER 34

The Don's interrogation of Madison, although civil, had been horrendous. He'd fired questions at her, one after the other, often just rewording previous questions, trying to trick her. Madison held up well under the pressure, never veering from her story. It was close to what really happened, making it easy to remember and be believable. The only problem for Madison was Tony's presence in the room. Every time she glimpsed him out of the corner of her eye, she felt unnerved. She found staring straight ahead at The Don was her best option. He was a formidable figure, but everything pointed to the fact that he wouldn't hurt her, at least not directly.

It relieved her that Carl could stay for the interview. They positioned him close to the door and out of Madison's sight, but his presence was reassuring. She knew she'd handled herself well, only answering the questions as he asked and not trying to fill in the lulls of conversation. After three hours, The Don called an end to the interview and instructed Carl to take her back.

Now that they were back in his room, Carl turned to Madison and signalled for her to be quiet. She knew he wanted her to ask him to play some music, thus allowing them to talk. What she wanted was a drink, something to calm her nerves. Not a repeat of the interview upstairs. But she knew they needed to talk while everything was still fresh in their minds.

"Um, do you think you could put some music on? I'm exhausted and would like to relax. I know you'll be heading back to The Don's office. That will leave me here alone for the rest of the day, and it would be nice to have something to break up the silence."

"Sure. No problem."

Carl walked over to his sound system and selected a classical piece, Handel's Water Music. It would achieve both desired effects. First, it would cover their voices and help Madison relax. He adjusted the volume so that it was loud enough to distort their voices, but low enough that it wouldn't distract them while they spoke. Carl knew The Don sent Madison back to his room for the day so he and Tony could watch her and observe his interaction with her. He couldn't display affection, even though he wanted to wrap his arms around her and comfort her. She'd done an outstanding job today, but this was the easy meeting. The next one would be more gruelling. He couldn't stop The Don from using Tony's methods if she wasn't cooperative. There was still so much for them to discuss and to come up with a plan to satisfy The Don's questions.

He glanced at her out of the corner of his eye and noticed that, although she'd trembled on the way back, now she was back in control. Carl found her ability to adapt and to remain calm, admirable. He knew deep down she was fighting her emotions every step of the way. He'd seen her temper at the ranch, half expecting it to show up here at any minute. There was a flash of it during the interview, but she restrained it. The more demure she was, the more The Don warmed to her, but that didn't mean The Don wouldn't order her death once he'd finished with her. It just meant he might use gentler methods to get the information he needed.

Madison sat down on the love seat and waited for Carl to join her. She hoped that she'd kept to the story and didn't veer from it. It was difficult for her to hold her tongue when all she wanted was to inform that smug, fat bastard of her opinion. But she couldn't. She was here for a reason, and that was to prove who killed Abby and get back to her own life. Yes. She would also help Dean get what he needed because it was all the same thing. Dammit, she wished she'd paid more attention to Abby when she spoke about the cases she was working on. She vaguely remembered Abby talking about a case where her morals and ethics were called into play. Her response had been to reassure Abby that she was one of the most honest people she knew, even if she was a lawyer. Abby had laughed at that and dropped the conversation. Abby never brought it up again, and Madison didn't think to ask.

Carl settled himself in a chair across from her, choosing to face her and away from the view of the camera. He also blocked her face as much as possible so they couldn't detect her expressions and reactions.

"Stay where you are. Where I'm sitting, I'm blocking the camera, so whoever is watching can't view your face. We have little time, because I'm sure we're being watched. When they realize we've blocked their vantage point, they will send someone down with refreshments, or to get me."

Madison swallowed, preparing to speak, when Carl motioned for her to remain quiet.

"Let me finish while we have the time. You did great in there. You impressed the Don. Although you gave him a brief glimpse of your anger, it benefited you. He does his research and would know the red hair had a temper to match."

Madison opened her mouth to retort, but closed it when she saw the warning look Carl shot her.

"The next meeting won't go as smoothly. You've already told me you don't know where Abby kept her back up files if she had any. That shit-head boyfriend of hers, from my understanding, tossed her house and couldn't find anything. I'm sure by now someone has gone through your studio and loft as well. There is no way The Don would believe you didn't know where she'd hide a file. Mitchell said

Abby told you everything. If it was important enough to risk her life for, she'd be sure to keep a copy and put it somewhere safe, even though she sent the original to the Crown Attorney's office."

"But I don't know where she'd keep a file like that. I'd think it would be in her office or home. The next logical place would be on her, but everything she brought with her got destroyed in the explosion. What happens when I can't answer the questions to his satisfaction?"

"I think you already know the answer to that. Don't mention that if she had a file on her it got destroyed it in the explosion. If you do, The Don wouldn't need you anymore, and he'd turn you over to Tony. If that happens, I'm not sure I could stop him."

"And I'd be dead."

"As I've already told you, he likes to take his time. He has his own torture chamber set up downstairs. Just follow my instructions and we can draw this out a little longer. If things don't go well, Tony will hit you, and that's not something I can stop. My hands are tied. I'll do everything in my power to prevent him from hurting you. The Don doesn't like to witness violence used on women, but that won't stop him if he thinks it will get him what he wants."

"O.K., so when I'm called back, will you be there?"

"I can't be certain. If I am, it will be to test my loyalty. If I intervene, I'm disloyal, so I won't be able to stop things once they start. But if it gets bad, I can step in because, at that point, The Don would expect me to."

"How bad?"

"You don't want to know."

"When do I get my gun back?"

"I fastened it to the back of your bedside table. If you need it, it's there. You'll know when it's time."

"I'm scared."

"I know. Believe it or not, so am I. Not for myself. I'm trained for this, but for you. I don't want to see anything bad happen to you. We are being watched, and I wish I could give you a hug of reassurance.

Before she could respond, there was a knock at the door. "See"

Carl whispered as he stood up to answer it. He found Tony on the other side, his disdain clear as he glared at Dean.

"The boss wants to see ya."

"That's fine. I'll be right there."

"NOW!"

Carl looked at Tony and replied, "I think you forget you don't give me orders. You passed your message on. I'll head up to see him in a minute." Tony moved to enter, but Carl used his body to block him from doing so.

"I don't think so. Miss Kerr is my responsibility until The Don says otherwise. So back the fuck off."

Tony looked past Carl at Madison, licking his lips. He'd get his chance with her and soon The Don wouldn't play these games for long. Then she'd be at his mercy. He could wait. It would be well worth it, especially if he made Dean aware of what he was doing to her. He'd make sure he did. Tony put his hands in the air and backed away. He turned and left, but not before muttering, 'she won't be so pretty when I'm done with her.' Ignoring Tony, Carl looked back at Madison to see if she'd heard his parting comment. She was still sitting on the sofa, and far enough away that she missed it.

"I'm heading to meet with The Don. Lock the door and don't open it without asking who it is first. If it's Tony, don't open it. I expect they'll bring your lunch down to you soon, so that's who should be at the door. Whoever it is will tell you they've brought your lunch. You can let them in. There's an armed guard out in the corridor, so don't leave."

"I'll just stay here like an obedient child and wait for your return."

"Now there's the smart mouth I know."

"Sorry. I'll pull out my Kobo and read."

She locked the door behind Carl as he left and walked over to where her backpack sat, since being returned to her after they searched it. So far, she had taken very little out of it other than her hairbrush. They'd supplied everything she needed. She reached in and felt for her Kobo, which she slipped into the bag just before they left the ranch. Carl had said to pack only the bare essentials, but he'd also told her she could be alone for periods of time. She knew she couldn't just sit and watch TV for hours. It would bored her to tears.

Madison found it tucked to one side. Next to it was also the small cosmetics bag she took from her purse and slipped into the knapsack at the last minute. She pulled that out as well. After turning on her Kobo, she opened the makeup bag for the first time since the explosion. Inside, she kept a compact blush, mascara, and lipstick. Those were inside. But there was also a second lipstick, one that she didn't remember packing. She pulled the unfamiliar lipstick out and opened it. Twisting the tube until she saw the stick of colour. She stared at it. It wasn't hers. It wasn't a colour she'd wear, but there was something familiar about the colour. Then it hit her. Abby! Abby wore that colour. She closed the lipstick and put the cap back on. This shouldn't be in her bag. Abby must have put it there for a reason.

With the lipstick hidden in her hand, she went into the washroom to investigate. It was the only place Carl assured her there wasn't a camera, so she'd be okay to sit on the toilet to examine the lipstick. She pulled off the lid and twisted it all the way out. It was shorter than normal for an unused lipstick, and it was brand new, but the stick of colour was half the size it should have been. She twisted the colour back down and examined the other end. Madison twisted it one way, then another. Nothing. She tried pulling it apart, but again, nothing happened. There had to be a reason it was in her bag. She looked at the decorative gold trim and ran her fingernail along it. The bottom of the tube popped open to reveal a small memory stick hidden in the end. 'Oh my god! This must be what they're looking for!' She put the lipstick back together and flushed the toilet. Then went back to where she'd left her Kobo and slipped the lipstick back in the bag and the bag back in her backpack. She picked up her Kobo and pretended to read, as her mind raced.

*'I wonder when Abby put that there. It had to have been at the bar after*

*Carl warned her about The Don.'* Looking back, she realized there were plenty of opportunities for Abby to have slipped it in her bag. Carl didn't know she had this. Would it persuade him to give up on his own vendetta? She doubted it, but it was leverage. She just had to figure out how she could use this to her advantage. It must be important, or Abby wouldn't have hidden it in a lipstick tube or put it in her bag. This also meant Abby knew she was in danger. Part of her wanted to cry, but she was also angry. Abby died for something so small, but part of a much bigger picture.

She had to keep it a secret. There was no way she'd let The Don get his hands on this. But, without the evidence to prove her innocence, she was no further ahead. Dammit. She'd have to continue with the charade a little longer. She couldn't tell Carl what she found. Despite her attraction to him, she still didn't trust him, even if Hank and Rose told her she could. They didn't know everything. As for the sex? Well, it was just sex. Good sex, but still just sex. She needed more time to think and figure out her next move. She was very thankful for this time alone.

# CHAPTER 35

The Don chuckled as Carl entered the room. "So, Dean, tell me how our guest is making out? You seem to have her wrapped around your finger. I thought she'd fight with you after she realized you tricked her."

"She was as mad as a hornet at first. I lied to her to get her to come with me. I could have knocked her out and bound her, but it would have been more difficult as we crossed the State Line. It doesn't matter, anyway. She's here, and now we can find out what she knows."

Carl strode across the room and sat in the chair across from The Don, noticing that Tony wasn't joining them. That was a good thing. Maybe he could convince The Don not to use Tony's tactics just yet. He didn't want Madison hurt and would do anything he could to prevent it. Anything that was except to reveal his true identity.

"So tell me, Dean, did you enjoy your little tryst with the girl last night? Was she worth the effort?"

Carl pretended to be shocked. It wouldn't do any good to reveal he was aware of the camera and microphone in his room. If he did, he'd blow the opportunity of speaking candidly with Madison. The Don would learn that it wasn't an accident the music always played when they were in the room or that he sat with his back to the camera, blocking its view.

"How did you know?"

The Don chuckled again. When he did so, the sound was grating and almost forced.

"Dean, I know everything that happens within the compound. You should know that. I hope your involvement with her won't complicate things. She's here for a reason. That won't change, no matter how many times you lay with her."

"You have nothing to worry about, Don. She's just a pretty girl. Chasing her got me riled up. I could have fucked her during the trip here, but I wanted her willing. That meant I had to gain her trust. If I forced myself on her before we got here, it could have proven problematic. I want you to know that I don't think she knows anything. She doesn't deserve to be handed over to Tony when this is over. Let me take care of her. You know I will make it quick and painless."

"I'll consider it. I don't like women to suffer, but Tony has been looking forward to taking care of her himself. He's taken her escape as a great insult to his capabilities. I think he deserves the right to finish the job, but I'll tell him to make it quick."

"We both know that won't happen."

"That may be true. Tony does like to draw out the inevitable and takes much pleasure in causing pain, but his methods have proven invaluable in the past. Why don't you leave it with me? We'll see how cooperative she is."

"Have you considered she knows nothing?"

"Yes, but it's unlikely. That Mitchell fellow assured me the two women were very close. They shared everything. There is another file out there somewhere. I'm certain of it."

"It may have been in the chalet and blew up with the Monroe girl."

"No. Tony went through the place while they were out. If it was there, he'd have found it. There has to be another hiding place. One we haven't considered. That's where Miss Kerr comes in. She'll know where it is."

"When did you want to meet with her again?"

"We'll have supper tonight, and tomorrow we have other business to attend to. So, depending on how long that takes, the next day will be fine, but I'll let you know."

"Whatever you say."

The Don pulled out a box of Cuban cigars and offered one to Carl. Carl selected and rolled one between his fingers, feeling the freshness of it. The Don then made his selection, trimmed and lit his own, before he passed the paraphernalia to Carl to do the same. The Don drew in the smooth, rich flavour of the tobacco before getting down to the business at hand. Madison was just one small spoke in the cog of The Don's day. There were so many other things that needed his attention, and Dean has proven himself again, so it was time to bring him deeper into the fold. Miguel would need a trusted advisor when he took over. Dean fit the bill.

BACK IN THE ROOM, Madison tried to concentrate on her book, but the lipstick with the memory stick hidden in the base made it impossible. She wished she had access to a computer so she could check what was on it, but that wasn't doable. Even if Carl had a computer in his room, she was sure all the computers were connected to some primary system, and inserting it would transfer the information to The Don. No. The best thing was to keep it hidden. If she survived this, that would be the time to check it out.

Time slipped away from her. Before she knew it, a couple of hours had passed. They delivered her lunch and had long since removed the tray. She wondered where Carl was and when he'd be coming back. Madison checked the clock on the stereo and decided she had better go through the closet to find something to wear for dinner and have a shower. She'd been told dinner was formal, so she needed to try. It wouldn't do to displease her 'host'.

The closet revealed they had brought another evening gown in for her during the 'interview' this morning. This one was pale ivory silk, with a low cowl deep in the back. She looked on the ground to see if there were shoes to match and found a lovely pair of matching ivory heels. The Don had good taste in clothing. It unnerved her that everything provided was her size. She realized nothing was private if someone wanted and knew how to get the right information.

She hung the dress on the back of the closet door. The back was so low. There was no way she could wear a bra with it, and the material was so thin it would cling to every curve. She figured he was trying to annoy Tony, who leered at her with lust and hate. She had enough of her figure already revealed by the hidden camera. So a dress that hugged her body was nothing in comparison.

She was thankful that she could shower in privacy. She turned on the water, waited for it to reach the temperature she preferred before she stepped in so that the heat and steam could both relax and refresh her. She washed and rinsed her hair, using a generous amount of conditioner to free up the tangles that occurred in her curls, lathered up her body, and snapped a fresh blade on the razor to shave. As she rinsed the conditioner out of her hair, she ran her fingers through it to loosen any major knots, staying under the stream of water until she was sure the conditioner washed away.

When she dried off, she wrapped the thick plush towel around herself and applied moisturizer to her face, arms, and legs. Next, she ran a comb through her hair and peered at herself in the mirror. The face that stared back at her differed from the one before the explosion. Her face was thinner, and there were shadows under her eyes. She dropped the towel, deciding to see what else had changed. What she saw surprised her. She was leaner. Her muscles were more defined from the training. She looked long and appreciated the difference. Her breasts were full and high, and one still bloomed with the purple bruises where Tony had squeezed it. But there was a definition in her core. Her arms and shoulders showed the most change. As she moved them, she could see the ropes of muscles twisting and flexing beneath her skin. Years of personal training hadn't accomplished what a few weeks of intense workouts and stress did as she fought to survive. She heard the door to the room open and scooped up the towel and wrapped it around herself. She stepped out of the washroom, expecting to see Carl, but she stopped dead when Tony's sneer greeted instead.

"What are you doing here?"

Tony pushed the door closed behind him and turned the lock.

"You stupid puta. You're making a joke out of all of us. Dean can't figure you out because he's too busy thinking with his dick. And the Boss has always admired beauty. If I ruin that beauty, this can be all over much faster."

Madison saw the glint of metal in his right hand and realized he was holding a knife. She swallowed, trying to appear calm before continuing.

"How do you think they'd react if you hurt me before I answer all The Don's questions?" She challenged, hoping to make him think before using that knife on her. She thought about her gun behind the bedside table, but knew there wasn't time. Tony closed the distance between them. Madison stepped back and found herself trapped against the wall as Tony's knife came up to her throat. His free hand yanked the towel away, leaving her exposed.

CARL TOOK his time as he walked back along the corridor to his room. He found himself lost in thought as he went over his conversation with The Don, trying to decide how best to protect Madison. Halfway there, he paused and turned. He looked up one way and back the other. Something wasn't right. Where was the guard? The hairs on the back of his neck stood up. 'Madison! Shit! Had The Don only distracted him to take her to another area of the compound? Or was it something else? Tony! Fuck! It had to be Tony.'

Carl reached into his holster and pulled out his Glock. He

released the safety and gripped it in both hands as he made his way down the rest of the hallway to the door. Carl tried the handle and found it locked. He leaned in and put his ear to the door as he listened for sounds coming from inside. Carl heard nothing. He had a key. But he needed the element of surprise. Kicking the door open would give him that. He took a step back and, with all the rage and strength he had, kicked the door, splintering the wood as the lock gave way and the door swung open.

NAKED, with a knife pressed against her neck, Madison's heart raced, and her body shook. The knife pressed deeper into her throat, causing bright bursts of blood to blossom along its sharp edge. Tony pressed his body into hers, his dark, soulless eyes only inches away. His free hand traced down her body and squeezed her already bruised breast. She flinched. The hand continued down over her stomach before pausing just above the apex of her legs. Tony sneered and forced a finger inside of her. She gasped in pain, which Tony mistook for pleasure.

"Soon, The Don will have finished with you, and you'll be mine."

Behind them, the crashing sound of splintering wood echoed through the room. Tony lowered the knife. Madison grabbed his hand and held it away from her body. His other hand was still between her legs as Carl made quick strides across the room. His gun gripped in both hands, aimed at Tony.

Carl took in the beads of blood on Madison's neck, her wet hair, and naked state before noticing where Tony's hand was. He also noticed how quickly she'd grabbed Tony's knifed hand when he dropped it from her throat.

"Let her go, Tony." Carl's voice was menacing.

"Fuck you, Dean." Tony's voice wavered, realizing he'd lost his advantage. He could break out of her grasp, plunge the knife into her chest but, Dean would kill him. If he killed Madison and Dean didn't kill him, he'd have to deal with the Boss. Shit. He didn't have a choice.

The audible sound of a click as Carl cocked the gun broke the silence in the room. Tony removed his hold on her and backed away. Madison released his arm and let him go.

"Get the hell out of here. NOW!"

Tony backed up, his eyes never leaving Carl's gun until he was out of the room. Alone, Carl turned to Madison.

"Are you O.K.?"

She ran to him and buried her face in his chest and cried. Her body shook from stress and fear. Carl wrapped his arms around her and pulled her close. He still held his gun in his right hand, and his free hand stroked her damp curls. His shirt became moist with her tears, and he continued holding her until she was all cried out.

# CHAPTER 36

When Madison gained control of herself, she stepped back and looked Carl in the eyes, embarrassed at her reaction to Tony's assault.

"Are you alright?"

Madison nodded. Carl went to the closet and brought her a robe to cover herself. She sat on the sofa with it tied around her waist. He then poured and handed her a brandy. The amber liquid warmed her insides, taking away the chill left by Tony's attack. While she recovered on the couch, Carl went to the washroom and wet a face-cloth, which he used to cleanse the blood from her neck. Underneath his calm demeanour, he was fuming at Tony's gall to have entered his quarters and attack Madison.

"Thank god! It's not much more than a scratch. I should have killed him."

Madison looked up at him. Her green eyes rimmed red from crying, which intensified their cool emerald depths.

"I'm O.K.. He scared the hell out of me. But that's what he wanted. If you didn't come in when you did, I don't know how far he'd have taken it. I'm glad you got here when you did."

"Me too." He replied as he reached over to brush a lock of hair out of her eyes. "I can call The Don. Let him know what happened. He may let you forego dinner."

"No. That would show weakness. We'd lose any ground we gained. Plus, I won't give Tony the satisfaction. Let The Don see my neck. Let him see the healing blood and fresh bruises."

She peeked down the front of her housecoat at the breast Tony squeezed. New bruises already bloomed, bright blue fingerprints branded her with Tony's intent. Madison drained the last of the brandy and stood up.

"I had better finish getting ready. It will take a lot of war paint to hide the swelling around my eyes from crying. I'm a little embarrassed about that. There wasn't anything to cry about."

"It would surprise me more if you didn't cry. Tony is an unpredictable psychopath. I hope you're watching, you slimy bastard. This isn't how The Don wants things handled." Carl yelled into the air. "I'll grab a quick shower first if that's O.K. There's no fear of Tony showing up again."

While Carl showered, Madison used a cool cloth on her eyes to reduce the swelling. She searched through the medicine cabinet and found some eye drops to minimize the redness. As for the bruises and cuts on her neck, she was going to display those with pride. She'd have another shower when Carl finished. Madison wanted to wash off the vile feeling of Tony's touch from her flesh.

She was still examining her bruises when Carl stepped out of the shower. Beads of water dripped down his body. As he grabbed a towel, he eyed the purple and blue marks and again cursed under his breath. Madison averted her eyes, but then thought better of it. After everything they'd been through, it was a display of false modesty. She reached past him and turned the shower back on. Carl raised his eyebrow in question.

"I have to wash the feel of Tony from my skin."

Carl just nodded as she slipped back into the shower, once again feeling the cleansing steam and heat. She scrubbed her flesh, turning it pink as she removed all traces of Tony's touch. Madison noticed pink spots on the towel as she dried off and realized her neck was bleeding again. She pressed a wet face cloth against the wound to stop the bleeding, then towel-dried her hair and stepped out into the room.

Carl took the time to shave while she was in the shower and was fastening his bow tie. His tuxedo jacket hung on the knob of the closet. She smiled at him. He looked as good in a tux as he did in blue jeans. She wondered if this evening would end as pleasantly as the last one had. Madison let the towel drop and strode across to get her dress. She slipped it on over her head, feeling the silk kiss her curves as it slid into place. Then she went back to the washroom and applied her makeup, taking extra time to cover the dark circles under her eyes. She piled her hair up on top of her head, allowing a few curls to spiral down and frame her face. A light touch of lip gloss, and she was ready. She stepped out of the washroom and twirled for Carl's approval. A low wolf whistle greeted her in response.

At any other time, Madison would wonder why she made such an effort for a dinner with someone who was holding her captive. But these were far from normal circumstances. To survive this, she had to appear gracious. The Don expected her to behave like a guest. Until that changed, she planned to do everything she could to continue portraying the part.

"I'm glad you didn't cover up the bruises. The Don needs to see that he can't trust his pet dog. I won't have to say a word. The cut on your neck and bruises speak for themselves. This could prove to be an interesting evening."

"If he asks, should I tell him what happened?"

"He'll know the minute he sees you, but if he asks, tell him. Lying wouldn't do either of us any good. It's time. We'd better head up."

Carl offered her his arm and escorted her up to the lounge for cocktails. They made their way and could hear what sounded like a string quartet coming from the lounge. As they entered, Madison's step faltered. Not only was Tony nowhere in sight, but a small gathering of well-dressed men and women mingled in the room, chatting and drinking champagne. Madison paused as a hush fell across the room, and all eyes turned towards them.

The Don was standing to one side with a group of men. She bit her lower lip, unsure of what to make of his sudden ability for movement. He turned and opened his arms in greeting. "Ah, Miss Kerr. Welcome. Please join us."

As she moved closer to shake his outstretched hand, he frowned when he noticed the bruises and cuts on her neck. His eyes flicked to Carl, who gave a small shake of his head. His eyes widened as understanding dawned on him, but he had other guests and was quick to recover.

"My dear. You had an accident, I heard. I hope it's not as painful as it looks. In the morning, I'll have to speak to the gardener to make sure he trims back the low branches. I wouldn't want anyone else getting hurt. Please accept my sincere apologies."

He was quick. Madison gave him that. He recovered and made up a plausible explanation at the same time. She put on her biggest smile and replied. "No need to apologize. Accidents happen. I'll also be sure to take precautions against further mishaps in the future."

A smirk played on his lips as he realized they were playing the same game to appease his other guests. He would make time to speak with her privately to find out what happened. He turned to the room. "May I present, Miss Madison Kerr. Cecile, I believe you're familiar with her work."

A young woman in her mid-twenties beamed. Her dark hair pulled into a neat chignon, displaying beautiful ruby and diamond earrings. Her red silk gown rippled as she moved forward to meet her.

"Miss Kerr, my daughter Cecile."

Madison's eyes grew wide. This was more than just a game. The Don had his family present. Recovering from her shock, she reached out and shook Cecile's hand. Carl and The Don moved on to mingle with others, leaving Madison alone with Cecile. As Madison watched the direction they took, she listened as Cecile chatted about fashion and her upcoming wedding. Without thinking,

Madison agreed to custom design Cecile's dress. Cecile squealed in delight, causing heads to turn in their direction.

Madison's mind reeled at the continued uncertainty she faced. Abuse, interrogations, and now dinner parties. She was a prisoner, but he'd invited her to a social event with his family. None of it made sense to her. She'd have to wait until she was back in Carl's room to find out what this was all about. But she felt Carl was just as much in the dark as she was.

At the end of the cocktail hour, they moved to the massive table in the dining room, which was set with place cards assigning everyone to a specific seat. Madison found herself between Cecile and Carl. The Don was at one end of the table and his wife, Arabella, at the other. Madison glanced her way, trying to get a sense of the woman who was married to her captor. She was a tiny woman, only five feet tall with a slight build. Silver shot her once dark hair. Her dark, knowing eyes missed nothing as they darted around the room. There was a calculating look in Arabella's eyes. Madison was certain Arabella was well aware of her husband's business and why Madison was here.

THEY ORCHESTRATED THE MEAL PRESENTATION, like a well-choreographed dance. With every course, an individual server appeared, serving each guest in unison. They left no one waiting. It was spectacular to watch. When the meal ended, they asked the guests to adjourn to another room for more entertainment. The servers reappeared and held the chairs as everyone rose to leave. Madison turned to follow Carl when The Don stopped her.

"Miss Kerr, will you wait for a moment? I have something to ask you."

Madison nodded and risked looking at Carl. His eyes moved between the two of them and gave a slight shrug. There was nothing he could do. She wouldn't come to any harm, at least not tonight, with a house full of guests. The Don remained seated. He patted the chair to his right, showing that she should join him. She made her way to the seat and sat down next to him.

"I need you to tell me what really happened to your neck."

Madison sighed. She wanted Tony to pay for what he did, but she also knew that it wasn't The Don's fault. He didn't order Tony to assault her, not that he wouldn't, but from what Carl told her, he didn't like when his men went rogue, either.

"I'm sure you have your suspicions. It was from Tony. He came into the room while Dean was meeting with you."

"Dean didn't leave a guard outside? I gave instructions that a guard was to always be outside your door."

"You'd have to ask him. There was one when my lunch arrived. After that, I don't know. I showered to get ready for this evening, and that's when Tony came into the room."

"You'll have to tell me what he did."

Madison looked him in the eyes. Did he want to know out of concern for her welfare? No. That wasn't it. Although there seemed to be a genuine concern in his eyes. She wondered how he could be the same man who ordered Abby's death. Maybe Carl was wrong. She told him the entire story from Tony's assault to Carl's rescue. As she recounted the events, he patted her hand like a caring father.

"Don't worry Miss Kerr. I'll deal with Tony accordingly. I'll have you escorted to where the others are, and I'll join you."

As if on cue, a servant appeared to lead her to the drawing-room where there was music playing. They filled the rest of the evening with music and dancing. The Don sat with his wife, watching their guests enjoy themselves. Madison danced with several gentlemen before ending up in Carl's arms. He leaned in and whispered.

"Did he ask you what happened?"

"Yes."

"You told him everything?"

"Of course! I won't cover for Tony. Although he asked whether you'd left a guard outside, I couldn't answer that."

"Oh, I did. He will be dealt with as well. It's possible Tony bribed him, held something over him, or threatened him. But he left his post, and that's how Tony got in. I'm very sorry about that."

"You can make it up to me by telling me what kind of punishment The Don will give Tony."

"The guard's punishment will be more severe. The Don needs Tony because he has certain talents that make him invaluable. He may have the guard executed."

Madison's grip on his hand tightened. "Executed?" She hissed.

"Madison, this isn't your world. The rules here are very different. You can't care what happens to anyone here. Your only concern must be for your own safety. Promise me you won't say anything." At her hesitation, he repeated. "Promise me."

"O.K. I promise. He showed actual concern when I told him what happened. I find it hard to believe he'd kill a guard for what might not be his fault."

"Don't forget why we're here. Justice for Abby. He hasn't shown remorse for that, has he?"

Madison was about to reply when a gentleman asked to cut in. It was a conversation that would have to be continued at a later time.

By the end of the evening, Madison had promised to sit down with Cecile to talk about designing her wedding dress. She knew it wasn't possible, but it appeased Cecile, which was the point. With the festivities over, she and Carl made their way back to his room. After taking her hair down, removing her makeup, she found she was too tired to continue their earlier conversation. She slipped under the covers, watched as Carl removed his tux, and before she knew it, she was sound asleep. Carl turned and looked at her sleeping form, thankful he wouldn't have to explain anything more tonight.

# CHAPTER 37

Madison stretched under the covers and reached out for Carl, but the bed was empty. Her eyes opened and searched the room, only to find she was alone. She slipped out of bed and made her way to the washroom to further inspect her injuries. While peeing, she noticed how tender she was, the urine burning against the torn flesh. The vibrant shade of plum had developed overnight, mixing with the faded yellows and greens of her swollen breast.

She splashed her face with cool water and brushed her teeth before showering. Clean and refreshed, she went to the closet, pulled out a pair of slacks and a blouse before running a brush through her hair. When she dressed, she padded barefoot to the door. Noticing for the first time that someone repaired the damage. Something she hadn't noted when they returned last night. The Don must have sent someone to fix it while they were at dinner. She turned the handle, surprised to find it open. She hoped to go in search of Carl and some coffee. When she pulled the door open, she stared at the backs of not one, but two armed guards. Hearing the door open, one guard turned to her and spoke.

"You're awake. We have orders to let the kitchen know to get your breakfast ready as soon as you woke up. Dean is with The Don. He'll return after their meeting. You are to remain here until further notice."

Madison just nodded at them, stepped back, and closed the door. She paced the room, waiting for her morning coffee while wondering what was so important Carl had to slip out without telling her. Soon, there was a knock at the door, and they wheeled a cart in, laden with a variety of breakfast items, a pot of coffee, and a large glass of pink grapefruit juice. When she was alone, Madison poured herself a coffee and chose a few items from the cart. She settled herself down on the sofa and turned on the news. Madison expected to hear more about the explosion, but it surprised her to find there was no mention of it. She knew she was still the prime suspect, but they didn't even mention that.

She wondered what she'd find waiting for her when she returned home. Her business and friends were there. Would they arrest her if she tried to cross the border? How would she cross? The explosion destroyed her passport. Of course, none of that mattered if she didn't survive this ordeal. Carl seemed confident he could get her out, but their sneaking in hadn't gone the way it he planned. Instead, they'd been the ones to be taken by surprise. Or had they? The more she thought about it, the more sure she was that Carl expected to be found. She felt the overwhelming urge to check if the gun was behind the bedside table.

Madison stood up and brushed down her slacks, removing any crumbs as she did. She walked over to the bed, relieved her side was out of view of the camera. Sat on the edge and angled her body so that she blocked the view of the bedside table. She leaned forward and, with her left hand, pulled open the drawer. Her right hand slid down the back, feeling for the gun. Her heart sank when she didn't find it. Then, a few inches lower, her fingers brushed against the leather of the holster, and she felt the distinctive shape of the gun inside. She let out a deep sigh. Carl told her the truth. She pulled her arm back up and leaned on it as she stood, continuing to rummage through the drawer, pulling out a pen and a pad of paper. At least now, if anyone was watching, it appeared like that was what she was looking for all along.

With the pad and pen in hand, she poured herself a second cup of coffee and sketched with Cecile in mind. She may not make the dress, but the least she could do was to come up with some ideas. The girl wasn't her father, and she deserved to have a beautiful gown on her wedding day. Once designed, Cecile could take the sketch anywhere to have it made.

When Carl returned, Madison had completed half a dozen sketches. She looked up when he entered the room and observed that he seemed distracted. He didn't seem to notice the sketches that were laid out on the table in front of him as he sat down across from her. He ran his hand through his hair and he leaned over to talk to her.

"It seems there's a glitch in the plan."

"Oh?"

"Last night, you promised to design Cecile's wedding dress. That's all she can talk about. This has annoyed The Don. He doesn't know how to take care of the situation with you without hurting his baby girl. I don't know whether to be impressed by your strategy or annoyed at the delay."

Madison burst out laughing and scooped up the designs from the table.

"It's his fault for putting us all in a social situation together. She knew who I was and asked. What could I say? I've already come up with some designs. She can take any of these sketches to a dress-maker and get what she wants!"

Carl looked down at the sketches she held out and smiled at her.

"You're brilliant. This may give you some freedom around the compound and help us get out of here. Do you often use a pen when you draw?"

"No, I work with a sketch pad and pencils. Why?"

"Well, if we show The Don these and tell him what you need, he will have the right supplies brought here for you within the hour. Then you can do some proper sketches for Cecile. Once you have a design she's happy with, he'll try to ensure everything that can be done will be done. This also means he won't resort to torture while trying to find out what you know. He can explain away one 'accident', but not multiple. If we can draw this out a little longer, we should be able to get what we need to clear your name and what I need to bring him down."

Carl's phone chirped with a text, informing him it was time to bring Madison back up to meet with the boss. She packed up her sketches, knowing that they'd come in handy if The Don asked her about Cecile or her dress. The chances were slim, but it was better to be prepared.

THIS TIME, when she entered the office, she felt an immediate release of tension when she realized Tony wasn't present. She remembered Carl telling her The Don would punish Tony for his assault. She dared to look Carl's way, but knew he couldn't say anything. Instead, he gave her a slight wink. She'd have to ask him later how The Don disciplined Tony and the guard. She felt annoyed at herself for not remembering to do so earlier.

"Miss Kerr. Please have a seat." The Don greeted her, motioning to the chair across from him.

Madison sat down, aware that Carl once again sat in a chair at the back of the room, close to the door. She crossed her legs, the sketches clutched in her hands, realizing for the first time she still wore the slacks she put on when she got dressed this morning. She cursed herself for not changing.

"Did you bring me something?" He questioned, pointing to the sketches she held in her hands.

"Uh, yes. Cecile mentioned she was getting married and asked me to design her wedding dress. Of course, I said yes, so as not to offend her. While I was waiting for Dean to come back this morning, I drew up some basic first draft ideas."

"May I see them?" His hand reached out for the sketches. Madison leaned forward and handed them to him. He spread the rough drawings on the desk and took the time to look at each one.

"These are quite good. You say they are only rough sketches. What do you need to do finished ones?"

"Just regular sketching supplies, sketch pad, pencils, gum eraser, that sort of thing."

He picked up the phone and barked orders to someone at the other end, asking that they bring drawing supplies to the office. Madison wondered how long it would take. Depending on where the supplies came from, could show how close they were to a town. When he hung up the phone, he turned to her again.

"It seems my daughter wants you to design her wedding dress and that you have talent. I'm going to allow you to design her dress. It will change a few things while you work with her. First, you will only meet when and where I say. Although I won't be there, I will listen to your conversations. So you will not talk about why you're here, what happened to your friend, and never mention Tony's assault on you. Do you understand?"

"Yes, of course. Cecile is a sweet girl. I would do nothing to upset her."

"Good. On that, we can agree. I'm glad we understand each other. I want to apologize again for Tony's behaviour. He overstepped his bounds, and I don't think he needs to be included in our chats."

Madison smiled at him. Her mind worked as she tried to determine what The Don meant by that when there was a rap at the door. The Don nodded to Carl, who stood up and answered it. Someone handed him a paper shopping bag. He paused and checked through the contents before taking it over to The Don and placing it on the desk.

"Is everything there?"

Carl nodded.

The Don pushed the bag towards her.

"Miss Kerr, I believe you'll find everything you'll need in there."

Madison grabbed the bag and placed it on her lap before opening it to check its contents. Inside, she found two sketch pads, a variety of pencils, and a gum eraser. She looked at the clock on the wall and couldn't believe that it had arrived in less than half an hour. There were only two things she could assume, one - they were very close to a town or two - the items were already here.

"Thank you," she murmured. "I can get to work on some designs right away."

"No, I think you should sit down with Cecile first. See what her vision is, then do some finished sketches. But please bring these rough sketches for her to look at. It may help her decide. I think we can postpone our chat for another day. But tell me first, once you design the dress, what then?"

"What do you mean?"

"I want to know happens after you design the dress? What is the next step?"

"Oh. I would work with the client and pick out the right fabric and trim. Then, I'd get the client's measurements and send the design to the pattern-maker. From there, the fabric is cut, and fittings started until the final gown is ready for pickup."

"I see. And how long does something like that take?"

"It's several months from concept to the finished garment."

"Well, we both know you don't have that kind of time available. Therefore, in this case, how do you see this proceeding?"

Madison hesitated and then replied. "I'll design it. Make suggestions as to the correct fabrics, and I can make recommenda-tions for a pattern maker and seamstress so that once I complete the design, my involvement is over."

"You're bright. I see we understand each other. Just design some-thing that makes my baby happy. Someone else can finish it. That works for me. I didn't bring here you to design Cecile's wedding dress. Dean, you will take Miss Kerr up to the family sitting room. I'll let Cecile know. She'll be there waiting."

Madison slid her sketches into the bag with her drawing supplies and clutched it. She stood up and thanked him for his generosity. The words were tough without sounding insincere. She turned towards Carl, who held the door open, and they left. Now she was certain that The Don had no intention of allowing her to live. She never believed Carl, but her life hung between the two of them. One she knew wanted her dead, and the other she still wasn't sure she could trust!

# CHAPTER 38

Tony paced around his tiny room. It was on the lowest level of the compound, situated down in the belly, with the guard quarters, but also near where he hid his torture chamber. He punched the wall, splitting the skin on his knuckles, leaving a bloody trail. He'd overstepped his bounds, and now that The Don banished him here while he figured out his punishment. The Don wasn't happy that he'd touched the slut.

*'What did they expect? She stood there naked, wearing only a towel. She was begging for it. Damn Dean! If he hadn't shown up when he did, things would have turned out differently. I wouldn't have killed her. I know now wasn't the time. But I'd have fucked her and messed her up a bit, marred her pretty face. Then Dean wouldn't want her anymore, and this could be over.'*

He fumed as he plopped himself down onto his bed. He was thankful he didn't receive the same punishment as the guard he had bribed. The Don had the guard taken out and shot. But there was a difference. The guard's and Tony's motives were different. Tony wanted to hurt her, and the guard was a greedy, untrustworthy employee. The Don wouldn't accept that. Tony's skills were more valuable.

The boss might be upset with him now, but in the end, The Don would turn the girl over, so he could dispose of her in his own way. He'd enjoy toying with her. He thought of how lush and plump her breasts were. Before he killed her, he'd cut them off, watch her contort in agony. The wait gave him the time to plan alternative ways to torture her. Yes, he was going to enjoy himself. In the meantime, he'd have to stay out of Dean's and the boss's way. When the time was right, he'd have his fun. It would be a good idea to record everything that he did to her. Then he could watch the tapes, reliving every moment. He needed to set up cameras in his torture room. Yes, there were many ways to inflict pain, and he was the master.

Tony settled himself into the semi-sterile holding area. They'd locked the door. He could leave, but it would be best to bide his time and wait. The Don would tire of the game, and then need him. Yes, he'd bide his time.

CARL LEFT Madison in the lounge to wait for Cecile after instructing her to stay put. He warned her there'd be trouble if she left. Then he decided it was time to have a chat with Tony. Deep in thought, he made his way to the guard's quarters. Tony's particular talent meant his quarters were on the same level. Tony didn't have the swank, well-appointed room he had, and Carl knew it irritated Tony, which was another reason they didn't get along. The other was Carl despised Tony's love of violence. He understood each player had a part to play, and he got along well with many other enforcers, but they only intervened when necessary. Carl's hatred for Tony was the sick pleasure he derived from inflicting pain. Carl vowed he would do whatever he could to prevent Tony from getting his hands on Madison again, even kill him.

He turned the corner closest to Tony's room, but when he heard music coming from the fitness area, he changed course, deciding at the last minute to go into the gym instead. He'd find Tony there, working out his frustrations. Carl pushed open the door.

Yes, Tony was there, working hard at the punching bag. A few other guards were also present, training on various machines. Noticing the look on Carl's face, the others got up and left. The room cleared, leaving Tony and Carl to either come to terms or to fight it out. Catching the sight of Carl in the mirror, Tony gave a firm right jab to the bag before turning towards him.

"Are you going to put the gloves on so we can have a match in the ring?" Tony challenged.

"No, I don't think so. Unlike you, I'm expected back upstairs, and I won't go against the boss!"

"Chicken!" Tony sneered.

"I'll tell you what. When Miguel is free, and the girl is no longer needed, you and I will settle the score. Until then, stay the hell away from her, out of my room, and away from me. If you can't handle that, I'm sure I can persuade The Don to send you off on another job for a while. One that takes you far from the compound!"

Tony glared at Carl, struggling to control the rage that boiled within him. He knew Carl could manipulate the boss into doing just that. For now, he'd have to play nice.

"Fine, I'll stay away from both of you for now. But I'll be looking forward to getting into the ring. You need to understand who you're dealing with! Since it will be after the girl is gone, I'll enjoy describing what I did to her!" He gave the bag a last punch for effect, his eyes never leaving Carl's.

CARL SEETHED AS he made his way back to the principal part of the compound. Tony was getting under his skin. He should check and see how Madison was making out with Cecile. If they were done, he couldn't let Madison wander around. Not yet, no matter how appealing the idea was. They needed more time for The Don to trust her and let his guard down. Without knowing it, Cecile had solved a lot of their problems by recognizing Madison and asking for her help. Carl continued along the route, but before he could get to the family lounge, he ran into The Don.

"Ah, Dean, can I assume from your scowl that you had a chat with Tony? I realize it was only a chat because I don't see any blood or bruises. Tell me how you accomplished that?" The Don asked and motioned for Dean to join him.

"I was heading to bring Madison back to my room."

"There's plenty of time for that. Cecile has ordered a meal to be served for the two of them. She seems to like Miss Kerr. It's too bad we'll have to dispose of her."

Carl followed The Don into the sitting room. That the two women were eating together worked out well, because the closer they became, the better the chances he'd find what he was looking for. It would also delay the final chat between Madison and The Don.

The Don settled himself into one of two oversized wing back chairs and waited for Carl to take the other. Then, The Don rang for coffee and dinner to be served.

"You will join me, of course, Dean."

Silence followed while the two men waited until servers set the meal up. They brought a table in for each man, a coffee urn placed between the two chairs, allowing them equal access. The supper comprised roasted potatoes, lasagna, garlic bread, and a salad. A tray of Cannoli was on the sideboard. The Don, once the staff left, heaped his plate with food, turned to Carl, and asked him to elaborate on his conversation with Tony.

"There's not much to tell."

"Now, Dean. I am well aware there is no love lost between the two of you. Any time you're in the same room, I can cut the tension between you with a knife. I'm just surprised you could control yourself and didn't start a fight. I know Tony has been itching for it."

Carl laughed.

"If he had his way, we would settle our differences in the ring.

But I figured you wouldn't approve, so I avoided the situation. I told him to stay away from me, Madison, and my room. Although I promised him, we could settle the score after we get Miguel back, and the girl is gone."

"Speaking of Miss Kerr, it seems I'm going to hold off on my final interrogation, at least until she designs Cecile's dress. This is very inconvenient. Miguel is rotting in a Canadian prison and the only person alive who may know where the last file of evidence against him is has become my house guest. We are no further ahead."

"I'm sorry about that. There was no way of knowing Cecile would be familiar with her designs. Or even that she'd want one for her wedding dress. I thought she wanted a Vera Wang design."

"My Cecile is fickle, but she deserves the best. Your job is to make sure that Cecile doesn't find out why Miss Kerr is staying here. If she knew, she'd move her to a guest room in the family area of the compound. That would never do."

"I'll make sure Madison knows that her situation here is contingent on her silence. Don't worry about that. When we've finished dinner, I'll collect her."

"Fine, but first, I want you to contact that Mitchell fellow. He was supposed to check the Monroe woman's house and office again to verify that they'd left no stone unturned. As her 'boyfriend,' he has keys and complete access to both. Who knows how thoroughly he looked while she was still alive? Make sure he knows his life depends on it."

They finished their meal, and Carl excused himself. With The Don's permission, he left and scooped up a cannoli on his way out, pulling out his cell as he went. He dialled Mitchell's personal line as he walked, looking for a private corner where no one would over hear him.

"Charles Mitchell."

"It's Dean."

"Um, uh, what can I do for you?" he asked.

"The Don wants to check on your progress."

"Not much has changed. I tossed her office. I even offered to pack all of her things now that she's dead. There was nothing there, no hidden files on her computer. No paper copies stashed away. The office was clean."

"What about her house?"

"Um, that's proven to be a little more difficult."

"How so?"

"Right after getting the news of her death, her parents moved into the house to sort through her belongings."

"That's not good. Get them out of there and get in there yourself."

"How am I supposed to do that?"

"I don't care! Figure something out, and fast. The Don doesn't like loose ends. He likes failure even less. If you don't get results soon, we'll have to take care of things. You know what that means, don't you?"

Carl could hear an audible 'gulp' before Charles spoke again.

"Yes, I know. I'll think of something."

"Make it fast."

Carl disconnected the call. Charles was a wimp, but his fear would motivate him to get Abby's parents out of her house and finish the search. If there was a copy of the file, that was the only place left to look. Carl slid his phone back into his pocket and made his way to the lounge.

The door to the lounge was ajar, so he peered in. Madison and Cecile were nowhere to be found. 'Dammit,' he cursed to himself. 'This isn't good. Where could they be?' He wondered if Cecile would take her off the compound. If she did, would Madison run? Another woman might be in her shoes, but Madison? It was hard to say. A maid entered from the side door to remove the dirty dishes.

"Do you know where they went?"

Startled, the maid turned to him.

"They went up to Miss Cecile's room. She wanted to show the lady her wedding book and samples."

Carl cursed again. This was not how things were supposed to go.

He couldn't go upstairs to the family's private quarters. He turned back to the maid.

"Could you please go to Miss Cecile's room and tell Miss Kerr I'm here to escort her?"

"But what if they aren't done?"

"I'm sure Miss Kerr can come back and meet with Miss Cecile. Please tell them I said they should set that up before Miss Kerr leaves. I'll make sure she gets back for the appointed time."

With that, the maid left the room, carrying the dirty dishes on a tray. Fifteen minutes later, the maid escorted a beaming Madison down to the lounge. In her arms, she carried scraps of fabric, Cecile's wedding book, and her sketch pad. She was in her element, strong and in control. This was a side he hadn't seen before. They made their way back to the lower level, away from the family section, and back to Dean's quarters.

# CHAPTER 39

The next day, surrounded by Cecile's wedding inspirations, Madison pulled out her sketchbook and began working on the thumbnail sketches she drew with Cecile. She combined several elements that Cecile considered musts in the gown, and when she finished, she had sketches for three stunning dresses. Each very different but still incorporating all the aspects.

Carl paused behind her and looked over her shoulder. He enjoyed watching her creativity. When this was over, he hoped to visit her studio and see her in her own environment. He didn't know Cecile well, but from what he knew, any of the designs would suit her. His chest swelled as he realized how talented Madison was. He turned on the music, poured himself a coffee, and stood across from her as he continued to watch. She put the sketch pad down and looked up at him.

"I think I've captured what Cecile is looking for, but it wouldn't surprise me if she requests changes. From what I can tell, she's used to getting everything she wants. Even if she loved one design, she'd make changes so she could feel she had more input."

Carl laughed. "You understand who she is in a short time. Would you like to make a small wager on which she'll choose?"

"A wager? What did you have in mind?"

A sly smile played on his lips. Madison raised an eyebrow in response, not sure of what to make of his wager idea. But after her discussion with Cecile, she felt confident about her designs. Plus, although she didn't let Carl know, Madison had another design in mind, in case she could persuade Cecile to wear two original dresses.

"If I pick the design she likes, you and I can re-enact the other night."

Madison laughed. "I don't need a wager for that."

Carl paused. His head snapped up as he looked into her eyes. He wasn't expecting her to want a repeat, especially under the circumstances. It didn't matter how much he knew she enjoyed it. He smiled as she continued.

"I'm not afraid to enjoy sex, and the sex was good. Why don't we come up with a better wager, one that takes the sex out of it?"

"Hmm, so you're saying we can still have sex?"

"Yup."

"This keeps getting better. O.K. You go first then. What do you want if you win?"

Madison chuckled. "It's not if I win, but when I win." She whispered her bet. "I want you to promise me that no matter what, you'll get me out of here and back to my own life. I want the proof I'm innocent of Abby's murder."

Stunned, Dean stopped cup to his lips. He took a sip while he considered his response. The whole idea was to get the proof they needed and then escape. It was obvious she still didn't trust him. This wasn't what he'd expected when he suggested the wager. She had guts. He had to give her that. But he couldn't promise something he couldn't control: there were too many variables. All he could promise was to do his best. However, she knew if he agreed, he'd die trying to keep his promise. This meant, whether she trusted him, she knew he was a man of his word.

"Well played Madison." He replied, keeping his voice low. "O.K. I'll agree to your terms, but here's what I want if I win. You should be prepared to look for the evidence when I say so. I know I told you not to, but I think we can take advantage of the fact that you're designing and working with Cecile. I can distract The Don while you look for it. With Tony forced to stay underground, we won't have to worry about you running into him. You'll also have to finish up with Cecile. The longer you drag it out, the longer you're trapped here."

"Now you want me to search? Isn't that what I've been suggesting all along? Of course, I'll look for the evidence! If you can get me past the guards and give me a chance, I'll find it. Why now?"

"There have been too many delays already. The longer you're here, the more dangerous it becomes. I've warned Tony off once, but that doesn't mean he'll stay away. You've had a taste of what he's capable of, and that's without consent. I think you can imagine what will happen if The Don decides you are no longer useful. He'll turn you over to Tony before I can intervene. It would be better for you to die than to end up in Tony's hands. He is a cruel, sick bastard. I don't even want to think about what he'd do to you."

Madison looked up and searched Carl's eyes. She saw the compassion and warmth he felt for her. She stood up and went to him, wrapped her arms around him to offer him comfort and to feel the reassurance she needed from him. He stood with his hands at his sides and allowed her to hold him before he enveloped her in his arms and pulled her to him. Breathing in the fresh scent of her, he felt his need for her grow. He leaned over and kissed her, knowing now wasn't the time.

"As much as I'd like to continue this, we're expected to have supper with The Don again. Tonight isn't formal. It's his way of keeping his eye on you. We can pick up where we left off when we get back."

"Mmm, that sounds good. Just let me change into a dress, and then we can head up."

She stepped out of her slacks and top, let them drop to the floor, and turned her back to him. With a quick wink over her shoulder, she padded to the closet in search of a dress. She knew she was teasing him, but that was half the fun. Things had become easy with Carl. So many times, she found she could forget the situation she was in because of him. He had a way of making her feel protected. She just hoped he could keep her safe.

She picked a simple dress from the closet, still surprised at the amount of new clothing that showed up from which to choose. The dress was a light grey knit wrap-around, with a three-quarter sleeve. It was perfect for a casual dinner, but still feminine. She slipped her feet into a pair of simple black pumps before going to touch up her makeup. When she was ready, she came back out to find Carl had changed into slacks and a blazer.

She slipped her arm through his as they headed to dinner.

THIS TIME they discovered the staff set the table for five, and both Cecile and Arabella were present when they entered the dining room. This changed things. Once again, she had to behave like a guest. The constant uncertainty unnerved her. She faltered as Cecile rushed over to greet them.

"You're here! Father said you'd be joining us." She linked her arm through Madison's and leaned in to whisper, "He also said you're dating Dean. I'd love to hear all about that. He's so mysterious."

Madison shot Carl a look. That must be how The Don explained her presence here to Cecile. At least she'd be able to play along. They may not be dating, but they'd been intimate and had gotten to know each other. They'd been in close confines for weeks. She relied on him and trusted him. The realization took her aback. Instead of responding, she ignored Cecile's comment.

"I have some good news. I completed the sketches and have some designs ready for you to look at. We could set up a time for me to show you tomorrow if you'd like."

Cecile squealed in delight and hugged Madison. The Don frowned from the end of the table where he sat enjoying a Scotch on the rocks. Arabella leaned over to her husband and whispered something in his ear. The Don's expression changed, and he smiled.

Carl stood back and watched the faces of those in the room. Arabella could manipulate The Don. He wondered how involved she was in the business, probably more than anyone knew. She was also a calming element for him. She reigned in his temper and levelled him out when needed. Carl had also witnessed her whisper a few words and watched as The Don brought wrath down on those around him. They both watched their daughter, whose excitement was contagious. Carl could only assume Madison told her about the finished sketches. This was good news! It meant they could move on with the search before they questioned her about the evidence, and they could get out of here.

Carl went to the sideboard and poured himself a Scotch. He turned and motioned to the bar to see if anyone else wanted anything before pouring three Cabernet Sauvignon for the ladies and handing them each a glass. Arabella moved to where her daughter sat, leaving Carl to sit with The Don.

"It seems your Miss Kerr has thrilled my daughter." The Don said.

Carl almost corrected him: she wasn't his Miss Kerr, but that would create tension at the table, especially as Cecile believed Madison was his. For all intents and purposes, she was. Also, she was his responsibility, and she could expose him by telling The Don his actual identity. But if she did, they'd both be dead. He needed to maintain his cover if their plan was going to work. He had a job to do. The senator was counting on him, Madison was counting on him, and the people back home needed him. Again, he wished he'd locked Madison up somewhere until this was over. Somehow, over the time they'd spent together, she'd got under his skin, which made the situation even more dangerous.

Arabella turned to address Madison as she approached.

"My daughter tells me you are designing her wedding dress. How wonderful! Can I assume by the excited greeting she gave you're done?"

"Cecile told me what she wanted, and I got to work right away. I just informed her I finished the sketches and they're ready for her approval."

"Oh, mother, wait until you see how talented she is. The rough sketches were so good. I can't believe she's already put all the things we talked about into last sketches."

"If she works so fast, are you sure she's good?"

Madison's jaw dropped. In one sentence, Arabella had insulted Madison's expertise as a designer and her daughter's ability to determine what best suited her.

"Mother!" Cecile exclaimed. "I can't believe you said that. Do you want to see what she has designed so we can prove how good she is?"

The Don shot his wife a warning look. It wouldn't do to upset Cecile and cause friction before they resolved Madison's real reason for being here. They both wanted Miguel freed, and Arabella knew this was one step towards making that happen. It was Arabella who insisted on including Madison in the gala. This whole situation was her fault. She wanted to see Madison, to learn what all the fuss was about. Now she'd have to deal with the consequences. They both would. One thing they agreed on was that Cecile deserved to be happy, and right now, having her wedding dress custom-designed made her happy.

"I apologize, Miss Kerr. That was rude of me. I shouldn't have spoken out of turn. I've never seen your work, so I have nothing to compare it with. If Cecile trusts you, so should I. Why don't we all sit down now that dinner is ready?"

Madison nodded at Arabella. She wasn't sure if Arabella was aware of the real circumstances that brought her to the compound. There was something about her that was more unnerving than her husband. There was cruelness behind her knowing eyes.

Throughout dinner, Cecile rambled on about her wedding plans, which achieved the effect of calming everyone. The tension was high when they first sat down. Cecile was so self-absorbed in her own issues, she was oblivious. Carl felt relieved Cecile's chatter deflected the attention away from him and Madison. He'd have to be more careful in the future, Arabella saw much more than her husband.

When dinner ended, Madison promised to meet with Cecile in the morning to go over the designs. Cecile turned and asked her mother if she wanted to be there, so she could see how good Madison's work was. However, Arabella declined, stating that she could wait and review the last choice before ordering the fabric. The only thing left was for Madison and Carl to excuse themselves from the room and head back to his quarters. Cecile had already rushed off to join some friends, leaving The Don and his wife to talk.

# CHAPTER 40

Once they were alone, Arabella turned to her husband.

"It seems things aren't going as smoothly as you thought. I want this business finished, and Miguel home!"

"Now! Now! My sweet. We have to bide our time. When Cecile chooses her dress, Miss Kerr has promised to recommend someone who can make it, so her part in this will be over. That's when I'll interrogate her. I may keep Dean away and have Tony present. If she isn't cooperative, I'll allow Tony to work his magic. He has ways of making people talk. Don't worry, my pet. This will soon be over."

"Tony is nothing more than a trained ape. His methods are disgusting. If you didn't treat her so well, to begin with, this would already be over!" Arabella abruptly stood and turned to leave.

"Arabella." The iciness of his tone made her blood run cold. She stopped and turned to look at him.

"I have always maintained control of this situation. You will not question my methods again. I WILL get Miguel back, and soon. Remember, it was you who insisted that she attend the gala." He dismissed her with the finality of his words.

Wife or not, she had no business questioning his methods or authority. At least she had the moral sense to wait until they were alone. This was all her doing. Arabella was the one who wanted to see who Madison was. That was the only reason the girl was at the gala. Neither of them knew Cecile would want Madison to design her wedding dress.

He pulled out a cigar as he watched his wife depart. He cursed his son for his foolishness. Miguel's recklessness put them in this situation. The impulsiveness of youth. His son had a lot to learn before he'd be ready to take over the family business. It was time to consider giving Dean more responsibility. Then, if he needed to step down before Miguel was ready, Dean would be there to guide Miguel. Dean had proven his loyalty. Even his attraction to the girl hadn't made him flinch, knowing Tony would be the one to finish her. He may still rethink that. After everything she's done, she deserved a quick death. Tony's behaviour and unpredictability were becoming a problem. He needed Tony's methods of intimidation, but allowing him to have the girl once she was of no use now seemed excessive.

He'd wait a couple of days before making his final decision. Cecile was meeting with Miss Kerr in the morning, and that should resolve the designing side of the problem. Once her part of the process was complete, he'd have Madison brought to him. If she was difficult or lied, Tony could supply the right amount of persuasion. He hoped they could get this resolved by the end of the week. It was time to get his house in order.

MADISON KICKED off her shoes the minute they returned to Carl's room and rolled her shoulders to release the stress of the evening. Carl stepped up behind her and kneaded her aching muscles. He swept her hair to one side and kissed the base of her neck, sending shivers down her spine. At any other time, this would be heaven. She willed herself to relax and give into Carl. Wanting to find pleasure with him and block out the open hostility Arabella had shown at dinner. She took a deep breath and released it, as his kisses traced up her neck and to behind her right ear. He paused and whispered.

"Do you want to wait until you show Cecile your designs?"

She could hear the jest in his words. Instead of answering him, she turned to face him. Looked deep into his eyes and saw for the first time the man he was. She saw him as Carl, not his alter ego, Dean, hard-assed, determined, calculating, but also caring and concerned. At that moment, she surrendered. Tomorrow didn't matter. There was only today. She slid her hands behind his head and pulled him down to her, switching her look from his eyes to his lips and back. Kissing him, feeling his arms wrap around her, crushing her to him, and deepening the kiss.

His lips never left hers as he guided her back towards the bed and eased her down, releasing her lips. She slid back across the mattress until her head was on the pillow. He climbed up beside her before straddling her, taking her face in his hands and kissing her.

"Are you sure?" he whispered.

"Yes." she replied.

He hopped back off the bed and turned out the lights, stopping to knock a book over in front of the camera lens. He considered turning on the music but knew the sounds alone would be enough to enrage Tony, who he was sure would be watching. Banished or not, Tony would want to be in the observation room to see everything.

He stopped and slipped out of his clothes and tossed them to the floor. He turned back to look at Madison, who had already removed her clothing. Three long strides brought him back to the bed. He took her into his arms and explored her body. This time he took his time, enjoying every sensation of where flesh met flesh. Sated, he pulled her close, and they continued to lie in each other's arms. He looked into her eyes as he reached out and stroked an errant curl, tucking it behind her ear. His eyes locked onto hers. He leaned forward and kissed the tip of her nose.

"You are so beautiful."

Madison smiled, preferring to languish in the warmth of his

arms than to respond. Suddenly, she realized he'd blocked the camera lens. She saw him do it and took that opportunity to undress, but the magnitude of the deliberateness of his action just registered.

"You blocked the camera. Won't there be repercussions?" She whispered.

"The Don isn't watching tonight, only Tony. He needed to know I knew he was watching, and that I wouldn't let him. It's part of the game of control. Tony needs to know he can't control me."

Keeping her voice low, knowing that although he blocked the camera, the microphone wasn't. "How long will you have to keep this up?"

"It's already been too long. I've been inside here for years. I believe The Don's father caused the death of my parents, which is why I first infiltrated the family. So I wanted to get the information to prove it. When the senator hired me to find the evidence to confirm Miguel's guilt, I just went in deeper. It's complicated, so long as I have all the information I need, I can get you out of here, and get myself out, too. I don't have my end plan in place yet, but I'm working on it. The one thing I have going for me right now is that no one knows who I am. If anyone learned the truth, it would be the end."

"Your parents?" she gasped. "You think The Don's father handled your parents' death! I can't believe you didn't tell me this before. Do Rose and Hank know?"

"Yes, but before you get angry, I swore them to secrecy. I didn't know how much information you could handle. Now I realize you need to know the full story. Hank kept telling me I should trust you with the truth. I'm sorry. I couldn't tell you sooner."

Carl whispered everything to her. When he finished, he waited for her response.

Her hands trembled as she reached out to stroke his cheek.

"I'm sorry you went through that. Losing your parents at such a young age must have been devastating. As you know, I lost mine when I was a teenager, so I understand. We have more in common than we thought. I'm glad you trusted me with the truth. I'll do whatever I can to help you find what we need."

Carl chuckled. He laid back and let out a deep sigh. He pulled her close, thankful for how well she handled this information.

Sensing the change in Carl's demeanour, Madison turned the conversation back to the blocked camera. She was worried there'd be repercussions. It was the last thing they needed.

"Will it upset The Don when he discovered you blocked the camera?"

"I doubt it. Tony was told to disconnect it and didn't. The only reason he set it up was to verify why I wanted you in my room. The Don has the answer to that. He may listen in to every room, but he respects my privacy within my suite. Tony has used it to spy on you and my interactions with you. He was hoping to find something to bring to The Don. Of course, he found nothing. After he attacked you, The Don was furious. Tony had orders to leave you alone, which included spying on you."

"Doesn't that seem odd, considering he wants me dead?"

"The Don is a complicated man, but everything has to be on his terms. Tony acted alone. And your injuries might have become an embarrassment at the gala. That could have been a disaster, so Tony is underground until The Don needs him again, on orders to stay far away from you. Now let's get under the covers. We need to get some sleep. You have a date with Cecile in the morning."

Madison chuckled, scampered up to the head of the bed, and slipped between the sheets. "Goodnight," she whispered as he crawled over her to his side of the bed and slid in beside her. "Goodnight." He whispered back.

In the viewing room, Tony cursed, running his fingers through his hair in frustration. First, Dean blocked the camera, and then everything they said got mumbled and impossible to hear.

*'Dean was up to something, but what? How can I get the boss to listen*

*to me? Fuck! If only I hadn't attacked the bitch. I should have waited. The boss promised I could finish her. But the bitch was always twitching her ass in my direction. She wants me. I know it. She only played at being upset when Dean came into the room. That manipulative bitch!'*

Tony envisioned how she wouldn't be teasing anyone when he finished with her. He'd have to preserve the pieces he planned to cut from her body. Tony wanted a souvenir for all the trouble she's caused him. He'd take her breasts, but before he removed them, he would bite her, leaving his teeth marks deep in her flesh, while she screamed in pain. Tony grew hard as he thought about it. Yes, he was going to enjoy humiliating her before he was done.

Dean wasn't immune to her charms. He'd become protective of her. That would only be a problem for Dean when the time came. They all knew she had to be disposed of. He had to let Dean know what happened to her. And then maybe they would settle this business between them. He wanted to be rid of Dean as well. Taunt him with how he made the bitch suffer until Dean came after him. He'd make sure their fight would end with Dean's death. The Don couldn't blame him. He knows that the two of them are already at odds. The Don didn't instruct them not to settle their differences. Dean's death would be the perfect end to this mess.

If only he could find proof Dean was up to something. Then the boss wouldn't mind if he killed Dean. He'd be doing The Don a favour. That would solve their problems. The Don would be pleased, and maybe he'd bring Tony further into the family. It was time to do some more digging.

# CHAPTER 41

In the morning, Madison sat across from Cecile with the final three designs laid out between them. Cecile picked up one and looked at it before putting it down and picking up another. She did this several times, never seeming to be satisfied. Madison wondered if she'd been wrong in her assessment of Cecile and what she was looking for. She sat back and waited for Cecile to say something, deciding she'd let Cecile speak first. If she didn't, she'd seem unsure, and she felt confident in her work. Madison knew that if none of the designs were right, it was because Cecile changed her mind about what she wanted. Soon, it became apparent to Madison that Cecile was trying to contain herself. She was very excited. She gave in to it, squealed with joy, threw her arms around Madison, and hugged her. Cecile pulled back, and her smile stretched from ear to ear.

"Were you worried?" She asked.

"Did you want me to be?"

"Well, after the way my mother was last night, I thought you might think she was horrible. I wondered if you were going to change your designs or make back-ups."

"Your mother has a lot on her plate right now. I understand that, so I didn't let what she said bother me. I trusted you knew what you wanted and stuck with the original designs I made after our meeting. Do you have a favourite?"

She picked up the one Madison knew she'd prefer. It was a long, simple sheath that was cut on the bias. It had a sweetheart neckline, attached to a chiffon halter that ended with a beautifully beaded collar. The back was low and scooped out; a minimal train finished the look.

"This is my dream dress, but I couldn't wear it in the church." She sighed.

Madison opened her sketchbook and brought out the second dress she'd planned to show Cecile, but kept hidden until she was one hundred percent certain.

"That's why you deserve two dresses."

The second dress was more demure but just as stunning. A fitted lace bodice, with long sheer sleeves and a high neck. The full skirt was tulle, with a lace and beaded edge. It was the princess dress the family expected and was church appropriate.

"This is beautiful, but it's what my family wants, not me."

"Think about it this way. The first dress is for the blushing bride. A young woman moving forward as a new wife. The ceremony ends. You change and are presented as a wife, a Mrs. Now you have the grown-up look you want."

Cecile's eyes filled with tears as she looked up at Madison.

"That's so beautiful. It's the perfect solution. Matthew doesn't care what I wear. He said I'd be beautiful in a burlap sack."

Madison agreed. It was what a loving man would say about his intended, and Cecile was a lucky girl.

"So what you're saying is that with two dresses, I can make my family happy, be respectful of the church, and still be true to myself. You understand what I need."

"The next thing we have to do is pick the fabric, find a pattern maker and a dressmaker, and you'll be all set."

"Wait, a minute! Aren't you going to make my dresses?"

"As much as I'd love to, I don't make the dresses myself anymore.

They're done at my studio, or I contract the work out. Because you are in the States and I'm Canadian, we should find someone local to do the work. Don't worry, I've already made a mental list of people who would be perfect."

"It's because you killed your friend. That's the real reason you don't want to make my dresses, isn't it?"

The silence that followed Cecile's odd question was deafening. Madison couldn't speak as she sat back. Cecile's words felt like a slap in the face. She struggled to control her fury, realizing she'd mistaken Cecile's character. The sweet, innocent act Cecile portrayed had taken Madison by surprise, but was now aware she also had a malicious self-serving side. Madison took a few deep breaths to compose herself before she responded. She needed to give herself time to decide whether to deny it or challenge Cecile. In the end, she decided ignorance was the best.

"What do you mean?" Madison replied in mock innocence.

"I saw it on the news. They said you killed your friend over her boyfriend. But that makes little sense. You're with Dean. I just wondered if there was any truth to it, especially since you won't make my dresses." Cecile finished with a pout.

Madison sighed, relieved she played dumb. Any other response would have made her look guilty or created a new slew of questions she didn't want to answer. It was obvious Cecile didn't know why she was here. She'd almost jumped to conclusions, instead of under-standing that the question came from a selfish but naive girl, whose family protected from knowing the true nature of their business.

Madison still didn't understand why The Don allowed her to work with his daughter, especially in such a close and personal manner. There was much more going on here than she knew. Madison decided the only thing she could do was to tell Cecile a little about what happened in order to put her mind at ease, so she'd be able to understand why the dresses needed to be made here, instead of at the studio.

"My best friend died a few weeks back, which you heard on the news. We'd been out together, and when we returned, she sent me to join some people at a neighbouring chalet, and she went back to my chalet to get something."

"It was your place? Then the news people are silly. You'd never blow up your own place."

"I wish everyone thought that way. I bought the chalet because my parents took me there all the time when I was young. After they died, the lawyers sold my family's home to close out the estate. So when I could, and it was for sale, I purchased the chalet to remind me of them. All of my family memories and keepsakes were in there, along with the best friend I've ever had. The explosion destroyed everything."

Cecile reached over and grabbed Madison's hand, squeezed it, and encouraged her to continue.

"I tried to go into the chalet after it exploded and help Abby, but someone stopped me."

"Of course they did. I'm sure it wasn't safe."

Madison knew she'd have to be careful of what she told Cecile. She knew The Don bugged the room. If she said the wrong thing, there would be no way to recover. Cecile shifted to the edge of her seat and leaned closer to Madison, eager for her to continue. Madison took a deep breath and went on. She chose her next words with care and decided that if she described what happened, it would shift the focus.

"It was one of the most horrifying things I've ever seen. She walked into the chalet. We'd been laughing and enjoying ourselves. Then the explosion hit. It threw me to the ground, and before I knew it, flames engulfed the building. I struggled to get up. When I found my footing, I ran towards the chalet. Everything was in chaos. People near the chalet got hurt, not just from the explosion, but also from pieces of flying debris. There was no way I could enter the chalet, even if I'd been able to reach it. The flames were too hot."

"Oh, my god! I can't imagine having seen that happen. That must have been shocking to you, but you said: 'one' of the most horrifying things you ever saw. What could be worse than that?"

Again, Madison sighed, her eyes welling up with tears. The

sadness she felt wasn't just reliving Abby's death, but the other horrifying death that still haunted her all these years later. Cecile noticed the tears and pulled Madison into a hug to offer her comfort. Cecile saw a deep sadness in Madison's eyes and knew something painful happened to her long before her friend's death. She coaxed Madison to tell her the rest, her curiosity getting the better of her.

"You can't mean you saw something else just as horrible?"

"Yes," Madison whispered, giving in to the first real comfort she'd felt since Abby's death. She knew it was wrong, but she needed the opportunity to grieve.

"What happened?"

"On the night of my prom, I saw my boyfriend get struck and killed by a train." There, she'd said it. It was out there.

Cecile gasped, pulling back so she could look at Madison. Cecile's face displayed a mixture of shock and horror.

"Oh my god, Madison. I'm so sorry. You've been through so much. It's a good thing you're so strong. I've even heard my father say so."

Madison's head snapped up as she looked at Cecile.

"Your father says I'm strong?" She said in disbelief.

"Yes, I heard him on the phone. He said: 'she's so strong it would take a lot to break her.' I don't know what he meant. Why would anyone want to break you? Do you think he was referring to your friend's death?"

"I'm sure it was an expression to show my strength, that's all." She refused to allow her tears to spill over. Instead, she blinked them away as she considered what The Don was referring to.

"Are you feeling better? Let me call up for some lunch. Maybe we should even have some champagne! We can celebrate my beautiful dresses!"

*'Leave it to Cecile to skim over one person's sorrow and change the focus back to herself.'* Madison thought as she sighed in relief, thankful not to have to go into more details.

# CHAPTER 42

After lunch, Cecile excused herself and left the room. Madison found herself alone in the family's private quarters. Unsure of what to do, she decided it was best to sit and wait, assuming Carl would come for her. More than an hour passed, and he failed to show. She figured if Cecile came back and found her still waiting, she'd ask questions that Madison couldn't answer. So she made her way back to his room on her own.

Madison peeked through the door that connected the family area to the rest of the compound to see if the coast was clear. The hallway was empty, so she stepped out into it and worked her way through the maze of corridors and passageways down to the lower levels. She moved at a fast pace as she went. Even though she'd been here before, she found herself lost and unable to recognize where she was. A cold sensation crept into the pit of her stomach as she realized she hadn't passed a single person, not even a stationed guard. Whenever Carl took her through the compound, they'd always passed at least a dozen posted throughout.

A tingling sensation crept up her spine, and a deep knot formed in her stomach. Something wasn't right. There was no way she should be able to wander about without an escort. She was a prisoner, and although Cecile had left her alone, someone should have come for her. The Don wouldn't leave the compound unguarded. She slowed her pace. Madison had to be careful and took the time to pause and listen for sounds as she passed by doorways. She turned left at the next passage. It was familiar, but she felt uncomfortable. She felt the hairs on the back of her neck stand up as she continued.

Madison heard voices ahead. She listened and recognized one of them as belonging to Tony. Without thinking, she backed up against the wall. Her eyes widened as she looked around for a place to hide in the barren hall. All she found were more doors to unfamiliar rooms. She could open one, but what or who would she find inside? Her hand grabbed the handle of the door closest to her. The knob turned without resistance. Finding it unlocked flooded her with relief. She slipped inside. With her back to the room, she peered down the hall and then closed the door. Alone in the darkened room, her forehead pressed against the door, she took slow, deep breaths to calm her racing heart.

Madison stepped back from the door and turned to see where she was. It took a moment for her eyes to adjust to the unlit space after the brightness of the hallway. It was too dangerous to turn on a light. If anyone saw it, it would expose her. A window stretched across the wall on the far side of the room, but the curtains were drawn. Only a slight filtration of light flickered around the edges.

It meant she was on the backside of the lower compound. Carl told her that only the back had windows as they built the compound on the side of the mountain. Carl explained that if anyone approached from the front, it would appear to be a majestic home. The lower floors remained undetected. But there were many levels, all hiding the sins of Don Fernando. Only the wall with windows could his family access. The other floors housed the darker, more sinister side of his business.

As her eyes adjusted to the poor lighting, her knees weakened when she realized she was in The Don's office. She couldn't believe she found the door unlocked. Of course, The Don wouldn't expect anyone within his 'family' to enter here uninvited. Her being here was an accident. If she wasn't so terrified that Tony would find her, she wouldn't be here, either. She realized if he caught her, it would be over.

As she got her bearings, she realized she had an unexpected opportunity. The Don would hide the evidence they were looking for in here. She needed to search for it, but she'd have to be careful. The room had to remain dark. Even opening the curtains would be risky. They'd find her if anyone noticed a disturbance in the room, and investigated. She made her way towards the massive desk. To her left, stretching along the wall, was a set of large mahogany filing cabinets. She figured that was a good place to look.

She tugged on several drawers, but they didn't budge. Of course, they were locked. She needed the keys. She went over to the desk and slid open the centre drawer. There was nothing important in there. All she found was the usual array of office supplies. The desk had a row of drawers on either side. She paused and considered her own. She was right-handed, and her important things were in the right-hand drawers. The Don was left-handed. It made sense that he'd be more likely to use the left-hand drawers.

She pulled open the top left drawer and found that it didn't run smoothly on the tracks. It caught before she could bring it all the way open it. That was odd. A man like The Don wouldn't put up with his desk drawer catching unless there was a reason for it. She pulled the drawer free from the desk and listened to the voices, which now were right outside the door. If she was going to find what she was looking for, she had to work fast.

She lowered the drawer to the floor and slid her hand inside, feeling along the tracking to determine what it got caught on. Her fingers poked around and felt for a clue to why the drawer stuck. At first, she couldn't find anything, but she was determined. There had to be something. She took a deep breath, and this time used her fingernails to feel for loose pieces of wood and seams inside the compartment. Her nail caught on a slight lift just above the tracking, and she ran her nail along the seam. It was small, only an inch wide and two inches long.

Her nails dug into the seam until she pulled the piece of wood free. Inside was a small compartment. Her fingers prodded the interior until she felt an object. She grabbed it and pulled it out. It surprised her to find a USB stick clasped between her fingers. She realized how important it was, or The Don wouldn't have hidden it. Madison could only assume that it contained valuable information, maybe even the files they were looking for.

She clutched it in her hand. Her fingers curled around it. She had to decide what to do. If she took it now, without an escape plan, and got caught, she'd never get out of here. The Don would have her killed. Chuck would get away with setting her up, and his part in Abby's death. The Don would get away with everything. Miguel, who was the reason all of this happened, would be free, and the senator wouldn't get his justice. Leaving it behind might mean giving up any hope they had to prove everything. Dammit!

She didn't have a choice. She had to put it back. At least she knew where it was. As long as no one caught her and she put everything back the way she found it, no one would be the wiser. She slipped the USB stick back into the hide-y-hole and put the piece of wood back in place. Feeling the edges until she knew it was secure. She lifted the drawer back up and slid it home. Now she had to get out of here and find Carl without getting caught.

# CHAPTER 43

Madison slipped back to Carl's room undetected. The only guard they'd posted she encountered outside of his room. She knew that when The Don found out, there'd be hell to pay. But Cecile left her alone. No one gave her instructions, and no one came to escort her. At least she made her way back undetected. She was careful not to leave any evidence of her detour into his office, so she felt safe. If asked, she'd tell them she waited. When no one came, she thought if Cecile found her still sitting in the lounge, she'd question Madison, so she headed back to Carl's room.

She paced, waiting for Carl to come back. Madison wondered what was keeping him. She had so much to tell him. With her unexpected discovery today, they had to make plans. They had to decide how they'd get away. But now, they also needed a plan to retrieve the memory stick. She debated whether to tell him about what she found inside the lipstick, but decided against it for now. It was her insurance policy. Since she discovered it, she started slipping the tube of lipstick into her bra each morning and back into her makeup kit at night. She wanted to be sure she had it with her at all times because if the opportunity to escape presented itself; it was too important to leave behind.

Hours went by, and there was still no word from Carl. Madison became agitated as she considered the cause of his absence. What if he didn't return, or if something happened to him? Then she'd be at The Don's mercy, and he would hand her over to Tony. She had to think. There had to be a way to get out of here. If she could figure out one on her own, then she'd go, even without Carl. A knock at the door interrupted her thoughts. She hesitated before she got up to answer it.

Madison opened it, and the guard greeted her with a cart of food. The guard brought the cart in and left, resuming his position outside. Madison turned to ask him where Carl was, but he ignored her and shut the door. Once again, she was alone with her unanswered questions. With too much time on her hands, her mind wandered. It wasn't a good thing. All she could think about was what would happen to her if Carl didn't come back. Those thoughts terrified her. She didn't know where he was. He didn't tell her anything. He'd never left her alone for such a long period.

She lifted the lid on the food and found a cold plate of sandwiches and salad. A far cry from the more elaborate meals they had served so far. Something wasn't right. She grabbed a sandwich and ate, chewing without tasting it. Finding it dry, she grabbed a bottle of water to wash it down. One thing Carl taught her when they were at the ranch was that food was energy, and you must fuel the body because you didn't know when you'd need it to perform.

She looked for a distraction and tried to read, but that didn't work. She found she couldn't concentrate on the words as her mind drifted off to consider different scenarios. Which one's put her most at risk? What if someone saw her? She didn't consider that there may have been cameras hidden in the office! Dammit! She was so careless. She'd never even thought to look. Frustrated, she got up and peered through the peephole to find there were now two guards at her door. This wasn't a good sign. Her body tensed with irritation and uncertainty, so she grabbed a hot shower and hoped that it would help relax her.

She turned the water on and waited until it was as hot as she could stand before she stepped in. Madison felt some of the tension eased from her shoulders. She scrubbed her body until her skin turned pink and continued to stand under the stream of water until long after she was clean. The steam from the shower clouded the glass door and filled the room. She hadn't bothered to close the bathroom door, as there was no need with the guards positioned outside. They wouldn't let Tony in, not after what happened to the last guard. For the first time since finding the hidden compartment, Madison relaxed.

She felt a shift in the room's temperature. A slight coolness broke through the steam. Madison looked up from under the spray of water and peered through the glass. It was too foggy to make out more than the shape of a man as he entered the room. He moved closer to the shower door before reaching out to open it. Madison felt dread in the pit of her stomach until her vision cleared and she realized it was Carl. He stood there with a towel in hand.

"Get out and dry off. We need to talk."

Madison took the towel and dried off. Carl's expression wasn't angry, but he kept his voice stern. So she wasted no time in wrapping a robe around herself, ran her fingers through her hair, and joined him in the main room. Carl sat in one of the two chairs. His foot tapped on the floor in agitation. There was a sense of seriousness about him she'd never seen before. As she entered the room, he motioned for her to have a seat and join him. She took the opposite chair to observe his expressions as he spoke. He ran his hand through his hair and paused before he began.

"How did you get back here?"

"I walked." She retorted.

"Being flippant won't solve anything."

"Why don't you tell me what's wrong, and then we can discuss it?"

"What's wrong? Are you kidding me? You left the family quarters and wandered about on your own. The Don is furious!"

"Well, then maybe someone should've come for me!"

"Madison, this isn't a joke. It was all I could do to get him to allow me to talk to you, instead of sending in Tony."

Madison gasped, with all the scenarios that played out in her mind. She'd forgotten about The Don's temper. If he'd sent Tony, it would be over. The reality of how bad things could have turned out flickered across her face as she fingered the still healing cut on her neck. Satisfied that she realized how dangerous her foray was, Carl continued.

"I've told you before that you can't wander around unescorted. You should have waited for someone to get you."

He shot her a warning look as she opened her mouth to speak, closing it again. She remembered the camera and audio. They were being watched. The Don would want to see her response to Carl's questions. If her answers didn't satisfy him, he'd hand her over to Tony.

"I'm sorry. After Cecile left, I waited, but no one came. I thought that if Cecile came back, she would find it odd that I was still there. I remembered how to get back to your room, so I just came back here. There was a guard outside when I got here. He can verify what time that was."

"We already have, but that leaves a lot of time unaccounted for."

"I don't see how. I waited for quite a while before I made my way here. Without a watch, I couldn't be sure how long it was. But Cecile and I had lunch before she left. I waited and then had to make my way in the maze of corridors, which was more difficult than I thought. I've been here for a while, wondering where you were and why I'd been left alone when food arrived. That about covers all of my time!" She couldn't help herself from sounding annoyed. She wanted this conversation to end so she could tell him what she found.

While Carl considered what she said, his phone rang.

"Dean speaking."

"Hello, Dean." The Don drawled. "I believe her. It was your fault for not finding someone to escort her back. Make sure it doesn't happen again. I think tomorrow I'll need to have a chat with Miss Kerr." The line went dead.

'Dam' Carl cursed under his breath.

"It seems you've satisfied The Don, at least for now. I want to watch the news. Why don't you pour us both a drink and join me?"

Carl ended the conversation. If The Don accepted her story, there was no reason to continue talking about it. Madison fought to control her anger. How dare he question her like that? He knew they were being watched. He made her feel like a wayward child who needed to be punished. Now he expected her to mix drinks and watch the news with him. Unbelievable! She would do it because she had to, but it still infuriated her.

Making sure the tie on the robe was secure, she made her way to the bar. She knew he'd want a Scotch on the rocks, but she wanted a glass of Chianti, a great big one. Madison looked through the selections of wine before picking a simple Ruffino. She opened the bottle and attached an aerator and poured herself a generous serving. She picked up both and handed Carl his Scotch. When he saw the size of her glass, he raised an eyebrow but thought better than to question her.

She took a long sip of her wine before settling on the sofa. He moved over to sit beside her. The local news broadcasted on the screen in front of them. Carl downed his Scotch and got up, and poured another. He deposited his glass on the table and went back to the bar. He came back with the open bottle of wine, Scotch, and ice bucket, which he also placed on the table. Madison shot him a look. It was then she noticed how tired he was. There were dark circles under his eyes.

With the television on to drown out their conversation, she contemplated how to tell him what she found. She wasn't sure if he still planned to help her. Madison could still be a means to an end, but she needed to take a leap of faith and hope for the best. She kept her eyes on the TV, and in a low voice, told Carl she didn't come straight back to the room. He had his glass raised to his lips to take a sip. Then he paused before he drained the amber liquid.

"Oh?"

"I waited. But I was tired of waiting and figured I could find my own way back to the room. I got lost. There were so many corridors."

Carl poured himself another drink and stayed silent while she continued.

"I didn't see anyone. Then I turned down another corridor, and things looked familiar. I heard voices, and at first, I wasn't concerned until I realized one of them was Tony. I knew if he found me wandering around alone, I'd be in trouble. So I ducked into the first unlocked room."

"You would have found them all unlocked. The Don doesn't hire people he can't trust, so he doesn't lock the doors. Except to the family compound."

"Are you going to ask me which room I entered?"

Carl looked her up and down. This had been a trying day, and he was in no mood to play games. The Don had a few 'items of business' that needed taking care of. He'd been putting out fires all day, only to return to find The Don irate about Madison's unescorted trip through the compound. The Don only calmed down after he took a strip off him. Together, they went to the audio feed to the room, and they could hear her move around just as the supper tray arrived. That's when The Don ordered Carl back to his room to question her. The day was endless, and he didn't want to play games. He sighed and asked where.

"The Don's office."

"What the fuck!"

"It's O.K., no one saw me."

"Do you know how lucky you are that no one did?"

"Yes, but I found something."

He turned to her and saw the excited expression on her face. She stopped to take a generous sip of wine.

"I think I found what we are looking for."

"Where is it?"

"I left it there."

"You WHAT? Are you crazy? If it's what you think, we both need it to get out of here!"

"That's the point."

Anger boiled beneath the surface as he took another sip of his drink. He struggled to calm himself before asking her to explain herself.

"It was a fluke that I found it. When I realized where I was, I thought I could look around while I waited for Tony to continue past the office. I tried the filing cabinets, but found them locked, so I went to the desk in search of a key. I keep my keys in the top right-hand drawer of my desk."

"So?"

"So. I'm right-handed, and The Don is left-handed. That's why I checked the top left drawer."

"You found the keys?"

"No. Something better! As I pulled open the drawer, I noticed it didn't open smoothly. That didn't seem right, so I pulled the drawer out to investigate. I found a small secret compartment with a memory stick hidden inside. I thought it must be important for it to be hidden so well."

Carl considered what she told him. Yes. That memory stick must be important. But she left it behind! Would they get another opportunity to retrieve it and get out of here? He topped up her wine as he struggled to find the words to continue. Knowing where the information was and retrieving it were two different things. He turned to her.

"If you knew how important it was, why did you leave it?"

"I didn't take it because we don't have a plan in place on how to get out of here! If I took it and they discovered it missing, say while I was here alone, what do you think would have happened to me? I figured, now that I know where it is, we needed to come up with both an escape plan and a way to get the memory stick."

He looked at her and smiled. She was right. He'd been so busy protecting her and dealing with the rising issues, he hadn't worked out how they'd get out. He grabbed the back of her head and pulled her to him, kissing her hard.

"You're right. I'm proud you found it. Now we have to come up with a plan. Get the memory stick and get out of here. Let me think about this overnight. We'll talk again in the morning. But now, I'm supposed to bring you to The Don for a chat tomorrow."

She leaned back as the news flickered across the screen. Madison sipped on her wine and wondered what the chat with The Don would be about. She wanted to ask Carl, but when she looked over at him, he was no longer paying attention to the television or her. He was staring into space, lost in thought.

When Carl awoke, it was with a firm plan of action in mind. It would be tricky. They still needed to grab the USB. He knew if The Don caught them, he'd have Carl shot, and the fate that awaited Madison was far worse. She knew the risks, but they no longer had a choice. He briefed Madison on his plan as they dressed for the day. She had a hard time concentrating on what he was saying, but struggled to pay attention. The Don had scheduled his private meeting with Madison for right after breakfast, and it weighed on her. If he was going to start his interrogation, that meant their escape window was closing.

She had to come up with a way to stall The Don and pretend she didn't know what he was looking for, although that wasn't true. She thought of the lipstick that she'd hidden in her bra. It was her safety policy. She'd destroy it before, allowing him to get his hands on it. She only hoped to use the design process for Cecile's dress to hold him off.

There were still a few things she had to do for Cecile's gowns to be made. But anyone could source out the fabrics and a seamstress. If The Don was aware of this, it was over. She forced herself to push the thoughts from her mind and tried to pay attention to what Carl was telling her.

"Madison! Are you listening to me?"

"Oh, I'm sorry. I'm distracted thinking about my meeting with The Don this morning."

"You have nothing to worry about. I can guarantee he won't let anyone harm you today. Not with the work you still have to do for Cecile. Now pay attention. This is important."

Carl continued to explain his plan and gave her suggestions on how she could prolong recounting the details of what she knew. The Don wasn't a fool. It wouldn't take him long to know she was stalling, as all he cared about was Miguel's freedom and destroying any evidence that could interfere with that outcome. The same evidence, she was sure, was on the USB she found in her bag.

Today she opted for slacks, wearing a chiffon blouse for the femininity preferred by her 'host'. From here on in, she was sticking to flats, so dresses were out. Heels would hamper their escape when the opportunity presented itself. Carl said she needed to be ready to run at a moment's notice, and that meant wearing the right footwear. She wished she could wear running shoes or the hiking boots she wore here, but that would cause suspicion. So far, Carl still hadn't permitted her to carry her gun, but she loved the security she felt knowing it was nearby. She often laid in bed and allowed her hand to slip behind the table and feel its location.

Once they were both ready, they left for the dining room. When they entered, she half expected to see Tony and the usual array of guards, but felt happy to find Cecile and her father alone and already seated at the table waiting for them. Cecile turned and beamed at Madison, very pleased to see her.

"You're here! Father said you'd be joining us. Mother ate in her room today so, it will be just the four of us. Do you think we can set up the suppliers and seamstress appointments today? I showed father the two dresses. He thinks they are perfect. He was happy you respected the church with the first one. When I told him how you describe the two dresses as my change from a princess to a married woman, I think he almost cried." Cecile gushed as she rushed to hug Madison and lead her to the empty chair beside her.

"Now, Cecile. Let's not be too hasty. I've asked Miss Kerr here today because I need to have a chat with her. I promise as soon as we are done, I'll have her brought to you so that you can finish the plans for your dresses."

Carl took the seat across from Madison and next to The Don. It wasn't long before they served breakfast. The Don, who preferred to eat in silence, motioned for the conversation to end. Cecile vibrated with excitement, and Madison could sense she wanted to continue talking. Madison could only focus on the relief she felt, knowing that The Don wouldn't torture her. Not today. Not when he'd promised his daughter would meet with her.

After breakfast, Cecile left, but not before telling Madison she'd be waiting for her in the lounge. The Don motioned to his staff that he was ready to head to his office. As he struggled to stand, he told Madison and Carl to wait ten minutes before joining him. They stayed and enjoyed a second cup of coffee while they waited, knowing that The Don didn't want them to see his lack of mobility. It put him at a disadvantage. He wanted to show his power by being seated behind his desk when they arrived. His restricted movements meant he'd use a wheelchair, and he felt it showed weakness, something he didn't want either of them to see. Knowing it was necessary and seeing him in the chair were two different things. To The Don, the chair had become a necessity, but he also knew that it threatened his authority.

When it was time, they made their way to the office. In the corridor ahead, they could see that two guards flanked each side of the door. A chair was just outside, against the wall. When Madison noticed the chair, she looked at Carl, her eyes questioning his. He only shrugged. They stood outside the door as the guard knocked to announce them, waiting for a response. The Don called them in. Carl opened and held the door as Madison stepped inside. When Carl went to follow, The Don stopped him.

"No, Dean. I don't need you here for this. I want to speak with

Miss Kerr alone, so take a seat in the hall and wait for us to finish. When we are done, you can escort Miss Kerr to the family lounge to meet with Cecile."

Carl did a quick visual scan of the room. He breathed a sigh of relief when he noticed The Don was alone before he nodded and stepped back out into the hall. The Don motioned for Madison to approach the desk and have a seat. As she crossed the room, knowing she didn't have Carl's support, she also looked around and the fact that Tony wasn't present comforted her. This meant that The Don wouldn't use intimidation during their 'chat'. Madison shifted back into the chair and relaxed.

"Miss Kerr. It is my understanding that you have almost completed the design process for Cecile's dresses. Is that true?"

"Yes, it is. We have to set up a supplier for the fabrics and a seamstress who can make the dress. I've already suggested a pattern maker so that I can send her measurements off."

"I see. You know what that means?"

"I think I do. You'll want to talk to me about Abby."

"You're a bright girl. Do you know why I've put this off?"

"So I could design the dress of your daughter's dreams."

He chuckled.

"Yes. That's part of it. But the other part is, if you don't co-operate with me, I'd have to use any means necessary to get the answers I want."

"You mean Tony."

"In part, but he is the last resort. I don't want to use violence during our chats. It can get messy, and if we understand each other, things will go more easily for you."

Madison took a deep, calming breath before responding.

"Tell me what you need, and I'll see if I can help."

The Don smiled. Things were falling into place.

"Tomorrow, the two of us will sit down again and continue this conversation. Tony will be here. Dean won't. Right now, I'm going to tell you what I'm looking for. That way, you'll have some time to think about where it might be. If you answer or at least don't lie to me, I won't need Tony's services. I want you to ponder where you think the item is. You may not even realize its significance, but think about your discussions with Miss Monroe. You may find you know more than you thought."

Madison nodded as he spoke.

"I'm looking for a file. It may be a paper or an electronic one. Your friend gave the Crown Attorney the original file, and he used the information against a member of my family. I'm sure you can understand the position that puts me in. We got the original, but it came to our attention she may have made a copy."

"Who told you that? Why would she need a copy?"

"Not that it's important, but her boyfriend overheard a conversation she was having on the phone. Because of what she alluded to during that phone call, we believe she made a copy for insurance."

"It doesn't seem like that worked for her."

The Don raised his head and glared at her. Madison regretted her outspokenness and shifted in her seat. He was trying to be nice, or at least appear that way. If she didn't control her outbursts, he might start tomorrow's conversation with Tony's methods instead of allowing her to respond to his request. She shrank back into her chair and mumbled an apology. The Don sighed before continuing.

"I suppose you are right, Miss Kerr, but that changes nothing. I believe there is a file out there. That Mitchell fellow hasn't located it, and not for a lack of trying. Trust me. We tried to convince Miss Monroe to hand it over, but she refused."

Madison gasped. In that one statement, he'd all but admitted his involvement with the explosion. Madison didn't believe there was time to question her before the chalet blew up. She supposed it was possible, but she also knew there was no way Abby would let him have the file. That meant Abby knew her life was in danger before they went to the chalet. Everything was making sense. Abby's sudden desire to leave criminal law and join the Crown's office. Something she'd only just divulged. Abby hated being the reason bad people went free. It went against everything she believed. No! Abby would have died before giving up the evidence, which she did.

She gave her life to protect what was on the USB stick. Madison vowed if she made it out of here, she'd add Chuck to the list of people she'd make pay for Abby's murder. The lipstick tube between her breasts felt heavy, a constant reminder of the danger it possessed should they should find it.

"Ah, I see you've made the connection. No worry. I knew you were an intelligent woman. The file means nothing to you. It's of no use to your friend anymore and may save your life. Think about it. You must know what she did with it. She may have alluded to it in an offhanded comment. You need some time, and it will come to you."

"But why me?"

"You were her best friend. From what I understand, the two of you were as close as sisters. If she told anyone, it would be you. If she didn't tell you to protect you, then you know enough of her secrets to know where she would hide something like this. That is why I am giving you the night to think about it. Do you understand?"

"Yes."

"Good. That's all for now. Dean can come back in and take you to Cecile. I'm sure she is very impatient waiting for you."

Madison thanked him and left the office and followed Carl to the lounge.

# CHAPTER 45

When she arrived at the lounge, Madison found Cecile surrounded by piles of inspiration, colour swatches, and design pages. Her wedding book was open. Sticky notes marked individual pages with comments and suggestions. She looked up and beamed at Madison as she entered. Carl stayed out of sight and slipped away before Cecile could see him, not wanting to explain why Madison needed an escort.

"Hi again. You brought nothing with you. How will we get everything organized?" Cecile pouted, noting Madison's empty hands.

"I need nothing more than a cell phone. Do you have one?"

"Of course!"

"I'm sorry. I forgot mine. If I can use yours, I'll call my assistant in Toronto and have him put a list together for us. He has access to all my contacts. If you have a pen and paper, I'll write everything he tells me down. Together, we can look over the list and decide who to call. I'll have samples sent over for you to look at and line up a seamstress. Today, I can also call the pattern maker and send over a copy of the sketches so that he can make the pattern. When the pattern is ready, he can send it to the seamstress so she can cut out the dress after you've chosen your fabrics. You'll want her to come here to do private fittings and take measurements, although she may accept the measurements I took for the pattern maker."

Cecile slipped her phone out of her pocket and hesitated before handing it to Madison. She wasn't supposed to allow anyone else to use it, but this was different. It was for her wedding dress, and Madison forgot hers, so it must be O.K. If they were going to set everything up, Madison needed a phone. She handed it over and prayed her parents didn't walk in and find out that she'd broken a rule.

Madison held Cecile's phone in her hands. If she were smart, she'd use it to call for help. But she knew that by the time help arrived, she'd already been dead. Who would she call, anyway? She didn't know where she was. Even if she did, would anyone come to her rescue? Yes, Hank would, and he'd know where they were. When she was at the ranch, he had her memorize his number just in case she needed it, but that wouldn't do her any good. She'd still be dead by the time he got here. Madison wouldn't put his life in danger, too. She wouldn't take any unnecessary risks.

She had to stick to the plan. The only call she'd make would be to the office for the information she needed. She keyed in the number to her studio in Toronto and listened as it rang. Something was wrong! Someone should have picked up already. They always answered calls on the second ring. Just as she was about to hang up, George answered.

"Madison Kerr Designs."

"Hi, George."

"Oh, my god! Madison, do you know the chaos going on around here?"

"George, I'm sorry. I don't know. I wish I were there to help."

"No, you don't. If you were here, you'd be in jail. Last night someone tossed the place. They broke into the studio and your loft. They were looking for something, but I don't know what. From what I can tell, nothing is missing. The police are here now."

"Don't let anyone know I'm on the phone."

"O.K. Tell me what you need?"

"I want you to go to my contact files. I need a list of the best seamstresses in the US and a list of suppliers who will rush out fabric samples to the States. The suppliers I'm looking for are for bridal wear. I'll give you a few minutes to gather the information, and I'll call you back."

She disconnected the call and looked at Cecile, who just stared at her. Madison was quick to explain.

"Things are crazy busy in the studio right now. I figured it was best to give him the time to put a list together. That way, when I call him back, he'll have what we need. There's no reason to wait on the phone while he puts together the list. My supplier list is pretty big to sort through." She laughed.

Cecile nodded and went back to the colour swatches. She was still trying to figure out her colour scheme before ordering the fabric samples. She held up swatches, trying to match different colours together. On seeing her struggle, Madison pitched in and help her sort and discard, paring down the enormous selection to a more manageable amount.

While she was sorting, Madison wondered how long someone had to be on the phone for a trace to go through. The police would have a warrant for her arrest, and the line might have a trace on it.

'No,' she thought, 'that was unlikely. They were there because of the break-in. Plus, I trust George. If he knew there was a trace on the line, he'd let me know.' She looked at the clock on Cecile's phone and figured she'd given George enough time to gather what she'd asked for. It was time to call him back. This time, he answered on the first ring.

"Hello?"

"George?"

His voice dropped to a whisper.

"Madison. I have what you need. Do you have a pen handy? We should do this before the police ask who I'm talking to."

"Go ahead, George."

She jotted down the contact names and numbers. The list wasn't extensive. Most of the suppliers she used were from Canada or Europe, and so it didn't take long.

"Is that all George?"

"Yes, but you knew the list wouldn't be big Stateside. Madison?"

"Yes?"

"Be careful. I don't know why you need this information or what's going on. I won't ask. All I can say is we need you back here. If there's anything else I can do, let me know. I'll do what I can. We need this mess resolved so you can come home."

"Thanks, George. I'm working on that now. I'll be in touch as soon as I can."

Madison looked at the list in her hand. It only comprised a few names, but any of them would be up to the task. She made notes beside each of the names, placing them in order of preference. Meanwhile, Cecile continued working on her wedding book, oblivious to what Madison was doing or that she had the list.

"Cecile?"

Startled, she looked up at Madison, realizing for the first time that Madison had compiled names and numbers on the paper she gave her.

"Oh, you have the list! Can you tell me something about each of them? Then maybe we can pick who to use and make some calls."

"Of course. I'm familiar with all of them by reputation. I've already made some notes for you and placed them in order of who we should call first. If you'd like, I can call them for you, as they know who I am. Together, we'll ensure that you get the best team in place to make your gowns."

"I still wish you were making them, but I understand."

Madison sat with Cecile and explained who everyone was and their area of expertise. She made recommendations about who her first choice was and why. Cecile, who knew nothing about this side of fashion, trusted Madison's suggestions. She asked her to make the calls, hoping Madison's influence could ensure that the top choices would work with her. Of course, Cecile knew her father could force people to do it, but she didn't want intimidation to mar her wedding day. When Madison agreed to make the calls, she hoped as she dialled the first number that they didn't know she was a murder suspect.

It didn't take long for Madison to call everyone she needed from the list and get them to agree to do the work. Cecile offered a post office box number for the samples to be sent and supplied an email address for the quotes. If anyone heard Madison's name on the news, they didn't let on. She was thankful for that. The last thing she needed was to explain to people in front of Cecile that The Don had set her up and she wasn't guilty of the accused crime. Cecile heard the news reports but believed Madison was innocent. She didn't know her father's involvement. Madison intended to keep it that way.

With everything in order and appointments set, her job was done. Now nothing was preventing The Don from moving forward in questioning her. Madison sat in silence as Cecile chatted on, oblivious to Madison's growing distress. From what she could tell, Cecile was unaware of her father's business and what he had in store for Madison. If she did, Madison wondered, would it make any difference to her? Cecile was gentle and innocent, but spoiled and self-centred. It was doubtful she'd go against her father to help Madison. Cecile excused herself and left the room. This time, her father instructed her to inform him when they were done. So that's what she did. She then told Madison to wait. Someone would come for her. It was time to head back to Carl's quarters and 'think' about things.

Alone, Madison drummed her fingers on the table and waited for someone to collect her. She hoped it would be Carl. At least with him; she felt safe. Things had preoccupied him last night, so something was going on. Something he hadn't told her about. But she could tell it was important. When she saw him, she hoped he'd have the holes in his plan filled in. When he told her what he had in mind earlier, there were still hurdles he had to work out. But with the file in the office, and the one she had, she was sure they had all the proof they needed. She didn't care who came for her. As long as it wasn't Tony. In the end, it was a guard who came to get her and bring her back to Carl's room. She followed him back into the bowels of the compound, struggling to keep up with the hurried pace he set.

# CHAPTER 46

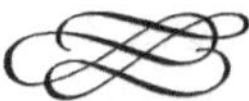

 $\mathcal{M}$ adison spent a quiet afternoon alone in the room. She used the time to consider how she would deal with The Don tomorrow. Now with her work on Cecile's dress finished, he'd clarified that they'd meet to go over the probable locations of Abby's missing file. Unknown to him, she had what she believed to be the missing file. Abby was brilliant to think of hiding the USB at the bottom of a lipstick tube. She had to have it made, so Madison knew there was a reason for it to be hidden. It must contain valuable information that Abby wanted to be impossible to find. If the colour was a shade she'd wear, Madison would have missed it for what it was. She was thankful she and Abby wore such different shades. Otherwise, she may never have discovered it. She brought her hand up to her chest to feel the lipstick still secure in her bra. Madison didn't dare take it out with the cameras, watching her every move, but it reassured her when she could feel its presence. She still didn't want Carl to know it existed. Madison planned on keeping it that way for as long as she could. She'd only tell him about it when they were away from here.

Madison tried to come up with an escape plan of her own, but she knew they locked doors to the underground tunnel. She couldn't go through the family compound. They kept the door connecting it to the underground locked. She could persuade Cecile to let her in again, but if anyone discovered her, they's take her to The Don. The only recourse was to buy some time, but that meant sending The Don on a wild goose chase to search for the file. But if she couldn't get out before he discovered she lied, he'd let Tony torture her. She had to think of somewhere they hadn't searched, somewhere obscure but believable. She knew Chuck searched Abby's home and office. Someone had rifled through her studio and loft, and the chalet was gone. Abby could have chosen any of those locations. Was it possible Abby had a safe deposit box no one knew about? No, Chuck would know if she did. As she considered other possibilities, she realized. Her SUV! She left it parked at the chalet and in the glove box was a USB with the preliminary sketches for her next collection. She hoped she could convince The Don that she remembered Abby fiddling around in the glove box and that she thought the behaviour was odd. Perhaps she might have hidden something there. He might believe her. Yes, that could work.

Satisfied that her idea would buy them some time, she leaned back and put her feet up. The Don believed Abby didn't give her the file, so that meant she'd have to think where Abby might have hidden it. By the time he found out that it was a decoy, she hoped to be long gone. If not, at least she would know she tried. It wouldn't be difficult to feign that she 'forgot' that she had a USB in there, especially under the circumstances. If she and Dean could get out of here with the evidence before The Don discovered her deception, she'd be O.K.

CARL RETURNED JUST as the dinner cart arrived. Madison knew they weren't joining The Don tonight. He wanted her to think about what she was going to tell him tomorrow and allow her the opportunity to avoid Tony. Although she knew he lied to her, he never intended for her to leave. The plan was for Tony to kill her. If Carl was right, Tony would take his time as he tortured her beforehand. She shuddered as she considered it.

Carl pushed the cart into the room and locked the door behind him. He paused at the stereo to put on some soft music. Tonight, they needed to talk. Madison pulled the two chairs over to face each other and moved a small table over for them to eat from. Carl wheeled the cart over to the chairs and lifted the cover from the food.

The aroma was enticing. Her stomach growled when she realized she didn't eat lunch and was ravenous. The cart held chicken parmesan, roasted potatoes, spaghetti and meatballs, fresh bread and oil dip, garden salad, and a small collection of pastries for dessert. A bottle of her favourite Chianti was there as well. The Don ensured those under his roof ate well. Carl opened the bottle and attached the aerator, poured them each a glass, and handed one to Madison.

They sat back and sipped on their wine before they loaded their plates. The salad, in typical Italian style, would come at the end of the meal, before dessert. Madison was eager to tell Carl her idea about the USB, but held off, sensing his mind was elsewhere. She ate in silence, looking up at him, waiting for him to let her know he was ready to talk. She knew he put the music on so they could, but she felt he should start. He had something to say. By the time they finished dessert, they'd only spoken half a dozen words. Carl cleared off the dishes and topped up their wine glasses before sitting back down. This time, he looked at her.

"I heard you've finished the arrangements for Cecile's dresses. You know what that means, right?"

"Yes, I'm well aware of what that means. It means The Don wants me to tell him where Abby hid the copy of the file, or at least where I think she did. I have been thinking of nothing else all day. But I have an idea on how to handle this and give us more time. Let me tell you what I'm thinking."

She told him about the USB in the glove compartment of her SUV. It wasn't the file The Don was looking for, but it was already there, and it would buy them some time. Now that she knew they'd searched both hers and Abby's home and office, there was nowhere else to look. She explained to him that when she called her office to help Cecile, George told her that there'd been a break-in and the police were there. The break-in could only mean that The Don sent someone to search for the file, especially since nothing was missing. They saw the chalet destroyed as flames engulfed it after the explosion, so anything inside was gone. That meant they were out of options. Madison thought the USB in the glove box was the best choice. It would take a few days before The Don discovered it was the wrong one. She still kept the lipstick a secret.

Carl looked at her and smiled. The first genuine smile he had for days.

"That's brilliant, and it's just plausible enough to be believable. The Don will send someone to look into it. When they find the memory stick, it will have to be brought back to him so he can check it out. It may just buy us the time we need. The Don won't send me. He won't send Tony either, but by the time it gets sent back here, and The Don reviews it, we should be gone. I have figured out all the details so we can get out of here."

"Thank God! You don't know how worried I've been. Tell me what the plan is. I was wondering if The Don would hand me over to Tony in a few days."

"You know I'd never let that happen! Here's what I've been up to today. I made a copy of the key to the underground passageway to the tunnel. I'll give it to you when we're in the bathroom. From now on, you're going to strap on your gun whenever you leave the room. So you'll have to wear slacks and secure the gun as high as you can around your ankle. Then, it won't be visible. I'll move it tonight and secure it behind the toilet so you can take it on and off, out of sight. One of us needs to get the file from The Don's desk. Which one of us will depend on who has the opportunity? Once we have the file, we have to run. Listen and memorize what I'm going to tell you. If you get the file, I want you to run. Don't worry about me. I promise I won't be far behind you."

Carl described the maze of tunnels under the compound to the escape hatch. If she was on her own, she needed to pay attention and memorize the way out. He reassured her that no matter what, he'd be right behind her. However, she needed to know how to get out on her own if she could. Everything depended on getting the file. He made her repeat the route back to him until he was sure she knew it and could run it blindfolded, if need be. If she made one wrong move, they'd catch her. He described the number of steps she'd have to take to find the hidden door in the hedge when she got out of the escape hatch. Then, when she was back in the woods, if he hadn't caught up to her, she'd need to make her way to where the jeep was. The keys were inside. If he still didn't show up, she was supposed to leave without him. Push the GPS to home and follow the directions back to the ranch. There was a cell phone on the console. As soon as she was a safe distance away, he wanted her to call Hank and alert him.

Once Carl knew she'd memorized what he told her, he placed the gun behind the toilet and gave her the key. Then they headed for bed. He also gave her the code to the door, to the escape tunnel to memorize.

'He had a good plan, but there were still so many factors to consider. One of them being; would she escape without him? If she had the chance to get out, would she be able to leave him behind?' As she lay in bed, her mind raced. She mulled over her options and reviewed the directions through the tunnel. She had to get it right. One missed turn, and they'd catch her. Then it was certain death. She tossed and turned, trying to get comfortable, unable to turn off her thoughts. Exhaustion set in, and she drifted off to sleep.

TONY LAY on his bed in his tiny cell of a room as a smile crept across his face. The boss told him tomorrow they'd start interrogating the bitch. He grew hard thinking of all the things he planned to do to her. Not tomorrow, he knew that, but soon. Now that the real inquisition would begin. He believed the bitch lawyer didn't make a copy of the files, but that wouldn't stop him from having his fun. He could still picture Madison's face when he held the knife to her throat. It terrified her. Her fear of him excited him all the more.

The Don gave him the space to set up his torture room on the lowest level of the compound. It was there that he did his best work, alone and in complete privacy. From time to time, The Don brought him people who weren't cooperative and needed convincing. He took his time getting them to talk. Those were the jobs he favoured, the ones where he could work undisturbed. It'd been too long since he had been a prisoner, but the wait was worth it. He was going to enjoy this one. He was going to enjoy hurting her. It was the pain in their eyes, the screams and begging for mercy or death that turned him on. This would be the first time a female visited his torture chamber, and he hoped not his last. When he dealt with women, it was away from the compound. Then he used the forests to hide their remains.

The lawyer's death was too quick and unsatisfying. He had to knock her unconscious to get The Don out before detonating the explosive. There was no pleasure in that. It was too easy, but he was following orders, and The Don's safety was more important. He did what they expected and no more, not with The Don there. Him wanting the stupid cow to know he was the reason she was going to die complicated things. It made getting the boss out the priority.

This time, The Don promised him the girl to do with as he wanted. The wait was long, but would be worth it in the end. The taste of her fear whetted his appetite for the kill. He had many ideas about how he would drag it out, making it last as long as he could. He set the video camera up so he could record everything. Something he planned to force Dean to watch. He knew it would enrage Dean, and they'd settle the score between them.

# CHAPTER 47

With the rise of dawn, Madison awoke from a restless sleep. She slid her hand across the bed to discover Carl was already up and could hear that he was in the shower. Madison shifted onto her back and stared at the ceiling, once again reviewing the escape route in her mind. She had to do her part if she was going to be ready when the time came. She wondered if she needed the USB in The Don's office. The one she had, she assumed, would convict Miguel and prove her innocence. The first chance she got, she should just run without the other USB and Carl. This wasn't her world. She wanted her life and her freedom back. Now she had a way out.

Carl walked back into the room with only a towel wrapped around his waist. He'd shaven, and the faint scent of his cologne drifted towards her. He smiled when he saw she was awake. She smiled back, but cursed under her breath. There was no way she'd run. He'd protected her, kept his word, and was trying to work with her. Somewhere, during all this, she'd developed feelings for him. She would wait for his signal and follow his lead. This was what he did. He'd know when the time was right. So far, he'd kept her safe, and she prayed he'd continue doing so.

"The bathroom is all yours. They'll bring breakfast down early. The Don left word: he wants to meet with you at 9 a.m. So get a move on."

Madison threw back the covers and jumped out of bed before heading to the shower. She wanted to be sure she had plenty of time to attach the holster to her calf and hide the lipstick and the key in her bra. Plus, there was the stupid rule of femininity for women within the compound. That meant even though she'd choose pants again, they had to be dress slacks and a blouse of some soft chiffon concoction. Today, if she could, she'd rather wear a t-shirt and yoga pants. The rules frustrated her, but she needed to adhere to them, even if it meant being treated like a fragile woman. She wanted to kick and scream, force her opinion on that fat, pompous ass, and shoot him between the eyes. Tony deserved to be shot in the balls before anyone fired the kill shot. But self-preservation prevailed, and now wasn't the time.

Clean and wrapped in a towel, she chose an appropriate outfit from the closet. She thought to herself, *'Was there such a thing as an appropriate outfit for an interrogation?'* After selecting the right combination of slacks and blouse, she went back into the washroom to dress. She slipped the key and lipstick into her bra, but struggled with the holster. She needed to make sure it was secure enough not to slip, but high enough that it wouldn't show when she sat or crossed her legs. After several attempts, she found the right spot and tightened the straps. She completed the look with some light make-up and ran a comb through her hair before joining Carl for breakfast. She heard the cart arrive while she was dressing.

The chairs were in the same position from the previous night, and Carl wheeled the cart over. Today's breakfast was French toast, scrambled eggs, sausage, and fruit. There was a generous pitcher of fresh-squeezed orange juice and a carafe of coffee. Madison took her place across from Carl and crossed her legs. Carl looked down at her ankles and gave her a questioning look. She nodded before stating it had been more difficult than she thought, knowing if anyone were listening to them this morning, they wouldn't know what she was talking about. They had plenty of time, so they enjoyed a leisurely breakfast before they had to meet with The Don. Once they had enough to eat, they pushed the cart aside and sat back, taking their time over a second cup of coffee.

"Do you think that you're ready?"

"I'm ready for anything. I spent most of last night going over everything in my mind." She alluded to their conversation from the previous night. The music wasn't playing this morning, so they had to be careful about what they said. "I think I have an idea where Abby may have hidden the file."

"That's good. I'm glad you came to your senses and decided to co-operate. It will please The Don."

"And of course, we want to keep 'The Don' happy." She quipped.

Carl scowled at her and had no choice but to play his role and rebuke her.

"I think you'd better remember your place, Miss Kerr. If it wasn't for The Don's good nature, you wouldn't have been so well cared for while a guest here."

"Guest my ass! I'm a 'well cared for' prisoner. A guest wouldn't have to share your room and could leave whenever they chose. I can't."

"Have I treated you poorly? It seems to me you have been quite comfortable in my room. Would you have preferred the alternative? I think you'll agree this was the best choice."

Madison sat back and took another sip of her coffee. She didn't want to say anything else that would start an argument. She knew why Carl was treating her this way, but it didn't make it hurt any less. To lessen the harshness of his words, he gave her a wink. They had a lot to lose if things didn't go according to plan. If they couldn't get what they needed from The Don's desk in time, they'd be out of options. The number of guards stationed around the compound made sneaking around a challenge, let alone escaping. Carl wished he could do more to ease her mind, supply her with a cell phone or something; so they could contact each other. But it was too dangerous. Just allowing Madison to carry the gun and have the key to the locked corridor was risky enough. If they found either on her, they'd both pay the consequences.

"It's time to go," Carl announced, just as there was a knock at the door.

They both stood, pushing the cart aside, and prepared to leave. Carl was the first to the door and answered the knock. When it opened, Tony greeted them. He stood there, wearing a satisfied sneer on his face.

"I thought I told you to stay away from my room."

"The boss sent me. He wanted to make sure you were on time. I guess he thought you might stay in bed, enjoying what time you have left with her."

"I've never been late before," Carl responded, ignoring the rest of Tony's comment.

"You've never been fucking one of his 'guests' before, either. Let's go."

Madison stayed as close as she could to Carl as they made their way to The Don's office. She wanted to put as much space as possible between herself and Tony. Just his presence made her skin crawl. He made it impossible for her to keep her distance, choosing to walk on the other side of her, sandwiching her between both men, pushing as close to her as he dared without setting Dean off. He knew Dean was going to be pissed when he found out The Don wasn't allowing him to sit in. The Don warned Tony that he wouldn't need his methods of persuasion, at least not yet. But that was O.K. He'd take pleasure knowing how uncomfortable she'd be just by his being there. The boss thought she'd tell them where the files were, but he still doubted there was a copy, and if there was, that she'd even know where to find it. Once The Don verified her information and learned if there was a file, or there wasn't one, then they'd need Tony to persuade her to talk or to finish her.

As they approached The Don's office, they noticed there were two guards stationed outside. Tony knocked and waited for The Don to invite them in. When instructed to, Tony opened the door so that Madison could enter. This time he got great pleasure from turning and stopping Carl from following. Carl growled at him, stepping closer to intimidate.

"What the fuck Tony?"

"Relax, Dean. I guarantee no harm will come to Miss Kerr today. I won't need you for this meeting. There are other things for you to attend. There is that matter of the Mitchell fellow we discussed yesterday. Please see to it. I will call you to collect her when we are done." The Don called out from behind his desk.

"Yes, Don. I'll get right on it. Let me know when you're finished."

He shot Madison a look of apology. There was nothing he could do. She knew it and smiled at him before giving him a brief nod, acknowledging she'd be fine. As long as The Don believed she was cooperating, she knew she'd be O.K. Madison took a deep breath and turned towards the room, smiling as she made her way across to the chair positioned in front of The Don. She stood waiting until he granted her permission to have a seat. Out of the corner of her eye, she noticed Tony had stationed himself to stand just inside the door. The Don may have decided not to use Tony today, but his presence was still intimidating, which she assumed was the desired effect.

"Cecile tells me you have completed your task, and she is happy. Thank you. That pleases me. That also means there is no longer a reason for the two of you to work together, so there is nothing left to delay our business. Thank you for achieving this. It would displease me if you'd dragged it out. So, Miss Kerr, that leaves us with only one question. Did you think about what we discussed yesterday?"

"It was all I could think about."

"I'm sure it was." He chuckled. "Do you know where Miss Monroe may have hidden a file, such as the one I'm looking for?"

"I thought it might be in her home or office, but you've already had those searched. When I was setting up fabric suppliers and seamstress appointments for Cecile, I had to contact my assistant for the names and numbers. He informed me someone ransacked my studio and loft. I'm guessing, considering nothing was stolen, it was to look for the files."

"You are very astute, Miss Kerr. But that still doesn't tell me where the files might be."

"I'm sorry. Yes, of course. If they were in the chalet, they're gone. There is only one other place I can think of."

The Don leaned forward across his desk, focusing, and motioned for her to continue. Tony cursed under his breath from the back of the room. Madison smiled to herself before continuing, relishing in knowing she annoyed Tony while doing so.

"When we arrived at the chalet, Abby opened the glove compartment of my SUV. It's something she's never done before. When I asked her what she was looking for, she said a tissue, so I handed her one from my console and thought nothing more about it. It wasn't until you suggested it might be an electronic file. That's when I remembered Abby opening the glove box and thought she might have hidden a USB stick in there without my knowledge. I don't know if it's there or not, but it's all I can think of."

The Don smiled. "Where is your car now?"

"I left it parked in the chalet's laneway. As I've told you, I took off on foot. If I'd been rational, I'd have hopped in it and headed back across the border as fast as I could. But grief overcame me and I wasn't thinking clearly."

"It's a good thing that it's still there. I will send someone to check it out. It may take a day or two for me to verify if a USB is indeed in the glove box, and if so, what's on it. You'd better not be sending me on a wild goose chase. I don't have time for games. My patience is wearing thin. If it's found, I'll have it brought here so I can verify it's what I'm looking for. In the meantime, you will continue to be my guest. When I have the file in my possession or discover it doesn't exist, I'll send for you again."

With that, she found herself dismissed. The Don picked up his phone and told someone on the other end that the meeting had finished. He sent Madison to wait in the hall with the guards until Carl showed up. She stood up, turned, took her time as she walked to the door, looked at Tony. Unable to stop herself, she gave him a satisfied wink. Rage flickered across his face when he saw the wink, but he was quick to control it. He hissed 'bitch' under his breath as she passed him. The Don, sitting at the far end of the office, was unaware of what transpired between the two of them.

"I'll take her back to Dean's room, seeing as you have him doing something else." Tony offered.

"No, Tony. If Dean doesn't return soon, the guard outside can take her. I want to discuss something with you. Come over and take a seat."

Madison breathed a sigh of relief. When she winked at Tony, she didn't consider that Carl wasn't there, and Tony might be the one to 'escort' her back. The thought of being alone with him brought a shiver up her spine. Madison left the office, and after a brief wait for Carl, made her way back to his room in the guard's company. He didn't engage in conversation as he walked with her. He brought her back to the room where another guard was in place and handed her off. This guard unlocked the door and held it open until she was inside. He instructed her they expected her to stay there until either Dean returned or The Don called for her again.

# CHAPTER 48

$\mathcal{M}$adison paced around the room in frustration. Once again, she found herself alone, waiting for Carl, hating the uncertainty that surrounded her. She felt like a lion in a cage, itching to break free. Madison checked on the guards in the hallway through the peephole, praying something would call them away from their post so she could try to sneak back to The Don's office. She felt she couldn't take the silence and uncertainty any longer. Then there was a knock at the door. Carl wouldn't knock! After she first peered through the peephole, she opened the door.

"Yes?"

"You're wanted upstairs." Replied the young guard as he stepped aside to allow her to get past, before motioning for her to follow him down the hall. She hesitated, not wanting to go, but realized she didn't have a choice.

Madison stared at the young man's back as she followed him, noticing that he was alone. Not more than half an hour ago, she looked out and saw two guards. He wasn't one of them. She felt a sudden rush of fear. This wasn't right. Where was the other guard? Why was he alone, and when did they switch? Her mind raced as she tried to determine what had changed. The guard wouldn't tell her why they wanted her upstairs or where Carl was. Had The Don already discovered that the USB was a fake? No, it was impossible. It was too soon. There wasn't enough time for someone to get to the chalet, search the car, and return, let alone for The Don to review what was on it. But if he had it and reviewed it, he'd know it wasn't what he was looking for. She felt dread spread into the pit of her stomach as she continued following the guard.

It wasn't long before she realized he was taking her to The Don's office. As they approached, Madison realized two things. One, the guards weren't outside, and two, the door was wide open. She took a deep breath and looked inside, expecting to see The Don at his desk, but the room was empty. She turned to question the guard. Before she could speak, he did.

"Carl says you have five minutes. Be quick." With that, he positioned himself outside the door and waited.

Her jaw dropped when she realized he used the name 'Carl'. The only way the guard could know that Dean was Carl was if they worked together. If The Don learned Carl's identity, the compound would be in chaos. Tony would be the one escorting her, not to the office, but to his torture chamber. This was it. She had to move fast. She rushed across the room to the desk and pulled out the drawer. Using her nails, she felt around for the slight lift in the wood that revealed the hidden compartment. She found it, pulled the piece out, and slipped her finger inside. Madison felt around and paused when she discovered this time, instead of one USB, she felt two! She plucked them both out and slid them into her bra, adding them to the key and lipstick. She put the piece of wood back in place as the guard hissed, 'Hurry'. When she got the drawer inserted on the track, she ran back to the door.

"Did you get what he needs?"

"Yes."

"O.K., get out of here. No one will notice you're missing for some time. I'll find Carl. Run. The Don has an emergency. The whole compound is in an uproar, and this is the only opportunity you're going to have to escape. Don't worry! Carl will be right behind you. Just get moving."

The guard smiled at her. It was the first friendly smile she'd received from a stranger since coming here. She wanted to hug him, but she returned his smile and ran. If she ever saw him again, she'd be sure to thank him. She turned and headed back through the corridor, past Carl's room, to the passageway out.

THE DON FOUND himself in the conference room meeting with a crew of guards. Someone had attempted to break into the compound. It was unheard of. In all the years he'd been here, this was the first time there'd been an attempt. The silent alarm notified them of a breach along the South wall. The first set of guards was already out investigating. He barked orders about security, instructing the guards to first check through the family area of the compound. As soon as the alarm sounded, he'd sent Arabella and Cecile off to New York for a shopping trip. He needed them as far away as possible from any danger. Arabella had dug in her heels, insisting this was her home and she'd make anyone who threatened it pay. But The Don pointed out how vulnerable Cecile was, so she agreed to go. Cecile was beyond excited at the thought of a spontaneous shopping trip, oblivious to the surrounding chaos.

"Get someone out there to check the security cameras. There is no way six went out at the same time. Someone get out there and investigate. Dean, come here." The Do barked.

Carl moved closer to The Don. He was eager to be given his assignment. The breach wasn't real. He'd arranged it as a distraction so that Madison could get the file and escape. Most of the cameras that were offline faced the South wall, but one was near the escape hatch. On that one, he'd cut the wires. By the time the others were up and running, and they checked the last one, he hoped they'd both be long gone. He'd received the signal that Madison had the file and was now on the run. He needed to get out of the conference room and join her before anyone was the wiser. His man had already left.

"Dean, I want you to check the cameras. The morons in the audio room missed something. Get down there and see who turned off my cameras. Go out and check each one if need be."

Thankful to be dismissed, he turned to leave.

"And Dean, find Tony. I don't know where he is, but I'll need him ready to use his special talents when we find who's responsible."

"Yes, Don."

With that, Carl was off. The thought that no one knew Tony's location bothered him. He needed to find Madison and get out of here without being caught. It was a stroke of luck that they assigned him to check the security cameras. The situation benefited them. It would give them the lead time they needed. By the time anyone discovered the cameras were still offline, they'd be O.K. unless the controller was already working on a solution. But if Tony found them first, he shuddered at the thought.

When everyone was called to the conference room to be briefed, Carl noticed Tony's absence. He prayed Madison got away and was already out of the building. It was only a matter of time before most of the cameras would be up and running again. He took off at full speed and headed to his room first. To make sure she wasn't there. Then, he ran to the tunnel. His man was trustworthy and was long gone, taking with him anything that could link either of them to the family. Madison had to be the one to retrieve the file. She knew where it was and what to look for, and time was of the essence. He knew she wouldn't give it to his man, but would have it on her. He prayed she secured it.

With all the guards off on other assignments, he knew he wouldn't pass anyone in the halls. Until they sealed the 'breach', the guards would be occupied elsewhere. The only wild card was Tony. He checked his watch. There were less than fifteen minutes to get clear of the building before the cameras went back online on their own. After that, it wouldn't take long for someone to investigate the remaining camera to see what the problem was. He threw the door open to his room. It was empty. He breathed a sigh of relief. She wasn't there. For once, she'd followed instructions, and by now, she should be well on her way.

He pulled his gun out of his holster and sprinted towards the tunnels. Unsure how far behind her he was, he tried to make up the time. He pushed forward as fast as he could, praying he didn't run into anyone, especially Tony. Then he heard it, the distinct sound of a gunshot echoing through the halls. He stopped in his tracks. Concerned, he grasped his gun in both hands and cocked it before continuing.

# CHAPTER 49

Carl kept his word and did everything he vowed to do in order to arrange for Madison's escape. He got her a key to the underground leading to the tunnel, and the hidden exit. He promised he'd be right behind her. After his man told her to run, she did. She knew she had to hurry. This was her only chance to get out. As she ran, the items in her bra chaffed her, so she transferred the lipstick and USBs to the pocket of her slacks, taking the key in hand to have it ready. This was what the training and preparations at the ranch had been for, she realized. It wasn't to get her here or survive being here. It was in order for her to make it out alive. The last few days of idleness had made her sluggish, but her muscle memory came back with each practiced step. Her feet pounding as she ran, echoing on the cold tiled floor of the lower corridors as she fled for her life.

Finding the right door was more difficult than she expected. But now it was all that stood between her and the escape hatch. She inserted the key and turned it, breathing a sigh of relief as the tumblers fell into place and the door opened to reveal a flight of stairs leading further down into the dark belly of the compound. She sprinted down the stairs to the maze of underground tunnels.

At the bottom of the stairs, she paused as she looked at the multitude of corridors jutting off the main hallway. The actual test to her memory and ability to navigate lay ahead, as she tried to recall which tunnel to take first. A moment's pause was all she needed to recall what Carl's instructions were. Madison could almost hear his voice telling her which way to go as she visualized the described escape, how many turns and corridors she still needed to take until she reached the right one. When the memorized instructions flooded back, she pushed off, taking the second passageway to the right, keeping her pace up, aware of her surroundings. She followed the many turns in the labyrinth under the compound; the area reserved for prisoners, torture, and training. She knew she would reach one more doorway before entering the last tunnel that ended with the trapdoor. That doorway had a key code lock. Carl gave her the code, which she repeated to herself as she ran.

She made the last turn towards the doorway and freedom, and stopped dead. Up ahead, the lights in the final passageway were out. She could see a figure stood between herself and the door. As her eyes adjusted to the light, she realized as the figure moved closer; it was Tony. He lunged for her before she registered his presence, knocking her to the ground. The fall forced her breath from her lungs as her body slammed against the concrete floor under his weight.

Tony took the opportunity and pinned her body beneath his as he swung his fist, connecting it with the side of her head. Pain flashed with a bright light radiating from her temple. A wave of nausea washed over her. Madison was aware she was losing consciousness and fought the bile that welled up inside her as she forced herself to stay awake. She knew that if she succumbed to the darkness, she'd be at his mercy and he'd kill her. Weakly, she tried to focus on his face as it hovered only inches above hers. He shifted and pinned her upper arms beneath his knees and sat back on her chest, forcing another breath from her lungs. Pain radiated across her chest. She wondered if she'd broken a rib. Still, she struggled beneath him, kicking her legs, trying to buck him off.

"Where do you think you're going, bitch?" He hissed. "I should've taken care of you days ago. The Don won't care what happens to you now."

He grabbed her blouse, tearing the fragile chiffon, exposing her bra. Tony reached into his back pocket and pulled out a switchblade, and flicked it open. He ran the blade along her skin, so lightly it was almost a lover's touch, before slipping it under the front of her bra and slicing through the fabric as her breasts sprung free. She'd never been more terrified in her life as he traced the tip of the knife around her areola, push the point into her tender flesh until a bloom of bright red glistened as blood sprung to the surface under the pressure. She wanted to fight back, needed to fight back, but the fear that doing so would force his knife deeper into her chest stopped her.

Tony sneered at her as he moved the knife away and licked the blood from her breast, allowing it to smear across his face. Lust flickered through his eyes, and the reality of what lay ahead snapped Madison into action. She kicked her legs out again, hoping to gain enough traction to push free. Tony enjoyed the fight, dropping the knife to grab her head in both of his hands and smashed it into the concrete. This time as the bile rose, she couldn't prevent it, and she vomited, spewing it out and all over Tony. Gagging on what remained in her mouth, she turned her head and spat out the rest.

"You stupid bitch!" Tony screamed, shifting his weight as he wiped it off his shirt.

This movement allowed her right leg to brush against her hand, and she felt the bulge of the holster against her calf. This was her only chance. She slid her hand down her leg and up under the hem of her slacks. Her hand felt leather and cold steel. Tony's distraction of cleaning off the vomit gave her the opportunity she needed. She had to take it. Madison slid the gun out of its holster, her head throbbing in pain as she kept her hand under her leg to conceal the gun.

He still pinned her upper arms under his knees, preventing her from bringing the gun up. In this position, she'd only be able to fire a warning shot, but who would she be warning? The pain in her skull washed over her like water crashing through rapids. If she lost consciousness, it would be over. She fought to stay awake, praying for the opportunity to use the gun before it was too late.

Tony cleaned most of the vomit off, wiping his hands on the tatters of her blouse. His eyes narrowed to slits as his hatred for her emanated from them. Once again, he picked up his knife and pressed it to her neck with one hand. With his other hand, he reached up and undid his pants. The shift in weight freed her right arm. With the gun in her grasp, she pulled her arm free, pressed the gun to Tony's chest, and without hesitation, pulled the trigger.

Shock registered on his face as he looked down at the spreading circle of blood on his shirt as it mingled with the remaining traces of her vomit. The knife slipped from his hand as he brought it up, trying to stop the flow of blood before his body collapsed, pinning Madison beneath him. Tears of relief pooled in her eyes as she realized he was dead. She lay there as a fog filtered through her brain, not registering the sound of approaching footsteps.

"Madison?" A voice called out, "Are you OK?"

Weakly, Madison turned her head to see Carl as he ran down the passageway towards her. In one swift motion, he pushed off Tony's body and helped her to her feet. She shook as she stood; the gun hung in her hand. Carl reached out and took it from her and stuck it in the waistband of his jeans. His eyes surveyed her for injuries before realizing that most of the blood belonged to Tony. He pulled the zipper of her jacket up, covering her nakedness. As her knees buckled, he caught her and pulled her into his arms.

"We have to keep moving," he whispered in her ear before kissing her on the forehead. "Can you manage?"

Madison looked into his eyes and saw his concern and compassion. She nodded and found the strength to carry on. Although her legs still felt weak, Carl released her and grabbed her hand, pulling her the rest of the way to the door. With each step, her head pounded as her brain sloshed within her skull. Another wave of nausea hit, but this time she swallowed it down, taking a deep breath of air. Carl keyed in the code. The door unlocked. He held it opened, allowing her to pass through. He stopped and withdrew a small device from his pocket and pressed it to the keypad. It was a small charge to render the keypad useless; he lit the very short fuse, and a small pop took out the entry lock. He forced the door closed and checked that the lock held. This would prevent anyone from following them through the tunnel when they found Tony's body.

Carl kept his arms around Madison, half dragging her along the route. Her steps faltered under the waves of darkness that still threatened to overcome her. He only hoped she could continue. He went up the ladder first to push open the escape hatch and ensure the way was clear. When he climbed back down, he found Madison in an unconscious heap.

# CHAPTER 50

arl looked down at Madison's prone body. Her injuries
were more severe than he thought. He could see that her
eye had already swollen shut. A bright purple bruise formed around
it, along past her temple, into her hairline. He lifted her head and
found the hair on the back of her head matted with blood. He
considered trying to wake her up, but dismissed the idea. She had a
head injury. Although he knew he should keep her awake, he
decided now wasn't the time. If he woke her, she could pass out
again at any moment, and if she was on the ladder, she could fall
and suffer greater injury. He ran his fingers along the back of her
skull under the matted hair and discovered a soft area that was also
swelling. He cursed under his breath. If Tony wasn't dead already,
he'd go back and kill him. Even if he got her to regain consciousness, there was no way she'd get up the ladder. He had only one
option.

Carl bent over, lifted her slight frame up and over his shoulders,
firefighter style. He prayed his strength would hold out, hoping
that she didn't gain consciousness during the climb. If she did, any
movement could throw him off balance, and he'd lose his hold on
her. He began his ascent up the ladder. As light as she was, he

strained under her added weight, losing precious seconds with each laborious step. If anyone else heard the gunshot, they'd investigate, find Tony's body and sound the alarm. He had to move faster.

Soon, he was far enough above ground that he could deposit Madison on the grass. There still wasn't time to check her injuries, so he closed the hatch and sprinted to the hidden gate in the hedge. He flicked the latch and ran back to where Madison still lay. He lifted her back up and over his left shoulder, gripping her legs as he made his way back to the gate. To avoid swinging her into the electric fence, he kept close to the hedge, his right side brushing across the thorns, tearing at his t-shirt and into his flesh. He couldn't prevent her from being further injured by the thorns, but he'd do his best.

Carl slipped through the gate and close it behind him, taking the time to look around, ensuring they weren't being watched. He looked up at the camera, noticing the light was still out, and breathed a sigh of relief as he started through the forest to where he hid the jeep. There was still a kilometre of woods to navigate through. Carl was already sweating under the exertion and the added burden of carrying Madison. Still, he pushed on. His foot caught a root, and he stumbled, almost dropping her. But somehow, he stayed upright and kept her from falling. Sweat stung his eyes, blurred his vision, and disoriented him. He should be close, but the sun was bright, and his eyes burned. As he got his bearings; a movement to his right startled him. With his free hand, he reached around to the small of his back, where he put Madison's gun. He pulled it out and cocked it.

"Carl." A voice hissed.

Carl turned and lowered the gun, overcome with relief.

"Thank god!"

Hank rushed towards him as Carl put the gun back in his waistband.

"What the hell happened?"

"There's no time for that now. Where did you park?"

"Your mole dropped me at the jeep. Give me Madison. You're exhausted."

Carl hesitated before handing Madison over. He wanted to argue, but Hank was right. He felt the exhaustion throughout his body and needed his strength. They weren't safe yet. He shifted Madison over to Hank, who led the way back to the jeep. Carl pulled his gun out of his holster to be ready in case they ran into anyone. His eyes scanned the dense woods as they went. It filled him with gratitude when he saw the jeep was already uncovered and ready. Hank had prepared. His guy on the inside deserved a bonus for this. Carl opened the door, and Hank laid Madison on the backseat and slid into the driver's seat. Carl once again scanned the landscape before he hopped into the passenger seat, gun ready.

"Let's move!" Carl barked when he was in.

Hank started the engine and put it into gear. Gravel flew off the tires as they sped away. Carl reached into the glove box and pulled out a small remote control device. He looked back and hesitated before pressing the button. The ground beneath them shook. An alarm screeched through the air. Hank turned to Carl.

"What the hell was that?"

"I set an explosive in the underground tunnels. Not enough to blow the whole place up, but enough to collapse part of the supports under the structure. Let's call it added insurance. By the time they get all the fires put out and gather the troops to find that Madison and I are missing, we'll be long gone."

"Good. Now tell me what the hell happened."

Carl filled Hank in on everything that had transpired since they left the ranch, choosing to leave out the more personal details. Hank sat in silence and allowed Carl to continue. Madison moaned from the backseat. Hank was in awe of the strength and determination Madison displayed, according to Carl's account.

"We need to get her to a hospital." Hank said.

"We can't. She's still wanted by the police. I'll call Rose and have the ranch doctor waiting for us. If we both take turns driving, we can be home tomorrow. Let me crawl in the back and try to wake her up. From what I can tell, she has a concussion, so we should keep trying to awaken her every couple of hours. If I can wake her, I'll get her to drink some water and then let her rest some more. We'll switch out caring for her when we switch out drivers."

As Carl climbed into the back, he could feel Hank's eyes on him in the rear-view mirror. He lifted Madison's head and placed it in his lap. He called out to her, stroking her cheek. Emerald green eyes blinked open, but closed just as fast. He tore part of his shirt off and soaked it in water, touching the wet cloth to her face. She groaned again and opened her eyes.

"Did we make it?"

Carl smiled down at her, brushing a strand of hair from her face. "Yes, we made it."

Madison struggled to sit up, but Carl stopped her.

"You need to rest. Hank's driving, and we're heading back to the ranch."

"Hank's here?" She muttered, confused. "How?"

"Don't worry about that now. You're safe. Can you tell me where you're hurt?"

"My head feels like someone hit me with a baseball bat. I wasn't, Tony… crap, where's Tony?" Madison struggled again to lift her head.

"Tony's dead."

"Oh yes, now I remember. I shot him." She whispered as she lay back down.

In the front seat, Hank raised an eyebrow as he caught Carl's eyes in the mirror. It seemed he left that part out. Hank wondered what else Carl wasn't telling him. He couldn't help but notice the compassion Carl was showing towards her.

"Madison, I need you to tell me where you're hurt. That's the only way we can help you."

Madison was drifting off again, but forced herself to focus.

"Tony punched me in the face, and he slammed my head into the ground. So the side and back of my head hurt. I also think he broke a rib when he landed on me. It hurts to breathe."

"O.K. You can rest now. We'll get you taken care of when we get back to the ranch."

Madison forced herself to focus so that she could reach into her pocket and pull out the lipstick and two USB sticks. She wanted to make sure they were in Carl's possession before she lost consciousness again.

"Here, you'll need these."

Carl stared dumbfounded at the items Madison had dropped in his hand.

"You found two USBs? That's better than we could have hoped for. But I don't think I need the lipstick."

"Yes, you do. I believe that's where Abby hid the file The Don was looking for." Madison mumbled as she closed her eyes and succumbed to the darkness.

Carl's jaw slackened as he looked from the objects in his hand at the battered woman beside him. He picked up the tube of lipstick and opened it, and twisted up the colour. He twisted it down and put the lid back on. She was confused, but in case she wasn't, he examined the other end. Noticing the seam, he worked at it until it opened and revealed the hidden USB. Dammit. She was clever. His chest swelled with pride as he looked down at the beautiful, battered, and bruised woman who lay in his arms.

# EPILOGUE

For several days, Madison drifted in and out of consciousness. During that time, Carl reviewed the information on all the USBs. Including the one hidden in the lipstick. Already, there was a team assembled to arrest The Don and members of his organization. The only surprise was how involved in the family business Arabella was. She used her position for personal vendettas; and manipulated people to get what she wanted. Now she would also spend the rest of her life in jail.

After the doctor examined Madison, Hank, Carl, and Rose took turns sitting by her bedside. She had two fractured ribs, a severe concussion and needed round-the-clock supervision. Carl hired a full-time nurse to care for her, but none of them wanted Madison to wake up to find a stranger at her bedside.

ALTHOUGH BRUISES still covered Madison's face, after a few days, she could maintain consciousness and sit up in bed, which was what she was doing when Carl entered the room and greeted her with a warm smile. She smiled back, grimacing as she did. Moving her facial muscles was still difficult because of the swelling and bruising. He motioned to Rose, who sat with Madison that she could leave. He was going to take over. Rose stood, stroked Madison's cheek, smiled at her, and with a nod to Carl, she left.

Carl bent over and kissed her brow.

"Finally," Madison said when they were alone. "Did you find everything we needed on the USB sticks?"

"Yes. Arrests are already underway. I should punish you for keeping the one hidden in the lipstick a secret." He smiled at her.

"I think I've suffered enough punishment, don't you? Will I be able to go home soon?"

"Yes, but first, I have a surprise for you." Carl gestured to the closed door. "You can come in now."

Madison lifted her eyes to the door and watched as it opened. A petite woman with shoulder-length dark hair entered with a smile that lit up the room. Madison's jaw dropped, unable to believe what she saw. How could this be?

Abby raced across the distance and threw herself onto the bed and into Madison's arms, pulling her into a firm embrace. Madison gasped as her still tender ribs compressed. Ignoring the pain, she wrapped her arms around her best friend. Madison squeezed Abby, speechless, and then pushed her back to get a better look. Tears streamed down both of their faces in an overwhelming flow of emotion. Abby was unharmed, and very much alive.

Now able to speak, Madison croaked a single word. "How?"

Carl stepped forward.

"When I met with Abby in the bar the night of the explosion, I warned her that her life was in danger. I arranged for a friend of mine to get her out before the chalet exploded. Don Fernando had to believe she was dead, or else he would have kept trying to kill her. So my guy got her out and kept her safe and hidden. I decided you couldn't know the truth, or your grief and anger wouldn't be believable. I'm sorry about that. You were supposed to have been inside with her. Then you'd both would have gone into hiding. When you stayed outside, that changed everything."

Madison wanted to yell at him, but the joy that Abby was alive curbed her impulse.

"I'm sorry, Madison. I didn't know when I told you to wait outside that the plan was to get us both into hiding. I was worried something would happen to you." Abby pulled a tissue out and handed it to Madison. "My parents know everything. I insisted they be told I wasn't dead, but that they had to act as if I was. That's why they never spoke with reporters. They weren't sure they could keep up the pretence in front of an audience."

"I'm just happy you're alive and that this whole thing is over." Madison pulled Abby back into a hug. Abby hugged her back before she pulled away.

"It's not over. Charles is still out there somewhere, and there's a warrant for his arrest. We will also both have to testify at the trial. But yes. The danger is gone. Thank you for what you did for me. You are one of the most resourceful women I know."

Madison blushed and reached her hand out towards Carl. He stepped forward, taking her hand in his.

"Carl kept me safe. He took care of me and made certain I wasn't hurt. Well! Beyond the inevitable. I can't say I always trusted him, but I can say I do now. It's funny how life works."

Abby looked from Madison to Carl and paused as she looked down at their still clasped hands. Whether Madison knew it, Abby was certain Madison had found someone who would always stand by her.

# ACKNOWLEDGMENTS

Writing is daunting, the blank page staring back, words twisting as fingers fly or stall on the keyboard. To write, there are many people on the sidelines cheering the author on. I've been blessed to have many supportive people in my corner.

First, I must thank my wonderful husband, Steve. Without him suggesting that the only way for me to write would be to take early retirement and 'just do it', I'd still be dreaming of writing, with false starts and interrupted attempts. He listened as I struggled with wordy paragraphs, made suggestions when asked, and became my grounding force in a world of make-believe.

Second, I want to thank my children, Darren, Tanya, and Cynthia, who recovered from their initial shock when I told them about my plans. I believe the first response was, 'no, what are you really planning on doing?' But when they discovered I was serious, they became my greatest cheerleaders.

The concept for the first book in the series came to me as I travelled coast to coast with my husband in his big rig. The previous year we were ships crossing in the night as we both travelled separately across the provinces. We decided we needed some time together. As we travelled, I made notes of locations, situations and things of interest which I peppered through the book.

Finally, a book isn't complete without the people behind the scenes who help check for consistency, believability, grammar, and spelling. They helped prepare the book for launch through guidance and critical reviews that improved my writing. Thank you, Wendy

Catalano, Tracy Wilson, Trevor Craig, Anne O'Connell, and Judy Gray.

My cover designer, A. E. Hellstorm, and the many members of Genre Writers of Atlantic Canada for the advice and knowledge.

To my readers, thank you. Because of you, I will always strive to be a better writer.

# ABOUT THE AUTHOR

J. E. Friend is an emerging author of crime thrillers. Her debut novel, Design of Deception, was first published in August 2020.

She lives in the beautiful Annapolis Valley with her husband Steve and their dog, Hartley. There she can enjoy the peace and solitude it offers so that she can write, whether in her writing room or on the deck. She has a Bachelor's Degree from the University of Waterloo. Her field of study was psychology. This enables her to get into the mind of a killer when writing.

She is a member of Author's Ink, a writing group in Nova Scotia, comprising published and non-published authors, and for the past few years, she has also been The Municipal Liaison for NaNoWriMo (National Novel Writing Month) for her geographical area. NaNoWriMo promotes writers with an annual challenge to write 50,000 words in November, which she has won each year since 2017.

She is an active member of the Writers Federation of Nova Scotia where she has reviewed and short-listed emerging authors in several competitions.

She is just finished writing the first novel, in her trilogy, that follows a serial killer across Canada. Redemption, The Trans-Canada Killer Series, Book 1 will be out in September 2022.